CLUB RED

Christopher Hoy

CLUB RED

ISBN-13: 978-1537321219

Cover design by Andrew Somerville

Acknowledgements

I would like to thank my sweet wife and best friend forever, Leslie Hoy, for her excellent work as my chief editor and story advisor. And I want to salute all my writing pals in the Professional Writers of Prescott, as well as the mysterious writers who meet in a small tight-knit group known as Suspicious Characters. Hanging out with these creative people is what has convinced me that writing stories is a perfectly normal thing to do.

Thanks to MotoeXotica Classic Car Sales for the usage of their 1960 Lincoln Continental Town Car photo as part of the front cover design.

Dedication

This novel is dedicated to my late father, Gerald D. Hoy.

CLUB RED

CHAPTER ONE

Sometime in the 90's . . .

Midnight . . . Camp David

The President of the United States stared into the dancing yellow flames in the fireplace at Aspen Lodge. He had the mother of all headaches. His armpits oozed sour perspiration. His bowels bubbled and squeaked.

Nearly overwhelmed with the nausea that he knew precedes a migraine, the President tried desperately to visualize success.

I have to kill that bastard before he kills me. It's that simple. And I must kill him in such a way that his death cannot be traced back to my office. Because if his people suspect that I personally ordered his extermination, they won't stop blowing things up until the entire free world is reduced to smoking rubble. Fortunately, this idiot thinks I have no choice but to seek a way to defend myself against personal threats that will satisfy the legal and ethical standards of my country. But he's dead wrong about that. When it comes to saving my own ass, I get to decide what's legal and ethical.

The President heard a Marine helicopter begin its noisy descent onto a landing pad a few hundred yards away. He knew that the chopper carried the second most ambitious man in America—the Director of Central Intelligence, Charles Talbot.

The President walked to an antique rocking chair and eased himself into it. A snifter of brandy and an unlit cigar sat on a low table

1

next to the chair. He closed his eyes, sipped the warm liquor and rolled the fragrant cigar under his nose.

Perhaps help is on the way . . .

Moments later, the President heard Talbot talking to the marine standing guard outside the door. Then the tall, handsome and impeccably groomed man stepped into the room.

"Good evening, Mr. President."

The President executed a perfunctory inspection of the most powerful American intelligence official since J. Edgar Hoover. Charles Talbot's wary dark eyes locked on the President's illegal Cuban cigar. He walked to a leather sofa directly across from his boss and sat down.

He didn't even bother to shake my hand because he's not going to waste time being cordial with a man he knows will be rotting in a crypt within the year. Especially if that man's sudden death benefits him. What an asshole.

"Last month," the President said abruptly, "I told you that a senior NASA official had related to me in confidence a story about an experiment in mind control conducted by the Russians during the Cold War. This official claims that a report describing that experiment is sequestered somewhere in your agency. I want NASA to have access to the information in that report. Did you find it?"

Talbot shook his head. "Sir, there is no such document hidden in my agency."

The President leaned forward, jabbing his cigar at the Director's face. "And you flew up here in the middle of the night just to tell me you can't locate the damned thing?"

"No, Mr. President, I wouldn't do that. It appears that at least one copy of the report still exists. However, we have not yet taken possession of it. My people talked to a retired agent, an old gentleman who says he participated in the interrogation of a KGB psychiatrist in the late 1960's. Most of the questions directed at this Russian doctor were about mind control. This senior agent has no medical training and admits he did not understand the clinical details about hypnosis discussed in his presence. But, even though President Johnson later demanded that every scrap of information collected by the team conducting the interrogation be destroyed, this man decided what he

2

had heard was simply too important to go up in smoke. He says he pilfered a copy of the final report and has kept it under lock and key all this time."

The President felt a mountain of dread slide from his shoulders.

My lucky streak continues! Salvation is at hand!

"This guy had the balls to ignore a direct order from President Johnson?"

"Yes, and he did it despite the fact that Johnson believed if details about the Russian experiment were somehow leaked to the public, there would be rioting in the streets."

The President jumped to his feet and hurried back to the fireplace. His heart was beating so hard he feared Talbot could hear it. His headache had vanished. He drank the rest of his brandy in one gulp, set the snifter on the mantel and lit his cigar.

Talbot walked over to stand beside his boss.

"Mr. President, this agent's only child, a fifty-year-old son, has liver cancer. The father says he'll hand over his copy of the report only if we arrange a liver transplant for his boy. He apologized for resorting to blackmail. Said he hated bargaining for his son's life with information that is clearly the legal property of the federal government."

The President laughed. "I like this old fart."

"Although he would not discuss specific information contained in the report, he did tell us that the CIA, working on a tip, snatched the KGB psychiatrist in South America in 1967 and smuggled him back to Washington. A panel of medical experts and senior intelligence officials questioned the doctor for two weeks. The doctor said he had developed a new hypnotic technique that enabled him to take control of Lee Harvey Oswald's mind and order him to assassinate President Kennedy. He bragged that he was paid a fortune for his extraordinary feat."

The President whirled and glared at Talbot. "Those chicken-shits! I can't believe they didn't retaliate instantly. We should have dropped a cluster of atomic bombs on somebody's country five minutes after we found out about this. Russia picked up the tab, right?"

"No, sir. The psychiatrist said that Fidel Castro paid him."

"Castro financed JFK's assassination? And we did nothing about it? If I'd been in Johnson's shoes, every tobacco plant on the island of Cuba would still be radioactive today!"

"I believe you, sir."

The President puffed hard on his cigar for a full minute before he spoke again. "Find a compatible liver, save the dying man, and secure the report. That's an order."

"Yes, sir."

"What happened to the Russian psychiatrist?"

"Sir, he suffered a fatal heart attack while being escorted back to Brazil."

The President hurled his cigar into the fireplace. "Sure he did. And my wife's father is the Pope. Okay, let's talk about what this means to us. Tell me how you plan to use this brilliant doctor's long-lost research to keep me above ground. Explain how your agency will now be able to create a robotic human assassin anytime I want one."

Talbot chuckled. "That's funny, sir. Reminds me of that old movie about mind control. Frank Sinatra and Angela Lansbury. What was the name of that thing? Scientifically invalid, but scary as hell."

The President stepped closer to Talbot and tapped his silk necktie with a rigid finger.

"Forget scientific validity and concentrate on what's possible. I choose to believe that the KGB doctor did, indeed, find a way to turn an ordinary mortal into a controllable killing machine. To assume otherwise is to close the door on the possibility that this extraordinary feat can be repeated. And I don't give a rat's ass if a previous administration thought it prudent to destroy clinical information about the good doctor's work. Circumstances have changed in ways our predecessors could not have foreseen. We both know that a psychopath has vowed to put a bullet in my brain in front of the entire world before another year has passed. He has the resources to do it, too. But this could be my lucky day, Charles. Because if your agency can figure out how this doctor pulled off his big trick, we can use that knowledge to keep me alive."

Talbot frowned and said, "Sir, foreign terrorists say all kinds of outrageous things just to make the evening news. You're the most heavily guarded chief executive in the history of the world. No one can break through our elaborate protective net to get to you. Furthermore, the particular terrorist you're talking about is just a minor player on the world stage. A fanatic doing whatever he can to get attention. He is not a serious threat to you."

"Bullshit," growled the President. "That nutcase has promised to kill me and there's nothing you or anyone else can do to stop him from trying. Certainly not by relying on conventional security methods. But if my own personal programmed assassin sneaks up on this bozo while he's napping in the shade of his favorite mosque? Game over."

Talbot lowered his eyes to conceal his astonishment. *This is incredible! The President is talking gibberish!*

"These oil-rich Arabs racing around the desert on diseased camels are crawling with twisted beliefs we Christians can barely fathom," continued the President. "They're willing to sacrifice their own lives and the lives of countless others just to see me destroyed. And don't bother arguing that psychological control over human beings is Hollywood hype, because I know better. It's as real as today's headlines. People are strapping explosives to their bodies and their vehicles and then blowing themselves up in our embassies and troop barracks overseas. They blast themselves to shreds because some authority figure has convinced them that they'll spend eternity as martyrs if they voluntarily die for their cause. Call it extreme brainwashing or black magic or voodoo. I don't care what you label it. It's the most effective weapon in the world today. The bad guys use it without hesitation and I want to be in a position to use it, too. So I can defend myself." The President paused to catch his breath. Then he muttered, "And the nation, too, of course."

Talbot squared his shoulders. "Mr. President, the mere existence of this Cold War report is not proof that my scientists will soon be able to create a controllable assassin. It isn't even proof that the KGB psychiatrist did it. According to our agent, several of the medical people present during the interrogation were not convinced that everything happened exactly as the doctor said it did. One of them flatly stated he thought the psychiatrist had offered no new insights into hypnosis at all. In other words, sir, the doctor might have been lying."

"Okay, so the report isn't final proof of anything," said the President. "Not yet, anyway. I understand that your people have to analyze the KGB doctor's methods to see if what he said he did can be replicated. But the existence of the file does prove that I have a new reason to hope. My worst nightmare disappears if you can create an assassin so familiar to our target that he's above suspicion and can get close enough to that slimy bastard to kill him. So let me repeat my order. Find a compatible liver, make it available to the agent's son and secure the report."

"Yes, sir." Talbot blinked rapidly as he pondered the horrendous implications of what the President had just ordered him to do. Then he said, "Sir, although there is much I do not yet know about all of this, I can promise you one thing. My people will fail unless they have adequate funding available to them for research. Especially since they'll be working with an extremely short calendar.

The President waved his hand. "Don't worry about money. This started when NASA came to me for help in locating classified information about practical uses of hypnosis. Managing boredom is at the top of their list. Their future expedition to Mars has to come off without a hitch. NASA can't afford to have astronauts lose their ability to function during the monotonous voyage. Congress is going to debate the space agency's budget request for that mission next week. I'll do a little horse-trading and see to it that the bill passes exactly as written. You can siphon the fat in their budget into your black books. Give NASA a filtered copy of the KGB report. Just enough new information about hypnosis to help them get the astronauts to Mars and back."

"Very good, Mr. President." *Breakthrough! At least I'm going to come out of this fiasco with a ton of new money. Now all I have to do is find a way to derail the President's crazy scheme without him discovering that I caused it to crash.*

The President clamped his hand on Talbot's shoulder and squeezed. "I'm willing to do whatever it takes to make sure this happens. A little bird told me you believe you're even more qualified for the top job in the world than I am. If that's true, Charles, then listen carefully, especially if you're having unpatriotic thoughts about sabotaging my project. I am the only man alive who can deliver the White House straight to your door. And I'll do exactly that if you promise to focus all of your agency's considerable talents on this plan. You have a crucial decision to make tonight. You must agree right now to keep me alive by demanding that your people try to create a customized killer in record time. Or admit to me that you cannot accept my bold idea and start working on your first and last campaign speech."

Talbot experienced a wave of dread, replaced almost immediately by elation. *The most powerful man in the world has just offered me the deal of a lifetime. I've prevailed in this bizarre confrontation, not because of something clever I said, but because I cleverly said almost nothing at all!*

"Sir, that is a very generous offer," said Talbot. "Because I have the utmost respect for your judgment, I will do everything in my power to insure that this project gets the attention it deserves. As far as the other matter, I haven't made a final decision about whether to seek our party's nomination when your term expires. But I will welcome your support if I choose to run."

The President released his grip on Talbot's shoulder. "Good. We understand each other. Obviously, this has to be our little secret. You must insure total deniability for me at all times."

"Not a problem, sir."

The President escorted Talbot to the door and shook his hand. Then he said, "Incidentally, if I were in your shoes, I'd secure that report before the agent's son goes under the knife. People sometimes die during surgery. We can't afford to have daddy get upset and change his mind about turning over the information we need if his little boy should happen to give up the ghost on the operating table."

Charles Talbot opened his mouth to say how much he appreciated that advice, but the President had already walked away.

CHAPTER TWO

Six months later . . .
Three Palms Trailer Court
Smithville, Florida

The cardboard carton was the size of a small suitcase. A husky young fellow, balancing the carton on his shoulder, lurched up the steps of Helen Rutz's small wooden porch. When she asked him if he would place it inside her trailer, he shook his head.

"No can do," he panted. "Company rules."

He dropped the carton from a height of five feet. It landed with a tremendous thud, almost knocking Helen out of her sandals. She lit a cigarette and watched through narrowed eyes as he roared off in his boxy brown delivery truck.

"Company rules, my dimpled ass," she muttered. "You're just another lazy, good-for-nothing swamp bum."

Her scraggly backyard—all four feet of it—bumped smack up against the eastern edge of the Everglades. Something made a splashing sound nearby and Helen peered out at the mysterious swamp, smoke drifting from her flared nostrils.

She slapped the side of her foot against the carton. Felt like it was full of rocks. She tugged a pair of metal-rimmed spectacles out of a deep pocket on the front of her cotton dress, put them on and leaned over to read what was written on the return address label taped to the top of the carton. It had been shipped by Malcolm Johnson, Attorney at Law, Boston. She knew that Johnson was the lawyer handling Walter's estate because of the letter he had sent to her a year ago officially informing her that the General had died in his sleep. According to Johnson, the General's will stated she was to continue to receive $500 each month for the rest of her life, the same amount of money Walter had been sending to her since their divorce in 1968. It had seemed like a lot of money back then, but it barely covered her grocery bill now. The balance of Walter's substantial estate was going to his widow, Faye, and their two adopted children.

Helen puffed furiously on her cigarette. She should write to that bastard Johnson and complain. Didn't anyone in the legal profession ever think about inflation? On the other hand, she knew she was lucky that the General had decided to leave her anything at all. He probably had been under no obligation to pay her a red cent for years. The divorce had taken place so long ago, she couldn't remember the exact deal they had agreed upon. There had been no children so the property settlement had been a relatively simple matter. She had lost the divorce papers somewhere in her travels, during her heavy drinking days, and had never bothered to try to replace them. Perhaps Walter had continued to send $500 each month after he no longer needed to because he couldn't remember exactly what the agreement was, either. More likely, he had sent it because he felt guilty about being filthy rich while she lived in comparative squalor. She had said a million times that it was only the General's susceptibility to guilt that had prevented him from being a perfect asshole.

Cigarette smoke curling up under her glasses into her watering eyes, Helen tugged the heavy carton through the front door of her trailer and into the middle of her living room. She cut it open with a pair of scissors. There was a white business envelope inside with her name written on it in a shaky hand. Malcolm Johnson must be a very old man, she thought. Walter had died at age eighty-five. His lawyer could be nearly that old, too feeble to still be practicing law. No fool like an old fool . . .

Helen sat down on her sofa and opened the envelope. There was a two-page formal letter inside that began with her full address: Mrs. Helen Rutz; Three Palms Trailer Court; Trailer Number 93; Smithville, Florida. Johnson's secretary had prepared the letter on a computer and printed it in large type. How thoughtful of her, thought Helen. She figures I'm so old I must be nearly blind by now.

"Dear Mrs. Rutz: As I was going through the last of Walter's things this past week, in preparation for closing the estate, I ran across several items that I believe must have belonged to you at one time. Apparently they were overlooked when the two of you divided your physical possessions in 1968. They were in an old trunk I found in the attic under the dress uniform your husband wore when he was stationed in Germany. I don't know if they have any value to you now, but I thought it best if you made that determination. There is a fur stole, a pretty decent winter coat, two ladies' hats and several black-and-white photographs in sturdy metal frames. One of the photographs is of the two of you posing arm in arm on the Old Bridge in Heidelberg."

Helen snorted. Oh thank you, Malcolm, she thought, for being so damned thoughtful. What I really need now is a pile of useless, mildewed clothing and a couple of faded photographs to remind me that I once had it made in the shade.

"I also found in that trunk a batch of old papers, letters addressed to you, all written in longhand by your ex-husband. Out of respect for your privacy, I did not read any of them closely. After skimming a few of them to verify that they were just personal communications and not official documents, I stopped and asked Faye Rutz if she wanted to examine the letters (protocol, you understand). I also needed her formal permission to send them off to you. She declined to look at them and said she was not interested in things that were more about your time with Walter than about his place in history. She did say (and I agree) that if you happen to run across anything of significant historical value in the letters, you should report it to me at once. Faye is the legal owner of all of the General's personal effects."

"Drop dead, Faye," muttered Helen. "Reporting anything of value I find in these letters is not on my list of charitable things to do this year, you crazy old witch."

"I trust the checks are arriving on time each month. If there is ever anything I can do for you, Helen, please do not hesitate to contact my office. I just turned seventy-eight and will be retiring in two years.

10

When I close my practice, you will receive instructions about how you can find me if a special need arises. In the meantime, I remain Malcolm Johnson, Attorney at Law."

Helen noticed a postscript in Johnson's spidery scrawl at the bottom of the last page of his official letter: "I sent the dress uniform to Walter's adopted son Bradley, who maintains a collection of his father's important military memorabilia. Everything else I found in the trunk I have shipped to you."

Helen Rutz sighed, leaned back on her sofa and lit another cigarette. She had hoped to stumble across something in the carton worth money, something she could sell. Five hundred dollars a month just wasn't getting the job done these days. There was her meager Social Security check, of course, but it wasn't enough to live on. She was seventy-two years old. Her former glorious looks were long gone—too much booze, too many smokes, too many years of reckless living. When she was beautiful, she had traded shamelessly on her sex appeal. Men fell at her feet. They took care of her, bought things for her, made sure she had everything she wanted. And then, almost overnight, her looks were gone and so were the men—or, more to the point, the kind of men who seemed to have lots of money to spend on good-looking women.

She looked around in disgust at her dingy trailer house. At least she owned this piece of crap. Ted, her last full-time boyfriend, had outlived all of his alcoholic relatives. When he died, he left her his rusty old one-bedroom trailer, his new color television set and a few pieces of drab furniture. She had kept Ted's ashes in a jar on top of her television set for a while but rinsed them down the sink one day two years after he died when she suddenly remembered the time she had caught him in the sack with that skinny Cuban slut in trailer number 98.

Helen stubbed out her cigarette, kicked off her sandals, got down on the floor and began to pick through the items Malcolm Johnson had packed in the carton. She sniffed the stole. Yuck. It had been a beautiful strip of fox fur at one time, but it was now just something old and stinky. The two hats were kind of fun. She tried them on. The winter coat, in perfect condition, was basically a joke down here in the tropics, but the people at Goodwill might be able to find a use for it.

Carefully wrapped in plastic bubbles were four framed photographs. In addition to the picture of her and Walter on the Old Bridge, there was one of Walter and several members of his staff posing on the steps of the command building. She recognized First Sergeant Alonzo Brill, Colonel David Canonico and the General's personal chef, Klaus Zimmer. In the background, their faces a bit fuzzy, were two military policemen standing at parade rest, one on each side of the front door. The third picture was of Checkpoint Charlie in Berlin. Walter had insisted that if you looked closely you could make out a dead East German citizen slumped in the gutter behind the guard shack. She examined the picture carefully, just as she had when Walter first showed it to her, but she still could not see anything that could be positively identified as a human body. There was *something* there, but apparently, you had to know it was a body in order to recognize it as one. The fourth framed picture, taken in Berlin, was of Walter and Vice President Lyndon Johnson. It had been an important day, she remembered that much, and Walter had returned to Heidelberg in a helicopter and found her drinking herself into a stupor at the Officer's Club. Furious and embarrassed, he jerked her out the door, drove her home and ignored her for an entire week.

Helen removed the letters from the bottom of the carton. Some of the pages had turned yellow, the edges curling with age. She arranged them in four stacks, each nearly a foot tall. Then she glanced at a sentence here and there. They were written in Walter's impressive masculine script. She could not recall ever having seen any of them before, yet they were all addressed to her. Finally, she realized they were not letters at all, just records Walter had made about certain events he had participated in between 1961 and 1968. Each "letter" began with several paragraphs of personal junk about the two of them and then abruptly changed to factual notes.

Helen suddenly recalled something Walter had said to her one night during dinner. He had raised his wineglass in a mock toast. "This is history in the making, my dear," he had proclaimed, referring, on that particular evening, to the attention being lavished by most world leaders on Berlin and its new wall. "I am a witness to history. More than that, I am an important participant in it. It is therefore my responsibility to write down every detail of what I am seeing, hearing and doing."

Shit, thought Helen. These were just Walter's "Cold War" notes. Helen remembered that he had decided to keep a sort of diary of particular activities he was sure would someday be important to military historians or political scholars. But Walter worried that unauthorized persons would find and read his material before enough time had passed that the sensitive details he was putting down on paper were no longer any sort of security threat to the United States. He had apparently decided to crudely disguise the notes as letters to his wife.

Ridiculous, thought Helen. Pathetically transparent. But, she chuckled, it *had* prevented the decrepit Malcolm Johnson from seeing what the papers really were. The aging attorney, probably overwhelmed by the mountain of career memorabilia he encountered when he inventoried the General's possessions, no doubt made a number of errors as he worked on the complicated estate. And Faye wasn't any mental giant, either. She wouldn't have known what Walter had been up to in the 1960s and wouldn't have cared if she had known.

Helen wondered why Walter had never published these memoirs. Had he thought that he'd been too close to history to report it accurately? Surely, all of the events detailed in his "letters" had been written about by real historians, people who had the advantage of looking at things from a distance. Walter had been seeing history firsthand, but history can't truly be grasped up close, can it? No one ever seems to get it right when it's happening. Events have to be put into context. Someone has to do meticulous research and link things together that no one could have known about at the time history was being made. Helen had heard a famous author say that on television one evening, a man who had become quite wealthy doing just that sort of thing.

Well, Walter, thought Helen, you're far away now. How does it look to you these days? My guess is you'd give up all your direct knowledge of "history" for just one more romantic dinner in Paris, one more dash down a snowy mountain in the Swiss Alps, one more passionate night with me in a gondola in Venice.

Helen stared at the pile of old papers she had stacked neatly on the floor and shook her head. She knew the kind of junk Walter thought was important to write about—troop locations, boring conversations with other military leaders about strategies for freeing landlocked Berlin, Russia's evil plans for East Germany, Pentagon politics, visits to West Germany by important people, experimental military technology and the obscene proliferation of espionage agents. She recalled that he had gone on and on about the way General Norstad had reacted to President Kennedy's abrupt assignment of General Clay to Berlin in the middle of all the tension. Both Walter and Norstad had been offended by that insensitive maneuver and they didn't like it much when Kennedy flew into Berlin and played the world hero, either. *"Ich bin ein Berliner!"* Pure public relations crapola. The German people had gone wild over JFK for reasons Walter had never been able to fathom.

Helen stared at the burning end of her cigarette. Maybe, she thought, the dashing young President would still be alive if he had been smart enough to hang out in places where people liked him, such as Berlin, instead of getting his brains blasted all over his wife's pretty pink suit in, of all places, *Texas*.

Helen glanced at the small clock on the wall behind her faded sofa. Two o'clock in the afternoon . . . approximately. The clock was not very dependable. It had rusted in Florida's smothering humidity like everything made of metal did down here. She looked again at the pile of dingy papers in front of her. She had to prepare for a dinner date, if it could be called that, with a sweet older gentleman she had met recently at the pharmacy. Murray Klein had said his arthritis had been troubling him lately, and Helen had told him that she could give him a therapeutic massage that would snap him right out of it. Murray had smiled shyly and said, "What do you charge for a massage, Helen?" Helen had batted her eyes and purred, "Oh, dinner would be payment enough, Murray. Just dinner." She got plenty of free meals with that line, and, once in a while, she got laid!

14

Helen struggled to her feet, opened a fresh pack of cigarettes and lit up. She could take a nap, then bathe and enjoy a cup of hot tea while she waited for Murray to arrive in his nice new car. When she got home (if she got home!), she could get into her comfy robe and read some of Walter's "letters." There must be some interesting paragraphs about their wonderful early life together, about their sweet time in Europe, before he lost interest in her. It would be fun to see what he was thinking back then. Walter had been so mesmerized with her physical beauty in the beginning, so consumed with desire, she had never doubted that she would last long enough to spend her share of his family's fantastic wealth when he inherited it.

Wrong again, thought Helen. It was plain, dumb, ordinary Faye who got to spend the Rutz fortune, damn her moldy soul.

What happened, anyway? Walter had never said exactly what triggered the divorce. It wasn't her drinking. Hell, he drank his share in those days. It wasn't her infidelity. He never knew about it. Anyway, it was only that one time. No, it had to be something else, something so bad that it would cause him to march into the house one day, his handsome face as cold and gray as a block of granite, and tell her it was all over.

Helen wandered back to her cramped bedroom, stubbed out her cigarette in a large tin ashtray overflowing with butts and slipped out of her dress. She stretched out on the lumpy bed, squirmed in a vain attempt to find a comfortable spot and closed her eyes. Almost immediately her mind was flooded with brilliantly colored pictures of her life in Heidelberg—the wonderful stone house the Army provided their commander, the dining room with that enormous old chandelier, the elegant dinner parties she and Walter frequently hosted there!

Oh . . . lovely women in fine dresses wearing obscene quantities of jewelry . . . and handsome men in expensive designer suits. And the food, prepared by Chef Zimmer, was beyond description. There were always fine wines from all over Europe and rich desserts to die for . . .

Helen was nearly asleep, her mind brimming with images of crystal wine goblets, silver serving platters heaped with delicacies and Walter Rutz, his chest ablaze with battle ribbons, rising to toast his cheering guests.

Oh no! Someone was spilling red wine! On her! All over her beautiful pink dress . . .

Helen's eyes snapped open and she sat up in bed and cursed. What the hell was that all about? She had never owned a pink dress in her entire life!

Helen lit her twentieth cigarette of the day and shuffled out to the kitchen in her underwear. She filled a small teapot with water and put it on the stove. Then she took a deep, shuddering drag on her cigarette. *Dreams, she thought. Go figure . . .*

*

Murray Klein drove Helen back to her trailer at nine in the evening. Dinner had been a success—her date had paid for it with cash. She believed that was always a good sign.

They had talked about interesting places they had been and famous people they had seen in the flesh. Murray had vacationed in Fiji, he had said, and one time his greatest wish had come true when he saw Joe DiMaggio eating clams in a fancy seafood restaurant in Manhattan. Helen had told Murray she had traveled extensively in Europe but was vague about how she happened to be over there. She hinted that she was in great demand as a subject for world-class magazine photographers for many years and later lived off her investments.

"I once saw Queen Elizabeth when I was working in London," she had announced, "and about ten years ago I rode an elevator in New York City with Marlon Brando. He tried to pinch me."

"And now," Murray had said with a sympathetic smile, "you live in a trailer house in Smithville, Florida, just a few feet from the biggest swamp in America."

"The stock market took an unexpected dip," Helen had said bravely, her lower lip quivering, "and my broker had just given me what turned out to be terrible advice. I've been forced to, uh, adjust my standard of living a bit in recent years." Murray said he was very impressed with Helen's ability to cope with her abrupt change in fortune.

He did not smoke, so Helen had politely kept her cigarettes in her purse all evening. When they stopped at Murray's fancy new double-wide trailer house—located in a deluxe mobile home park on the other side of Smithville from Three Palms—for a dish of chocolate ice cream, Helen had been sure he was going to ask her to give him a massage. Instead, he had coyly said that he thought they should have another dinner date or two before he took off any of his clothes, even his shirt. With obvious pride, Murray gave her a tour of his home and pointed out numerous framed pictures of his family, including several of his late wife. Murray said he had five grown children and nine grandchildren. They all lived in or around Long Island. He said he had owned two bakeries on the island and had worked like a dog from before dawn until after dusk six days a week until his dear wife passed away and he decided to retire.

"Thanks for a lovely evening, Murray," said Helen as they pulled up in front of her decaying trailer in his sparkling new Oldsmobile.

"Helen," said Murray nervously. "May I call you next week?" Murray was seventy-five years old, bald and thin as a diabetic crane. But he looked and acted like a sixteen-year old boy on his first date.

Helen flashed him a dazzling smile she knew would keep the old man awake half the night planning their next evening together.

"If you don't, I'll be devastated," she whispered. Helen could do a dead-on impression of Marilyn Monroe's sultry whisper and this seemed like a good time to drag it out because she suddenly recalled that Joe DiMaggio, Murray's hero, had once been married to the blond bombshell.

Helen stood on her tiny porch, sucking ferociously on her first cigarette in several hours, as she watched Murray drive away. Nice guy, she thought. Probably has a few bucks tucked away someplace. I'll have him naked and whimpering in two weeks, tops. Just like shooting fish in a barrel.

Of course, she knew Murray would leave everything he had to his five kids. But he was going to be an easy touch for the basics—food, transportation, a bauble now and then. She doubted he'd be much of a lover, although you could never tell about these old men. Some of them were still randy as goats. Murray was careful and excessively polite right now, but he was terribly lonely and desperate to be touched. The key with a guy like Murray Klein was patience. He'd come around nicely if she just didn't put too much pressure on him.

Helen went inside, filled her teakettle and placed it on the stove. She exchanged her dress for an old terry cloth robe. Then she sat down in front of the stacks of "letters" written to her by Walter Rutz. I'll read these for an hour or so, she thought, then hit the sack. The next day was Saturday. She figured she could amuse herself with the letters most of the weekend if reading them turned out to be fun. I'll keep the best and burn the rest, she chuckled to herself.

Helen settled back, put on her reading glasses, lit a fresh cigarette and picked up the first sheet of paper. "Dear Helen," it began, "I have been thinking about you all day . . ."

*

Early Sunday morning Helen Rutz wearily removed her glasses and brushed a veil of cigarette ash from the front of her robe. She stared off into space, shaking her head slowly from side to side. The letters, once neatly stacked in front of her, were now scattered all over the trailer. There were sheets of paper in the bathroom, the kitchen, on top of the television set, strewn across her unmade bed and wedged between the cushions of the sofa. Some of the letters were stained with tea, strawberry jam or cream cheese. Several were decorated with wide purple underlines and exclamation points.

Helen struggled to her feet, stretched and yawned. She needed a bath. Except for two brief naps, she had read continuously since Friday night, stopping only to prepare a light snack or run to the bathroom.

"I'll . . . be . . . damned!" she said aloud. "Walter, I just love your tight little military ass. I really do, honey. Thank you! And thank you, too, Malcolm, you befuddled old fart. This is it, boys, salvation! *Money* for me and lots of it. All I need to do is think everything through carefully. There surely has to be a way to make this pay off."

Helen reached into the carton and retrieved the four photographs she had quickly scanned earlier. She looked again at the picture of Walter and the members of his personal staff taken as they posed on the front steps of the command building. She slipped her reading glasses back on and held the frame close to her eyes. Squinting, she could just make out the black metal nametags with white lettering fastened to the front pocket of each man's uniform. The tags on the two military policemen standing on either side of the front door were the hardest to see. Helen rummaged around in a drawer in the kitchen, finally producing a small magnifying glass she used when studying the tiny print on prescription labels. She bent over the photograph and placed her face as close to the lens as possible.

"Aha," she said aloud, "that's him! Just a boy he was, but a very *naughty* boy! How could I forget a name like that?"

She marched into her bedroom, picked up the phone on the small table next to her pillow and dialed the number of her friend and hairdresser, Brenda Quinn.

"Hello," said Brenda, slightly out of breath.

"Brenda, this is Helen."

"Oh, hey. You need an appointment? No. You were just in a few days ago. Advice? You meet some guy?"

"Yeah, I need advice. Honey, didn't you tell me one time that you work for a collection agency off and on? Filling in when somebody goes on maternity leave or vacation? Something like that?"

"Skip tracing. Pays pretty good and I can do it sitting down. Flexible hours, kind of interesting. Why? You need a job?"

Helen snorted. "Not anymore. I want to know if you can find someone for me."

"We can find anybody. There's a fee, though. I can't do it for nothing, Helen. And, it helps if you have the person's Social Security number. Why? Someone owe you money?" Brenda paused and screamed at one of her kids.

"Exactly. This individual owes me money. But, I don't have his Social Security number."

"Then it costs a little more, Helen. I mean, we can get it, the Social Security number, but it takes longer so it costs more."

"How much are we talking here?" asked Helen. Her savings account had a balance of nine hundred dollars and change.

"Hang on a minute while I strangle one of my kids. Be right back with you." Brenda dropped the phone and Helen could hear the ferocious battle that ensued. Brenda won.

"Okay, I'm back. Don't ever have kids, Helen. I'm serious as a kidney stone. It just isn't worth it," said Brenda.

"Okay, I won't have kids. I was asking you how much this is going to cost me, Brenda."

"Right. You know, I don't get into the billing that much, but I think if it was more than fifty bucks I'd be surprised. I'm sure it would be less than a hundred if all you need to know is this man's present location."

"Great. Sounds like we can do some business, Brenda. Look, I want to think about this a little more and then I'll give you a name, okay? Maybe I'll come by the salon early next week. You working?" Helen was thinking so hard she almost forgot to wait for Brenda's answer before she hung up. *Cambridge, Massachusetts. I think that writer I saw on television lives in Cambridge, pretty close to Malcolm Johnson's Boston law office.*

"Does the pope wear a funny hat?" asked Brenda. "I'll be there every day next week. I'm scheduled to do the skip-tracing thing on Tuesday and Thursday nights this month. Hey, I've gotta run, Helen. My other kid just committed a mortal sin. I'm serious. He's going to spend the rest of his natural life in purgatory."

"See you, Brenda," said Helen just as her friend broke the connection.

As Helen was turning to leave her bedroom, the phone rang.

"Helen? It's Murray Klein."

Helen glanced at herself in the dusty mirror over her dresser. I look like shit, she thought. Why do they always call when I look like shit?

"Murray. I didn't expect to hear from you so soon."

"I know. I said I'd call next week, but Helen, I . . . I . . ."

Helen could feel the dread in his voice. Damn. This guy was pathetic. She was going to have to say it for him.

"You need a massage in the worst way, don't you, Murray?" purred Helen. It occurred to her that Murray could come in handy very soon. She might need a ride someplace in his big new Oldsmobile. Like the airport in Miami.

"Well, I . . . ."

"Say no more. I know it's difficult for you to ask for help. But, relax, Murray, it's okay. *I want to do it for you.*"

That almost always got 'em, thought Helen, flashing herself a naughty look in the mirror. When you said you wanted to "do it" for them, they invariably translated that to mean whatever they wanted it to mean. Men! If they weren't so incredibly useful now and then, they'd be a total waste of flesh and blood.

She could hear Murray burbling with glee.

"Well, Helen, if it wouldn't be too much trouble," he said in a deeper voice. "I've got a couple aches and pains that are really screaming for attention."

"Give me an hour, Murray. I have to shower and change clothes. Then come on over here. We should do this on my bed."

Murray Klein was panting into the phone, so delighted he was actually unable to speak.

Helen smiled at herself in the mirror. It really is like shooting fish in a barrel, she thought.

Bang . . . bang . . . bang!

CHAPTER THREE

Lionel Cooper and Bret Barringer strolled into Barnacles, a popular seafood restaurant near Harvard Square, and were promptly ushered to their preferred table. The two celebrities met regularly in Cambridge, where Cooper lived, to discuss the author's latest blockbuster book on political corruption or Barringer's take, as CNN's senior reporter, on national and world events. Usually, Barringer tried to give Cooper the impression that he was there primarily to help the author in some way. Perhaps to arrange a confidential meeting with a powerful government insider or track down the source of a nasty rumor. Cooper's goal was always the same—to leave Barringer gasping in disbelief. He wanted the pragmatic reporter to go back to his office in a panic, thinking "That son of a bitch knows something so important it could start a war, but he won't tell me what it is! I need to stay on his good side so that, when he finally decides to confide in someone, he thinks first of Bret Barringer."

Cooper was dressed casually in a black silk polo shirt, tan slacks and black tasseled loafers. He had arranged his long white hair so that it looked attractively disheveled. Just over six feet tall, he was distinctive in appearance but not handsome. Although often seen in the company of beautiful women, he had never married. He was lean as a bean, almost bony, and his skin had a blue-white cast, like skim milk.

A chest-thumping atheist and acid-tongued political pundit, Cooper was a popular guest on late night television talk shows. He delighted in making intentionally provocative statements about organized religion and corrupt politicians. His fans relished the fact that Cooper considered decadent evangelists and power-mad public officials to be his natural prey.

Bret Barringer wore an off-the-rack navy blazer, wrinkled gray slacks, a pink button-down shirt and no tie. Short, plump and nearly bald, he had a knack for appearing to be distracted when he was actually riveted on the matter at hand. When he was on camera, he magically changed from one of the most forgettable faces in the room to an animated and charming performer. He lived near Washington D.C. with his wife Lillian and his mentally challenged daughter, Norma.

On the far side of the dining room, a handsome, broad-shouldered, powerful-looking man named Jim Redline sat alone at a table for two. He sipped lemonade and picked at his food. Redline was Cooper's chief of investigations and security. When circumstances required it, he also functioned capably as the famous author's bodyguard. Redline had counted a total of thirty-six customers in the dining room. Eleven were female. There were six waiters and two busboys flitting about. Fourteen tall windows let copious quantities of daylight into the square wood-paneled room. Two were open. No one in the restaurant appeared to pose a threat of any kind to Lionel Cooper.

Redline didn't always inventory everything in sight over lunch, but he did have a compulsion to do something productive during idle moments. He found it satisfying, often useful, to assimilate random details in his immediate vicinity and then see if they could be arranged into a meaningful pattern. He had once discovered that his boss was being tailed by an agent from a hostile foreign government when he scanned every face on a DC-10 midway to Beirut and realized he had recently seen one of the male passengers at least twice before. Jim Redline would not allow himself to believe something like that could occur naturally. Not when he was being paid top dollar to protect his famous boss.

A waiter delivered a steak sandwich, cooked rare, and a half-bottle of Merlot to Cooper. Barringer, who never ate red meat, had a shrimp and lobster scramble, sourdough biscuits and Earl Gray tea.

"Tell me about that devilishly good-looking man sitting over there pretending he's not keeping an eye on us," said Barringer. He inclined his head in the general direction of Jim Redline. "He's big enough to hunt bears with a tack hammer. Is he your bodyguard or what?"

Cooper reached for his wineglass. "I thought you were only interested in mainstream stories, Bret. The kind that could bring you another Pulitzer. I mean, you're a man who routinely dines with kings. A man with instant access to senators, generals, spies and corporate titans. The president of the United States is flattered when you ask him for an exclusive interview. Why would you want to talk about an ordinary mortal like that fellow?"

"Just curious," said Barringer diffidently. "I noticed he got here well ahead of us. The last time I was in the Cooper Building I saw him working in a big office near the front door. I remember thinking, that guy is a security consultant or something. Am I right?"

Cooper smiled. "I'll tell you a little about him, Bret, but I want you to consider this confidential information. His name is James T. Redline. His father was the best investigator I have ever known. William Redline worked cheek and jowl with me on the Russo case. In fact, without his help, I would never have solved that mystery. The elder Redline was nearly finished training Jim to take over his business when . . . well, when he suddenly died under suspicious circumstances. I immediately hired Jim to replace his late father."

Barringer chewed his food and silently reviewed his lunch companion's meteoric rise from a popular writer of mystery fiction to the most famous author in America. In the late 1980s, Cooper's true crime book *The Glass Coffin* disclosed the U.S. government's criminal complicity in the murder of Detroit mobster Sonny Russo. Cooper stunned the country by revealing that Russo had spent millions to get inside information on key people in the federal government and had then set about blackmailing some of the biggest names in Washington, forcing them to commit acts of near-treason as they manipulated Congress in ways that benefited organized crime. What set *The Glass Coffin* apart from other books of its type was that Cooper, after months of painstaking research, had been able to produce physical evidence that proved even his most outrageous claims concerning the crime were true.

He revealed names, dates, methods and motives. He explained who in the government had ordered the hit on Russo and exactly how it was done. Driven by an obsessive need to be seen by the reading public as a fearless crusader against abuses of power by elected officials, Cooper had managed to uncover everything there was to know about the case—including Russo's cement-covered, bullet-riddled remains.

Two things happened after the book was published. A number of important people in the government abruptly resigned from their jobs. Two went to jail. And Lionel Cooper, suddenly wealthy beyond his wildest dreams, became a national hero. Most Americans still felt that Cooper, now approaching seventy years of age, deserved to bask in glory, even if he never wrote another important word in his life.

"You say William Redline died under suspicious circumstances?" asked Barringer. "Surely you don't mean he was a direct casualty of the investigation into the Russo matter?"

Cooper nodded. "That's precisely what I mean. The coroner said William died when an artery in his brain collapsed. His insurance company accepted that finding, but I believe the man was murdered. I can't prove it in a court of law, Bret, but I believe someone got to him just seventy-two hours before I delivered the final draft of *The Glass Coffin* to my publisher. William was brilliant, experienced and extremely cautious. Only a professional could have killed him and made it look as if he died of natural causes. Fortunately, my own safety was never at risk. As soon as *The Glass Coffin* was under contract, I was protected by my fame and visibility."

"Good grief," said Barringer. He dropped his fork on his plate and looked around the room as if he expected to see a masked killer lurking nearby. "An investigator in your employ murdered! And you say there is nothing you can do about it?"

"Not a thing," said Cooper. "Jim Redline is even more convinced than I am that his father was murdered. He tried to find out who did it, of course, but he failed. You'd never know it by looking at him right now, but he is an extremely bitter young man. Scares me to think what he might do someday if all that bottled up rage boils over."

Barringer looked directly at Redline. The big man was calmly reading a newspaper.

"A powerful animal like that walking around with a thorn in his paw," muttered Barringer. "Bad news for someone, that's for sure."

"Jim doesn't carry a gun, but he's an expert in unarmed personal combat," said Cooper. "He keeps an eye on me when I'm out and about, in case some lunatic tries to tear my head off. That's happened twice so far. Both times the attacker ended up in surgery and I walked away without a scratch. Jim's a pleasant fellow, Bret, but when circumstances demand it, he can tap into a bottomless well of subconscious fury. I feel perfectly safe when he's around. It's a shame I'm going to lose him soon."

"Lose him?" While staring at Redline, Barringer had dropped a biscuit on his lap and was trying, with little success, to remove a blob of melting butter from the crotch of his wrinkled slacks.

"He hasn't said so yet," said Cooper, "but I know he's going to quit. He's not enjoying the jobs I've assigned him lately. Petty investigations compared to the volatile stuff we were digging into when his dad was around and I was younger. Jim works hard and provides me with a steady stream of scandals that feed my newspaper column. And, of course, a few peppery bits I can amuse the audience with when I'm on television and radio talk shows. But nothing earth-shattering these days, I'm afraid."

Barringer, who had a prodigious sweet tooth, signaled the waiter and ordered a piece of blueberry cheesecake. Cooper declined dessert and asked for a cup of decaf.

After the waiter served them both, Cooper looked sharply at Barringer and rapped the table several times with the handle of his spoon.

"Don't think I'm telling you that I'm slowing down, Bret, because I'm not. I keep a lot of balls in the air, even at my age, and I'm still the only writer in the business who doesn't peddle manufactured pap to the masses in order to make a buck. I showed them all how it's supposed to be done when I wrote *The Glass Coffin* and I'm still showing them!"

Barringer nodded in silent agreement, his mouth full of cheesecake. He was thinking that if Jim Redline had a brain in his head, he'd quit tomorrow. Nothing lasts forever and in Cooper's rather desperate declaration, there had been an odd noise that sounded very much like a death rattle . . .

"One thing that limits my output, of course, is my insistence that everything I say or write about is true," continued Cooper. "You know that I deal only with stories that can be supported by physical evidence. Other writers create provocative more-or-less possible scenarios out of thin air and write about them as if they are fact. There's big money in that game, but it has never appealed to me."

"I have nothing but respect for your remarkably high standards, Lionel," muttered Barringer. I'm going to have to spice this conversation up a bit, he thought drowsily, or I'll fall asleep. "Not to change the subject, but I heard something around the water cooler recently that might interest you."

"Really?" Cooper stifled a yawn and looked out across the dining room, hoping to see something that would prove he was still at the top of his game. He saw nine people he knew by name and a dozen who wished they knew him well enough to say hello. Pretty good numbers, he thought smugly. Nothing's changed yet. It will someday, of course.

"The brass at CNN are considering doing a major piece on Jay Jessup. Prime time, the whole nine yards," said Barringer. He glanced at Cooper in time to see a panicked look surface behind his pale blue eyes.

The author gripped the edge of the table and hissed, "Jay Jessup? That two-bit charlatan? What the hell are you talking about, Bret?"

"Jay has been getting considerable media attention lately with his public comments about our nuclear energy plants. He says not only are they vulnerable to the Y2K snafu, as many scientists have warned, but they also have structural flaws that are being covered up by the government. Jessup claims the shell and pea game started immediately after the Three Mile Island scare some years ago. And, he says the plants are sitting ducks for domestic or foreign terrorists, too."

"Oh, *please*," moaned Cooper, "spare me!"

"Jay Jessup believes a nuclear accident in this country is more than just a statistical possibility, it's inevitable. He says we're going to experience a Chernobyl-type meltdown within the next five years. The

CNN brass are convinced there'll be a riot in the streets when his new book comes out. They say the big enchiladas in the Department of Energy are paralyzed with fear of Jessup. He apparently got it right this time, Lionel."

Barringer pushed his fingertip against the last two crumbs of cheesecake on his plate, jammed his finger into his mouth and sucked. There were very few experiences left that a man with his long, rich history could still enjoy. Sticking little pins into a narcissistic fading star like Cooper was one of them. Cautiously, of course. He didn't want to permanently offend the popular writer. A bit too soon for that.

Lionel Cooper stared into his empty coffee cup, the muscles in his jaw vibrating with rage. He was thinking about Jay Jessup, a prolific writer blessed with youth, talent and boundless energy. Jessup was very adept at self-promotion. But he had not yet lived up to his real potential, primarily because his publisher had pushed him into the fast-fame, quick-money game available to those writers audacious enough to produce one sensational bestseller after another, even if the information in their books was not one hundred percent true. None of Jessup's work, in Cooper's judgment, had even come close to meeting his own lofty standards. Still, that did not mean that Jessup wouldn't pull off a major coup someday. Getting the truth was expensive and Jay Jessup had probably cobbled together enough money by now to buy a small piece of it. Or worse, a hunk of mind-boggling near-truth.

Cooper swept the palms of his hands across the long white hair on his temples and took a deep breath. "Jay Jessup," he hissed, spitting out the name as if simply pronouncing it created an unpleasant taste in his mouth, "is running down a dead-end road, Bret. I looked into that nuclear energy rumor three years ago. I found nothing. If Jessup says there's a serious problem, he's lying. It's a ghost story, totally unfounded in fact. Long after the last man on earth has died of thirst or plague, those sweet little nuclear generators will be humming along perfectly. You heard it here first."

Barringer shrugged. "Perhaps. But, most authors just figure out what sells and then write about it. Fear outsells everything else two to one, Lionel. People want to have their worst nightmares described for them in excruciating detail by writers talented enough to create at least the *illusion* of plausibility. Stories don't have to be absolutely true anymore. They just have to be *possible*. Absolute truth no longer exists, anyway. It's been replaced by absolute uncertainty. And Jay Jessup is uncannily good at creating vast amounts of uncertainty where none existed before. The big brains at CNN are understandably impressed with him."

Cooper pushed himself away from the table and rocketed to his feet, knocking over his coffee cup and spilling Barringer's tea all over everything. He waggled a long finger in Barringer's face.

"Jay Jessup is the kind of low-life scum that tries to fool people into believing that things that are only possible are *real*! Not only *real*, but *true*!" Cooper's voice boomed across the elegant dining room. Several people appeared to be annoyed at the spectacle of the white-haired, wild-eyed author scolding the famous CNN reporter, but most were obviously quite delighted. Jim Redline jumped up quickly and began watching everyone in the room at once.

"If CNN is going to report all the news that's just possible instead of sticking to the news that's true, then we might as well have the Disney Channel covering national and world events! Because that's Mickey Mouse, damn it, Mickey Mouse!"

Cooper wheeled around and, to scattered applause, stomped out of Barnacles Restaurant.

After a moment, Jim Redline sat down and resumed working on a crossword puzzle in the Boston Globe. Barringer tossed his napkin on the floor and crossed his arms in an effort to appear monumentally disgusted. Four distressed waiters rushed to his table and began to put things back in order. The maitre'd hiccuped and fled to the safety of the kitchen.

Redline needed a four-letter synonym for the word "eviscerates." Aha, he thought, I think I know this one. He printed his answer with great deliberation: G-U-T-S.

CHAPTER FOUR

It was six o'clock in the evening when Tina Romero walked into Lionel Cooper's office carrying a manila file folder and a silver ice bucket. Tina had short black hair and sparkling cinnamon eyes. Thirty years old, she was single, attractive and a workaholic. As Cooper's personal secretary and factotum, she was responsible for paying the author's bills, coordinating his appointment calendar, screening his calls and trying her best to keep the eccentric old man from doing something so outrageous it would land him in jail. She was privy to nearly everything going on in Cooper's muddled life.

Cooper thought of Tina as a sexy organizational genius whose exceptional skills enabled him to function in the midst of chaos. Her duties forced him to allow her access to many of his most private activities. Consequently, he had moments when he felt unusually close to Tina. Once, at the end of a long boozy office party, he had made a grotesque pass at her. She had rebuffed him cruelly, her beautiful eyes crackling with disgust. He had never tried it again.

Cooper was sitting behind his massive mahogany desk in a high-backed green leather executive chair, deep in thought, his white hair fanned out around his patrician head in a frenzied borealis. He clutched a highball glass half full of twenty-five-year-old single-malt scotch.

Tina placed the file folder in front of him and then used silver tongs to extract three ice cubes from the bucket and drop them, delicately, so as not to cause a splash, into the pale liquor.

"If you have a moment, Jim would like you to scan this file. He's on the phone but will be in shortly to talk to you about it," said Tina.

30

"What time is it?" asked Cooper. The brass clock on the paneled wall directly across from him displayed the time in six different places in the world, but he rarely looked at it. It interferes, he had once explained to an exasperated Tina Romero, with my intense concentration on the here and now.

"It's six o'clock. You have dinner at eight in Boston with those pointy-headed liberals from National Public Radio."

Nothing happened for several seconds. Then Cooper stretched and peered around the office as though he had never seen it before.

"Tell Jim I'm ready to talk when he is," said Cooper. He took a sip of his freshly chilled drink, settled back in his chair and opened the file folder.

Jim Redline walked into Cooper's office just as Tina was making her way out. She flashed the big man a warm smile, but he did not appear to notice. She walked briskly away, wondering, as she had many times before, if the day would ever come when Redline would smile first.

Redline sat down in one of the four green leather guest chairs arranged in a semi-circle in front of Cooper's desk. He waited a couple of beats to see if his boss was going to offer him a drink. But the author was studying the file and did not look up or speak.

Finally Redline said, "After you, uh, left Barnacles this afternoon, Mr. Barringer took a tape recorder out of his pocket and turned it off. Then he called someone on his cell phone. He signed the lunch ticket, apologized to the staff for the mess you made, shook hands with two or three people and wandered away."

Cooper took a slow sip of scotch and nodded.

Redline inspected the magnificently appointed office and tried to figure out if anything had been moved since the last time he'd been in the room. He had just finished an inventory of the interesting items on Cooper's credenza when the author spoke.

"Okay, I've finished the file on Helen Rutz. I see nothing here of interest to me, Jim. You know as well as anyone that I've been presented with countless oddball leads on the JFK assassination over the years and none of them, not a single one, has ever panned out. What's special about this one?"

Redline shrugged. "Maybe nothing. I took Mrs. Rutz's call yesterday when both you and Tina were out of the office. I thought that what she had to say sounded pretty good. Helen was married to General Walter Rutz during the early sixties when he was commander of the U.S. Army in Europe. They divorced in 1968. Walter died last year and the lawyer handling his estate shipped a box of old papers to her residence. Said he thought she might want them for sentimental reasons. Dozens of letters handwritten by her late ex-husband and addressed to her. Turns out they aren't letters at all. They're confidential documents Helen Rutz says prove there was a foreign conspiracy to assassinate JFK. A little voice in my head said, 'well, why not'?"

"In other words, you're playing a hunch," said Cooper.

"Yeah. And that's all I'm doing. Playing a hunch."

"General Walter Rutz," said Cooper. "I met him once. His father had offices in Boston and New York. Karl Rutz invested heavily in the reconstruction of Europe after World War II and made a ton of money. Even dabbled in politics for a while. I ran into General Rutz when he was stationed at the Pentagon. Chatted with him for an hour or so. He looked exactly like you'd expect a general to look."

"Like Jimmy Stewart?"

"Like Clark Gable."

"Helen Rutz said she put the new information in Walter's letters together with something she recalled from her time in Europe with him and suddenly realized she had stumbled across proof of a conspiracy," said Redline. "Physical proof, not a theory. She insisted it would be impossible for anyone else in the world to know what she knows."

"Oh, sure," said Cooper. "Jim, I can't begin to count the number of times someone has called this office claiming to be the only person alive who knows what's really going on with this or that major world event. Crackpots, every one of them."

"I know that," said Redline. "Anyway, Mrs. Rutz asked me to set up a meeting with you as soon as possible. I said I would talk to you about this and get back to her promptly. She said, 'that's nice, but be sure and tell Mr. Cooper that if he's not interested, I will take my story to someone else in a heartbeat.'"

"What sort of physical proof is she offering, Jim?"

"I have no idea. She insists that you meet with her first and sign a contract before she'll reveal her proof."

"Sign a contract?" said Cooper, rubbing his eyes. "She wants a signed contract and probably a hunk of money up front before she'll tell us exactly what she has? Does that sound fair to you, Jim?"

"No. Mrs. Rutz told me she decided to make this offer to you first because she caught your act on television one night, some talk show. Said you announced that if anyone could provide you with physical proof establishing who was actually responsible for the assassinations of Martin Luther King or Robert Kennedy, you'd split the profits from the book you would write with the source. She said you claimed the profits from a book like that could run into the millions."

"And she figured proof of a conspiracy to kill JFK would also qualify for that deal?"

"Yup," said Redline. "Lionel, Mrs. Rutz probably does not have final proof of a foreign conspiracy to assassinate JFK, as she believes, but I doubt her story is entirely bogus. Could be something worth knowing about buried in those so-called letters from the general."

"I don't share your optimism about this at all," said Cooper bluntly. "Not yet, anyway. I need more information."

"I thought you'd say that," said Redline. "That's why I'm offering to fly to Florida and talk to this old woman face to face. She lives in a house trailer on the edge of the Everglades. Said she's fallen on hard times in recent years."

"Aha," said Cooper. "I knew it! We finally come to the real reason Mrs. Rutz is desperately trying to parlay the general's stuffy old love letters into cash. She's dead broke."

"Could be," admitted Redline.

"Let's say she really does have something you feel is worth my time and money, Jim. You want to bring her back with you?"

"Yes. But if she can't or won't show me enough of her so-called proof to justify a meeting with you, I'll just thank her for her time and leave."

Cooper closed the file folder and pushed it across the desk.

"Okay," he said, "I'll gamble on your hunch, Jim. But know this. It won't be easy to persuade me that Helen Rutz is the real deal, no matter how plausible her story sounds to you. I don't believe the JFK mystery will ever be solved, period. Don't forget to do a background check on this lady before you buy a plane ticket. She could be an alcoholic flake sitting around in her underwear eating cat food."

Redline stood, grabbed the file folder and headed for the door. "I started the background investigation yesterday," he said. "So far, so good."

Tina Romero, drinking from a can of diet cola, strolled back into Cooper's office. She sat down in a guest chair and crossed her legs, alluring in patterned hose under a short navy skirt.

"What do you think about the Helen Rutz thing?" asked Cooper. He stared at Tina's legs, mostly because he knew it annoyed her.

Tina tugged at her skirt. "I think Jim could use some away time. Whenever he starts mumbling into his morning coffee about beaches and surf and palm trees, it means he needs to take a trip."

"I agree," said Cooper. "He'll enjoy Florida for a couple of days and come back with a nice tan and not much else."

"He really does need a break, Lionel," said Tina. "He's been pacing back and forth in his office like a caged tiger for months."

"I expect him to go off on a boondoggle now and then," said Cooper. "Part of the cost of having a high-energy guy like Jim on my payroll. But this Rutz story is obviously a scam. As soon as I opened that file folder, I detected the familiar aroma of swamp gas. Speaking of swamp gas, I surely have some reason for agreeing to have dinner with those talkative clowns from NPR?"

"As a matter of fact," said Tina, "you don't. That's why I'm still here. Jim and I thought you'd appreciate a suggestion or two to help get you through the night. He's picked up some fascinating scuttlebutt about the head of the FCC that will have your dinner companions hanging on your every word."

Cooper grinned. "Fantastic," he said.

A few minutes later, Cooper was on his way to Boston and Tina was back in her office, shutting down her computer and organizing the papers on her desk in preparation for tomorrow's hectic day. She thought idly about Jim Redline's "boondoggle" to Florida. No one is better than Jim at interviewing women, she reminded herself, even women of Helen Rutz's vintage. If she knows anything new at all about the JFK assassination, she's going to tell charming Jim all about it. One dazzling smile from him and Mrs. Rutz will talk like a magpie.

CHAPTER FIVE

Jim Redline drove into Smithville, Florida at three o'clock in the afternoon. He cruised all three blocks of Main Street and noted the location of two scruffy motels, a new pancake restaurant, a post office, the police station and a busy medical clinic. There were senior citizens on every corner, clad in colorful beachwear and floppy sandals. They laughed and bounced around as if they hadn't a care in the world. Just happy to be alive, to be anywhere, even a backwater burg like Smithville.

Redline drove to the edge of town and parked his dark blue rented Taurus sedan under a leafy tree. When he got out to stretch, the sun smacked into his wide back like a steam iron, plastering his damp polo shirt to his thick upper body. He checked out an antique shop and a candy store, then ambled into The Oldies But Goodies Café in search of a late lunch and something cold to drink.

Except for two elderly people dining quietly at a corner table, the café was empty. Redline plopped down on a stool at the counter and squinted at the lunch specials printed in blue chalk on a piece of paper tacked to the wall. Breaded sea perch with fries, a roll and salad bar. BLT with fries and salad bar. Fried clams, fries and salad bar. Jim glanced at the nearby salad bar—a big glass bowl half full of pale coleslaw floating in a pool of murky ice water. Two plastic relish trays sprinkled with shriveled carrot sticks and blobs of limp celery bobbed in the water next to the bowl.

A large woman materialized behind the counter. Her mouth was shellacked with a thick layer of orange lipstick. She was draped in an orange tent dress that was trying desperately to conceal her chubby thighs and wide behind. She wore a silver ring on each of her fingers and a gaudy necklace made of coral seashells. Her coarse black hair, cut close to her square skull, was flecked with silver. The plastic tag pinned to her dress said, "Rose Blanchard, Owner/Manager."

Rose flashed him a goofy grin, revealing her multi-colored front teeth above a wide yellow chin dotted with stiff black hairs.

"Hi," said Rose heartily. "Welcome to my little café. What'll it be?"

"BLT special," said Redline. "Got any lemonade?" Ernest Borgnine, he thought. Rose could be Borgnine's double.

"Best lemonade in Florida," chortled Rose. "BLT SPECIAL!" she shrieked at someone in the kitchen. Then she took a dented metal pitcher from an old Kelvinator refrigerator and poured lemonade into a tall plastic tumbler full of crushed ice.

"You've never been here before," announced Rose as she slammed the tumbler on the counter. "I would have remembered a handsome devil like you." She tilted her head and flashed Redline a bawdy wink.

Redline took a thirsty pull on the lemonade. His lips twisted and he shuddered from head to toe. "Wow," he gasped. "Bitter!"

"Too much sugar ain't good for ya," boomed Rose. "You moving here? Or just passing through?"

"I won't be here long," said Redline. "Day or two."

"Rats," sighed Rose. "Friday we're having an all-you-can-eat fish fry and homemade key lime pie. Perfect meal for a man your size. You played football, right?"

"In college," said Redline. "Long time ago."

"Figures," said Rose. "What's your name? You married?"

"My name is Jim. I'm single."

Rose leaned on the counter and tapped Redline's forearm with a finger the size of a jumbo frank.

"You might consider moving to Smithville, Jim. It's a terrific place to live. Most of the people here are over fifty-five. Quiet, law-abiding and respectful of others. We're way off the tourist trail so we have hardly any drugs or burglaries at all. Of course, we do have some insects and vermin and reptiles and the like because of the swamp."

Redline tried another sip of lemonade. He coughed against the back of his hand. "Sounds wonderful," he said, blinking tears from his eyes.

"And I don't care what people say about killer alligators stalking around town and all that hee-haw. Why folks want to make up scary stories like that is beyond me."

"Alligators stalking around town?"

Rose grinned. "Well, here's what it is, Jim. We've had some seniors disappear at night when they're out walking alone. The police have done their best to explain how that happens, but people want to believe that alligators are picking off the geezers one at a time. They say Smithville is a very popular snack bar for man-eating carnivores."

"What do the police say?"

"They say a few befuddled and over-medicated folks have wandered into the swamp, stepped in quicksand and bubbled out of sight. Mystery solved."

A distant bell clanged. Rose whirled and waddled off to the kitchen. The other two customers in the café, an old gentleman accompanied by a frail woman supporting herself with a cane, waved in the general direction of the counter and tottered out the door.

Rose hustled back with a mammoth sandwich and a jungle of curly fries draped across a plastic platter.

"I'll let you eat this in peace, Jim," said Rose. "Don't forget to try our fabulous salad bar." She smiled warmly and went to sit at a table near the front window. Sipping coffee from a pink mug, Rose watched the traffic go by, an expression of intense fascination on her face.

Jim ate slowly and, between bites of his sandwich, turned around on his stool and inventoried objects in the café. Eleven square tables with white tablecloths and clear glass ashtrays. A calendar tacked to the wall near the restrooms that featured a dramatic painting of a sailboat struggling with a storm at sea. A genuine Wurlitzer jukebox. Redline was tempted to play some music but didn't have any change. Besides, he thought, all the tunes are sure to be oldies but goodies.

Suddenly, Rose clambered to her feet and pointed at something outside.

"Well, I'll be go-to-hell," she bellowed. "There goes Ted's new Dodge pickup and, get this, *Ted ain't in it!* I can't see who's driving that sucker!" She looked at Redline and wobbled her head in amazement. "I mean it, Jim, if you sit by this window long enough, you'll see everything there is to see in this world. Everything!"

Redline dropped some wrinkled bills on the counter and found his way to the men's room. It was spotless and smelled of citrus air freshener. As he washed his hands, Redline examined his face in the mirror mounted above the stainless steel sink. There were fat beads of greasy sweat on his forehead. He needed a haircut. His eyes were bloodshot. Been trapped in that boring office too long without a break, he thought. And I could use a good night's sleep.

He smiled when he noticed a line of graffiti carefully printed across the top of the mirror with a black marker. *You can never know for sure . . . you know.*

"Tell me about it," he said out loud.

*

Redline drove straight to Three Palms Trailer Court. Some of the trailers were decent, a few were boarded up, and one or two looked like they'd been there since the dawn of time. The narrow gravel road that meandered between the trailers was a minefield of treacherous chuckholes.

Redline pulled in beside trailer number 93. He sat for a moment staring through the windshield at the vast tangled swamp directly behind Helen Rutz's home. She lives less than ten feet from a jungle crawling with flesh-eating reptiles, he thought. Must be a laugh a minute. He got out of the car, climbed three steps to a small wooden porch and knocked on the trailer's cheap aluminum door.

The door popped open and Helen Rutz appeared, smoking a cigarette. Her blond hair was nicely done, her makeup skillfully applied. The skin on her neck sagged a bit and her cheeks were laced with tiny varicose veins, but it was obvious that Helen Rutz had once been a real looker. She wore a yellow sundress and white leather sandals. There was a slim gold topaz ring on her right hand and a gold watch on her left wrist.

Redline smiled at Helen while he did a quick assessment. She appears to be in her early seventies, used to having plenty of money, but doesn't have any now, he thought. Always expected to be beautiful and sexy. Can't handle getting old. Still vain, probably spoiled, likely stubborn.

"Please come in, Mr. Redline," said Helen sweetly. Redline stepped into the small trailer and paused while his eyes adjusted to the dim light. Plain as a used tea bag. A miniature kitchen with a small oak breakfast table, two stick chairs, a white refrigerator, a two-burner gas stove and a tiny counter with nothing on it but a shiny stainless steel toaster. Helen led him into the living room. It was inexpensively furnished with a drab brown corduroy sofa and two matching club chairs. There were two lamp tables, scuffed from top to bottom, glistening with lemon-scented furniture polish. No family pictures in sight.

A narrow dark hallway led from the living room to what Redline assumed would be a bathroom and a bedroom. An air conditioner of uncertain vintage on the roof of the old trailer thumped and wheezed, somehow managing to keep the interior relatively cool.

The radiant Helen Rutz looked totally out of place in the musty old trailer house, like an aging movie star stranded in a ghetto. This woman's in trouble, thought Redline.

Helen could not have been the original decorator of the trailer's uninspiring interior, he realized, but she might have purchased the fancy white shades for the two old fudge-brown ceramic lamps in the room and perhaps the maple rocking chair parked in front of the modern television set. Next to the rocking chair was a cardboard carton that appeared to be half full of loose sheets of yellowed paper. In a pile near the carton were two ladies' hats, a thick winter coat and a fur stole.

"Please sit down," said Helen, waving him toward one of the club chairs. She took a seat at the end of the sofa so she could flick her ashes into a large tin ashtray on a nearby lamp table. She held her cigarette like a painter's brush, daintily and at a rakish angle.

"May I offer you something to drink, Mr. Redline?"

"No thank you," said Redline. "I just finished lunch. And please call me Jim."

"You ate lunch here in Smithville?"

"A café called Oldies But Goodies."

"Rose Blanchard's place," said Helen. "She spends every waking moment in that place. No rocket scientist, looks like a truck mechanic, but has a heart of gold. Thinks coleslaw is one of the four basic food groups."

"I noticed her fascination with coleslaw," said Redline. He abruptly produced a small spiral notebook and a pencil. Apparently, the cordial introductions are already over, thought Helen.

"I'm sure you have a lot of questions for me, Jim," she said. "Fire away."

"Okay. How did you end up in this old trailer house next to the Everglades?"

"Same way you did."

"Meaning?"

"I drove down here one day to visit someone and just never left." Helen took a deep drag on her cigarette. "What's that old saying? 'Life is what happens while you're making other plans'?"

Redline scribbled in his notebook. "Yeah," he said. "Okay, next question. Why am I here?"

"Because I know something that could be worth millions of dollars to Lionel Cooper," said Helen. "Something no one else could possibly know. I thought of Mr. Cooper right away when that cardboard box over there was delivered to my doorstep. Your employer is wealthy and as you can plainly see, I am not. This is about me getting my hands on some big money before I'm too damned old to enjoy it."

"Helen, are you saying proof of a conspiracy to assassinate President Kennedy is in that carton?"

"I can't believe you asked me such a ridiculous question," said Helen sharply. "Of course not! Do I look like I was born yesterday, Jim? The location of the proof is known only to me. That's how it has to be until Mr. Cooper and I have signed a contract." Helen squared her shoulders and threw Redline a disapproving look.

Redline rolled his pencil up and down his chin and contemplated the cardboard box. Helen used the break in conversation to look him over carefully. He appeared to be in his early thirties and was well over six feet tall. Powerfully built, very muscular chest and shoulders. Huge hands. His strikingly handsome face was framed in curly light brown hair. He had steady, clear blue eyes and straight teeth. He was dressed casually in a white polo shirt, tan slacks and tan loafers. A thinker, Helen decided, enjoys solving puzzles. But an athlete, too. Reserved. Distant, even. Looks tired, as if he hasn't had much sleep lately. No wedding band. Helen wondered what kind of social life a hunk like Jim Redline—

"Helen," said Redline suddenly, "do you really know where the proof is? Or do you just hope you know where it is? Or once was?"

His question was reasonable enough, but his voice had an irritating, condescending sound to it. He's trying to provoke me into blurting out the truth, thought Helen. He wants to find out in five minutes or less what I've got and then get the hell out of here.

"You have to understand, Helen," continued Redline, "Lionel Cooper gets calls all the time from people who claim to know something about something. And most of them sincerely believe they do know something unique and important. But guess what? Almost without exception, they turn out to be wrong."

Helen's felt her blood pressure spike. This guy is a professional prick, she thought. I'd like to slap him silly! But there's a lot of money at stake here. No matter what he says or does, I have to stick to my plan. Everything depends on it. She took a deep breath and tried to bring her mounting rage under control.

Redline appeared not to notice Helen's discomfort. "You see," he went on, "Lionel Cooper pays only for genuine, bird-in-the-hand physical proof. Not theories. If you don't have that proof, Helen, right here, right now, then you don't have anything that would interest him."

Redline sat back and waited for his words to sink in. He had given a version of this speech to many people under similar circumstances, and he knew most of them were not prepared for it. The blunt talk marked the beginning of the end of their fanciful dreams.

Helen sat stiffly on the sofa, her lips compressed, her hands twisting in her lap. She needed to begin her pitch immediately. She had to say something that would grab Jim Redline's attention or he was going to get up and walk out. But she was so angry that the first three things that occurred to her were too filthy to say to anyone, let alone a man she needed desperately to impress.

"Is the proof here or not, Helen? Yes or no?" Redline got to his feet and put his pencil and notebook in his pocket. He was bone tired and suddenly very disappointed. This broke, pitiful old woman, he thought, is just trying to figure a way to nail somebody for a few bucks. She has nothing. Oh well . . . win some, lose some.

"In 1961," said Helen abruptly, "my ex-husband was the commander of the U.S. Army in Europe. We were stationed in Heidelberg, Germany. Walter was very gregarious, a real people person. We both loved hosting dinner parties in our beautiful home. There were plenty of interesting people around. We enjoyed putting on a big feed and talking to our fascinating international guests about important world events. One night we invited the Spanish ambassador to the United States, Juan Ortega. He brought along his niece Maria, a student at the University of Heidelberg. There were two unusual things about that particular night. First, the main course was wild boar. Walter had bagged one in Bavaria, and he wanted everyone to know about it. It was the first and only time we served wild game. Second, in spite of the fact that she was just a child, Maria was by far the best-looking woman in the house. Better looking than me and in those days, I was a knockout."

Helen lit a fresh cigarette. Redline was still standing. He looked longingly at the door. With a calmness she truly did not feel, Helen plunged on.

"I was jealous of the attention Walter paid to Maria that night. He was a very attractive man. And, he came from one of the wealthiest families in New England. All I had going for me was my pretty face. I was painfully aware that I was fortunate just to have met a man like Walter, let alone marry him. Maria was infatuated with Walter the moment she set foot in our home. They were sitting side by side at the table, and every time I looked over there, he was whispering in her ear or peeking down the front of her dress at her big knockers like an oversexed teenager. I got a little drunk and it wasn't long before I was totally pissed."

Helen stood up and began pacing around the small room, trailing a ribbon of smoke. Each time she walked past Redline, she looked into his eyes.

"I didn't say anything to Walter about how angry I was. But I wouldn't make love to him, either. Not that night, for sure, and not the next night, either. He was a lusty fellow and he knew I was punishing him for something. But he couldn't figure out what he'd done to make me so furious. Several rather tense days went by and I finally calmed down. Decided I'd probably overreacted. As far as I knew, Walter had always been faithful to me. And, I thought, why would this worldly, sophisticated man fool around with a mere *child* anyway, when he had me? I began to feel guilty about how I'd been treating him. I decided to surprise him, go to his office and seduce him. He loved to have sex with me in weird places. The weirder the better. One time we . . ."

Helen's voice trailed off and she shook her head as though clearing it of an old and inappropriate memory. Redline turned his face to the side and smiled.

"Never mind. Anyway, I got all dolled up and drove to Walter's office in the command building late in the morning. The sergeant major said the general was out but would return shortly. I waited in Walter's huge office. In a few minutes I was bored stiff. His office was all gobbed up with his military trophies. Weapons and awards and photographs and so on. He had served in Korea and had been decorated for heroism too many times to count. I tried to amuse myself by looking at his things, even though I had seen them many times before. I remember thinking there couldn't be anything more stupefying than staring at pictures of Douglas MacArthur posing with that ridiculous corncob pipe. Eventually, I sat down behind Walter's desk and began to rummage through his drawers. It felt wicked but fun."

Helen suddenly wheeled and barked at Redline, "Either sit down and listen to this or get the hell out of here, Jim! We can't both stand up in this tiny fucking room!"

Redline reacted like he'd been caught with a left hook. He tumbled into his chair and jerked out his pencil and notebook.

Helen puffed on her cigarette and began to pace again.

"I found an odd package in his desk. It was wrapped in ordinary brown paper. What caught my attention was the return address. It was from Maria Ortega. In the corner she had written, 'Personal and Confidential.' Walter had opened it, looked it over and then stuffed it in the drawer, out of sight. That little *bitch*, I thought. Turns out she had sent him a simple jewelry box, very inexpensive, the kind you could buy in any tourist shop in Heidelberg. Wooden, lacquered finish, a small painting of the famous Heidelberg castle in the center of the lid. There was nothing in the box. It was just an empty jewelry case lined with cheap blue velvet cloth. When I picked it up, I noticed a note folded underneath it. Maria's English was excellent and her handwriting perfectly legible. The note said she was faced with some kind of terrible problem, something she thought Walter would want to know about, and she needed to talk to him face-to-face as soon as possible. She said she felt that they had established a special bond at the dinner party, an unspoken connection that caused her to think of him as soon as she encountered her difficulty. She said the problem had to do with the jewelry box and how it had come into her possession. She provided her dormitory room phone number and signed off with some mumbo-jumbo that I interpreted to be a naked promise that Walter, if he helped her, would find her willing to express her gratitude in any way that pleased him."

Helen paused to stub out her cigarette. She noticed Redline was writing in his notebook. He looked up and asked, "Any idea why your husband invited the Spanish ambassador to the dinner party?"

"Yes," said Helen, barely able to keep from giggling with relief. *This is working, she thought, just like I hoped it would. He's writing everything down!* "Walter's father was interested in doing business in Spain. But he wanted to visit personally with President Franco before he invested money there. Karl Rutz asked my husband if he could persuade the ambassador to arrange for a meeting with Franco in Madrid. "

Redline nodded. "Okay."

Helen lit another cigarette and drew the smoke deep into her lungs. "When I found the jewelry box and the note from Maria, I was blind with fury. Here I was in Walter's office, feeling ashamed of myself, prepared to submit to his wildest sexual fantasies to make up for my inexcusable behavior, and what do I find? I find proof that he is about to trade favors with an exotic young girl. I'm quite sure I was, at that moment, as jealous as it is possible to be. I might even have been temporarily insane."

"So you took the jewelry box," said Redline.

"Yes, I took it," snapped Helen. "I hid it in my purse and ran for the front door. The sergeant major tried to stop me. He said the general was only moments away. I mumbled something about suddenly remembering another appointment and I fled. I drove straight home and made myself a stiff drink. I read Maria's note over and over again. Each time I read the damned thing, I got more jealous. In an hour, I was totally out of control."

Helen looked in the direction of her kitchen. "Speaking of a drink," she said, "would you like one? I'm parched. I think there's a cold beer around here someplace."

"Got any lemonade?" asked Redline. He was writing rapidly in his notebook.

Helen returned from the kitchen with a bottle of citrus-flavored soda water for Redline and what looked like orange juice for herself.

"That's as close as I can get to lemonade," she said, handing Redline the soda. "I'm drinking fruit juice. Haven't touched booze in ten years. I keep beer around so my alcoholic friends won't shake themselves to pieces when they stop by." She took a sip of her juice. "Where the hell was I, Jim?"

"You were about to tell me what you did as a result of being temporarily out of your mind with jealousy."

Helen smiled and her voice suddenly became husky. "Oh yeah. Well, that's kind of fun to tell. I did what any normal, red-blooded young woman would do under those circumstances. I went outside and grabbed the young military policeman standing guard by our front door, hauled him into my bedroom, filled him with liquor and screwed him silly."

Redline looked startled. *"What?* That's what a normal woman does when she suspects her husband may have attracted the interest of another female? Commits adultery with the first man she sees?"

"Why not?" snarled Helen. "What was I supposed to do? Cry my eyes out? Bake a cake? Call my mother?" Helen looked at the floor, remembering, her skin turning pink. "There was always some young MP guarding our house. One of the perks that came with Walter's job. This one was cute. Tall guy, not as muscular as you, but about your height. He was astonished by my behavior, but delighted, too. We played the radio, danced in our underwear, had a great time. I showed that kid more about sex that afternoon than he could have learned in two normal lifetimes. You know what, Jim? He was grateful."

"I'll bet," muttered Redline.

Helen let out a long breath of air and smoke, then sat down on the sofa. She picked up her cigarette pack and peered at the label.

"I know what you're thinking and you're dead wrong, Jim. That was the one and only time I ever cheated on Walter. I'm not proud of it, even though I do enjoy remembering it. Human beings make mistakes. Now, all these years later, I can see that I had other options that day. Better options. At the time, I believed I was doing exactly the right thing."

"Yeah," said Redline. "So, the military policeman, besotted with sex, wandered away in a daze. Why are you telling me about him? Is he somehow part of the conspiracy to assassinate JFK?"

Helen laughed. "Not exactly. Just before the soldier went away, I handed him the jewelry box. Send this to your sweetheart, I said. You must have one back home. And when you see this box again, think of me and remember what we did here this afternoon. Then I grabbed him by his gun belt and said, but, don't ever speak to a soul about this. If you tell anyone, even a priest, and the word gets back to my husband, I'll convince him that you broke in here and assaulted me.

The General will track you down like a dog. You'll be in Leavenworth for the rest of your life. Then I kissed him and turned him loose."

"Great speech. Did he tell anyone?"

"How the hell do I know? The whole thing was so outrageous, I doubt anyone would have believed him even if he had wanted to brag about it. He'd mentioned to me that he was scheduled to ship back to the States in a few weeks. I never saw him again. I burned Maria's note and the wrapping paper in the fireplace. Then I just waited for Walter to come home. When he showed up, he said the sergeant major had told him I stopped by his office to see him earlier in the day. He wanted to know why I hadn't waited for him. I said, well, because I had something else I needed to do, Dear. Walter just stood there looking at me. He knew I had found the jewelry box in his desk and taken it. But he never asked me about it. How could he? If he had asked me directly, I would have said I had no idea what he was talking about. Then he'd have had to quiz his entire staff to find out who else had access to his office that morning. To protect himself, the sergeant major would have said that I was the only person who could be responsible for the theft. Everyone in the command building would have been talking about us in the most unsavory way imaginable. Walter was a strategic thinker. I think he decided that the cost of forcing me to confess that I had taken the box was greater than the benefit of finding out what I had done with it. He just let it go. I have no idea what he told Maria. Probably never even called her. I'm certain he didn't see her again. I think she would have interpreted his silence as rejection."

Redline pointed his pencil at the carton on the floor. "What is the connection between that box of old papers and the story you just told me, Helen?"

Helen dug a tissue out of a pocket on the front of her yellow dress and dabbed at tears that had suddenly begun racing down her cheeks.

"I found the answer to the biggest question in my life in that box a few days ago, Jim. You see, Walter divorced me in 1968, not long after we moved to Washington D.C. He had just started his new job at the Pentagon. One night at dinner he looked across the table at me and said, Helen, our marriage is over. Finish your supper, pack your

48

suitcase and get the hell out of my house. My husband tossed me out in the street with nothing but the clothes on my back and a couple thousand bucks in my purse. He never told me why. I asked him, of course, repeatedly, but he simply refused to discuss it. He hired an expensive lawyer and I hired my cousin, a bum who had flunked out of law school twice before finally bribing someone to help him cheat on his bar exam. Walter's lawyer offered what seemed to be a decent financial settlement. My stupid cousin advised me to take it and that was that. Now, thirty years later, I finally know exactly why Walter abandoned me."

Redline looked up from his notebook and sighed. "I'm on pins and needles," he said. "Seriously, Helen, I don't want to be insensitive but so far you have said absolutely nothing that Lionel Cooper would pay money to know. Could you skip the hearts and flowers and jump to the part I came here to find out about, please?"

"Patience, Jim," sniffed Helen. "I'm getting there. I have to be sure you have all this background information so you'll see everything the same way I do."

"Okay," said Redline wearily. "By all means, don't leave anything out."

Helen looked forlornly at the cardboard carton. "Naturally, you'll want to verify what I'm about to tell you by reading about it in Walter's own handwriting. But you will do that only after Mr. Cooper and I have negotiated a satisfactory contract, not before."

"Whatever," said Redline. He stifled a yawn and peeked at his watch.

"After President Kennedy was shot in Dallas in November of 1963, all hell broke loose in Europe. You can't imagine how emotionally destabilizing it is to be in uniform overseas when the Commander in Chief goes down. We all felt extremely vulnerable. Most of the people Walter worked with believed the assassination had to be a Russian plot of some kind. Many smart people said, this is it, we're definitely going to have a nuclear showdown with the Commies now. The Russians denied having anything to do with the assassination, but we didn't dare believe them. Our entire military apparatus was on full alert worldwide. Walter was up to his neck in meetings with the CIA, the Secret Service, Military Intelligence, the British and French, and anyone else who might know something about what had happened. He and his people looked at every rumor, no matter how bizarre, trying desperately to discover who was responsible for the assassination. Walter dragged in every night completely exhausted. At first, he was one of those who thought that war with the Russians was unavoidable. He shuffled his troops, he flew to Berlin every other day, and he was on the phone with the Pentagon constantly. He was as tense and bristly as if he actually was at war."

"Sounds grim," said Redline.

"It was. Of course, no one came up with one single thing that could be pinned on the Russians or any other foreign power. President Johnson set up the Warren Commission to conduct an investigation and we all know what they said. No evidence of a conspiracy. One crazy shooter. Case closed."

Helen took a long sip of her orange juice and looked at Redline.

"You listening to me, Jim?" she asked. "You look drowsy. I wouldn't want you to sleep through the punch line."

"I'm listening," said Redline. "But I don't know why because I already see where this is going. The United States government has investigated the JFK assassination twice since the Warren Commission announced its findings. The last time they admitted there probably had been a conspiracy of some kind. They said they will never know for sure who was involved, but it looks like it was organized crime. Is that what you're about to tell me, Helen? The mob killed Kennedy? Because that's not news anymore."

Helen shook her head. "Give me a little credit, Jim. I didn't invite you down here to tell you something you can read in a book. Listen closely. I learned all of this by studying my ex-husband's notes. Walter had been assigned a cushy job at the Pentagon in 1968. One afternoon he had lunch in his office with the retiring chief of Military Intelligence. The man asked him to talk about what had gone on in Germany immediately before and after the assassination of JFK. Walter asked, why are you interested in that? It's all a matter of record. The man said that the CIA had recently debriefed a veteran Cuban spy who had been persuaded to come over to our side. The spy had operated under deep cover in West Germany from 1957 until he defected in late 1967. He told them many things they had never heard before. But, the Chief said, after reviewing the case with experts from Military Intelligence, the CIA had decided that most of what the old man told them had to be false. Just fancy stories that would make the spy seem more valuable than he really was so we'd pay him a lot of money and hide him in a safe place. But, one of the more interesting things he told them was that in 1961 two young Cuban agents were in Heidelberg posing as students at the university. They were just hours away from traveling to Minsk for some special KGB training when the CIA picked them up for questioning. The spy said he had been able to warn the young men just before they were arrested. One of them tried to escape as they were walking him into the CIA building. He broke free, ran two blocks and was hit by a taxi. He died in the street. The CIA covered up that story, of course, and the young man's death never made the German papers. The other student was questioned for two days and then shipped back to Cuba. The interesting thing, according to the spy, was that the student who was killed had been hiding a wooden jewelry box in his room that contained classified information. If the Americans had noticed that box, the spy said, they could have discovered evidence of a joint Russian and Cuban plot to kill President Kennedy. Of course, the chief of Military Intelligence said to Walter, the CIA didn't know about the jewelry box and had no reason to ask the student agents where it was hidden."

Redline was alert now. "This is the same jewelry box you took from Walter's desk? The one Maria mailed to him? The very one you later gave to the young military policeman?"

Helen sniffed. "Yes," she said softly. "That one."

Redline thumped the eraser on his pencil against his notebook. "Okay, then stop right there. How did Maria Ortega get her hands on that jewelry box?"

"I don't know," said Helen. "Maria was a student at the university. Maybe she and the Cuban students were friends. My guess is if Walter had talked to her, she would have told him one of the young Cubans had asked her to hide the box in her room for him. I doubt she knew why the box was important, but when she heard that the Cuban students were actually Communist spies, she must have realized there was a good chance she had been dragged unwittingly into something that might be dangerous. I think she was planning to ask Walter to vouch for her innocence to the American intelligence authorities. Walter would have done that for her and then immediately turned the jewelry box over to the CIA."

"I get it," said Redline. "Walter is sitting in his office at the Pentagon in 1968 having lunch with this retiring big shot from Military Intelligence and he discovers that he once had his hands on something that might have prevented the JFK assassination. And he thinks to himself, damn, my jealous wife stole that jewelry box from my desk and I didn't have the guts to ask her what she did with it."

"Exactly," said Helen. Her face crumpled. "It gets worse, Jim. Walter realized that if I had not interfered, he would have had a fateful talk with Maria, one that might have changed history. If he had turned the jewelry box over to the CIA, they would have found what was hidden in it. President Kennedy would not have been assassinated in Dallas in 1963, certainly not by Lee Harvey Oswald. Once Walter understood what had happened, he made a snap decision to say nothing to the chief of Military Intelligence or to the CIA. His notes reveal that he did not think telling the government what he knew about the jewelry box would be in the best interests of the country. In fact, he was afraid it would lead to an armed conflict with either Russia or Cuba or both. Remember, Jim, this was 1968. Things were still very dicey between the United States and the Communists. And, both Kennedy and Oswald were dead. Nothing Walter could say or do would change that. The information hidden in that jewelry box would only have been useful to the government if Walter had been able to get it to them in 1961."

"Damn," said Redline. "Walter must have had a hard time finishing his lunch that day."

"Yes," said Helen, an expression of pure misery on her face. "He had to do something, of course, and right away. He couldn't just carry on once he realized that he might have prevented the death of his Commander in Chief. Somebody had to pay for this horrible mistake."

"Oh, I see. He divorced you because, as far as he was concerned, you were the guilty one? Walter blamed you for the death of President Kennedy?"

"Yes," whispered Helen. "It would have been impossible for Walter to live with me once he knew what had happened as a result of my irresponsible actions. He understood that I had no idea what the jewelry box was all about, of course. That I was just a foolish woman, an innocent, jealous foolish woman. But he was a disciplined military man, a three-star general. Generals don't bear fools lightly, Jim. I had to go."

After a moment, Redline said, "This is not a good time to ask you this question, Helen, but I must. What did the Cuban spy say was hidden in the jewelry box?"

Helen dabbed at her eyes with a tissue. "He said there were several things concealed in a cleverly designed false bottom. There was a small key to a safe deposit box in a Swiss bank, a box full of money. There was a coded message from the Cuban government to their Russian contact in Minsk. And then there were three tiny photographs. Two of the photographs were of the young Cuban agents. The other one was of an American defector. I assume you can guess who that was."

"Lee Harvey Oswald," said Redline. "If I remember correctly, he defected to Minsk in 1959 and was working in a factory there."

"Correct. If the CIA had seen those photographs, Jim, and unscrambled the coded message, they would have understood what was being planned in Minsk. Oswald would have been under their magnifying glass for the rest of his life. He would never have had the chance to shoot President Kennedy in Dallas because he would have been picked up and detained days before the presidential visit."

Redline drained his citrus soda and sagged back in his chair. He sat thinking for a long time while Helen smoked and stared morosely at the floor. Then he said, "I have the picture so far. Now tell me what the spy said was happening in Minsk."

"You're going to have trouble believing this part, Jim," said Helen. "Because you won't want to believe it. No one will."

53

CHAPTER SIX

Although Dr. Irving Katz was the senior psychiatrist working for the Central Intelligence Agency, he had never before been a guest in the Director's elegant townhouse in Silver Springs, Maryland. But now he had been summoned to a late afternoon meeting in the official residence and he knew why—because this particular conversation was not only top secret, but strictly off the record.

The fifty-year old doctor was a tiny bearded fellow, barely five feet tall, who believed himself to be a miniature replica of his hero, Sigmund Freud. He was urbane, erudite, civil, conservative, perverted and insecure. His friends thought of him as a dedicated public servant, a gifted man who had unselfishly given up the opportunity to become wealthy in private practice because his deep sense of patriotism demanded that he devote his skills to his country. But, his subordinates in the agency were unanimous in their belief that the pint-sized man simply lacked self-esteem and, like many people who did not have the courage to compete in the real world, had eagerly taken shelter behind a government desk.

The two men sat near each other in Charles Talbot's dignified study, surrounded by emblems of the Director's successful career. The walnut-paneled walls were covered with plaques, certificates, awards, commendations and autographed photographs of famous and powerful people. Talbot's wife, an athletic woman with long tanned legs and a silver ponytail, had brought in a carafe of hot coffee and two mugs. She had exchanged pleasantries for a few moments with Dr. Katz and then excused herself to go jogging.

"What a delightful room," said Dr. Katz. He gazed admiringly at the objects around him. "Everything in its proper place."

"Thank you," said Talbot. "My wife deserves credit for that."

"Clearly a talented woman," said Dr. Katz. He could feel his stomach knotting up, as it always did when he left his familiar surroundings and sallied forth into the domain of a superior.

"I take it you have read the report and are prepared to tell me what you make of it," said Talbot. "You do understand the fundamental question before us, Dr. Katz?"

"Yes," said the psychiatrist, "you want to know if we can create a programmable assassin capable of taking out the President's number one enemy in the Middle East." He fanned the pages of a thick bound document resting on a table near his right hand. "Fascinating reading, to put it mildly. I had heard rumors that this report, if it had ever existed at all, had been destroyed. I never thought I would hold it in my hand."

"As far as we know, that is the only copy to escape destruction. It came to us in a most unusual way."

Katz smiled and said, "Before we deal with the main question, sir, I think it might be useful if I briefed you on what hypnotism is and is not. But, perhaps I should first ask how much you know about hypnotism lest I bore you with information already in your possession."

Talbot nodded curtly. "My exposure to hypnotism is almost negligible. I once saw a stage performer in Las Vegas convince a lovely young woman that she was a chocolate chicken and in great danger of melting in the sun. To the delight of the audience, she immediately removed all her clothes and ran around in circles looking for shade. And, two of my relatives claim to have been cured of their smoking habit by a traveling hypnotist. Their so-called hypnotherapist was later picked up by the police and charged with molesting a female patient while she was under his spell."

"Ah," said Dr. Katz. "Interestingly, the same fate befell Franz Mesmer, the man who gave us the word 'mesmerized.' He, too, was accused of molesting a female patient while he had her in a hypnotic trance. In the eighteenth century, he was forced to flee Austria for

Paris to avoid prosecution. King Louis the Sixteenth appointed an investigative commission chaired by none other than Benjamin Franklin, our first ambassador to France, to determine whether Dr. Mesmer was legitimate. The commission found that he was a complete fraud. But, I digress. It would appear that the information about hypnotism I am going to give you now will be critical to helping you understand my conclusions."

Talbot glanced at his Rolex. He was not interested in memorizing scholarly footnotes about the history of hypnosis. He decided he would allow the doctor only a few minutes to establish a foundation for their talk and then insist that they get quickly to the answers he required. He took a sip of his coffee and tried to assume an air of quiet attentiveness.

Dr. Katz tented his small fingers beneath his thick beard, crossed his ankles, and began to speak in a measured, professorial voice, as though he were conducting a private graduate seminar.

"There is broad disagreement in the medical field about the exact nature of hypnosis. It may surprise you to learn that hypnosis is a poorly understood practice searching for a single unifying theory. There are several popular theories that attempt to explain hypnosis, as well as a rapidly growing list of therapeutic applications. We do not know for sure what is going on inside the brain of a patient who is in a hypnotic trance nor how to describe the phenomenon to each other in clinical terms. We just know that it works."

"That certainly does surprise me," said Talbot. "I assumed it was an ancient practice, understood by everyone in your profession."

"Ancient, yes," said Dr. Katz. "Understood, no. There are records of its use going all the way back to the beginning of recorded history. In modern times hypnosis is routinely used as a treatment for anxiety and certain personality disorders, specific chemical addictions and, occasionally, even for something as serious as schizophrenia. Recently, hypnosis has also been used with remarkable success by dentists and surgeons as a means of pain control."

"Pain control?" asked Talbot. "Why would they opt for hypnosis over standard chemical anesthetics? To cut costs?"

"Some people are so allergic to chemicals," replied Dr. Katz, "that they would die if an anesthetic were used to suppress pain during an operation or a lengthy dental procedure. Hypnosis is often the only option available to such patients."

"That would seem to prove that there really is a mind-body connection, would it not?" Talbot seemed intrigued with this insight. "It means that the mind can control the body when it wants to do so."

"There is no doubt that the mind and the body are connected in powerful ways," said Dr. Katz carefully. He focused on a spot a few inches above the Director's head. "Exactly how that connection works is anybody's guess. Several theories have been advanced that attempt to define not only the mind-body connection, but the precise nature of the entire phenomenon called hypnosis, as well. One widely accepted notion is that the mind consists of multiple cognitive structures, arranged in a hierarchical system of some sort, and 'managed' by a single dominant structure called the 'executive ego.' According to this theory, during hypnosis the hypnotist takes the place of the 'executive ego' and is thus in a position to speak directly to the other structures. Another theory is that some kind of interaction takes place between the patient's will, imagination and faith. By the way, this idea led to the term 'faith healing.' Yet another explanation is that the hypnotized patient, following suggestions planted in his subconscious mind by the therapist, replaces actual reality with an imagined version, one that has more flexible boundaries and will thus permit things to happen that would otherwise be impossible to conceive."

"Tell me a bit more about the theory of hierarchical structures," said Talbot. "That one sounds more plausible to me than the other two."

Dr. Katz uncrossed his ankles and stroked his beard. "The key to that theory lies in the belief that a patient's natural defenses can be gradually neutralized so that the therapist can gain access to the hidden internal structures and assume the authoritative role of the 'executive ego.' The patient is persuaded to relax the vigilance he normally maintains over his private mental functions. It goes without saying that natural defenses are there for a good reason and should never be set aside unless it is absolutely necessary. A person who willingly turns over control of his mental functions to another is extremely vulnerable. Trust is the key. The therapist must find a way to convince the patient that no harm will result if he abandons his normal psychological defenses."

Talbot nodded slowly. "And I assume numerous techniques have evolved over time that hypnotists can use to establish trust with a patient."

"Yes," said Dr. Katz. "But here's where it gets tricky, sir. The human mind is numbingly complex. It would not be correct to say that a therapist need only master a few parlor tricks and, shazam, he's in. Neutralizing the defenses of an individual mind is a highly customized task involving the skills and personality of the therapist, the motivation of the patient, the ability of the patient to relinquish reality-bound thinking, his tendency toward compliance when confronted with an authority figure and many other variables too subtle to be fully cataloged or explained. And, I should point out that I'm talking about people who volunteer to undergo hypnosis, who willingly submit to the process because they expect something good to happen if they do. Not people who, if they were aware they were being hypnotized for questionable purposes, would resist with every fiber of their being."

Talbot looked at his watch. "It's cocktail hour in Manchuria. I propose we have a drink and toast the inscrutable Asian mind. Do you know why I might be thinking of Manchuria at this particular moment, Doctor?"

"I can guess," said Dr. Katz. "You're probably remembering a popular film made over two decades ago in which mind control was a central element in the plot."

"No," said Mr. CIA. "I'm thinking about the real-life event that launched the most expensive research project in the CIA's history— MKULTRA. Following the Korean conflict, some American prisoners of war passed through Manchuria as they were being returned to us and later said they could remember nothing whatsoever about their travels through that particular part of Asia. Their testimony caused a panic attack in the intelligence community. People here believed that the Communists had finally mastered so-called 'deep programming' and, by doing so, had created the ultimate weapon."

Talbot walked to a small wet bar. He picked up a bottle of scotch and two square highball glasses. As he returned to his seat, he said, "We spent a lot of money over many years to see if we could master mind control in the same way we assumed our enemies had done. But our investigation failed to produce anything of real value, or so we have been told. The report I asked you to read is the only physical evidence in existence that suggests it might be possible to totally control a human being's mind, even if he has not consented to the process. So let's get to the real question, Doctor. Is it your conclusion that the KGB psychiatrist quoted in that report was able to take over Lee Harvey Oswald's mind, as he claims he did, and direct him to shoot President Kennedy? Wait, don't answer yet, there's more. Assuming that the psychiatrist was able to do that, does the report tell us precisely how he did it? Even more importantly, does that report represent everything we would need to know if we wished to repeat what the Russian doctor did?"

Mr. CIA handed his guest a highball glass half full of scotch. "I think I intuitively know the answers to my own questions, of course. But I would like to hear them expressed in medical terms."

The doctor stared into his scotch, a humorless smile on his small face.

"Ah," he said softly, "those truly are interesting questions, sir. I'm sorry to say that I cannot answer you with a simple yes or no. However, I believe I can explain what that report tells us, as well as what it does not tell us. As you know, fewer than half of the people who listened to the KGB doctor's forced testimony thought he had the right to claim success. The majority of the people in the room that day said he had failed to prove one single new thing, at least medically. Now, the fact that Oswald did come back to America from Russia and eventually did shoot Jack Kennedy would seem to support the notion that the doctor might have had some influence on his behavior. But it does not actually prove, clinically, the psychiatrist's specific contention that he achieved total control of his patient's mind and used that power to take out our president. There are just too many other, far more reasonable, explanations for Oswald's tragic behavior in Dallas that day."

"I don't care about other explanations," said Talbot sharply. His mood had changed. He was no longer the rapt student, patiently absorbing the wise professor's abstract ideas. He was the Director of the CIA again and he wanted concrete answers he could act upon in the real world. "You studied the report. I want to know what you learned from it. What do you think happened in Minsk and how much of what happened could we use if we wanted to build a Lee Harvey Oswald of our own?"

Dr. Katz felt his gut contract sharply. He looked straight ahead for a long moment before he spoke, his eyes hooded and unfocused. "I think that we can never know for sure whether Oswald was under the psychiatrist's direct control at the moment he pulled the trigger in Dallas, or not. Too much water under the bridge, too many people gone. But I can tell you how that could have happened and why, even if it did, most of the medical people who listened to the Russian's testimony were correct when they concluded that what he was telling them was of no practical use to this agency whatsoever."

"Perfect," said Talbot. He raised his glass. "To Manchuria," he said. "and to every American soldier who has ever been there, or who wonders if he's ever been there!"

*

It was just after midnight. The President of the United States and Charles Talbot sat facing each other in the Oval Office. The President's sleeves were rolled up and his tie loosened. He looked remarkably fresh for a man who had been working nonstop since five o'clock that morning. Talbot, the bags under his eyes smudged with fatigue, sipped strong black coffee as he organized his notes.

"I've had a long talk with the senior psychiatrist in my agency about the secret report and MKULTRA and several other related pieces of intelligence we have in our files," said Talbot. "Based on his analysis of that material, Dr. Katz thinks it could have happened this way, Mr. President. The KGB doctor was obsessed with proving that his theory of hypnosis should be of extreme value to his government but, for some reason, he was unable to get adequate financial support from Khrushchev so that he could continue with his research. The doctor was chagrined but undaunted. He continued to work on his theory in secret. Somehow he attracted the attention of Fidel Castro. Castro had correctly divined that the Kennedy brothers had marked him for assassination. Undercover, he sent money to help motivate the doctor to continue to work on his bizarre ideas. Over several years, the doctor had attempted to program literally dozens of individuals and had come up short every single time until he met Lee Harvey Oswald, who was literally hand-carried to him by senior Cuban intelligence agents. According to Dr. Katz, the odds that those two individuals would encounter each other at that exact moment in history were so remote it defies understanding. But they did meet and it changed the world forever, because Oswald was exactly the person the KGB doctor had been looking for, Mr. President. If the doctor had sent the specifications for his dream patient to God himself, he could not have expected a more perfect fit than the American who stumbled into his office in Minsk in 1961 and said, "What can I do to help Communism defeat the free world?"

The President beamed. "A bona fide nut case who was willing to do anything his new country asked him to do in order to earn their allegiance. Oswald probably needed very little in the way of a subliminal suggestion from the Russian doctor to launch him at Jack Kennedy with murderous intent."

"Possibly, Mr. President. But, according to Dr. Katz, it's amazing how many complex variables must be in play during the relationship that develops between the therapist and the patient if deep programming is to succeed. Compatible personalities, the patient's unconscious motivation, a list as long as my leg. But here comes Oswald, almost over-prepared psychologically to relinquish control of his life to the first Russian authority figure who treats him with respect. He was also extremely susceptible to visual cues. The doctor's military uniform and KGB insignia were powerful icons to Oswald. They represented a political system he had formed a deep intellectual bond with over many years. You can imagine how significant those things were to the process we are talking about. Without each of them already in place, it might have been impossible for the doctor and

Oswald to exchange the immense quantity of cognitive and emotional information that ultimately formed the basis for their singularly intimate rapport."

"Fantastic," said the President. "Oswald was a blank slate. The doctor must have slobbered all over himself when he realized the opportunity that had magically come to him. Dr. Frankenstein beholds, for the very first time, the potential to create a controllable human being from a miraculous convergence of impossibly rare variables."

Talbot nodded. "You're right about that," he said.

It was clear from the expression on the President's face that he was absolutely delighted with what he was hearing. "Fate had to be directing this whole drama, Charles. And now you're going to tell me that because of all these marvelous random circumstances, our KGB doctor was finally able to do the unthinkable. And then, when we brought him in for questioning, he described for us every single step of his unique process."

Talbot raised a cautionary finger in the air. "I'm going to tell you that Dr. Katz believes it is possible that the KGB psychiatrist did get some measure of control over Oswald's mind for an unknown period of time and may have been able to exert tremendous influence on his behavior. Possible, Mr. President, because we know that almost all of the critical variables that determine the outcome of an experiment like this one were not only present, but aligned in a fiendishly favorable way. But, according to Katz, this is a classic example of a medical result that will probably never be seen again because the odds against circumstances like those repeating themselves are so astronomically remote, they are beyond our ability to calculate. Nearly everyone involved in the interrogation of the KGB doctor concluded that, if this happened at all, it was just some kind of dark miracle, a statistical anomaly that had disastrous consequences for President Kennedy. The consensus was that the CIA could do nothing with this information. Almost no one believed that, using just the information provided by the Russian, we could consistently produce a totally programmed human being."

The President frowned. "Wait a minute. Are you saying . . ."

Talbot raised his hand, palm forward. "Hang on. I'm not finished, Mr. President."

"I certainly hope not," said the President. "I haven't heard what I need to hear yet."

"When Dr. Katz reached this point in his conversation with me, I said to him, let's get to the bottom line. If we looked hard enough, isn't it true that we might find an ideal candidate for deep programming just as the Cubans did? He said while that is undeniably a statistical possibility, it would cost a king's ransom to conduct such a search and, even if we found someone who seemed to fit the profile, the attempt to create another Oswald could fail anyway, for reasons we might never understand. Remember, he said, while it's mathematically possible that we could locate the perfect candidate and somehow pair him with the perfect therapist, to try to do so when we have no real idea if all that effort and expense will pay off would be foolish. There's no point, he said, in trying to create a scientific result that we already know cannot be replicated whenever we wish."

The President made an impatient gesture, jumped to his feet and began to pace restlessly around the room.

"At that point I thanked the doctor for his advice and sent him on his way, Mr. President," said Talbot. He sat back and closed his tired eyes. There was absolutely no doubt in his mind that he knew what his boss was going to say next. *Come on, you arrogant bastard,* he thought. *Do it!*

The President whirled around suddenly and made a noise like a wounded bear. He pointed a rigid finger at Talbot.

"Is Katz that little shit I met last year at my birthday party? Got a fancy beard and tailored clothes, struts around like a bantam rooster? Wake up, damn it! I'm talking to you."

Talbot slowly opened his eyes and nodded. "Yes," he said. "Katz is just a few inches shy of being a midget. I'm told he spends most of his salary on beautiful clothes and big cars in a pathetic attempt to impress women."

"Well, take it from me, he's got a midget brain," rasped the President. "I'd be nuts to take advice from an inconsequential pipsqueak like him. You know why? Because he'll never see the potential of something like this the way I do. Odds are not all mathematical. Ask anyone who's ever won the lottery. Odds finally come down to individual luck. And the only leader in the Western Hemisphere luckier than Fidel Castro is me. If that son of a bitch can find his Lee Harvey Oswald right when he needs him most, so can I!"

Talbot smiled. "Yes, Mr. President, you've always been very lucky."

"Damn right. I'll take shithouse luck over skill any day," said the President. "Luck is a gift from the gods or the devil, take your pick. I've never been afraid to take a risk when it really mattered because I knew I had a much better chance of coming out on top than an ordinary man had a right to expect." He was quiet for a moment and then sat down again. His bright blue eyes crackled with determination.

"Here's another thing Dr. Katz can't see," he said. "Some of the people who were present when the KGB shrink testified believed every word he said. If I'd been there, I know I would have been the most vocal member of that group. I'm a possibility thinker. I see what can happen, not just what is. I'm a visionary, probably the most visionary man ever to set foot in this exalted office. A shrimp like Katz could never see the world the same way I see it. Never!"

"I agree," said Talbot. "And we both know you've demonstrated an uncanny ability to interpret and even shape reality when it was necessary for you to do so."

"You're damned right I have! Now then, how much money do you need to give this project a realistic chance to succeed?" asked the President. "Just how much is a 'king's ransom,' anyway?"

"I should run some numbers," said Talbot, pretending to be thinking hard. "Let me have a couple of days. I wouldn't want to give you an off-the-cuff answer right now and come in too high or too low."

"Right. Okay, in two days we'll meet again and you can present me with your final budget. Ask for every dime you need. Thanks to the Mars project, I'm not worried about finding the money and you shouldn't be, either. By the way, did you bring the secret report with you tonight?"

Talbot, momentarily confused, said, "Yes, sir. It's here in my briefcase."

"How many copies of that report are there?" asked the President.

"I have the only copy in existence."

The President rubbed his chin thoughtfully. "I think it may be one copy too many. I listened carefully to what you said tonight and unless I missed something, your staff is not going to need to examine that report line by line in order to do the research for this project. This is about finding the right individual to program, not about mastering a technique in hypnosis invented a long time ago by a Russian doctor, right?"

"Yes, that's substantially correct. Katz told me the formal technique the KGB doctor used in the 1960's, when compared to what is being done now, would be considered archaic. I suppose I could simply extract the few original ideas in the report, rewrite them and make them available in a sanitized house document of some kind. But, it seems unwise to destroy—"

"Shred that report," interrupted the President. His eyes were tiny cobalt slits. "It represents the only physical evidence in the world that could connect me to this project. If something should go amiss when we launch our assassin, I don't want any physical clues that could link me to any part of what you've been doing. If certain people were to see that report, and then demand access to your books, they might be able to determine that only one person could have funneled to your agency the amount of money this research requires. And that person is me."

"But sir," exclaimed a stunned Talbot, "are you positive you want me to shred the report? What about its value as evidence that the Russians and the Cubans were involved in the Kennedy assassination? The historical significance of that information alone is a good argument for keeping this document intact. Not only that, we might be able to use that information someday to blackmail the Cubans or Russians. Surely you don't think the CIA is incapable of keeping a secret, Mr. President?"

The President laughed out loud. "Are you kidding me? Secrets like this are for sale on the open market every day. If certain people get wind of the existence of this report, they'll hunt it down and do everything in their power to expose us. Think of Nixon and his stupid tapes. He would have walked away from the Watergate scandal unscathed if he had just destroyed them. Shred the damn report. That's not a request, it's an order!"

"Yes, sir," said Talbot softly. "I'll take care of it immediately."

"Two more things," said the President. "First, get rid of Dr. Katz. He can't be allowed to corrupt this project with his negative thinking. He's already come to the conclusion that it can't be done. That's unacceptable. I want someone else in charge of the clinical work, someone with an open mind who won't prematurely abandon the research."

"Agreed," said Talbot. "What else?"

"I want your personal guarantee that you will eliminate instantly any physical evidence that could link me to this project. Shredding the report is a good beginning. But for all we know, there could be other things around, too. Things that could crawl into the light of day and bite me in the ass when I least expect it. If such things exist, find them and destroy them."

"What things? You mean other reports that might be out there?"

"How the hell do I know what things?" bellowed the President. "Use your imagination. Things! Remember when all the networks showed that forensic archeologist chipping the cement away from Sonny Russo's head? Russo was nothing but a thing by then, but look what happened around here! Careers crashed! People died! Because a thing surfaced, a thing everyone thought was buried forever."

"Oh," said Talbot. "Things like that. Now I understand what you're saying. Never fear, sir, there will be no nasty surprises caused by things. You have my word."

The President, his face slowly turning from bright red back to healthy pink, stood up and extended his hand. Charles Talbot shook it, picked up his briefcase and started toward the door. He paused and looked at the President's desk. *And to think, he mused, that maniac sits behind his desk every day with his finger quivering over the big red button.* Then he opened the door and walked slowly away.

The President removed his tie and folded it into a square. He stood bouncing it in his hand, his eyes twinkling merrily. *Talbot, he thought, is a dense, but sometimes useful, fellow. He exists because I say he exists. He's important because I have given him important things to do. Take me out of the picture and that man would disappear, not just into the night . . . but from reality altogether.*

CHAPTER SEVEN

Lionel Cooper's four-story gothic mansion occupied a half-acre lot less than a dozen blocks from Harvard University. The impressive ivy-covered structure served as both his business headquarters and his primary residence. Built in the early nineteenth century, it had been the county's first private insane asylum. Local wags liked to say it was hard to imagine a more appropriate home in Cambridge for the famously eccentric author.

Cooper purchased the mansion for a song in the early '80s from a nearly bankrupt historical trust and spent over a million dollars remodeling the place. The most extravagant item he added was a deluxe elevator with shimmering polished brass doors and floor-to-ceiling mirrored walls. The elevator was an essential upgrade, Cooper told his architect, because of the mansion's perilously narrow stairways and his own creaky knees.

A brass plaque fastened to the stone wall near the front door announced in scarlet letters that the structure was now called "The Cooper Building." A seven-foot tall iron spear-point fence surrounded the huge lot. Dozens of hardwood trees were liberally sprinkled across the property. A blue-green duck pond glistened like a frog's eye in the center of the perfectly manicured lawn. In the spring, the somber black fence came alive with a border of pink and yellow roses.

Jim Redline and Tina Romero worked in commodious private offices on the main floor, strategically located near the front door so they could intercept the occasional unexpected visitor. Other rooms on the first floor included a kitchen, a dining room that could seat thirty and a charming den furnished with leather club chairs and rustic pine tables. The second floor was used for storage. Lionel Cooper's private business domain took up the entire third floor. He had hired and fired, in rapid succession, six famous interior designers and squandered half a million dollars searching for ways to create the ideal environment in which to work. Finally, more from exhaustion than a sense of completion, he had declared the third floor to be marginally habitable.

Too suspicious of human nature to ever consider marriage, Cooper lived alone in an apartment on the fourth floor. The apartment was off limits to everyone else. The deluxe elevator would not go to the fourth floor unless a special key was inserted into the control panel. Jim Redline and Tina Romero had been given copies of the key for emergency use only.

Under another name, Cooper maintained several smaller luxury apartments around the country so that he could pursue his legendary amorous conquests without detection by the ever-vigilant paparazzi. But, as he entered what he assumed would be the last decade of his life, he found that his desire for trophy sex had waned considerably. He spent far less time with voluptuous young women and much more time basking in the pleasures of solitude.

Twice a week, a cleaning service was permitted access to Cooper's apartment. Tina Romero had cultivated a talking relationship with one of the maids. Flattered by the attention, the shy Asian woman had revealed a few rather interesting details about the apartment. "In spite of the fact that the rest of the building is decorated traditionally," she told Tina, "Mr. Cooper's residence is ultramodern. There is a black marble jet tub in the master bath and a matching black toilet with a crimson seat shaped like human lips. All of the furniture is upholstered in black suede. There are three huge walk-in closets, and one long wall in the living room is completely covered with framed photographs of Mr. Cooper standing next to other celebrities—Woody Allen, Norman Mailer, Barbara Walters."

Damn, Tina had said to herself, no anatomically correct inflatable dolls draped across his bed? No porno magazines stuffed under his pillow? Why won't Lionel let any of us go up there? What is it he doesn't want us to see? That his toilet seat kisses his ass every morning?

What had originally been a two-story carriage house near the back boundary of the corner lot had been converted into a five-car garage and a modest second-level apartment. Three of the parking spaces in the garage were reserved for cars owned by Lionel Cooper—a forest green Jaguar, a midnight blue Mercedes-Benz sedan and a white Land Rover. Jim Redline and Tina Romero parked their vehicles in the remaining two spaces.

The groundskeeper and handyman, Lyman Wolfe, lived in the small apartment above the garage. Lyman, an extremely introverted man, was in his late fifties. In his floppy overalls, faded denim work shirt and sweat-stained baseball cap, he looked like a blue ghost as he floated around the property, casting his eyes here and there, hoping to find something to tighten, snip, saw, glue or hammer. Sometimes Lyman would take one of Cooper's cars and disappear for several days. No one on the staff knew what he did when he was gone. No one on the staff knew anything about Lyman at all. One thing they didn't know was that, late at night, Lionel Cooper frequently visited Lyman in his little apartment and talked to him until dawn.

*

Jim Redline parked his vintage Thunderbird in the garage next to Tina Romero's dusty Hyundai hatchback and then walked rapidly down the long curved driveway to the Cooper Building. It was 5:05 in the afternoon. Redline used his coded key to bypass the electronic security system. He let himself into the darkened entry, walked past his own office and stopped in front of Tina's compulsively organized desk.

She was on the phone. Even from three feet away, Redline could hear a man's angry voice grating on the other end of the line. Tina covered the receiver with her hand and whispered, "Go on up, Jim. He's expecting you. Be aware that he has to leave here no later than six o'clock."

Redline took the elevator to the third floor and stepped into Cooper's cavernous office. The author was seated at his mahogany desk, clutching a fat black ink pen and writing energetically on a yellow legal pad. He was wearing a crisply starched white dress shirt and a black silk tie patterned with red and gold peacocks. A black silk blazer hung on an antique coat tree near the door. Cooper did not look up. His white hair was even more tousled than usual, boiling around his head like a cloud of steam.

Redline eased his large body into a guest chair and began silently studying everything in the office. Cooper scrawled for several minutes, then groaned, capped his pen and tossed it aside. He blinked his watery blue eyes at Redline and shook his head.

"I love to write," he said wearily, "but sometimes I get so bored with trying to string the same old words together in a new and fascinating way that I feel like bagging this job so I can go do something fun. Like selling vacuum cleaners door to door. Well, let me look at you, Jim. Just back from your vacation to Florida. Judging from that superb tan, I'd say you spent nearly all your time down there flat on your back at the beach."

"Not true," said Redline, feigning indignation. "I worked like a field hand every minute."

"Sure you did. Tina probably told you I have to leave in a few minutes to tape an interview in Boston with Dan Rather. He wants to ask me why I don't have a new book coming out this year, one so full of ghastly secrets about the crooked politicians in Washington that half of them will instantly resign. At least, that's what his advance man told me. But I think Dan's going to ask me why no one's shot me yet. I'm going to say, 'well, no one's shot me yet precisely *because* I don't have a new book coming out this year.'"

"Good answer."

"I thought so," said Cooper. He reluctantly flicked his eyes toward the clock on the wall in front of him. "I've got time for a condensed report on the Everglades scam. So, how long did it take you to figure out that Mrs. Rutz is just one more in a long line of nut cases who believe they know who is *really* responsible for the death of JFK?"

Redline shifted in his chair. "Stand by for a shock, Lionel. I was extremely impressed with Helen Rutz and everything she had to say. I think it is more than just possible that she can back up her claim that she knows where there is physical proof of a foreign conspiracy to assassinate President Kennedy."

Cooper slammed backwards in his chair like he'd been hit in the chest with a cannonball.

"You're mad, Jim," he rasped. "You're suffering from sunstroke!"

"The notes written by General Rutz strongly suggest there was a Communist conspiracy to bring down JFK. And Helen has personal knowledge of the existence of an old German jewelry box equipped with a false bottom that was used by Cuban intelligence agents to convey information to—"

"Stop!" Cooper held up his hand. "I can't stand it! Listen to yourself, Jim! Notes written by a dead man? A jewelry box equipped with a secret compartment? What are you going to tell me next? That Helen Rutz is in contact with the spirit world? That she gets her information directly from God?"

"Please hear me out," said Redline calmly. "Helen does not have the jewelry box, but she knows who had it last. She even knows where that person is living now. I want to try to retrieve the box for her, Lionel. If it still exists, I can find it. And when I do, and you sign a contract with Helen, you'll own the most incredible story of this century."

Cooper rubbed his long face and moaned. "Jim, please back up and tell me exactly what Helen Rutz said and did while you were in her presence. Don't leave anything out, not even a burp or a potty break."

Redline worked his way carefully through most of Helen's story. When he got to the part concerning the reason Cuba planned to send two of their young agents in Heidelberg to join Lee Harvey Oswald in Minsk, he paused to consult his notes.

"This is the clincher," he said. "The two Cuban agents were supposed to hook up in Minsk with a KGB psychiatrist who had been working for years on something called 'deep programming,' a hypnotic technique so powerful it would give him full control of an individual's mind. The idea was to use hypnosis to create a human assassin who could be manipulated like a robot. Khrushchev denied this doctor's request for more research money, but Fidel Castro, who believed the

Kennedy brothers had ordered the CIA to kill him, was desperate enough to pay the doctor to continue his controversial experiments. The two Cubans were supposed to carry the jewelry box to Minsk and turn it over to the doctor. In the secret compartment were a key to a Swiss safe deposit box, photos of Lee Harvey Oswald and both agents, plus an encrypted note from Cuban authorities explaining exactly what they wanted done. The safe deposit box contained the money the doctor needed. Of course, the three young men didn't know they were just guinea pigs for the shrink. There were delays and other problems, but eventually everything worked exactly as planned, at least in Oswald's case. Programmed to follow Castro's wishes to the letter, he returned to the United States and shot President Kennedy."

Cooper grimaced. "Jim, listen to me. In 1962, Frank Sinatra and Laurence Harvey made a movie called *The Manchurian Candidate*. Perhaps you've seen it. The plot is eerily similar to what you just described. Furthermore . . . "

"I know that," said Redline quickly. "I'm quite familiar with that movie. Lionel, I was in Florida yesterday looking straight into Helen's eyes, listening intently to every word she said. Trust me, she's the real deal. The general's notes and her personal experiences are the basis for what she told me, not the fictional plot of that movie. This is not a fairy tale concocted by an old woman who said to herself one rainy day, I know, I'll just embroider that great Hollywood story with a few new wrinkles of my own and clip Lionel Cooper for a ton of money."

Cooper sat as still as a wax statue, staring down at the white hair on the backs of his hands. Finally he raised his head and said solemnly, "Jim, would you know the general's handwriting if you saw it? The answer is no. If the attorney handling the general's estate sent those notes to Helen because he failed to notice that they were important historical documents, not personal letters, who do you suppose legally owns them? I can tell you this—it damn sure isn't the general's ex-wife. If I try to use the information in those notes as the basis for an investigation and a book, I'm going to get sued until the cows come home. And that jewelry box. Even if it is what Helen says it is—which it cannot be—what makes you think, after all these years, you can find the damned thing? There is nothing of value here, Jim. Nothing. This is a just the pathetic dream of an addled old lady."

Redline shook his head. "I respectfully disagree. We should at least try to find the jewelry box and, if we succeed, decide then what to do next."

Cooper sighed, waved his hand in the air, then sighed again. "This conversation is going to make me late for my interview with Dan, but I think it's critical that I straighten you out right here and right now, Jim. You've obviously fallen under this old widow's spell. I couldn't sleep tonight if you left this office believing what she told you could possibly be true."

Redline crossed his legs. "Okay. Say what you have to say."

"Listen to the voice of experience, young man," said Cooper. "Even though I was making a good living writing mystery fiction in the early '60s, I wasted many valuable hours trying to figure out who was responsible for the Kennedy assassination. I wanted to rock the world with a true crime book that would make me a billionaire overnight. Something strange had happened in Dallas the day Kennedy was shot and I believed the authorities were frantically trying to cover it up. I was just sure I was the perfect writer to finally tell the whole world what it was. There were abundant clues that a cover-up was underway, Jim. The Warren Commission investigation stunk to high heaven, important witnesses to the assassination were mysteriously dying left and right, and the anecdotal evidence that a criminal conspiracy of some kind had driven this tragedy was overwhelming. Among the various theories being bandied about in those days was the very one you are talking about now—mind control and robot assassins and so on. I can still remember clearly the night four of us young writers were trying to get drunk in a seedy tavern on the outskirts of Dallas, and I coined the term 'Club Red' to put a label on a set of conclusions I had reached about the so-called 'deep programming' theory."

"Club Red?" asked Redline. "Sounds like a strip joint."

"I suppose it does. Seemed clever as hell at the time. I said to my inebriated and completely disinterested colleagues, as we all know, last year Hollywood made a memorable movie about a U. S. soldier, hypnotized by Communist agents, who comes home and is directed *against his will* to shoot a presidential candidate. That film created a new monster in the public consciousness. Anyone who saw *The Manchurian Candidate* couldn't help but wonder if such a thing was possible. And now the unthinkable has actually happened! A former U.S. marine, a weirdo who defected to Communist Russia, has come back to America and killed our president. Naturally, some people are going to think Oswald was programmed by the Russians and ordered to shoot JFK."

"Exactly," said Redline. "Oswald *was* programmed. That's what I'm trying to tell you, Lionel. And, with a little help from us, Helen Rutz might be able to prove it."

"No, she will not prove it," said Cooper firmly. "Jim, free people fear a loss of control of their minds, memories and wills more than any other single thing. More than the atomic bomb, more than a biological attack, more than death itself. In a democracy like ours, the idea that a human being could be forced by an enemy to unwittingly do something evil is beyond terrifying. It's totally unacceptable. The Communists must have been overjoyed when they first noticed our peculiar vulnerability to this fantasy. I told my friends in Texas that night that the Reds had obviously developed a propaganda machine to put into play at every opportunity the sinister idea that they—and they alone—knew how to program people and manufacture robotic killers. They found many subtle ways to make us question the almost universal belief that man has an immutable soul, a divine center that cannot be touched by anything but the hand of the Creator. I pointed out that, as an atheist, I could step back and analyze this stunning heretical tactic from a perspective not available to my religious colleagues. As I recall, one of them fell drunk on the floor at that precise moment in my monologue and my insightful idea failed to take root."

"And you named this propaganda machine 'Club Red'?" asked Jim.

"My research convinced me that the Russians, Chinese and Cubans were working that diabolical machine in tandem. It was a near-perfect weapon, capable of causing a very durable uncertainty among our citizens, Jim. Uncertainty is a source of unbearable pain for most people, you know. It's a form of psychological torture and probably the main reason organized religion is so popular. People will go to shocking extremes in their efforts to avoid uncertainty. Some will even seek shelter in delusion. But I saw the whole thing for what it was— the dangerous product of a fraternity of shameless manipulators doing everything in their power to create irrational fear across entire populations by spreading a story that could never be proven one way or the other. I planned to write a book about 'Club Red,' canceling with one swoop of my mighty pen the distressing effect it was having on people all around me. People who should have known better than to allow themselves to be taken in by something as absurd as this."

"But," said Redline, "you didn't write that book, did you?"

"No. For many reasons, most of them difficult to recall or explain now. But maybe I should have written that book, Jim. I suspect many people in modern times, confronted with daily reports of suicidal fanatics willing to blow themselves up for no logical reason, must be thinking that anyone who does not recognize the existence of some degree of mind control in the modern world—apparently available to our enemies, but not to us—is simply not being realistic. Those people would be guilty of gross oversimplification, but I can certainly understand their thinking. After all, they've never heard of 'Club Red.'"

The door to the office opened. Tina Romero stuck her head in and said, "I'm sorry to interrupt, but Mr. Rather's assistant is on the phone, Lionel. She wants to know when you'll be arriving for your interview."

"Tell her I'll get there as soon as I can," said Cooper stiffly. "But don't apologize."

Tina nodded and gently closed the door.

"So, Jim, you can see why it's nearly impossible for me to believe that Helen Rutz has physical evidence that mind control resulted in the JFK assassination. My long-ago research determined to my satisfaction that 'Club Red' was solely responsible for that fictitious idea. By the way, 'Club Red' still thrives and has many enthusiastic new members. A fresh wave of evil wizards have caught on to this notion that uncertainty and dread can be artfully manufactured from the raw stuff of rumors and nightmares and forcibly injected directly into the minds of unsuspecting people everywhere. The contemporary fanatics are even better at creating psychological destabilization with this weapon than its original architects were because they've had years to perfect their art. But, this question about whether human minds, or even one human mind, can be or ever has been accessed, programmed and used for evil purposes can never be answered, once and for all, you know. 'Club Red' owes its very existence to that disturbing truism. And because I made the decision long ago to write only about things rooted in indisputable fact, Jim, I'm not sure I could write this story, even if, by some miracle, Helen Rutz turns out to be the one person in the world who truly knows what happened to JFK."

Redline sat rigidly in his chair, a stubborn look on his face. "That's all very interesting," he said. "I understand. But I still think we should at least look for the jewelry box. If I find it and we can satisfy ourselves that Helen's story is mostly true, well, who knows? Maybe you'll find a way to write a book about 'Club Red' that will knock everybody's socks off, Lionel."

Cooper drummed his fingers on his desk and looked at the clock on the wall. The door to his office opened again and Tina's head appeared. She arched her eyebrows. "They're getting pretty irritated, Lionel," she said. "Do you want to cancel?"

"Damn it," said Cooper. "Just a moment, Tina. Jim, even if you can run this old jewelry box down, it will only bring us trouble. Can't you see that?"

Smiling, Redline cocked his head to one side and said, "A dollar says you're wrong, Lionel. No, make that five dollars. That's how confident I am about this deal."

Cooper looked at the clock again. Oh, screw it, he thought. Sometimes the only possible answer is "yes," even if it's wrong. "Ten dollars," he said gruffly. "Not one red cent less."

Redline leaned across the desk and shook Cooper's hand. "Deal," he said. Then he eased past Tina and walked away.

I could swear Jim just smiled at me, she thought.

"Tina, tell whoever's on the phone that I'm leaving the building right now. Have Lyman bring the Jaguar around."

Tina trotted off toward her office. Cooper hurriedly slipped into his silk blazer and headed for the elevator.

So, he thought, should I tell Dan Rather that I'm late for this interview because, thanks to a stubborn investigator, a senile old hag and a stack of dusty notes written by a dead general, I'm working hard on a new book that will not only reveal the solution to the crime of the century, but also destroy the most sinister propaganda machine ever built by the enemies of freedom?

Cooper smiled at his elegant image reflected in the mirrored walls of his elevator and said aloud, "Not unless he's smart enough to ask me!"

CHAPTER EIGHT

Dr. Barbara Bowmaster had visited Director Talbot's home only once before and that time, too, his wife had been elsewhere. Barbara and the Director had spent an hour alone that chilly winter afternoon and she had left their meeting feeling that he was the most charming man she had ever met. Her assessment of him was validated when other agency staff members began to openly discuss Talbot's chances to someday be President. Although Barbara, a single woman in the prime of her life, found her boss extremely attractive, she knew it could be fatal to her career to telegraph her feelings. Still, she hoped that Talbot might somehow accidentally discover how she felt about him and . . . well, she didn't dare think about what might happen next.

A thin, pallid, bespectacled woman, Barbara wore her dark hair short and her dark skirts long. The thick lenses in her glasses magnified her gray eyes to twice their actual size. She lived alone in a small townhouse with a parrot and a miniature poodle. Obsessed with personal safety, Barbara kept two vials of pepper spray in her purse to ward off rapists.

After they had exchanged pleasantries at the front door and retreated to his elegant study, Talbot said, "As you know, Barbara, Dr. Katz is on indefinite medical leave. His unexpected absence has created a problem for me with a sensitive project I recently asked him to handle. I've invited you here this evening so we can discuss that project in private. To be frank, I'm going to offer you the opportunity to take it on."

Barbara felt her face flush. How extraordinary! She tried hard to assume the proper degree of professional reserve.

"Sounds interesting," she said. "It would be an honor to serve you, sir." Oh, she thought, and I mean that in every way imaginable! No sooner had that naughty thought crossed her mind than she felt an urge to burst into girlish giggles and slap herself.

"Yes, but before you give me your final answer, I want you to have an opportunity to consider this matter fully," said Talbot. "You may find that you do not wish to associate yourself with the project for ethical reasons. For example, no one else in the agency can be told precisely what you're working on. Of course, you'll require considerable staff support and those people will necessarily be close to certain elements of the work. But I'll be the only person with whom you discuss the results of your research. If your associates ask for details about the overall purpose of the project, you must tell them I've ordered you to maintain strict silence."

"Not a problem."

"Furthermore, I expect you to fail."

Barbara's eyes flickered anxiously.

"Certainly not because I doubt your competency," said Talbot quickly. "On the contrary, I picked you because I think you're exceptionally well qualified for this particular project. I expect you to fail because the task is . . . well, let me put it this way. I don't have a medical background, but I think it's safe to say it would be nothing short of a miracle if you succeed. That's the bad news. The good news is, in every way I can imagine, failure is the most desirable outcome."

In the silence that followed his dramatic statement, Talbot got up and walked to his wet bar. He glanced at his thoroughly bewildered guest and said, "May I offer you a drink?"

"Sherry, please," whispered Barbara.

Talbot returned to his seat and handed the doctor her drink. He peered at the tiny ice cubes floating in the tawny scotch in his glass and smiled.

"I'll explain shortly why failure would be good news," he said. "But first, cheers."

"Cheers," said Barbara automatically. She was trying to sort through wildly conflicting thoughts and emotions. Talbot had singled her out for a special assignment, one that would put her face to face

80

with him frequently. That was definitely exciting. On the other hand, he expected her to fail! Did that mean he had selected Barbara to fail because . . . he liked her? Was he doing her a favor or deliberately sacrificing her career? If she failed, would he truly be pleased or would he fire her for bungling an important project? Could she trust this man?

"Listen carefully, Barbara. I want you to try to create a completely programmable human assassin. One who will accept instructions planted in his mind while he is in a deep hypnotic trance. I want to be able to confidently dispatch this individual to the Middle East with orders to kill a fanatic who represents a direct threat to the life of the president of the United States."

Barbara set her glass on the floor beside her chair. "No one can program an assassin," she said bluntly. "That has been tried by every intelligence agency in the world. It has never been done and it never will be done. I believe you know that, sir."

"Are you absolutely sure it has never been done?" Talbot leaned forward and placed his hand on Barbara's knee. "You're not only a doctor, Barbara, you're a scientist. Aren't you open-minded enough to consider the possibility that even if it hasn't been done yet, it might be done someday? Does the term 'impossible' have any meaning in the modern world? Isn't it just a matter of time before we eliminate all the barriers to scientific knowledge we have collectively believed in for centuries and solve every mystery still out there? Even this one?"

Barbara looked down at Charles Talbot's large hand, felt its warmth pulsing through the fabric of her skirt. Her heart began to pound like an African drum. She raised her eyes to meet his. Had he touched her spontaneously? Or was he trying to arouse her?

Talbot suddenly pulled back and clutched his drink in both hands. "Barbara, I'm so sorry," he said softly. "I shouldn't have been that intimate with you. Please accept my apology."

Without thinking, Barbara blurted, "That's quite alright, sir. I've actually been hoping you would someday . . . I mean . . . oh goodness, what am I saying?" She grabbed her drink and twisted the glass in her hands, tempted to bash herself in the forehead with it. Damn, she thought, now I've done it!

"I'm surprised that you wanted me to, um, touch you, Barbara," said Talbot. "But quite flattered, too. Still, I shouldn't have done it."

Barbara pressed her thin lips together and nodded.

"I like you," said Talbot. His voice had deepened. To Barbara, he sounded like a lion in heat. "And I assure you, if I weren't a married man, I would want to touch you . . . often."

Barbara took a deep breath. Fantasizing about Charles Talbot is one thing, but this is too much to handle, she thought. For now, anyway . . .

"Sir, I'd feel better if we could return to our discussion about the project," said Barbara in a shaky voice. She met Talbot's dark eyes, tried to maintain a steady gaze. "Wouldn't you?"

"Yes," said Talbot. He cocked his head to one side and looked at her with shocking familiarity. "But, I confess I'm glad I unintentionally broke the tension between us."

Barbara allowed herself a shy smile. "Yes," she said. "Maybe that was something that needed to happen."

"Well, then, let's proceed." Talbot sat up straighter in his chair. His voice was normal again, his manner formal. The moment had passed. "I'm going to give you a report tonight that you must read immediately—an intelligence document prepared by my agency during the 1960s that deals with this concept in detail. Draw your own conclusions, but remember this—it is just as important for the CIA to know for certain that humans cannot be totally programmed as it would be for us to develop a reliable technique for doing it. Do you know why, Barbara?"

"Well—"

"Because," interrupted Talbot, "if the CIA can't do it, then it's reasonable to assume that our enemies can't do it, either. Once someone figures out how to do this, Barbara, the world will never be safe again. It will be a horror story without end."

Barbara licked her lips. "So you want me to—"

"I want you to work on this as if your very life depended on succeeding. Do everything you can to avoid failure. But, when you do fail, feel good about it, Barbara. Feel very good about it because you will have demonstrated, once and for all, that the human mind is beyond the reach of science. It cannot be tricked into serving two masters."

"Yes, sir," said Barbara. Damn, she thought, this is the worst assignment imaginable. No wonder Dr. Katz asked for a medical leave!

"I know that this is the worst assignment I could possibly give you, Barbara. But, do this for me and I promise to shepherd your career for the rest of your working life. It's that important, not only to me, but to your country. If you will commit yourself totally to this project, my gratitude will know no bounds."

Talbot went behind his desk, opened a drawer and pulled out a thick bound document. He returned and handed it to Barbara. "Please read this tonight," he said. "And let me know what you think of it first thing tomorrow morning."

"Well," said Barbara, "I suppose if someone has to work on this monster, it might as well be me. I've been interested in mapping the limits of hypnosis for a long time."

"I'm well aware of that." Talbot sat down and crossed his long legs. "By the way, that report is probably the most incendiary document in the world. All other copies of it were destroyed years ago by people who believed the information in it should never be allowed to see the light of day. I was ordered to shred that copy by the President himself. But I decided to let you look at it first because I thought your trained eye might spot something important others have missed. Barbara, if that report should ever fall into the hands of the wrong people, in or out of the federal government, we're both finished."

The skin on Barbara's narrow face contracted painfully.

"Now you know how much trust I'm putting in you," said Talbot. "Can you imagine the consequences to this country if our enemies somehow discovered what we're up to? If the world media got wind of this, they'd soon have every man, woman and child on earth convinced that the United States was routinely using controlled killers to advance its secret agenda to dominate the planet."

Barbara nodded solemnly. "I'm having no problem imagining all sorts of undesirable consequences that would result from a breach of security, sir."

"When you read the report, you'll discover that selecting the proper candidate to undergo this experiment is more than half the battle. You won't have to develop an entirely new approach to hypnosis in order to succeed. But you will need to find the proverbial needle in the haystack, an extremely rare individual, one who has a powerful subconscious need to be controlled. And, as if that weren't enough of a statistical improbability, that individual must also be able to access our wary target. In the back of that report, you'll find that I've provided you with a list of names of people who meet the second of these two criteria. The list is divided into two categories—militant terrorists from the Middle East who are either in one of our federal prisons right now or who could be picked up for interrogation, and certain foreign diplomats working in the Washington area. If you can't find a suitable candidate for this project within those two categories, we can discuss extending the search to include similar lists our allies might be willing to share with us. Particularly if they don't know why we are asking for such peculiar information."

Barbara scanned the list clipped to the back of the report. She bit her lip as she recognized some of the names.

"It is extremely important that you thoroughly document your work, Barbara, because I'll have to defend your . . . failure . . . to the President. When I do that, I must be able to say with confidence that this effort was comprehensive and conclusive. Record everything—every dime spent on research and how many man-hours were dedicated to the task. Explain your conclusions in plain English. It would be best if you can say that your work has convinced you that completely controlling human behavior with hypnosis is impossible. If you should, by some fluke, come to a different conclusion, you must talk to me before you write your report."

Barbara drained the last of her sherry and handed the empty glass to Talbot. "Bourbon," she said. "Make it a double, please."

As the Director prepared her strong drink, Barbara admired the impressive objects in his study. This is one of the most influential men in the world, she thought, and he's asking me to work privately with him on a top-secret project concerning the most audacious idea ever conceived by science. Is this turning out to be the absolute best day of my life, or what?

She gazed at Charles Talbot's lean body. He has a great chin and a cute butt, she thought. And someday, when that butt is seated firmly behind the famous desk in the Oval Office, I'm going to walk in there and find out exactly how far the boundaries to his gratitude can be extended.

Talbot returned and handed Barbara her drink.

"I'd like to propose a toast," she said.

"Here, here," said Talbot. He held his glass aloft.

"To you, sir." Barbara tilted her glass in the direction of the report. "And to the day when I come to you and proudly announce that, in spite of the revelations in this old hunk of paper, I have failed miserably to produce a robotic killer."

CHAPTER NINE

Helen Rutz smoked five cigarettes in rapid succession as she sat in The Oldies But Goodies Café waiting for Jim Redline. She had just spent 45 minutes under a hair dryer in Brenda Quinn's salon. In an effort to look her best, she was wearing a black cocktail dress and her most expensive costume jewelry. Rose Blanchard had approached her table twice to ask if she wanted something to nibble on while she waited. No thank you, Helen had said the first time, I'm just fine. The second time Rose loomed into view, Helen simply glared at her and blew daggers of smoke through her nose. Rose got the message and quickly backed away.

Helen wondered if Jim figured showing up late would somehow put him in control of the agenda. Or did it simply mean that he had something to say that she wasn't going to like? It seemed clear that the next step in the process was for Mr. Cooper to agree to meet with her in Cambridge to talk contract terms. Of course, she would hold all the trump cards during that discussion. Well, maybe. Mr. Cooper had been around the block a time or two and was probably a canny negotiator. One thing is for damn sure, she thought. No young whippersnapper like Jim Redline was going to charm her into anything she didn't like. If push came to shove . . .

"Ah, there you are, Helen. Great to see you again."

Smiling broadly, Jim Redline grabbed a chair and sat down. He was wearing a tan summer-weight suit, a pale blue dress shirt and a knit tie the same shade of brown as his curly hair. He looked confident and happy, a vigorous young man who obviously anticipated a long, prosperous and exciting life. For some reason, that made Helen feel like kicking him in the shins.

"Damn it," she rasped, stubbing out her cigarette. "I thought you'd been kidnapped or something, Jim! Where the hell have you been?"

Redline looked at his watch and frowned. "On the phone," he said.

Wearing a white sailor's cap, white sandals and tent-sized denim coveralls over a green tee shirt, Rose Blanchard waddled up to the table, glanced nervously at Helen, and then beamed at Jim. "Hi, handsome. You're back in town already? I knew you'd like this burg. Are you two related or something?"

"Hi Rose," said Redline. "Nice outfit. Helen and I are working on a business deal. What's the special tonight?"

"Crawfish gumbo," said Rose. "I also have fresh frog legs. They're extra yummy if you dip them in our wonderful seasoned butter. Or, you can order from our extensive dinner menu. I'll be back in a few minutes." She tossed two greasy menus on the table and padded off to wait on other customers.

"Rose Blanchard," chuckled Redline, "the human spy satellite. I'll bet she blurted out all the latest rumors as soon as you walked in the door, right Helen?"

"She did," said Helen. "As she escorted me to my table, she told me there's an old coot down at the nursing home who has infected half the widow ladies on his floor with a ghastly venereal disease. And one of the town cops has gone missing. Some of the seniors believe he was too fat to run and an alligator got him. The others think he ate one too many donuts, exploded into a trillion pieces and is now part of our colorful landscape."

Redline laughed. "If Mike Wallace ever comes to town, it'll be Rose Blanchard he interviews first. That is, after he figures out he's not looking at Ernest Borgnine's twin."

"Borgnine?" asked Helen. "No way, Jim. Charles Kuralt."

"Hmmm," said Redline. "I hadn't thought of Kuralt."

"Not to change the subject too abruptly," said Helen. She forced herself to pause and light a fresh cigarette. "But, as you might imagine, I'm dying to know what Lionel Cooper said when you told him my story. How come I'm not in Cambridge tonight sitting around a big conference table with Mr. Cooper and a team of contract lawyers?"

"That will happen," said Redline. "As soon as I locate the jewelry box."

Helen stared at Redline like she had just noticed he had leprosy. "What the hell does that mean?" she asked. "He thinks I'm going to tell him what I know about the possible location of the jewelry box without a signed contract? You're serious?"

Rose Blanchard returned, winked at Redline and boomed, "Okay, who's ready to chow down?"

Irritated at the interruption, Helen snapped out an order for crawfish gumbo. Redline politely asked for frog legs with seasoned butter. Rose congratulated them both on their excellent choices, scribbled furiously on her order pad, scooped up the menus and rumbled off toward the kitchen.

Redline pulled two sheets of paper from his coat pocket and spread them out on the table in front of Helen. "Lionel Cooper is a successful businessman, Helen. He's willing to take a risk now and then, but only if it makes sense. He's intrigued by your story, but he knows that without the jewelry box, he can't convert it into a profitable book. And, he thinks the odds that we can find that box are not in our favor. Nevertheless, I persuaded him to cover the costs of a thorough investigation into its whereabouts. This is a letter to you from Mr. Cooper that says if I find the jewelry box and it hasn't been tampered with, and we can establish that it contains the key, the photos and the encrypted message from the Cuban government, and the notes in your trailer really were written by General Walter Rutz, then he will invite you to Cambridge to finalize a book deal."

Helen said, "Shit." Her face registered massive disappointment. "What do you mean by that?" asked Redline.

Helen sneered at him. "You two must be joking! You think because Lionel Cooper is too high and mighty to . . . and you think that I'm so old that I . . . well, let me straighten you out right now, college boy! There are dozens of other famous writers who will be delighted to offer me a contract for my story whether they can ever find that damned jewelry box or not!"

"That's probably true, Helen," said Redline soothingly. "But you will never find a business partner the equal of Lionel Cooper. His international fame is your guarantee that you'll become a wealthy woman *overnight* if he decides to write this book. And, he will write this book if I can find the jewelry box and it turns out to be everything you say it is."

"I should just get up and walk out of here," sniffed Helen, her eyes suddenly swimming with tears. "I would, too, if I could see the damned exit."

"Please don't leave, Helen," said Redline hastily. "Not until you've thought this through carefully. Tell me this. What do you have to lose by accepting Lionel Cooper's offer?"

"Everything! That's what I have to lose, Jim. Everything I have left in this crappy world," sobbed Helen. A tear rolled down her cheek and she dabbed at it with her paper napkin.

"Helen, you need to face facts. It's pretty clear you don't actually know where the jewelry box is or even if it still exists. You just know who had it last and you're hoping he'll tell you where it is right now. If you think that young military policeman you gave the box to that fateful afternoon in Germany just put it on his nightstand and it's still there, you're kidding yourself. But, if it hasn't been lost or destroyed, I can probably find it. And if I do, you're in the chips."

"Drop dead," said Helen. Her eyes were puffy and she was still sniffling. "I can call that guy as easily as you can. If he still has the jewelry box, he'll give it to me. I know he will. You may not know it, but I'm an expert at talking men out of their possessions."

"Maybe. But, even if he still has the box—and that's unlikely—he may not hand it over to you out of the kindness of his heart," said Redline. "Not if he's smart. And you can't afford to be turned down flat when you ask him for it. You need to be in a position to make him an offer if he refuses to part with the box. How much money do you have in the bank, Helen? How much cash could you fork over if the man insists on being paid?"

"Screw you," said Helen. She blew her nose loudly into her napkin.

"If he doesn't have the box," said Redline, "and claims not to know where it is, he needs to be questioned by someone who knows how to do it. Someone who can draw old memories out of him. Someone who is a seasoned investigator. Someone like myself."

Helen hurled her balled-up napkin halfway across the dining room. It bounced on the floor and rolled under a table occupied by two elderly men wearing matching Hawaiian shirts. They didn't seem to notice they were under attack. "I hate you, Jim," she muttered.

Redline sighed and turned his attention to the other customers in the café. Fourteen people, one a small boy. Somebody's visiting grandson, he thought. Two people were blind, three were in wheelchairs and several had green oxygen bottles at their sides. He saw Rose Blanchard headed toward his table, a tray full of food balanced on her shoulder.

"Here comes dinner," whispered Redline. "If you don't want to become one of Rose's new rumors, stop bawling and try to look like you're having a good time."

Helen opened her mouth to say something nasty but changed her mind. She composed herself as best she could and sat quietly while Rose arranged the food on the table.

"Will there be anything else at this time?" asked Rose mechanically. Then she grinned at Redline and added, "Or any other time?"

"Don't think so," said Redline. "But later we can talk about pie."

Rose trotted off. A long moment of silence followed her departure. Redline popped a buttery frog leg into his mouth and gasped.

"Wow," he said. "Spicy!" Helen maintained her silence. The little boy ran past them on his way to the restroom. He waved joyfully at everyone in the café.

"Cute kid," said Redline. He bit into another frog leg and drained his water glass. Tiny beads of sweat appeared on his forehead.

"Well," said Helen at last, "if I agree to this pitiful deal, what happens next?"

Redline noticed that Helen's eyes had taken on a shrewd look, the look of a woman who had made up her mind to prevail over adversity no matter what. Even if it meant she had to trust two men she barely knew.

"You tell me the name of the guy who had the jewelry box last and where he's living now," said Redline. "Then I get on a plane and get the ball rolling."

Helen took a tiny bite of her gumbo. "I almost never eat here," she said, "because the spicy food is too hard on my digestive system. I'll be on the pot all day tomorrow if I eat this whole thing."

Redline handed her a ballpoint pen. "Sign on that blank line at the bottom of the letter," he said. "Just to acknowledge that you've read it and understand the terms."

The little boy wandered back through the café. He smiled shyly at Redline and Helen as he traipsed past their table. Then he paused to stare curiously at a white-haired old woman with a sharply bent back shuffling painfully toward the exit.

"Relax and order some pie, Jim," said Helen. She waved her hand over her head to get Rose's attention, then signed the letter. "After you finish your dessert, let's go over to my place. I'll show you an old photograph of the guy you'll be talking to. I might even make coffee if you behave yourself."

CHAPTER TEN

Jim Redline's morning flight from Miami to San Diego was delayed for three hours by a torrential downpour. He bought a cup of coffee and a bagel, sat down at a table in a busy food court near his departure gate and used his cell phone to call Raven Investigations in Los Angeles.

Rex Raven was a security expert and private investigator who specialized in all forms of electronic surveillance. He and his staff were the best in the business when it came to the covert acquisition of audio and video information. Most of Raven's business came from insurance companies, some from technology start-ups in Silicon Valley willing to pay outrageous sums of money for industrial espionage and, occasionally, a bit of action came in over the transom from individuals like Jim Redline. Raven Investigations was the most expensive surveillance enterprise in California for a very good reason—the word "impossible" was not in their vocabulary.

Rex answered his phone on the first ring.

"This is Jim Redline calling, Rex. I'm delighted to find you in your office this early. I'm flying into San Diego later today and I need something done chop-chop."

"Chop-chop costs extra," said Raven crisply. "Expensive to talk to me about chop-chop."

"I know that," said Redline. "How much would it cost me to find out your real name?"

"I don't have a real name. Wait a minute," said Rex. Jim could almost hear him slapping himself on the forehead. "I forgot who you work for, Jim. The guy who owns Fort Knox."

"Correct," said Redline.

"Okay, let's do some business."

"There's a man named Tom Sawyer living at 118 Temple Street, Apartment D in National City. I need a thorough background check on him. And I need his apartment bugged before he goes to bed tonight."

Rex chuckled. "Tom Sawyer? Come on, Jim. Everybody knows he lives in Hannibal or St. Louis or someplace like that. I only work in California."

"I'm going to drop in on Sawyer tomorrow morning," said Redline, ignoring the banter. "After I leave his place, I need everything he does next recorded and forwarded to me. I'll be staying at the Holiday Inn Express in San Diego. Here're the fax and phone numbers."

"Got it," said Rex. "Is this guy living in a fleabag, Jim? Much easier to plant bugs in a modern office building than in a tarpaper shack infested with crooks. They're extremely observant."

"I'll pay for your deluxe surveillance package, the one that goes the extra mile and takes into consideration special hazards."

"Now we're talking," said Rex.

Redline could hear Raven chuckling as he slurped coffee. The man loved to make easy money. In spite of his cautionary remarks about the difficulties of accessing and bugging a flophouse, Rex knew this job would be cake compared to the stealthy miracles his company was routinely asked to perform.

"If this guy leaves his posh quarters for even fifteen minutes today," said Rex, "we'll be in, do the job, read his mail, rinse out his socks and take out the trash before he gets back. Call me when you arrive at your motel, Jim."

Even though the two men were separated by thousands of miles, Redline could feel Rex relishing his own peculiar brand of fiscal rapture.

"Hey," said Redline, "remember that job you did for us two years ago? The Chinese scientist the Department of Defense decided to put in charge of building atomic bombs?"

"Sure," laughed Rex. "You and your boss thought the man was building a nuclear device in his basement so he could drop it into the

San Andreas Fault on the Fourth of July. Turned out he was just stealing routine military secrets and peddling them to his pals in Beijing."

"So you say. The word on the street is you updated your earthquake insurance an hour after you wrote your final report on that guy. Listen, thanks for making room for this today, Rex. Appreciate it."

"My pleasure, James. And my accountant thanks you, too. If you get some free time while you're out here, come up to L.A. so we can talk private-eye stuff. You'll enjoy looking at some of the new gadgets we're using these days. We can actually track people through solid walls now. Heat sensing equipment. Next we'll be able to read minds with these damn things."

*

Redline arrived in San Diego late in the afternoon. He rented a car, drove to his motel and immediately called Raven Investigations. Rex told him that Tom Sawyer had wandered across the street from his ratty apartment house shortly after noon to visit a neighborhood bar. He drank a pitcher of beer, ate three pickled eggs and won twenty dollars shooting pool. He stayed in the bar for two hours and forty-six minutes.

While Sawyer was in the bar, one of Raven's people slipped into his crummy apartment and installed several listening devices. The operative conducted a thorough search of the place and discovered a nine-millimeter pistol hidden under the mattress.

"The reason Sawyer lives like a wharf rat in a National City slum is because, until two months ago, he was locked up in Chino Prison," said Rex. "He was a San Diego cop until he slipped over to the dark side. Spent ten years in the slammer for extortion and assault with a deadly weapon. Sawyer is past his physical prime but still a dangerous man. He's armed, he's dead broke and he's desperate. Watch yourself with this guy, Jim."

Redline drove to the Gaslamp Quarter on San Diego Bay and enjoyed an excellent dinner in a classy seafood grill close to the beach.

He bought a map of the San Diego area in a drugstore, strolled around for an hour looking at ships and enjoying the cool salty air, then returned to his room. He spent a few minutes calculating the driving time from the Holiday Inn Express just off the Harbor Highway south to nearby National City. On the back of the map, he found a blurb explaining that the blue-collar, low-rent South Bay community of National City derived its name from its primary employer—National Steel and Shipbuilding Company. Temple Street paralleled the Sweetwater River, close to the Highway 805 overpass. The highway continued south to Chula Vista, San Ysidro and Tijuana, Mexico. Later, Redline lay in bed listening to the energetic night sounds of San Diego, thinking about what time the next day he should start hammering on Tom Sawyer's front door.

*

Ten minutes after sunrise, Jim Redline was standing in front of 118 Temple Street. He sniffed the foul air that permeated the decaying riverfront neighborhood. It was a nauseating blend of diesel fuel, smoke, rotting fish and industrial waste. He did a quick audit of the objects he could see from where he stood—four old rusty cars, two without license plates, one with a smashed windshield, one with bullet holes in the hood. An old Suzuki motorcycle with a bloodstained sheepskin seat cover and a windshield sticky with mashed bugs. Four bicycles chained to a bent metal rack, and an assortment of broken bottles, used syringes, cigarette butts and soggy fast-food cartons.

118 Temple Street was a decrepit three-story clapboard firetrap that had recently been painted dreary black. In days gone by, the apartment building had probably been a desirable riverside address, thought Redline. But now it was the end of the line, a slum occupied by miserable people who were one bad day away from being completely homeless.

Redline glanced at his rented Pontiac sedan. It looked like a maraschino cherry with a sign on the windshield saying, "Steal Me." He decided to keep his initial discussion with Sawyer short and to the point so he wouldn't have to take the bus back to San Diego.

*

Tom Sawyer was jarred rudely into consciousness by someone knocking on his apartment door. He rolled over on his back, licked his parched lips and struggled to remember what day it was. His first instinct was to grab his pistol and start blasting at the asshole making that ungodly racket. The knocking continued, louder now. Wearing only Jockey shorts, Sawyer rolled out of bed and lurched into the living room. He stood a few feet from the door and tried to clear his gummy throat.

"You'd better be my mother, you sorry son of a bitch, or I'm going to kick your ass!" he croaked.

The knocking stopped. Someone slowly pushed a new one-hundred-dollar bill under the door.

A strong male voice said, "Free money, Tom. Let me in and I'll explain how you can make many times that amount without lifting a finger."

Sawyer scratched himself, belched, stepped forward and plucked the bill off the floor. He shoved it under the elastic band of his underpants.

"Who the hell am I talking to?" he growled.

"Let me in," said the voice.

"Well, hold your damned horses," said Sawyer. "Let me put some pants on, for God's sake."

He shuffled back into his bedroom, put the hundred-dollar bill under his pillow and pulled on a pair of faded jeans and a Grateful Dead tee shirt. He thought about his gun again but decided he didn't need it. He went back into the living room, took a deep breath and jerked the front door open. The large young man standing there didn't look especially menacing. On the other hand, he didn't look very friendly, either.

Sawyer looked Redline over carefully. Good haircut, nice clothes, snazzy shoes. Too relaxed to be a cop. A jock with money.

"Just you and me?" asked Sawyer.

Redline nodded.

"It's pretty early in the morning to be talking business with a total stranger, but I reckon you can come in for a bit," said Sawyer. "Want some coffee?"

"No, thanks," said Redline. He sniffed the air as he stepped through the doorway. Stale cigarette smoke, spoiled food, body odor.

"Come in here," said Sawyer.

Redline followed Sawyer through the shabby living room into a tiny kitchen and sat down at a table coated with food crumbs. Sawyer rattled around making himself a cup of instant coffee. He was taller than Redline by an inch, gaunt and bony, with soft ropy muscles in his long arms and neck. His hair was dyed black and pulled into a short ponytail, his grimy fingernails bitten to the quick. He had oddly shaped yellow eyes that made him look like a battle-scarred alley cat that had fought every dog in town just to stay alive. He clopped around the kitchen in old rubber shower thongs, a sour smell trailing along behind him, as if he had slept for weeks in dirty sheets.

The kitchen was disgusting. The gray linoleum floor was pitted and streaked with filth, the small stainless steel sink overflowed with dirty dishes. The tiny countertop was littered with bread wrappers and empty soup cans. The gas stove was coated with a thick layer of rancid grease. A flyspecked full-length poster of a naked woman was scotch-taped to the wall above the stove. In the corner, an ancient refrigerator shuddered and tweeted.

"Get your story out quick," grumbled Sawyer. "I got more important things than this to do today." He sat down across from Redline and slapped his coffee cup down on the table like it was the ace of spades.

"You don't look like you have important things to do today," said Redline.

"Oh yeah? Well, either do you," said Sawyer. "Start by telling me your name. That might be important."

"No, that's not important," said Redline. "Just listen to me. I'm going to explain how you can make some money this morning."

"Okay, I'm listening," said Sawyer. He took a sip of coffee and looked at his wrist as if he expected to see a watch there. "But hurry up."

Redline locked eyes with the older man. "If you still have the jewelry box Helen Rutz handed to you in Heidelberg, Germany on a particularly memorable afternoon over thirty years ago, I'll give you cash money for it right now. If you don't have it, but think you know where it is or might be, I'll pay you the same amount of money for disclosing that information. You don't ask me any questions, Tom. You just take the money and chalk this up as one of the luckiest days of your life."

It was all Tom Sawyer could do to keep from falling out of his chair. He went rigid from head to toe. His yellow eyes bulged. He started to stand up, then crashed back into his chair.

My God, thought Sawyer, Helen Rutz? She shows up now, after all this time? What the hell is going on here?

Sawyer had no problem recalling the afternoon he had spent in bed with Helen Rutz. It was the most astounding thing that had ever happened to him. He could recall specific things about that erotic encounter in clinical detail. *But what was this crap about a jewelry box?*

"Take your time," said Redline. "It'll probably come back if you don't panic."

And then it was there. Sawyer could see Helen plain as day, stark naked, pressing the wooden box into his hands seconds before he walked out of her bedroom. It was a silly gesture, important to her but not to him. All he cared about was that he had somehow scored with the general's beautiful wife. But the jewelry box? He couldn't even remember what it looked like, let alone what he did with it. And now the damned thing was worth cash money to him if he could lay his hands on it again? Oh, man! No way this could be happening on this very day, when he was just one bad poker hand away from the gutter.

Sawyer leaned back in his chair and fastened his shrewd yellow eyes on the big man sitting across from him.

"You know Helen?" asked Sawyer.

"No questions, remember? You're dealing only with me. Where's the jewelry box, Tom?"

Sawyer continued to stare at Redline while he racked his brain. Why would that stupid little box be valuable to Helen now? More importantly, what the hell had he done with it? Tossed it away? Lost it? Left it in Germany? Then, like an old dream, the memory came floating back in bits and pieces. He saw himself handing the jewelry box to that company clerk, that nerdy kid who sat right outside the captain's office. Had a strange name. Shane. No, Lane. Not Lane, *Zane*. Gene Zane! That was it! Strange guy, Gene Zane. From the desert. Always talking about lizards and tarantulas and dust storms. Lived in Phoenix. Or was it Tucson?

"I'll bet you're a good poker player, Tom," said Redline. "I can't tell if you're deep in thought or asleep with your eyes open."

"Where are you staying?" asked Sawyer. He took a sip of cold coffee and glanced at his naked wrist again. He was feeling a little better. He knew what to do next. And it was obvious there was a lot more money to be made here than what this stiff was offering. After all this time, if Helen Rutz wanted that stupid jewelry box so badly she was willing to hire a guy to go out looking for it, something big was in the works.

I always knew a woman would make me rich someday, thought Sawyer. I just never imagined it would be Helen Rutz! She must be worth a bundle by now . . .

"I'm staying nearby," said Redline.

Sawyer began to chew on what was left of one of his fingernails. "How long are you planning to be in the area?" he mumbled.

"Depends on how much you can tell me about the jewelry box. If you don't know where it is, I'm gone today."

"Okay, smart-ass, let me put it another way," snapped Sawyer. "How long do I have to come up with the fucking box?"

Redline shrugged, flicked his eyes toward the ceiling as if he was thinking the question over. The ceiling was black with smoke, grease and dead gnats.

"I'm flexible," he said. "How much time do you need?"

"You say you'll pay me cash money for the box. How much money?" asked Sawyer.

Redline looked at the messy kitchen. "Why don't you give me a figure and I'll see if I can handle it. How much would it take for you to drop all the other important things you're working on today and concentrate on locating the jewelry box?"

Sawyer smiled. "I don't suppose you'd like to tell me what this is all about?"

"No," said Redline.

"Oh, I get it." Sawyer's eyes flashed anger. "You mean a loser like me could never understand the sophisticated world people like you and Helen live in? Old Tom, who lives in a flophouse and drinks instant coffee and can't afford shoes made in Italy just wouldn't comprehend the complicated high-class environment you two hang out in?"

"Not exactly," said Redline. "I mean an ex-convict like Old Tom, a felon, a man on parole without two dimes to rub together, is just not the kind of guy I'm willing to share any information with, period. So stop huffing and puffing and let's get to your number. How much do you want?"

"So you found out I'm an ex-con," said Sawyer. "Interesting. Then you probably know I'm an ex-cop, too. You must have run a background check on me. You're a private investigator?"

"It doesn't matter what I am," said Redline.

Sawyer grinned. "Okay, wise guy, we'll play it your way. I may run into some expenses looking for the box. I need five thousand dollars in advance right now. When I have the jewelry box, we'll meet again and negotiate my final fee."

"No dice," said Redline. "The advance is fine. But when you track the box down, you tell me where it is and I'll go pick it up. I'll pay you an additional five thousand if your information is accurate. That should easily make this the most profitable morning you've had in a long time."

Sawyer stood up and walked to the sink, his rubber shower sandals making sticky noises on the linoleum. He poured cold coffee from his cup across the stacks of dirty dishes, taking his time, making sure he didn't miss a single plate. Then he clopped back and sat down.

"Put five thousand dollars on the table and walk out of here," said Sawyer. "Come back one week from today. It'll take me that long to verify my hunch about where the box is now. If I'm right, it'll cost you another ten thousand dollars for that information. Then you can go and chase the damn thing yourself. I'll be out of the deal."

"So your number is fifteen thousand," said Redline. "For fifteen thousand dollars, you'll try to come up with the location of the box? And then you'll step back?"

"Sure," said Sawyer. "I remember Helen Rutz as a decent lady. If this helps her out in some way, I'm more than glad to do it for her. And that money will get me out of this dump and back in the game. That's all I want. You have my word on it."

"Your word is your bond?" said Redline, smiling. "When Tom Sawyer makes a promise, he always keeps it?"

Sawyer's hands balled into fists and he said, "Fuck you and everybody who looks like you."

Redline pulled a thick roll of bills from his pocket, counted out five thousand dollars in hundreds and tossed the money on the table.

"Here's some free advice, Tom," said Redline. "Don't lie to me. If you truly believe you know where the jewelry box is and you turn out to be wrong, that's okay. But if you lie about it, I'll be very unhappy. And you don't want to make me unhappy, old man."

Sawyer's yellow eyes narrowed. "You're really scaring me with that kind of rough talk, mister. I'm shaking all over."

"See you one week from today," said Redline. He got up and walked out the front door.

After Jim was gone, Sawyer sat at the table ogling the pile of cash. He picked it up and rubbed the crisp paper against his unshaven cheek. Five thousand big beautiful dollars, he thought. Just for being alive!

Gene Zane, you better be alive, too, little buddy. Be someplace where Old Tom can find you. We need to talk about the good old days.

*

Sawyer waited fifteen minutes to make sure his visitor wasn't coming back. Then he called directory assistance in Arizona and asked for a listing for Gene Zane.

"What city, sir?"

"Let's try Phoenix."

"We don't show a Gene Zane in Phoenix, sir."

"How many folks named Zane do you show in Phoenix?"

"Four," said the operator. "Frederick, Robert, Alice and Benjamin."

"Give me their numbers," said Sawyer.

It took five minutes. Frederick and Robert didn't know Gene. Alice wasn't at home. But Benjamin was very helpful.

"We're related," he told Sawyer. "Cousins. I don't see him much these days. You say you're an old army buddy of his?"

"That's right," said Sawyer. "I want to let him know about a reunion our outfit is putting together. Where can I reach him?"

"He lives north of here, up in the mountains. I'll give you his work number. You'll have better luck catching him there at this time of day. This is great. Gene could really use a party. He's had some tough luck recently."

Sawyer said, "I'll make sure he enjoys himself."

He dialed the number Benjamin gave him.

"Rocky Rim College, English Department, Ginger speaking."

"Gene Zane, please."

"I'm sorry, sir, Professor Zane is on his phone. May I take a message?"

Sawyer cursed under his breath. "This is urgent, Ginger. Be sure and deliver this message as soon as Gene is available."

"Okay," said Ginger. She snapped her gum. "Would you spell your name for me, sir?"

*

Jim Redline parked near the beach on San Diego Bay and spent the morning taking in the sights. He ate a leisurely lunch at Planet Hollywood in the Horton Plaza shopping mall at Fourth and Broadway. Then he killed two hours poking around in the upscale shops. Finally, he called Raven Investigations.

"How did you and Tom Sawyer get along?" asked Rex Raven.

"He wants to be my new best friend," said Redline.

"Bad idea," said Rex. "Trust me, he isn't qualified to be anyone's best friend. Here's what we know. Shortly after you left Sawyer's apartment, he called Directory Assistance in Arizona and asked for a man named Gene Zane. He tracked Zane to Rocky Rim College in Red Valley. Ever heard of Red Valley, Jim?"

"Isn't it an old black-and-white movie starring John Wayne and thousands of stampeding cattle?"

"I don't know. But the Red Valley I'm talking about is a little town two hours north of Phoenix, up in the piney mountains. I've actually been there. Loaded with Indian museums and cowboy saloons and stuff like that. Every business in town proudly displays Wyatt Earp's actual hat in their front window."

"The Old West," said Redline. "It will always be with us."

"Gene Zane moved to Red Valley a few years ago to take a teaching position at Rocky Rim College. Here's the big news. We did a background check on the professor and discovered he was in the army and stationed in Heidelberg, Germany in the early sixties. So was Sawyer. In fact, Zane was the company clerk for Sawyer's outfit, which was a military police unit."

"Aha."

"Jim, don't turn your back on Sawyer. He's definitely nasty. Got his ass fired from the San Diego police force after more than thirty years of notably undistinguished service. He took bribes, used excessive force, tampered with evidence, associated with known felons and so on. Not long after he was let go, he went into business with a woman he picked up in a bar. Scammed her for a nice piece of change but she turned him in. The police never recovered any of the money he stole. Sawyer told them he frittered it all away in Vegas. He's been out of prison just a short time and is almost destitute."

"Good work, Rex. Let me know if Sawyer suddenly decides to leave town."

"He can't afford to leave town."

"He can now. I just gave him a little traveling money."

Rex chuckled. "This guy won't be able to think about Gene Zane or Red Valley without me knowing about it. If he leaves National City, I'll be able to tell you exactly where's he headed and whether he's wearing clean underwear or not."

CHAPTER ELEVEN

Mustafa Rashid had no reason to suspect that Dr. Ian McTavish was not really a prison dentist. He sensed nothing amiss when the doctor told him that yet another wisdom tooth had to come out. The third one this month, even more severely impacted than the other two, pronounced the somber doctor.

So, thought Mustafa, free dental care in the American prison system? Bonus! What else are these filthy Christian pigs going to do with all the money they steal from the rest of the world? Build more laser-guided weapons? Stockpile more Saudi oil? Clutter Allah's sky with more spy satellites?

Mustafa relaxed in the comfortable dentist's chair. Even though his arms and legs were restrained with thick elastic straps and there were two armed guards standing just outside the room, he found the time he spent in the clinic enjoyable. It was certainly better than wasting away in his dreary prison cell, battered by the incessant din of obscene complaints from his fellow inmates. He concentrated on the tinny music floating down from a sound system concealed behind the ceiling tiles above his head. The Americans are such sappy romantics when it comes to music, he thought. Apparently, they are obsessed with their biological urges and frustrated in their search for ideal love. Clearly in America it is considered normal to prolong puberty until the last possible moment.

Dr. McTavish glided into the room wearing a mint green smock and a virus-proof mask that covered his nose and mouth. He glanced at Mustafa, then bent over a metal tray resting on a table near the dental chair. The doctor tugged on a pair of latex gloves, picked up a shiny metal instrument and examined it carefully. His slender assistant, Miss Rogers, walked into the room and stood beside him. She wore a mask, too, but no smock or gloves. Miss Rogers came close to Mustafa and peered down at him through the thick lenses of her glasses. He studied her hugely magnified gray eyes. She pressed the palm of her right hand gently against his forehead and said, "Trick or treat." A moment passed in silence. Then Mustafa took a deep breath, let it out slowly and began to blink his eyes rapidly. Miss Rogers snapped her fingers.

"Boo," said Mustafa.

"Good afternoon, Mustafa," said Miss Rogers. "Please go to sleep now and remain asleep until I summon you." Mustafa closed his eyes and immediately began to snore. Miss Rogers waited a full two minutes. Then she said, "Asad, I wish to speak to you."

"Asad is here," said the prisoner.

"Excellent. Please rest for a moment, Asad. I will be with you shortly." Miss Rogers turned to Dr. McTavish, motioning with her head that she wanted him to leave the room. Without a word, he turned and walked away.

Miss Rogers made a complete circle around the dental chair, examining every inch of the prisoner's body. Mustafa Rashid was short, muscular and heavily bearded. Not quite forty years old, he had pockmarked olive skin, a bulbous nose and thick black hair. Miss Rogers pulled a chair close to the prisoner's head and sat down, her face less than six inches from his. She flicked a piece of lint from his moustache with her fingernail.

"Asad, you may now speak to me," she said.

"Hello, Miss Rogers," said the prisoner. He stared happily at the musical tiles above him.

"We have many things to discuss today," said Miss Rogers. "I trust you are looking forward to our talk as much as I am."

"I am eager to talk with you again, Miss Rogers."

"Good. When we are finished talking, Dr. McTavish will return and extract one of Mustafa's teeth. But you will not be here while the doctor is working, Asad. Do you understand?"

"What will I be doing while Dr. McTavish is removing Mustafa's infected tooth?"

"You will be considering the concepts I am going to introduce to you today. They are complex. I want you to think about them long and hard."

"Of course. You are going to tell me how I can earn my freedom?"

"Eventually," said Miss Rogers. "But before I do that, I want to be sure you have accepted the new ideas I am going to discuss with you now."

"Please begin at once," said the prisoner.

"Asad, you do not tell me when to begin," said Miss Rogers sharply. "We settled the issue of who is in charge of these discussions the last time we talked."

"I am sorry. I did not mean to—"

"Hush." Miss Rogers put her index finger on the prisoner's hairy neck and located his pulse. "Listen carefully. Eliminate from your mind any and all distractions. Your ability to recall later every word I say today could very well determine whether we are going to continue with these dialogues or not."

"You are thinking of terminating our dialogues?"

"Only if you fail me," said Miss Rogers. Her fingertip recorded a dramatic increase in the prisoner's pulse rate. Excellent, thought Miss Rogers. Asad is terrified that I may decide to abandon him.

"I will never fail you," said the prisoner. "That is my promise."

Miss Rogers reached into a deep pocket on the side of her long dark skirt and retrieved a small tape recorder. She looked at the prisoner for a moment and reflected on his progress. Asad was bright and highly motivated. He was definitely becoming more self-confident. That was important because he would need an abundance of courage when the time came for him to emerge from his protected place and test himself against the fierce personality of Mustafa. That confrontation was unavoidable if Asad was to function independently in the real world.

Asad believed Miss Rogers was an angel sent to him by Allah, a warm and compassionate spiritual messenger willing to guide him along the path to eternal grace. So far, Asad had embraced all her suggestions without hesitation.

"Asad," said Miss Rogers, removing her fingertip from the side of his neck, "let's talk now about the defects in Mustafa's belief system. Defects that cause him to be radical in his political views . . . and terribly dangerous to you and me. Oh, and one other thing. From this moment on, you will refer to me by my real name, not the one I use when I am talking with Mustafa. You may call me Doctor Bowmaster."

*

"You're telling me you've accomplished the impossible?" asked an incredulous Charles Talbot. "You've already found someone you can control psychologically who is also personally acquainted with our target?"

The doctor shifted her eyes away from his and looked around the study without actually seeing anything. "Where is your wife tonight?"

"Shopping," said Talbot.

Barbara Bowmaster twisted in her chair. She tugged at her lower lip, removed her heavy glasses and rubbed the bridge of her nose. When she put her glasses on again, she stared down at her shoes. Dark and sturdy, she thought, just like Mustafa Rashid.

"I'm waiting, Barbara."

"Suppose I tell you what has happened," said Barbara, "and then you decide if I've done the impossible or not."

"Fair enough."

"Mustafa Rashid is in a federal prison because—"

Talbot said quickly, "That is redundant information. I know all about Mustafa Rashid. Where he was born, how many innocent Americans he's killed. The whole ghastly story."

"Sorry, sir. Well, like the majority of violent criminals in the world, Mustafa suffers from Dissociative Identity Disorder. DID is a complex neuropsychological process often linked to early childhood abuse. It's a natural defense mechanism, a way for a traumatized child to disconnect his consciousness from repetitive and unbearable pain. When he reached the age of five, and until he was strong enough to defend himself, Mustafa Rashid was regularly abused by his own father. Since this occurred during the critical time when his brain was being physically sculpted by his experiences, the impact of that torturous stress left an indelible imprint on his personality."

"How sad for him," said Talbot. "I'm tempted to weep. So now we know why Mustafa became a ruthless killer. Why do we care about that?"

"Individuals suffering from DID are remarkably easy to hypnotize," said Barbara. "I had no trouble putting Mustafa into a deep hypnotic trance the first time I met him. Later, I also injected him with an experimental chemical the agency has been testing. It allowed me to put him into an even deeper trance."

"Fascinating," said Talbot. "And then what happened?"

"We repeatedly brought Mustafa to a dental clinic near the prison, telling him he needed extensive work on his teeth and gums. He liked the process and reveled in the idea that we were servicing his body at the expense of the American government. On his second trip to the clinic, I discovered by accident that Mustafa manifests Multiple Personality Disorder."

"You mean he has a split personality?"

"Yes. Persons suffering from DID can be tested and tracked along a well-documented continuum. Their symptoms can range from simple depression or low self-esteem to extreme rage and hyper-vigilance. At the far end of the scale we sometimes encounter what is called 'alternative states of consciousness.' Mustafa is one of those extremely rare individuals who actually has a second human personality lurking in a dark corner of his brain."

"And it's the second personality you're interested in?"

"His name is Asad," said Barbara, "and that alone makes him interesting. When an alternate personality has developed to the point that it identifies itself by name, it is capable of a significant degree of independent thought and action."

"I see. How does Asad differ from Mustafa?"

"They are both manifestations of the same core personality. But Mustafa is a true believer, a fanatic who has dedicated his life to eliminating the enemies of his people and his religion. He particularly relishes killing Americans. He is brutal, canny and easily the most focused person I have ever met. He thinks about nothing but how to use violence and terror to advance his agenda. In contrast, Asad would like nothing better than to be accepted and valued by others. He has not yet lived in the real world so he's basically a blank personality waiting to be formed by experience or—and this is the good news—by a mentor. Right now he seems to have no fixed values, no permanent beliefs of any kind. He's just a young man with one priority—to get out of the bizarre predicament he finds himself in."

Talbot thought for a moment. "And you are positioned to become the mentor Asad needs if he desires independence from Mustafa?"

"Exactly," said Barbara, flushing with pride. "Asad and Mustafa are aware of each other, but they do not seem to know much about each other's thoughts or actions. Asad senses that Mustafa is violent, but he has no specific memory of any particular act his alternate personality may have committed. Mustafa has an impression of Asad as a puzzling but useless fragment of his own personality. A voice in his head that doesn't have anything useful to say. He doesn't know that I'm working with this 'splinter,' strengthening him, nudging him toward a state of mind that will enable me to use him in any way I choose."

"That sounds promising," said Talbot. "But difficult."

"Difficult, but not impossible. Asad is convinced that I have been sent to him by Allah to show him the one true path to freedom and eternal life. His blind faith in me is what grants me the power to forge him into a lethal weapon."

"Are you saying . . .?"

Barbara smiled. "For Asad Rashid, the miraculous experience of encountering me is the equivalent of a Christian stumbling blindly through the wilderness and suddenly coming face to face with Mary of Nazareth. To Asad, I am a divine figure. He has assured me he will do absolutely anything to please me. He would kill someone if I asked him to, even if he had to forfeit his earthly life to do it. In fact, he is strongly attracted to the idea of dying while serving me because he believes then we will be together in heaven for eternity."

110

Barbara relaxed and settled back in her chair to watch her boss assimilate her astounding report. She was gratified to see that he was simultaneously experiencing shock and pleasure.

"I thought Muslims had no respect for women," said Talbot. "How can—"

"Asad hasn't experienced the same rites of passage other young men of his faith are subjected to," said Barbara. "He appears not to know that women are treated like chattels in his culture."

"And all you need to do is tell him who you want dead and he'll do everything in his power to make it so?" Talbot was rapidly analyzing what he had just been told. This is amazing news, he thought. But it could be the worst amazing news imaginable. If the President learns of the presence of the malleable Asad Rashid, he will insist that I proceed immediately with his paranoid plan to . . .

"I believe Asad's offer to do my bidding is sincere," said Barbara.

Talbot cleared his throat and said, "Uh, this is not what I expected you to tell me today, Barbara. It is stunning, of course, and you are to be congratulated on your ingenious work. But I had hoped you wouldn't . . . that is, if I tell the President . . . well, for you to discover a human being who can be controlled is actually . . . frightening. Was the report I gave you to read a major factor in your success?" *Damn it, thought Talbot. I should have shredded that document the instant the President told me to! What the hell was I thinking?*

"Sir, let me be more precise about what I'm telling you," said Barbara quickly. "I learned nothing clinically useful from reading that old report. As far as I'm concerned, there are only two significant revelations to be found in it. One is that fate arranged for Fidel Castro to have a hand in the death of JFK. Even he must realize by now how incredible it was that Lee Harvey Oswald turned up just at the precise moment Castro needed him. What were the odds? The KGB doctor had failed with every other person he had worked with. If Oswald, a man truly born for his role in history, hadn't gone to Minsk and begged for a chance to serve Mother Russia, President Kennedy would still be alive today. The other remarkable thing I found in that report was that this agency successfully resisted the temptation to endorse the KGB doctor's singular accomplishment. The majority of people who interrogated the Russian psychiatrist were right to conclude that the Oswald phenomenon was a statistical fluke. The idea that the CIA, using the information the doctor gave them, could go on to develop a scientifically reliable way of creating a series of robotic human assassins was nonsense. And most of the people present that day knew it."

That's exactly what Dr. Katz concluded, thought Talbot. "You're saying that, although in Asad Rashid you *may* have found a weapon we can use, it was a stroke of luck, not a scientific feat? Are you also saying that two 'accidental' successes in three decades cannot be taken seriously? That even you, Dr. Barbara Bowmaster, skilled hypnotist working in a controlled environment, with the aid of modern hallucinogenic drugs, could attempt this mind-control experiment with an infinite number of candidates and it is a certainty that you would fail almost every time?"

"I would bet my reputation that I would fail almost every time," said Barbara. She was thrilled to finally see a smile brighten Talbot's handsome face. "I didn't prove that human beings can be hypnotized and made into killers. Hypnosis was just the key that opened a locked door and put me in front of a unique personality I would otherwise never have met. The odds against that happening again are extremely low. But saying that something *almost* never happens is quite different from saying that something can never, *ever* happen. My colleagues and I often celebrate that truth because the uncertainty factor in the world is what makes our profession so lucrative. More than half the people on this planet are suffering from some form of psychological pathology that we can trace back to their inability to cope with the absence of reassuring predictability in their lives."

Talbot did a drum roll on his thigh with his fingertips. He had quickly formulated a plan that would produce the results he was after. "I like this," he said. "I can win twice. Once when I tell the President that our extensive research proves conclusively that trying to create robotic assassins using hypnosis and drugs is a bad idea. We can't do it and neither can our enemies. And I win again when I tell him that, in spite of our failure to find a scientifically valid process, we have succeeded, by chance, in locating a weapon capable of taking out his target."

"Exactly," said Barbara.

"If we send Asad Rashid, posing as Mustafa Rashid, back to the desert to get close to the target and his resolve abandons him just as he is about to do the deed, well, I can't stand to even think about what that might mean for this country. Have you considered that?"

"Yes," said Barbara. She got up and walked over to Charles Talbot. She put her hand on his shoulder and leaned forward a bit so that her breasts were just inches from his face. "Don't worry about that, sir. I promise you Asad will not flinch when the moment comes for him to carry out his mission. And he will be riddled with bullets an instant after he makes his lethal move against our target. He won't be alive to tell anyone who ordered him to kill his leader."

Talbot double-checked his intricate plan. One thing is clear, he thought. Barbara is determined to please me. But her hormones are in control of her brain, not common sense. Mustafa Rashid hypnotized and helpless? Fat chance. The man is a rabid terrorist. It's unlikely that this lonely lady has found a bona fide way to make him kill his own leader. But it is possible that Mustafa and his 'alternate personality' would allow themselves to be manipulated for a while if they thought it might afford them even a slight chance to escape.

Talbot glanced at Barbara's hand, now lovingly stroking his arm. They exchanged sizzling looks, then Barbara blushed and awkwardly returned to her chair.

Talbot thought, *she's more in love with me than Asad Rashid is with her!*

Barbara thought, *he's close to caving in to his desire to ravish me! We're bonding! Some evening, he'll knock on my door and . . .*

"I see that you are ready to take a chance on Asad's commitment to perform," said Talbot, "but I'm afraid I don't have the same level of confidence in this process that you do, Barbara. Not yet, anyway. Let me suggest a way to test Asad that will provide the kind of verification of his reliability that I require."

"Test?" said Barbara.

"I think we should order Asad to kill someone for you. Not the final target. Someone else."

"Oh, I see," said Barbara. "Well, I guess that makes sense. Do you have someone in mind, sir? Is there a list of people you wish were dead?"

Talbot chuckled. "Oh, that's rich, Barbara! A list of people I wish were dead?"

"A secret hit list," said Barbara.

"Well, let me think," said Talbot, his eyes twinkling. "There's always my counterpart at the FBI. And then there's that wily senator from Nebraska who keeps derailing my budget."

Barbara smiled and clasped Talbot by the hand in a spontaneous gesture of affection and solidarity. He lifted her fingers toward his lips.

The door to the study suddenly opened and Mrs. Talbot stepped into the room. She stood rock still for a moment, studying the intimate tableau before her.

"Excuse me," she said, flashing Barbara a withering look. She shifted her gaze back to her husband. "I didn't know you were working late, Dear." She spun on her heel and left, slamming the door behind her.

Talbot rubbed his forehead, sighed, fought back a self-conscious grin and looked at Barbara out of the corner of his eye. "I know what you're thinking, Barbara, and the answer is no. I can't put my wife at the top of my secret hit list."

CHAPTER TWELVE

Gene Zane was sitting alone at a table in the faculty lounge, sipping coffee and nursing a vicious hangover. Paul Quimby suddenly materialized beside him.

"Good morning," boomed Dr. Quimby in his sepulchral baritone. "I need to see you in my office, Gene. I'm headed there now."

Gene nearly choked on a mouthful of boiling hot coffee.

"Okay," he croaked, "be there shortly."

Dr. Quimby marched away on his stubby legs, waving a hairy hand at some people seated on the far side of the lounge. No one waved back.

This is bad news, thought Gene. Dr. Paul Quimby, chair of the English Department, rarely spoke to anyone unless he had something toxic to impart. It was understood by everyone that Quimby spent most of each day staring out his office window at the pine-studded foothills that bordered the campus of Rocky Rim College, thinking up crafty ways to demoralize the instructors who labored in his department.

Rocky Rim College was located ninety miles northwest of Phoenix in the popular mountain resort town of Red Valley. The school's president, Dr. Milton Canfield, had let it be known that he was on a mission to establish Rocky Rim as the state's leader in graduating technologically-enabled kids who could succeed in the "rapidly expanding digital universe." Dr. Canfield, nearly seventy years of age, had never touched a computer in his life and had no intention of doing so.

As a middle-aged associate professor of English at Rocky Rim, Gene Zane came across to his hip students as a laid-back, environmentally aware, slightly-over-the-top intellectual. He had long brown hair, sun-bleached at the ends, wire-rimmed spectacles and a bushy mustache.

Gene specialized in teaching the literature of the American West. He liked to show students the films that had been adapted from the novels they were studying, films like *The Ox-Bow Incident*, *The Big Sky* and his personal favorite *Shane.* After screening the 1954 Alan Ladd classic, Gene would sometimes hear his students in the cafeteria or parking lot mimicking the child actor Brandon DeWilde: "Zane! Come back, Zane! Mother wants you! I know she does!"

Three years after he joined the faculty at Rocky Rim, Gene's wife died of cancer. Patti had been fifty-two years old when she was diagnosed with the disease, not yet fifty-three when she succumbed to it. His friends immediately began to see signs that Gene couldn't handle the tragic loss of his wife. They soon realized that the only thing keeping him alive was his fierce devotion to his daughter Sissy and his grandson Gene Junior. Frequently hung over and often morbidly preoccupied, Gene somehow mustered the energy to work as hard as ever.

*

Dr. Quimby's office looked like an indoor landfill designed by John Belushi in collaboration with Andy Warhol. Papers, books, maps, posters, gadgets and heaps of twisted junk littered every square inch. Paper clips, rubber bands, note pads, file folders, tape holders and writing instruments lay in a loosely connected mound over all sorts of other mysterious things. There were no framed photos of family or friends in evidence. No plants, no flowers, no art. The murky office was dimly illuminated by a tiny cone of pale yellow light from an antique lamp crouched on a messy credenza behind the desk.

Gene sniffed the air as he groped his way through the gloom to a guest chair. Apparently, Quimby had recently eaten a spoiled egg salad sandwich at his desk . . .

"How have you been, Gene?" asked Quimby. He jerked his reading glasses off and tossed them into the pile of flotsam in front of him. They instantly burrowed out of sight. Quimby's chocolate brown eyes, so dark they appeared to be black, looked calmly into Gene's sky blue eyes, his chubby face completely expressionless.

Gene didn't bother to respond. When you were summoned to Quimby's office, you were expected to listen patiently as the great man pontificated, not chat about yourself. Gene stared blankly into space for a time, then tried in vain to read the title printed on the spine of a hardback resting on the corner of his boss's desk.

"I have just come from a rather depressing meeting with President Canfield," said Quimby. He sighed and rubbed his forehead with his left hand, showing off his class ring from the University of Notre Dame, something he did whenever possible.

Damn, thought Gene. This is going to be bad.

"As you know, Gene, enrollment is down," continued Quimby, "and our budget is in tough shape. Consequently, although you'll be employed at Rocky Rim next year, I'm afraid you'll be teaching part-time. To be precise, we have decided to cut your hours by half."

Quimby's slimy eyes slithered over Gene's face like swamp leeches. Paralyzed by the unexpected news, but determined not to show it, Gene sat like a statue and stared off into hell. Holy shit, he thought. Financial extinction! Fiscal apocalypse! Economic annihilation!

Quimby idly pushed some papers around on his desk and made pointy arches out of his tangled eyebrows. "Terrible news for a man of your vintage, isn't it, Gene? I imagine it's going to wreak havoc with your retirement plans."

Gene looked out the window at the beautiful green trees on the hills just beyond the campus. The world was still there.

"I want you to know," said Quimby, "neither President Canfield nor I are pleased about this. You're one of the most popular teachers on the entire faculty. But numbers rule, Gene."

You lying prick, thought Gene.

Take that, you bastard, thought Quimby.

Boy, a drink would taste good right now, thought Gene. He felt his guts twist into a painful knot and said to himself, whatever you do, don't let this ape see your fear. Don't give him the satisfaction. If he can fake compassion, you can fake courage.

Quimby retrieved his glasses from the mess on his desk and began polishing the lenses with a grimy handkerchief. He locked eyes with Gene, savoring the moment.

Gene felt a bolt of pain race across his chest. He had a nearly uncontrollable urge to claw at his shirt collar. He knew student enrollment was steady, not down. I'm being punished, he thought. It must be that gender discrimination suit I won for the teachers' union last year. These assholes want their money back and they intend to get it from me!

"Please tell President Canfield I appreciate any work he can give me," said Gene. "Maybe next year things will improve enough that we can get back on my old schedule."

Quimby turned completely around so that his back was to Gene, plucked a piece of paper from his credenza and pretended to examine it with great interest. "That's what I told Dr. Canfield you'd say, Gene. You've always demonstrated remarkable strength in the face of adversity. Someone told me you had a large life insurance policy on Patti. Said you have a chunk of money in the bank. I was delighted to hear it. That money will help you to get through this temporary decline in your income."

Gene dug his fingernails into the wooden arms of his chair. Outrageous! Everyone on the faculty knew that Patti's sudden illness had pushed him to the brink of bankruptcy, that he had been caught with almost no life insurance on his wife at all. Barely enough to cover her funeral expenses!

I can't stay in this office another minute, thought Gene. I'm going to do or say something nuts! He jumped to his feet and, even though Quimby was not looking at him, glanced theatrically at his watch. His heart was pounding, his legs were turning to jelly. He was having a panic attack that, he knew, could kill him.

"Gosh, look at the time. I'm late for class," said Gene. He whirled and staggered for the door. He heard Quimby's chair squeak and knew the pudgy man had spun around, knew he was twisting his class ring, grinning as he watched his mortally wounded quarry run for cover.

Gene stumbled down the hallway until he reached the safety of his own office. He fell into his chair and gulped for air. Compared to Quimby's garbage pile, Gene's office was a model of organization. It was also chock full of warm human things. There were framed pictures of Patti and Sissy and Gene Junior everywhere. Some were over twenty years old. Patti as a young bride. Patti pregnant. Sissy riding her first bike. Christmas pictures. Birthday parties. A great shot of Gene Junior sleeping in his crib. The last picture of a smiling, healthy Patti.

Gene struggled to his feet, locked his office door, then folded back into his chair. He grabbed a pint bottle of peppermint schnapps from a drawer in his desk and took a long thirsty pull.

The phone rang. Gene grabbed it and growled, "Yeah?"

"Hi, Dad."

"Sissy! I was just thinking about you. How's life in Boulder, Colorado?" Gene reached for a picture of Sissy when she was thirteen years old. His eyes misted. Spitting image of Patti, an angel in human form.

"We'll get to that. First I want to know how it went for you yesterday."

"Yesterday? Well, I had breakfast. Then I came down here and had lunch. After lunch I took a nap. Then I went home for supper. Pretty full day." Gene burped into the receiver. He could burp anytime, as often as he wanted. Patti had protested whenever he did it, but Sissy always said burping was one of his best tricks.

"Dad, be serious. What was the outcome of your appointment with your cardiologist?"

"The cardiologist said if things improve soon, no problem. If not, he wants to put a new valve in my heart."

Gene suddenly had an encouraging thought. He could schedule the heart operation during the summer, maybe as late as August. His disability insurance would pay his salary until he was able to return to work. Could be six months, he thought, maybe longer. He could protect his income for at least half of the next academic year. Assuming, of course, he survived the operation . . .

"Daddy," said Sissy. "I'm scared for you."

119

"Don't be scared. The doctor said if I lose forty pounds, quit drinking, change my diet, and exercise properly, I can put this whole thing behind me in no time. And that's exactly what I'm going to do, Sissy. I really mean it this time."

"Forty pounds? Last week you told me you were only twenty pounds overweight!"

"Last week I *was* only twenty pounds overweight! But enough about me. All of my problems have easy solutions. Let's get to the hard stuff. What's up with you and Gene Junior?"

The line was silent for a moment. "Damn," said Sissy. "Now I don't know whether to tell you or not."

Gene snapped upright. "Spit it out! What's wrong? Is Gene Junior sick?"

"No, he's healthy as a horse. But I lost my job at the restaurant. Couldn't seem to make my schedule fit with theirs. And Gene Junior's father, that creep, is trying to get custody again. He says he can prove I'm not a responsible parent. He's taking me to court. I talked to a lawyer, but he wants a five thousand dollar retainer before he'll represent me."

"My God," said Gene.

"And," continued Sissy, "my car stopped in the middle of the street today as I was taking Gene Junior to the day-care center. The mechanic says he isn't sure what's wrong with it, but he doesn't think it's anything simple. Dad, I hate to dump all this on you when you're facing a heart operation and everything. I feel like such a failure."

Gene took another long pull from his schnapps bottle. In the background, he could hear Sissy's television set. It was tuned to one of the popular soap operas. "You're not a failure, Honey. You're just going through some tough times. They never last, you know that."

"But what should I do, Daddy?"

"I'll help you," said Gene. "Don't I always?"

"You're so great," said Sissy. "The best daddy in the world. Um, my rent is due on Monday and I don't have all of it. Maybe . . . "

"I'll mail it tonight," said Gene. "Put the car-repair bill on that credit card I gave you. Let me think about the lawyer thing. Maybe I can offer him a personal guarantee in lieu of a retainer."

Sissy sniffed and said, "Thank you, Daddy." Gene could hear the volume on the television set go up slightly.

"Give Gene Junior a hug for me, okay? Tell him Grandpa's going to take him fishing soon." Gene made a kissing sound and gently hung up the phone.

He peered at the ornate label on the schnapps bottle. Forty-percent alcohol. Doesn't taste that strong, he thought, taking another swig. Then he reluctantly put the bottle away.

Gene buried his face in his hands and considered Sissy's new problems. Money was the main issue and always would be. I can sell my personal computer, he thought. No, I need that. But I could sell the freezer. Never use that damn thing anymore. Maybe a garage sale would bring in a few bucks. My old golf clubs are worth something. And that set of fondue pots. They say fondue is back. Hey, retro stuff! I've got a ton of it! Clothes, neckties, vintage books.

I could ask Sissy to move back to Red Valley, thought Gene. That would cut my expenses by a bunch. No, she loves Boulder. Besides, she doesn't want to live with her old dad anymore. She's all grown up now. Well, sort of . . . it would be nice if she finished college one of these days and got a real job.

I'm such a sap, thought Gene. Here I sit making one bad decision after another. The first step in the evolution of a loser. He stared at a picture of Patti. Beautiful light blue eyes. With those eyes and her pale skin, she always looked best in dark colors. Gene thought of Patti in her coffin, wearing a beautiful black dress . . .

Someone knocked on Gene's office door.

The problem with giving up entirely, he thought, with making one rotten decision after another and not caring enough to stop, is that it directly affects Sissy and Gene Junior. My failures will eventually impact their lives in a very bad way and that's unacceptable. Camus was right. Either play for keeps or shoot yourself and get the hell out of the way. Or did Sartre say that? I should know. I get paid to know that.

Gene opened his desk drawer and fumbled for the bottle of schnapps.

Someone knocked on his door again, much harder.

"I'm not here," said Gene. "Isn't that obvious?"

"Open up, Gene. Got a phone message for you. Trust me, you'll want to see this one."

Gene climbed out of his chair, unlocked the office door and flung it open. The department's secretary, Ginger McCormick, stood in the hallway, smiling and holding a bright pink message slip in her hand. She was barely five feet tall. Her glasses had slipped halfway down her nose and her eyes were sparkling with merriment. Ginger was thirty-two years old and had six kids. Her husband, a skinny guy with a wild gypsy mustache, drove a delivery truck and was a drummer in a rock band.

Ginger stuck her head in Gene's office and sniffed. "Smells like mouthwash in here," she said. Then she gave him a penetrating I-know-you've-been-hitting-the-schnapps look and strolled away.

Gene closed his office door and peered at the message slip. The call had come in while he was talking to Sissy. Ginger had recorded it with a heavy black marker.

CALL TOM SAWYER. URGENT!!

There was a phone number preceded by an unfamiliar area code. Must be a joke, thought Gene. He lowered himself into his chair and tossed the message slip on his desk. Of course, he had once known someone with that name. A long time ago, in another life, another world. Could it be? He tried to think back but couldn't force himself to concentrate. He needed a drink before he did anything else. A real drink. He'd have to deal with the weird message some other time.

Gene bolted from his office and hustled down the hallway. He passed Ginger's desk on a dead run. From the corner of his eye, he spotted her watching him. She opened her mouth but he was out the door before she could speak.

Wow, thought Ginger, Gene is really upset about something. His face is beet red and he's practically sprinting to the parking lot. Then she spotted a piece of pink paper on the floor near her desk. It was the message she'd just delivered to Gene, the mysterious call from Tom Sawyer. Ginger bent over and picked it up. I'll give it to him again tomorrow, she thought. He'll be glad I saved it before the cleaning people swept it up. She giggled. Maybe if you're an English professor, you just get calls like this. Tom Sawyer phones from the spirit world with an urgent message.

Dr. Quimby walked out of his office, his reading glasses dangling from his fingertips, a puzzled look on his face.

"Ginger," he said, "what the hell is going on out here? I heard someone running."

Ginger flashed him her Mona Lisa smile, close-mouthed and mystical. She covered the message slip with her hand.

"You know what I think, Dr. Quimby? They aren't kidding when they say the truth is out there somewhere. Know what I mean?"

"No, Ginger, I don't know what you mean. What truth? Out where?"

"I can't say exactly," said Ginger. "But it's like, you know, kind of cool how things work out sometimes."

CHAPTER THIRTEEN

The huge man working behind the bar called himself Tiny. He was six feet six inches tall and weighed three hundred and forty pounds. On his island home of Samoa, men his size were not an uncommon sight. But in National City, he was considered a freak of nature. He kept his stiff black hair cut short and his flat brown face shaved close to the bone. His steel-hard head sat on a neck as thick as a fire hydrant. His massive forearms and hands could crush bone.

Tiny made it out of Samoa and into California when a scout from Stanford University spotted him at a high-school wrestling tournament and immediately offered him a full-ride athletic scholarship to play tackle on the Cardinal football team. Midway through his first season, the head coach abruptly dismissed him from the team.

"Maybe they'll let you play like that in the NFL," said the nervous coach, "but you can't get away with it in college, young man. Sooner or later, you're going to cripple someone out there. But you're not going to do it at Stanford."

The Oakland Raiders talked to him. So did the San Diego Chargers. Things looked promising for a while. There was a lot of money on the table, genuine excitement in the air. After Tiny breezed through his physical, both teams asked him to take a battery of psychological tests. Just routine, they said, all the guys take them. But when the test results came back, negotiations ended abruptly. Tiny was never told exactly why.

He found employment for a few months as a bouncer at a jazz joint in Los Angeles, got fired for brutalizing the customers, then went to bartender's school in San Diego. He mixed drinks for three weeks at a fancy place on the Bay but was terminated when he got into an argument with an inebriated customer and broke the man's jaw in six places. Tiny moved from bar to bar for two years. Then he walked into Sharky's Black Dog Saloon on Temple Street. He was an instant success. Within twenty-four hours everyone who frequented Sharky's understood one thing very clearly—Tiny ruled.

Dick Sharky was a former jockey who was barely tall enough to see over his own bar. He took one look at Tiny and knew he'd found the man he'd been dreaming about for years. Before the big jock hired on, expensive bottle-breaking brawls were almost a nightly occurrence in the shabby saloon. Sharky's overhead had threatened to put him out of business. Tiny immediately brought order to Black Dog. Now, no matter how furious or intoxicated the combatants were, they nearly always took their fight outside.

Dick Sharky paid the giant generously for his time and talents. Tiny had found a permanent home at last and he protected it like a rabid dog. He settled down, worked hard and even began to salt away a little money. Sharky's was a perfect haven for a powerful freak of nature cursed with the volcanic temper of a homicidal maniac.

The saloon attracted a colorful and varied clientele. There were always at least a dozen gleaming motorcycles in the parking lot. Sunburned men and women stood around the bikes adjusting their helmets, posing in monogrammed black leather jackets and saucy bandannas. Small bands of wiry Filipino merchant marines gathered at Sharky's to play poker. Asian and African-American drug dealers used the place to conduct business on their cell phones. Sharply dressed Mexican pimps and their tired whores met there in the wee hours of the morning to split up the evening's take. Nearly everyone who lived on four-block long Temple Street considered Sharky's to be a second home. Of course, nearly everyone who lived on Temple Street was a thief, an addict, a psycho or an ex-con. Most Temple Street residents desperately needed a second home, one with bright lights and a jukebox and a working john, because their primary abode was either a cardboard packing carton or a tenement with no heat and broken plumbing.

Tiny knew all of his regular customers by name but avoided forming close friendships with any of them. For one thing, they were losers and Tiny didn't think of himself as a loser. He believed he was a gifted athlete who had never been given a real chance to show the world what he could do. He made one exception to his rigid rule about getting close to bar patrons—the lanky ex-cop, Tom Sawyer.

In just six weeks, Sawyer had become Tiny's best friend and only confidant. The islander bonded with the lynx-eyed outlaw quickly, because the two of them had discovered they had many important things in common. Neither man was content to live with the lousy cards he had been dealt by a cruel and indifferent world. They were both ready and willing to risk everything, including life itself, to get away from Temple Street and back to the good times they had once enjoyed. When the right opportunity came along, they vowed they would do anything for a shot at returning to the golden days of tasty food, beautiful women and easy money. They talked about it constantly, and it was those intense discussions, brimming with hope and possibility, that kept Tiny from running amok in the filth and desolation of Sharky's Black Dog Saloon, from losing control completely and tearing someone to pieces with his bare hands.

*

Tom Sawyer strolled into Sharky's at noon on the day following his visit from Jim Redline and sat down at the bar. He had just concluded a long and promising phone conversation with Gene Zane. Sawyer was on cloud nine. Suddenly, life looked good again. There was money to be made and plenty of it. Of course, there was still much to be done, he reminded himself, before the money would actually be in his possession. He was eager to get started.

Tiny was standing behind the bar wiping his hands on the grimy blue apron he wore around his thick waist. He shot Sawyer a curious look before pushing a glass of beer in front of him, then quickly waited on several other customers before finding a calm moment to speak to his friend.

126

"Okay," said Tiny. "Let's hear it. It's written all over your ugly face, man. Something must have happened. Something good."

Sawyer grinned. "I knew I should have worn a mask in here today."

"You got a mug like a neon sign," said Tiny. "Make my day, man. Tell me all about it."

Sawyer took a slow sip of his beer and pointed to a jar of pickled eggs next to the cash register.

"I'm starving. Give me a couple of those eggs."

Tiny fished two eggs out of the brine and plopped them on a small paper plate. He set the eggs down next to Sawyer's beer glass and licked his fingers. Several customers called for service, but Tiny ignored them. His intense brown eyes were riveted on his pal.

Sawyer quickly ate one of the eggs and washed it down with beer. He wiped his mouth with the back of his hand, then pulled a wad of hundred dollar bills from his pants pocket. He peeled one off the stack and tossed it on the bar, making sure Tiny got a good look at the rest of the money before he put the wad away.

"Keep the change," said Sawyer. "Cause I sure as hell won't be needing it."

Tiny twisted his fingers in his apron and smiled. "You fell into it, didn't you?" he asked. "Just like you've been saying you would. You fell into it and came out covered in money."

Sawyer nodded. "That's right," he said. "This is it, Tiny. This is the one I've been waiting for, the chance I knew had to come along someday. It's happening right now."

Tiny bellowed with joy and slammed the bar with the palm of his huge hand. Everyone in Sharky's froze and looked around, eyes wide. The only sound for a moment came from the jukebox, Patsy Cline warbling about sweet dreams. But when the roof didn't cave in, the bar didn't explode and no one dropped dead, conversations resumed.

Tiny put his face close to Sawyer's and whispered, "You son of a bitch!"

"Thanks buddy," said Sawyer. "Listen, I got things to do, people to see and places to go that are kind of far away. I'll be back in town in a couple of days. We'll talk then. I think I'm gonna need some advice."

"I'll be right here," said Tiny. He watched his pal walk jauntily out of the saloon.

I'll be damned, he thought to himself. It looked like Tom had a couple thousand dollars in his pocket. He's on his way. No more shitty Temple Street life for that bad boy. He's done with month-old pickled eggs and flat beer for eats. He's gonna be knee-deep in dumplings and gravy. Damn, I almost can't stand it . . .

Tiny mopped his round brown face with a bar towel. I'm next, he thought. If it can happen to Tom Sawyer, it can damn sure happen to me. It *will* happen to me! I'll be the next one to break into the clear, by God! I can't wait to hear how he did it.

Two Mexicans shooting pool began to argue in staccato Spanish, softly at first, then much louder. The short fat one suddenly hit the short skinny one with his pool cue, knocked him down and started kicking him in the face.

A woman screamed. Someone threw a plate of nachos at her.

In a flash, Tiny was around the end of the bar, running hard, eyes blazing. He drew a bead on the Mexicans, both now writhing on the floor.

I reckon these guys have never been in here before, Tiny exulted as he bore down on the struggling fighters. Virgins, by damn! He sailed through the air and landed on the stunned Mexicans like a killer whale on twin baby seals. The other bar patrons roared with delight.

The woman screamed again. Someone bounced a heavy motorcycle helmet off the side of her head.

One of the waitresses, Anne Marie, watched Tiny working on the Mexicans for a few moments, then put down her plastic tray and sauntered to the pay phone near the front door. She took a hunk of pink bubble gum out of her mouth, stuck it to the side of the phone, punched in 911 and requested that an ambulance be sent to Sharky's Black Dog Saloon.

"That would be on Temple Street," said Anne Marie automatically, even though she knew the ambulance guys could drive to Sharky's with their eyes glued shut.

Shrieking at the top of her lungs, the injured woman hurled her beer glass at Tiny. A chunky female biker slugged the woman on the jaw, grabbed her by the front of her shirt and dragged her out the front door.

Anne Marie peeled her bubble gum from the side of the phone and popped it into her mouth. Then she waded into the excited crowd, looking for thirsty customers.

CHAPTER FOURTEEN

"I know less about Mars than I know about the World Wrestling Federation," said Lionel Cooper. "In other words, absolutely nothing. Same thing when it comes to space travel. I'm aware that it's important to someone, but that someone isn't me."

Stuart McManus chuckled. "Doesn't matter. I'm going to tell you everything you need to know about Mars and space travel in the next five minutes, Lionel. I haven't made a truly bad investment decision in over thirty years, knock on wood, and I think this may be the best opportunity to make money I've ever seen. Better than war."

Stuart McManus was plump, bald, brilliant and rich. He was an internationally renowned economist who had an uncanny knack for making lucrative investment decisions even in bad times. Both Harvard and M.I.T. had tried unsuccessfully for decades to hire him to run their respective business departments. He was one of only three men Lionel Cooper regularly consulted for advice on how to grow his money.

It was early in the morning. The two men sat next to each other in guest chairs in front of Cooper's desk sipping coffee and munching donuts.

"Nonsense," said Cooper. "There's nothing better than war for making money. Of course, since Mars is the god of war in Roman mythology, maybe there's a connection."

"The ancient Romans have nothing to do with this. Besides, everyone knows there won't be another war anytime soon. Or, to be precise, not one expensive enough to interest major league investors like you and me."

"Quit stalling and start talking," said Cooper. He peered down his bony nose at his friend and waggled his finger. "You barged in here this morning without an appointment, Stuart. A box of cheap donuts is not much of an inducement to get me to talk business when I have writing on my mind."

"Kiss my big floppy ass," said McManus affably. "You'd rather talk business than write and we both know it. Now listen up and prosper. Occasionally I waste a few hours with the retards in the business departments at Harvard and M.I.T. Most of the professors teaching in those hallowed institutions can't spell profit, let alone earn one, Lionel. But I enjoy sniffing around and, believe it or not, every now and then I find an unspoiled student who is alert enough to make an immediate contribution to my organization. Or I hear a tantalizing rumor or even stumble across a solid investment tip."

Cooper helped himself to a second donut. It was so brittle he could barely chew it even after he had dunked it in his coffee. "Where did you get these pathetic donuts?" he complained.

"I'm thrifty. Donuts cost a lot less when they're a week old," said McManus. "Anyway, to return to my gripping tale. There's an old saying—even a blind hog finds an acorn now and then. Quite by accident, I recently discovered that some gifted students from Harvard got drunk with some brilliant students from M.I.T. and the result was they created a gold-plated team that is about to form a corporation to fund and direct the first manned mission to Mars. Mostly private money, Lionel. Big corporations working in partnership with scientists from NASA and the governments of a half-dozen wealthy nations. America, of course, and Russia. France. Perhaps even China."

McManus bit down on his donut, moaned, fished it out of his mouth, stared at it in dismay and then flipped it into a nearby wastebasket. "A week might be a bit longer than thrift demands," he muttered.

"These kids think they can beat Uncle Sam at the space game?" asked Cooper. "And they expect to make a profit doing it? That's sheer arrogance."

McManus grinned. "When I first heard about this, I thought it sounded nuts, too. But then I asked some questions. Turns out our government is about to screw up this whole Mars exploration thing worse than they did Vietnam. The project is too big and too complex to be accomplished by any one entity, especially an inept entity like our government. But that won't stop them from trying. This will be a huge multifaceted gig so complicated it will push the scientific community to the far edge of its present technological capability. It's a one-shot project that could cost fifty billion dollars or more. It's Kennedy's moon shot all over again but a lot more ambitious and harder to do. Does that sound like something you want your government to try to handle all by itself, Lionel?"

"Of course not. But then, I don't see the point in going to Mars in the first place," said Cooper. "I like this planet. The food's pretty good and we have a market economy."

"You don't see the point right now, but you will when I'm finished talking," said McManus. "If we send people to Mars and we find evidence of life there—and the smart money says we will—it's going to change our perception of reality forever, Lionel. People will be forced to see the universe and God and mankind in a whole new way. Life on Mars would be proof that life is ubiquitous and that man must have cousins living in galaxies far, far away. We're talking glory unlimited to anyone associated with helping to accomplish such a philosophically significant voyage. It will fling open the public funding door and permit perpetual space exploration, the colonization of other planets and so on. And that's critical to the long-term survival of the human race. Don't forget, in five billion years our sun is going to burn out and we'll need to be living someplace other than here."

"I think about that all the time," said Cooper. "Just yesterday I was asking myself what the hell I'm going to do when the sun finally shuts down for good. By the way, Stuart, don't forget that I'm an atheist. It would never occur to me to wonder if a benevolent God has made provisions for the perpetual existence of human beings by thoughtfully placing a planet near us that's littered with clues about the origin of life and the possible existence of other sentient beings."

"Then let's think about this pragmatically," persisted McManus. "Consider the economic spin-offs from mineral rights, new technologies, broadcast licenses, medical information and untold other goodies, Mr. Atheist. A successful trip to Mars will supercharge the economy on earth permanently. Even faithless curmudgeons like you enjoy making and spending gobs of filthy lucre, Lionel, and I believe anyone who invests in a trip to the Red Planet will become rich beyond his wildest dreams. That would be me, by the way, and maybe you. That is, if I can overcome your reluctance to confront the naked truth and see that a huge payoff from this venture is virtually assured."

Cooper stared into his coffee. "How long is this fantasy trip to Mars supposed to take? In case I'm interested in going along to protect my investment."

"Using existing rocket technology," said McManus, "about two and a half years. It turns out Mars is only close enough to earth to make the trip practical once every twenty-six months. So you'd spend six months getting there, about five hundred days exploring the place and then another six months coming home. You'd have a great time."

Cooper rolled his eyes. "Two and a half years? No thank you. Stuart, I'm not a psychologist but my gut tells me that an astronaut sent on a trip like that is going to be a babbling idiot by the time he gets back to Mother Earth. Could you stay locked up in one of those little rockets for a year without strangling somebody? Could you hike around a dead planet like Mars in red dust up to your balls for five hundred days without bashing your best friend in the face with a golf club? I'll grant you we may have the science to make this project technically feasible and we may even be able to raise enough money to pay for it. But we're never going to find people who can tolerate a mental strain like that."

McManus feigned amazement. "Pshaw! Don't you read Tom Wolfe? He says astronauts are people born with the 'right stuff.' They can and will do anything they're challenged to do. Especially if we give them fast machines to fly."

"Bullshit," said Cooper. "The astronaut hasn't been born who could handle a trip that isolates him for that long. Even Wolfe knows that. They'll have to send machines to Mars, Stuart, robots of some kind."

"Aha," said McManus, beaming, "we've finally arrived at the crux of the situation. I'm always impressed, Lionel, by your ability to drill right to the heart of the problem. Some very famous scientists believe robots are the only realistic option we have for exactly the reasons you've just mentioned. Others say that without people along to do crucial on-the-spot thinking and subtle decision-making, the cost of going to Mars will exceed the return in useful information. I'm in that second camp. You say the astronaut hasn't been born who can tolerate the rigors of a trip to Mars? I say the robot has not been built that can come home from such a voyage and tell us what we need to know if we want to change the world forever."

"Nevertheless," said Cooper, "I'd favor sending robots to minimize the risk of abject failure. In fact, as soon as you leave here this morning—and that will be momentarily, Stuart—I'm going to call my broker and tell him to put some bucks into the companies working on artificial intelligence and robotics. I thank you for your sage investment advice. Now run along."

Stuart McManus peered over the rim of his coffee cup. "Is this a soundproof room?" he whispered.

"As a matter of fact it is," lied Cooper smoothly.

"If I tell you something that is absolutely top secret, will you promise me you will never reveal it to another soul?" McManus looked around the office as if he expected to discover a reporter hiding behind a potted plant.

"You have my word," said Cooper. His pale face was inscrutable but his brain was buzzing fiercely. Top secret? Two of his all-time favorite words!

"Don't ask me how I know this, Lionel, but it has been revealed to me by a credible source that NASA is collaborating right now with the CIA on a form of mind control that will enable them to manage the behavior of the astronauts on this voyage. Turns out the CIA has been sitting on information about this for decades, information that NASA can easily adapt to their purposes. The President himself ordered the CIA to cooperate with NASA scientists to help refine this secret technique."

"You don't say," said Cooper mildly. He picked up another concrete donut and bit through it effortlessly.

"I believe this changes everything," said McManus. "The human beings selected to fly to Mars will be under the control of their superiors at all times. They will perform flawlessly because they will not be destroyed by lethal levels of emotional distress. If I didn't know about this and thought we'd have to depend on ordinary men and women to behave themselves on the long voyage, I would agree with you that this investment opportunity was far too risky."

"Quite fascinating, Stuart," said Cooper. He was stunned and enthralled by what he had just heard but determined not to show it. "Do you know where the CIA got their hitherto unrevealed information about mind control?"

McManus shrugged. "No one wanted to discuss that very much. One professor did get a little tipsy over lunch and told me he'd heard a bizarre rumor that the information came out of an old file on the JFK assassination. But I think rumors of that kind are a dime a dozen, don't you? Rather like UFO sightings. When people see something they can't explain but desperately need an answer, they just start babbling about flying saucers and all that stuff."

"Yes," said Cooper. "That's what people do. Let me say before you go that I'm rather more likely now to invest in this project than I was when you first started telling me about it. You've done an excellent job of stimulating my interest. Understand, I would need to hear some very convincing details before I would actually write out a check to a bunch of inexperienced students, no matter how precocious you think they are."

McManus stood up and brushed a few donut crumbs from his tie. He arched his bushy eyebrows. "The minimum you would have to cough up to be accepted into the Mars project is twenty million dollars, Lionel."

Cooper waved his hand. "Money is not the issue here, my friend."

"I didn't think it would be," said McManus. "I'll be in touch." He said goodbye and let himself out the door.

Cooper sat down behind his desk, poured himself another cup of coffee and punched the intercom button on his phone. Tina Romero answered immediately.

"I'm going to that damned book festival on the Harvard campus in a few minutes. It's a waste of time, but Norman Mailer asked me to meet him there. Find Jim and tell him to call me at exactly five o'clock tonight," said Cooper. "And then put the Helen Rutz file on my desk."

"Sure. By the way, Jim called me while you were talking to Mr. McManus," said Tina. "He said he's made contact with the man he was looking for and things look promising."

Cooper smiled. Yes, he thought, things do indeed look promising. Almost out of this world, in fact . . .

CHAPTER FIFTEEN

"Jim, great to hear your voice," said Lionel Cooper. It was five o'clock in the evening. He had just taken his first sip of iced scotch. "I understand you've located the man Helen Rutz sent you to find and have already talked to him."

"I did," said Redline, "and that conversation may be about to bear fruit. He's booked a flight to Arizona and made arrangements to meet up with one of his old army buddies. I think he's on the trail of the jewelry box. I've got my fingers crossed that he'll come up with it quickly."

"Me, too," said Cooper. "More than ever."

"Really? Why is that?"

Cooper sniffed his scotch and smiled. "I'll tell you when you return with the box, Jim."

*

A freshly showered Tom Sawyer lay dozing on a king-sized bed in his motel room in Red Valley, his damp head resting on a pillow wrapped in a thick white towel. When the phone next to the bed rang, Sawyer's eyes popped open. He swung his legs over the side of the mattress and cleared his throat.

"Talk to me, Ace."

"The man just drove away from his house. I'm going in now."

"Do not go in now, you idiot," said Sawyer. "He's a scatterbrained professor. Probably forgot his wallet or something. Wait at least a half hour to make sure he's not coming back."

"Whatever. Tell me more about this jewelry box."

Sawyer could hear Ace chewing food with his mouth open, like a dog. He figured to be sitting in his rental car a few yards from Gene Zane's house, wearing dark glasses and a sweat-stained baseball cap, eating potato chips and sipping Jolt.

"This one was made in Europe in the sixties. Are you listening to this, Ace? Because if you find one that has a Wal-Mart sticker on it, that's not what we're looking for. They didn't have Wal-Mart stores in the sixties. How hard can this be?"

"Things that sound simple are the hardest to do," said Ace. "Don't ask me why."

"Your job is to get into the man's house without tripping an alarm or being spotted by a nosy neighbor, Mr. Professional House Burglar. Concentrate on that problem and stop imagining that you won't recognize the damned jewelry box."

"I know what I'm doing," said Ace. "I should leave a message at the desk when I'm done?"

"Call my room and if I'm not here, leave a message on the voice-mail system. I don't want to wave goodbye to the professor tomorrow without knowing for sure if that damned box is in his house or not."

Ace burped softly. "Got it. Anything else?"

Sawyer rubbed his damp hair with the bath towel. "Don't take anything out of the house except the jewelry box. I don't care if you find a solid gold nugget. Leave no clues that would tell the professor or the police that someone has been in his house."

"Never fear. Ace is here."

"I'm meeting the professor downtown in an hour. I'll make sure he doesn't come home before midnight. That should give even an idiot like you plenty of time to look at everything in that house."

Sawyer hung up, cursed, dropped the towel on the floor and walked into the bathroom. He pulled his hair into a stubby ponytail and secured it with a black rubber band. Then he stared at his reflection in the mirror above the sink.

This better work, he thought, because there is no Plan B.

*

138

Gene Zane drained the beer in his glass, waved it at the bartender, then turned around on his stool and scanned the busy saloon again. Tom Sawyer was already fifteen minutes late.

It was so bizarre to hear Tom's voice on the phone, thought Gene. And the timing of his call was miraculous. If I'd racked my brain for the best guy in the world to get drunk with tonight, I couldn't have come up with a better choice than Tom.

Tom had been strangely vague when Gene had asked him why he had chosen this particular moment to surface. But the "why" of it didn't matter anyway. What mattered was that Gene was stressed to the max from obsessing about his personal problems and he desperately craved a distraction, even if it was just for one night. The opportunity to spend an evening drinking with an old army buddy was exactly the excuse he needed to stop thinking about the mess he was in.

I'm definitely up against the blade, thought Gene. He stared glumly into his beer. There are some extreme options, things I could do to avoid bankruptcy. But they're more than just unpleasant to contemplate. I could get a second job pumping gas or waiting tables. I could sell life insurance over the phone. Or, I could ask my relatives for a loan. But I'd rather flee to Mexico and sleep in the gutter than admit to them that I've failed as a provider.

Hell, thought Gene, I can't be expected to cope with this much crap all at once. Thank God for Tom Sawyer. The man couldn't have picked a better time to reappear in my life and help take my mind off this horrible mess for a few hours.

It was almost too good to be true.

*

Sipping a soft drink, Jim Redline sat near the phone in his motel room. He was doing something he almost never did at home—watching television. An attractive female face told him sweetly that there had been a devastating warehouse explosion in Chicago, a fiery commuter plane crash in New Jersey and a bomb threat at the Vatican. The Dow had slipped twenty points, the Detroit Tigers had split a

doubleheader with the Cleveland Indians and the president of the
United States was relaxing at Camp David.

Redline studied the label on his soda can and wondered idly why
anyone would want to know those things. The phone rang.

"Mr. Redline, this is Dan Maples, Javelina Investigations, calling
from Red Valley, Arizona. How are you this morning, sir?"

"Couldn't be better."

"I'm calling to give you an executive summary of what went down
here last night. Thirty minutes after Mr. Zane left to keep his
appointment with Mr. Sawyer, a man broke into the professor's home.
He used illegal lock picks to gain entry. He spent almost five hours
inside the house. Shortly after Mr. Sawyer returned to his room, which
was around one o'clock this morning, the burglar called him and said
that he had not found the jewelry box. Mr. Sawyer told the man to get
his ass back to California."

"How were you able to monitor the call between the burglar and
Mr. Sawyer?"

"While Mr. Sawyer was meeting with Mr. Zane, we slipped into
his motel room and bugged his phone. We also checked his luggage.
No weapon."

"What did Sawyer and Zane talk about?"

"They met at a cowboy saloon downtown. I had two people there
equipped with concealed directional microphones. We have the entire
conversation between Mr. Sawyer and Mr. Zane on tape. They spent a
couple hours rapping about the army experiences they shared during
the time they were in Germany. Mr. Sawyer told Mr. Zane that he was
a retired police officer who lived in the lap of luxury in a condo
overlooking San Diego Bay. Mr. Zane said he had been a teacher for
many years. Near the end of the evening, a thoroughly intoxicated Mr.
Zane spilled his guts to a sober Mr. Sawyer about his personal
problems. The recent death of his wife, his current financial dilemma
and a life-threatening health issue. Mr. Sawyer said little in response.
They agreed to meet for lunch today. In fact, Mr. Zane just phoned Mr.
Sawyer and they set up a rendezvous at a pancake house close to
where Mr. Zane lives. I've got people there now who will record every
word they say to each other."

"Zane told Sawyer he has serious money *and* health problems?"

"Yes, sir. He said he's under enormous financial pressure. He also has a potentially fatal heart condition that requires corrective surgery."

"They never talked about a jewelry box?"

"That is correct."

"Thank you, Mr. Maples. After Zane and Sawyer conclude their visit in the pancake place, let me know immediately whether they discussed a jewelry box."

"Yes, sir. I've been doing this kind of work for over twenty years, Mr. Redline, so I know it's unprofessional to ask this question, but I'm curious. What's in the jewelry box?"

"Jewelry," said Redline. He hung up the phone, turned off the television and stretched out on the bed. Come on, Professor Zane, he thought. Make my day.

*

Tom Sawyer stared across the table at a pale and trembling Gene Zane.

"Man, you're trashed," he said.

Gene splashed coffee from an insulated carafe into a thick white mug. He made a feeble attempt to smile through the excruciating pain of his hangover.

"I'm proof that the phrase 'better living through chemistry' does not apply in every situation," he muttered.

Sawyer grinned. "No kidding. Gene, I don't know if this is the right time to bring this up but last night you asked me again why I'd picked this particular moment to contact you. I had a simple answer ready, but now that I've had a night to think things over, I'm going to change that answer and tell you it must have been your guardian angel that directed me to call your office the other day."

Gene's tongue flicked across his parched lips. He poured himself more coffee and watched in somber silence as steam rose from the dark liquid.

"Because," continued Sawyer earnestly, "what I came here to talk to you about could well be the answer to all your prayers, buddy. I represent the chance you never thought you'd get to solve every problem on your plate. So, it can't be just dumb luck that brought me to Red Valley yesterday. A higher power must be looking out for you."

"Tom, if this is an Amway pitch, you can forget it," grumbled Gene. "There are some things even I won't do."

Sawyer frowned. "Just listen to what I have to say and try to keep an open mind. You'll either know the answer to the question I'm about to ask you or you won't. If you do, your life is going to get better in a hurry. If you don't, well, look at it this way, Gene—you got a free night on the town courtesy of an old pal. A night that helped you set aside your troubles for a while."

Gene stirred two packets of sugar into his coffee and looked around for a waitress. "Yeah," he mumbled. "Let's order some grub."

"Let me lay a little foundation for you," said Sawyer. "Back in the sixties, on the very day I left Germany to rotate to the states, I walked up to your desk and handed you an object. I said, 'You'll never believe where I got this thing, Gene.' I promised I'd write when I got back to California and fill you in on the whole story. I never wrote, of course. The last letter I wrote was to the IRS and it damn near put me in front of a firing squad."

"Fascinating," said Gene. He yawned and rubbed his face with both hands.

"Pay attention! This is important. Do you happen to remember what I handed you that day?"

Gene shook his head and immediately regretted it. "Ouch! Damn, I think my brain is bleeding. Uh, sorry, but I remember absolutely nothing about anything that happened on that day. Why don't you just tell me what this mysterious object was and end the suspense?"

Sawyer leaned halfway across the table. "It was a wooden jewelry box, Gene. About so high, so long. I think there was a painting on the lid."

"Oh, *that* object. Sure. You handed the box to me and I thought, what the hell is this? Tom Sawyer bought me a gift? I was stunned."

Sawyer almost fell out of his chair. Gene remembered! After all these years, Gene Zane remembered the jewelry box! Whoa!

"If you can answer this next question," said Sawyer, his voice taut, "you can kiss all your problems goodbye. *Where is that box right now?*"

Gene took a careful sip of his coffee and appeared to be concentrating intensely. But he wasn't thinking about the present location of the jewelry box. That was a no-brainer. He was thinking that Tom Sawyer had not come to Red Valley to visit an old army buddy at all. He was here to try to screw that buddy out of something valuable! I might have known, thought Gene. Just another kick in the face, another shit sandwich. One more hideous event in a conga line of humiliating moments in the interminable downhill slide of Professor Gene Zane. If it weren't for the fact that I'm responsible for Sissy and Gene Junior, I'd stab myself in the throat with my butter knife and end this pathetic nightmare right now!

A twenty-something freckle-faced waitress glided up to their table, order pad in one hand, pencil in the other. She snapped her gum, rubbed her nose with the back of her wrist, and coughed.

"Excuse me! I can't seem to shake this horrible cold," she rumbled in a deep voice any radio announcer would have been proud to own. "Shouldn't even be working today. What'll it be, gentlemen?"

Delighted by the interruption, Gene promptly answered, "A stack of blueberry pancakes with a double order of crispy bacon on the side. Maple syrup, extra butter."

"Just toast for me," said an annoyed Sawyer. He drummed his fingers on the table and tried in vain to translate the odd expression on Gene's face. Did the bastard know where the box was or not?

"What kind of bread for that toast, sir? Wheat, raisin or sourdough?"

"Sourdough!" snapped Sawyer.

"Any juice today?" asked the waitress, unperturbed. Geezers, she thought. Hair-trigger tempers, every damned one of them. She blew a big pink bubble with her gum and stared out the window at the passing parade of people and cars.

"Yes," said Gene. "V-8 juice, please."

"Nothing for me," growled Sawyer. "Look, miss, we're talking here. Do you mind?"

143

"Large or small V-8?" The waitress coughed in Sawyer's direction.

"Large," said Gene. He wiggled the empty carafe. "Another jug of coffee, too."

Sawyer shut his eyes and ground his molars.

There was a tiny squeak as the waitress twisted her rubber-soled sneakers against the tiled floor and shuffled off toward the kitchen, coughing against the back of her hand.

Exasperated, Sawyer said, "Did you hear what I asked you just before Miss Congeniality showed up with her stupid quiz show, Gene? *Do you have any idea where the box is now?*"

"I know exactly where it is now," said Gene casually. The long harangue with the waitress had given him time to organize his jumbled thoughts. Behind his wire-rimmed glasses, his bloodshot eyes radiated a blend of caution, cunning and something like controlled outrage. "Let me just say I find this turn of events more than a little disturbing, Tom. I thought you came to Red Valley to visit me because we were once pals. Turns out you're here because of money. Furthermore, it's hard for me to get excited about this when I don't have any idea how that ratty old box could solve all my problems. Didn't you just say that you'd planned to write to me and tell me the whole story someday? Okay, why don't you tell me the story right now? What makes the jewelry box so valuable, Tom? What's in it, the map to the Lost Dutchman Mine?"

Sawyer was so relieved at Gene's matter-of-fact declaration that he knew where the jewelry box was, he almost screamed with joy. He made an odd gurgling sound and dropped his eyes to hide his excitement. Then he forced himself to quickly review the strategy he had worked out in case this very situation came up.

"Something like that," he said. "But the best thing for both of us would be that I get my hands on that box right away. Where is it?"

"I'm not going to tell you," said Gene firmly. He gave Sawyer a frigid look. Some primitive instinct buried deep in Gene's subconscious mind had clawed its way to the surface and counseled him to ignore the pain of his hangover, as well as the deep

144

embarrassment he was feeling, now that he knew the real purpose of Sawyer's visit. "Survive," said the voice, "and prosper!"

"Obviously you believe the box is worth big money," he said. "So I think we should negotiate a deal that is fair to both of us right here, right now. Getting my hands on the box is not going to be a problem, Tom, *if* I'm properly motivated. But if I'm unhappy with the terms you have in mind, well, it's hard to say what I might decide to do. Or not to do, as the case may be."

"That was damned good," said Sawyer. He was genuinely impressed with Gene's gritty response. "It took you less than sixty seconds to change from a miserable bookworm suffering from a near-fatal hangover into a professional contract negotiator. But in case you've forgotten how we got into this conversation in the first place, Gene, let me suggest you think about the fact that I flew here at my own expense just to bring this golden opportunity to your attention."

"Oh, really?" said Gene. "Look at it from my side of the table. You know I'm broke. You can hardly expect me to fork over the box just for old time's sake, Tom, and settle gratefully for whatever pittance you feel you can spare after you convert it into money. My guess is you're going to sell the thing five minutes after I hand it to you and I'd be shocked if you didn't already know *to the penny* how much it's worth. What do you figure my share will be? A third? Half? Since I can actually produce the box and you cannot, shouldn't I be the one to sell it? Keep the lion's share of the money for myself and pay you a reasonable commission for bringing this deal to my attention?"

Enormously satisfied with that speech, Gene enjoyed a silent moment of pleasurable self-congratulation.

"Without me," said Sawyer, his yellow eyes boiling, "you couldn't convert the box into anything but sawdust because you could never figure out *why* it's valuable. Only I know that and I'm not going to share that information with you just yet. Don't get any grandiose ideas about doing this deal on your own, Gene, or taking the biggest share of the profits. Think, man! What I'm offering you is a gift!"

"You've got a lot of talking to do if you expect me to believe any of the preposterous things you just said," said Gene.

"I plan to tell you everything you need to hear," said Sawyer, silently patting himself on the back over his clever choice of words. The beauty of being me, he thought, is that I'm not handicapped with a conscience the way Gene is. If he thinks fifty percent is what he deserves, hell, I'll agree to that. He'll deliver the jewelry box and actually expect to be paid half of what it's worth! The man is a patsy!

"I'm very pleased to know you feel that way, Tom," said Gene. "If a deal isn't a win for both parties, it's a bad deal. That's long been my business philosophy. We're both civilized men. I know we can work this out satisfactorily."

"I agree," said Sawyer amiably. "Hey, here comes our food. Can I have some of your bacon?"

*

"Good afternoon, Mr. Redline. Dan Maples again."

"Talk to me."

"Mr. Sawyer and Mr. Zane have just finished lunch. Mr. Sawyer asked Mr. Zane if he remembered the jewelry box and if he knew where it was right now. Mr. Zane said he does know where it is right now. Mr. Sawyer said if Mr. Zane would hand over the box, he could consider his current money problems solved. An intense negotiation ensued. Mr. Sawyer agreed to give Mr. Zane fifty percent of any profit he made when he sold the box. Mr. Zane eagerly accepted when Mr. Sawyer assured him fifty percent meant a minimum of fifty thousand dollars. Mr. Zane attempted to shake hands with Mr. Sawyer but accidentally knocked their coffeepot over as he lurched across the table. Mr. Sawyer complained loudly and profanely about painful burns on his legs and crotch. A waitress dumped a bucket of ice on Mr. Sawyer's lap. Then the two men hastily departed the restaurant."

"Zane didn't reveal the location of the box before they left?" asked Redline.

"No, but we caught a break at that point," said Maples. "They went to Mr. Sawyer's motel room so he could put some ointment on his scorched skin and change into clean pants. We weren't able to hear what they said to each other in the room, but the phone bug we planted there yesterday enabled us to record a call Mr. Zane placed to his aunt

146

in Belgrade, Montana. Her name is Kitty Carson. We traced her phone number to an antique store she owns called Kitty's Katchall."

"You got lucky."

"Yes. Mr. Zane asked his aunt if she still had the jewelry box he sent her from Germany in the sixties. She said, it's right here on my desk where it's been all these years. Mr. Zane said, I'm coming up there in a few days to go fishing and I want to buy it back from you. His aunt said, why would you want this old thing? He replied, I'll explain that when I see you. His aunt said, be sure and stay at my house, not at the motel here. I've got lots of space and the Gallatin River runs right past my back door. Mr. Zane said, I'll let you know in a day or so exactly when I'll arrive. Then he asked her how the fishing was and she said it was pretty good this year."

"Did Zane say exactly when he's leaving for Montana?"

"Not during the phone call. Mr. Sawyer and Mr. Zane went down to the lobby of the motel and that gave us one more opportunity to use our directional microphones. Mr. Sawyer said, I'm going back to San Diego tonight. I'll notify my buyer that I have a lead on the location of the jewelry box. In three days, I'll fly to Belgrade and get a room at that motel your aunt talked about. You throw your fishing gear in your pickup truck and get up there as fast as you can. Call me when you get into town. I want to be there when your aunt gives you the box. Sells me the box, Mr. Zane corrected him. She has to profit from this, too, or the deal's off. Mr. Sawyer said, her profit comes out of your share, so you do the math. Fine by me, said Mr. Zane. And that was it. Mr. Zane left the motel and Mr. Sawyer limped back to his room."

"Outstanding job, Dan."

"Thank you. By the way, I figured out what's in the jewelry box," said Maples. "And it isn't jewelry."

CHAPTER SIXTEEN

Jim Redline worked out for an hour in the motel exercise room, showered, dressed and then called Dude Daniels, a personal security expert based in San Diego.

"Dude, this is Jim Redline. Remember me? Couple years ago? We did a thing together involving some pimps from Mexico. They were smuggling their hookers out across the bay at night to rendezvous with a well-known senator on his yacht. Ring any bells?"

"Sure, I remember you, Jim. Mr. Deep Pockets from back east. What's up? Money burnin' a hole in your pocket again?"

"How'd you guess? I'm throwing money around like there was no tomorrow."

"Love your attitude, man."

"Can you come to my motel and talk to me right now?"

"I'm halfway there already. What's your location?"

While he waited for Daniels, Redline reviewed his notes from his last phone conversation with Dan Maples. Things seemed to be falling neatly into place. This could be embarrassingly easy, he thought. Too bad. I was hoping to sink my teeth into something nasty for a change. Redline made a fresh pot of coffee and was about to call Helen Rutz to let her know he was closing in on the jewelry box when he heard a heavy rap on his door.

Redline opened the door and Dude Daniels sauntered into the room. The two men shook hands and sized each other up. Although Redline was six feet four inches tall and weighed two hundred and thirty-five pounds, Daniels made him look like a kid who hadn't filled out yet. At six feet eight inches, he weighed nearly three hundred pounds. He was coal black, massive and intimidating. Dude Daniels could stop most men in their tracks just by scowling at them. He made a living providing protection services for a number of people, some of them with rather unsavory professions.

The two big men sat down at a wooden table.

"Coffee?" asked Redline.

"Never touch the stuff," said Daniels. He was wearing a black silk shirt, black designer jeans and black ankle-high boots. His hair was cut close to his skull. He sported a pencil-thin mustache and elegant tapered sideburns.

"You look almost the same as the last time we got together," said Daniels. "Then you were pale and puny. Now you're tanned and puny."

"Thank you," said Redline.

"So much for small talk," said Daniels. He rapped his big knuckles on the table. "Time is money. Tell me what you need done. By the way, my rates have gone up. Inflation."

"I understand inflation. Here, I wrote everything down for you," said Redline, pushing a piece of paper across the table. "The address and a few other details. The man's name is Tom Sawyer. I want to meet you near his dump in National City tomorrow morning. We'll keep an eye out until he shows up. Be prepared to waste most of the day. You can listen in while I talk to him. He's going to be livid. Sawyer's past his prime but he's an ex-cop and an ex-con. He's got a pistol hidden under the mattress in his room. My spies tell me we shouldn't let Sawyer's age or seedy appearance fool us, Dude. He's nasty enough to strangle babies for their toys."

"And what do you want from me, Jim?"

"Containment," said Redline. "Sawyer has to stay home for the next two days. He thinks he's about to go on a lucrative business trip, but he's wrong."

"Say what?"

"His gun is our trump card. Sawyer is a felon and possession of the gun is a violation of the terms of his parole. If he complains that his civil rights are being violated, we threaten to call his parole officer and blab about the firearm."

Daniels shook his head. "This is not cool, Jim. My conscience won't let me charge you my new rate for a simple job like this. Dude Daniels squatting on an unarmed toothless old coot? You're using an atomic bomb to kill a mouse. Waste of money."

"I can afford to waste money," said Redline. "In fact, I'll pay double your new rate if you do this for me. That should ease your conscience a bit."

"It does. But, this old fart gives me grief, he could get bruised."

"Bruised is acceptable," said Redline. "Even broken. But if Sawyer is crippled or he dies because he gave you grief, don't bother sending me a bill. I never heard of you. This is a handshake deal. No paper trail."

"I understand," said Daniels. He waved a hand as big as a truck tire and walked out of the room.

*

"You should call before you come here, you inconsiderate bastard," roared Tom Sawyer. He was standing in the open doorway to his apartment wearing nothing but boxer shorts and shower slippers. "There's no reason you have to work so hard at being disagreeable. I was just about to hit the sack. Been a long day."

"I apologize for interrupting your slumbers," said Redline, "but we need to talk."

Sawyer shook his head in disgust, turned around and began to flip-flop toward his shabby kitchen. Redline motioned with his hand and Dude Daniels materialized behind him. The two men slipped quickly into the apartment. Redline closed and locked the door.

"I suppose it isn't all bad that you're here," said Sawyer. He stood with his back to Redline. "I've got some encouraging news for you and, uh, your partner in fraud, Helen Rutz."

"I know you do," said Redline.

Sawyer spun around, the question forming in his eyes, and saw the mammoth black man standing beside Redline.

"Oh, I get it," he said. "Now I'm dealing with *two* creeps. One wasn't enough because I'm so dangerous, is that it? Like this changes anything."

"Tom," said Daniels, "this changes everything, man."

"You son of a bitch," said Sawyer, ignoring Daniels. "What was all this talk about honor and a man's word? All that high and mighty crap? Then you pull this low-life shit. I knew you were scum as soon as I laid eyes on you."

"Get his gun," said Redline.

Daniels headed toward the bedroom. He glanced over his shoulder at Redline and said, "You didn't tell me this place reeked."

Sawyer shot a nervous glance at Daniels' broad back as the big man faded into the bedroom. "I don't believe *this*," he said. "You're going to shoot me with my own gun? How the hell did you know about that, anyway?"

"Your services are no longer required, Tom," said Redline. "I'll take it from here." He tossed a fat wad of cash at Sawyer's feet. "There's the finder's fee I promised you. Ten thousand dollars."

"What the hell are you talking about?" hissed Sawyer. "I'm just getting started!"

Daniels reappeared with the gun wedged under his belt. Then he sniffed at Sawyer's greasy hair.

"This man is filthy," he growled. "First thing I'm going to do is dip him in some hot soapy water. Then he's going to scrub this rat's nest from top to bottom."

"I agreed to pay you a fee and there it is, right next to your big toe," said Redline. "You can keep that money if you stay in your apartment for forty-eight hours and make nice. My friend has graciously consented to hang around so you won't be lonesome. He'll see to it that you don't run out of lard or instant coffee or flypaper and that you have agreeable companionship every minute."

"You like gin rummy, Tom?" asked Daniels. He grinned and clapped his giant hand on Sawyer's skinny shoulder. "How about strip poker?"

"You bastard," said Sawyer, his cat's eyes still trained on Redline. "I'll track you down and blow your brains out. You're a dead man, pal."

"First you have to survive without getting yourself crippled," said Redline. "Dude hates to lose at cards."

Sawyer slapped Daniels' hand from his shoulder and bent over to pick up the cash. He counted it, spat on the floor, lurched across the room and sank down on the sofa.

"You can't hold me here," he said. He jerked his head up and tried to drill a hole in Daniels' implacable face with his angry eyes. "I can deal with this ape. I've put a thousand men just like him in jail. You two have no idea who you're dealing with."

"Look at it this way," said Redline. "If you cooperate, we won't have to tell your parole officer that we found a firearm in your possession. You get to keep all that cash without worrying that you might be headed back to prison. Don't get greedy and ask for more than you're entitled to, Tom. And don't fret about your good friend Gene Zane, either. I'll see to it that he makes out just fine on this deal."

"Oh, now I get it," said Sawyer. "You must have had a lot of help to do what you've done. Well, I know exactly where you're going when you walk out of here. Better keep looking over your shoulder because I'll be right behind you. And when I find you, boom, you're dead."

"Hey," said Daniels, looking at Redline. "Maybe you better clip a little rearview mirror to your hat. This old fart is going to track you down."

"I'll enjoy watching you die," said Sawyer, chewing on each word. "I'm going to carve your beating heart out of your chest and feed it to the pigeons one sliver at a time."

Daniels stood in the doorway to the kitchen, hands on his hips.

"Man, this is a pit. We're gonna make some changes around here, Tom, because old Dude is not going to live like this. This is squalor, baby, squalor!"

CHAPTER SEVENTEEN

The Director of the FBI, Conrad Morse, closed his eyes and relaxed as he waited for Charles Talbot to join him for a private meeting at FBI Headquarters. The two Directors met periodically to exchange opinions about events of mutual concern. They tried to make their get-togethers enjoyable as well as productive. The host Director provided refreshments. If the meeting convened before noon, gourmet coffee and pastries were served. But if the meeting took place after lunch, they nibbled on salty snacks, cookies and soft drinks.

Well in advance of the meetings, the two men exchanged copies of key foundation documents. Their discussions were not officially recorded, but both Directors scribbled notes on legal pads—to be discreetly shredded later—if dates, names, numbers or anything else that would be difficult to remember came up.

This meeting was scheduled for one o'clock in the afternoon in a soundproof paneled conference room located adjacent to the FBI Director's spacious office on the top floor of the J. Edgar Hoover FBI Building. Beneath a large framed black-and-white photograph of a grim-faced Hoover, the Directors would sit side by side at a mahogany table built to accommodate twenty-four people.

Charles Talbot stepped into the conference room at precisely one o'clock. Tall and sleek in his beautifully tailored suit, he carried a ribbed aluminum briefcase equipped with double combination locks.

Stacked neatly in front of Conrad Morse, next to a glass of root beer, were three file folders with "Top Secret" stamped in wide red letters on each light blue cover.

"Good to see you," said Talbot cordially, as he filled his glass with diet cola. "My God, look at the size of those cashews! I'd heard there were some colossal nuts in this building, but this is a bit of a shock!"

"The most gargantuan nuts in the country can be found here in our modest little agency," said Morse.

The FBI Director had smooth blond hair, a skier's tan and flinty blue eyes. He was in his early fifties, a lawyer with a reputation for being unusually aggressive in an environment where anything but extremely cautious behavior was considered downright reckless.

Charles Talbot was also a lawyer. Conrad Morse considered him to be a nakedly ambitious predator who could never be trusted with the whole truth about anything.

"I'm going to abandon my proposed agenda today because I have something urgent to talk to you about," began Morse. "This item may appear at first blush to be inconsequential, but hear me out. I'm sure you'll find this interesting."

"Wonderful," said Talbot, pawing at the cashews. "I'm never happier than when I'm listening to your hypothetical doomsday concerns. They make my own apocalyptic fears seem so much more reasonable."

"I doubt you're aware that we've been covertly monitoring a controversial American author, Lionel Cooper, for several years now," said Morse. "We were, uh, more or less ordered to do so after Cooper nearly crippled the entire federal government with his book on Sonny Russo."

Talbot made a face. "*The Glass Coffin.* I have two friends who are in mahogany coffins right now because of that damned book. Of course, I can't prove that. And I have other friends who are permanently unemployable, thanks to Cooper. I *can* prove that but they won't let me. They say they'd rather starve to death in dignified silence than endure any more unsavory publicity."

"Our President," continued Morse, "has made it clear to me that he will not tolerate an unexpected blast like the one his predecessor took when *The Glass Coffin* hit the streets. He believes Cooper is an intrepid foe of the United States government with as much potential to

154

harm this country as Saddam Hussein. Fortunately, we have a paid informant on Cooper's staff who keeps us advised about all of the man's activities. We know in advance who he's conniving with, who he's sleeping with, who he's bribing and exactly what he's planning to say when he appears on radio or television. We also review what he's writing about when he finds something juicy to disclose in excruciating detail to his doting public. He has a column syndicated in most major newspapers and regularly contributes controversial articles to radical periodicals that specialize in criticizing the actions of our government."

"What a guy," said Mr. Talbot. "All that talent and he chooses to waste it slinging mud at decent public servants."

"Interestingly, he hasn't found a topic suitable for a book-length work since *The Glass Coffin*, but we know he's constantly scanning the horizon for the perfect scandal, something he can really sink his fangs into. He'd love to end his career with a shocker that would add a few hundred years to his literary reputation."

"Blind ambition. Gotta love it."

"A few hours ago," said Morse, "our informant provided us with a bit of astounding news that I wish to discuss with you now."

"I'm all ears."

"Our mole is Cooper's personal assistant, a young woman named Tina Romero. She consistently provides us with accurate, reliable data about the author's numerous sins. Hang on to your hat, Mr. CIA, because you won't believe what she says the old goat is up to now. Cooper is trying to take possession of information that will prove that in 1961 a KGB psychiatrist, financed in secret by Fidel Castro, hypnotized Lee Harvey Oswald and successfully programmed him to assassinate JFK. This event allegedly took place in Minsk while Oswald was living there."

Charles Talbot felt his belly catch fire. He debated with himself at lightning speed whether the President's highly classified project involving NASA and his own agency might now be at risk of being exposed by the federal government's most relentless adversary, a man with awesome financial resources and the trust of every ordinary

American citizen. The possibility was almost too horrifying to contemplate.

"Romero used the word 'prove' in her report. Keep in mind, Charles, she's an amateur. Those of us who are trained in intelligence realize that no JFK conspiracy theory can be proven at this late date. Not in a court of law. Furthermore, all the savvy people who were trying to prove the conspiracy thing abandoned that quest years ago. This is yesterday's mystery. Which begs the question—why would a successful writer like Lionel Cooper waste time on this? Can he know something about this strange story that we do not?"

Talbot was shaken to the core by what he had just heard but was confident that Conrad Morse had not observed his agitation. He rapidly assessed this new situation. There was plenty of bad news to worry about, but the good news was that Morse had clearly said Cooper was "trying to take possession" of the proof. That meant the author didn't have it yet. There might still be enough time to intervene and prevent a catastrophe.

Talbot cleared his throat and reached for a chocolate mint cookie. "I'll be damned," he said. "I haven't heard a good JFK conspiracy story in years. This one isn't new, of course. It was obviously plucked directly from the plot of that popular old movie. You know the one I mean. Famous flick about mind control and an attempt by the Red Chinese to arrange for the assassination of an American presidential candidate. I think we can safely assume that what you have here is just one more in a long line of corny ideas that originated with that movie."

"Perhaps," said Morse. He had detected a subtle change in Talbot's voice and instantly interpreted it to mean the man was trying to conceal his extreme reaction to Romero's report.

"Romero forwarded us copies of the contents of Cooper's confidential file on this matter," Morse continued, "along with a transcript of her long conversation with him. A woman claiming to be the former wife of the late General Walter Rutz called Cooper's office recently. General Rutz commanded the U.S. Army in Europe during the sixties. His ex-wife Helen said she can prove that Oswald was a guinea pig in a successful deep-programming experiment conducted by the KGB and bankrolled by Castro."

"When pigs fly," said Talbot. He had eaten six cookies and emptied his nut bowl. "What sort of proof is she talking about? A sworn statement by Castro admitting to all this?"

"Helen Rutz says she was recently sent some papers by the late general's confused old probate attorney, a batch of secret notes her husband had written years ago. The notes were disguised as personal letters to her. Information in the notes alerted her to where to look for the proof."

"Oh, I see," said Talbot. "Then this is just idle speculation, a weird idea the general was toying with decades ago. A set of possibilities he imagined could possibly be true. I don't have to tell you that the general's private thoughts, no matter how credible they may sound to a layperson like his ex-wife, do not constitute legal proof of anything, Conrad. At best, this would appear to be an example of informed conjecture. You know how it is with these JFK stories. They all sound believable at first. Then it invariably turns out they contain a flaw, much to the dismay of legions of conspiracy buffs. Cooper will soon discover the problem with the Rutz story and the whole matter will go away like a bad odor."

Morse stole a furtive glance at Talbot before he spoke again. He's barely breathing, he thought. I wonder how much longer he can hold out. And if he can't stand to hear what I'm telling him, what does that mean? Morse felt a surge of pleasure as his competitive juices began to race through his body.

"I would agree with you," he said slowly, "except for the *physical* evidence that Helen Rutz claims to know about."

"*What* physical evidence?" barked Talbot. "The damn notes? I just said—"

"Not the notes," said Morse calmly. "It's obvious the notes alone don't carry much freight. But Cooper was interested enough in this story to send his chief investigator, a man named Jim Redline, to interrogate Mrs. Rutz. She told Redline the final proof that the statements in the notes are true is hidden in the false bottom of an old wooden jewelry box. That proof consists of photographs of Oswald and two Cuban spies, a key to a Swiss safe deposit box full of cash and an encrypted note from the Cuban government. Combined with the

notes—which provide a credible explanation of what was going on—
that kind of evidence might be rather compelling."

"An old jewelry box?" said Talbot, rolling his eyes. "With a false
bottom? You can't be serious."

"In 1961," said Morse, "the jewelry box was mailed to the
general's office in Heidelberg, Germany by someone known to the
Rutz family who had unexpectedly come into possession of it,
someone who didn't know if the box was important or not. Helen Rutz,
who was completely in the dark about the significance of the box at
that time, plucked it from the general's desk while he was out and,
within hours, gave it to someone else. Romero says it is that very
jewelry box that Jim Redline is pursuing. Redline faxed a report to
Cooper's office today that reveals the present location of the box and
his plans for securing it. When Romero read the report, she
immediately got in touch with her FBI contact. Cooper is in New York
and is expected to return to his office later tonight. He'll find the report
on his desk."

Talbot poured more diet cola into his glass. He looked at
everything in the conference room except Conrad Morse. Then he took
several noisy gulps of his drink, picked up the empty soda can and
squinted at it.

"Your question to me is, what could Cooper possibly know that
has him salivating over this absurd story?" asked Talbot.

"I thought you might have some unique insights into this puzzling
situation."

Talbot did his best to conceal his mounting apprehension under a
cloak of false bewilderment. "Why me?"

"Well," said Morse, "if anyone would know whether the Rutz
story had any basis in fact, it would be you or someone in your agency.
Did the CIA uncover anything like this when it looked at Russia and
Cuba following the JFK assassination? To get right to the point, will
anyone in your organization drop dead of shame if Lionel Cooper
retrieves the jewelry box and writes a scandalous book based on what
he finds inside it? Cooper may be an annoying crackpot and the
President may consider him a dreaded enemy of truth, justice and the
American way, but he's still a United States citizen. He can write

books about any damn thing he wants, courtesy of our esteemed Constitution. But if the book is subsequently shown to be bogus, the humiliation would silence the old fart forever and provide a lot of people in the government with a great deal of belated satisfaction. Personally, I think the reason Cooper is chasing this story like a rabid bloodhound is that he's so desperate to write another bestseller before he dies he's temporarily lost his mind. He's about to make the first mistake of his career."

"Sounds right," said Talbot.

"Yes, but let me hasten to confess that I have a problem with my own keen analysis," said Morse. "I want to believe that Cooper has gone over the edge. But the great Lionel Cooper fascinated by a story as cheesy as this one? A transparent knockoff of that old Cold War spy flick? I can convince myself that ordinary mortals might fall for this crap. But not Cooper. Something else must be going on here, I tell myself, something I'm not seeing yet. If we assume for a moment, Charles, that Cooper is fully aware that the Rutz tale is a fantasy but he's chasing it anyway, then the evidence in that jewelry box isn't what matters most to him. He's after something else entirely. Do you know what that 'something else' might be?"

Morse, delighted with the way he had set his trap, settled back to wait for his distressed colleague's response.

Charles Talbot got to his feet and began to stroll around the conference room. "Give me a minute," he said. Damn it, he thought, could someone in my agency have leaked information about the President's secret project? How else could Conrad be so sure there's something going on that a man like Cooper would kill to find out about? No, that can't be right. Morse knows nothing. Not yet, anyway.

"I should probably tell you," said Morse, "when this matter came to my attention today, my first thought was: 'the answer to the JFK assassination is not going to be found in the bottom of a five dollar jewelry box that has been bouncing around the world for thirty years.' That sounds like something Ian Fleming would put into one of his trashy James Bond novels. Then I started thinking about the espionage techniques of the Cold War era. Invisible ink and encrypted notes, spies using mechanical gadgets of every imaginable kind to get the job done. Isn't it true that in the sixties, the CIA was desperately trying to kill Fidel Castro with poisoned pens or exploding clams?"

Talbot, relieved to be diverted for a few minutes from the necessity to make a tough decision, slid back into his chair and nodded vigorously.

"I'm almost embarrassed to say the CIA was involved in those days with some very crude attempts to eliminate Castro. We failed to get him, but that doesn't mean we didn't try. You're also right that the notion that spies might pass crucial information along in a wooden box equipped with a false bottom is perfectly consistent with the way things were done back then. By today's standards, computers were barely functional. Even routine intelligence information had to be moved around the old-fashioned way. Hand-delivered by fallible human beings employing weird props and elaborate stagecraft."

"And that means," said Morse, "the false-bottom-in-the-jewelry-box story is plausible."

Talbot reached for his drink. His trembling fingers slipped on the wet glass and he almost tipped it over. "Mind telling me where the box is alleged to be at the moment, Conrad?"

Morse consulted the contents of one of the blue file folders. "Jim Redline's fax says it's in Belgrade, Montana. Sitting in the middle of a desk in the office of an elderly woman named Kitty Carson. She owns an antique shop called Kitty's Katchall. Redline intends to buy the box from Ms. Carson and deliver it to Cooper."

Talbot glanced at his watch, grabbed his briefcase and jumped to his feet. "I'm sorry but I'm going to have to cut this meeting short. I just remembered something important. To answer your earlier question, I can't imagine why Lionel Cooper is interested in the Helen Rutz story. Nor can I guess what he might be trying to accomplish. As you say, he's probably just desperate for attention and is willing to take a chance with his reputation to get it. In other words, I fully support your analysis. Let the man write his ridiculous book."

Still seated, Conrad Morse reached up and shook hands with Charles Talbot. He tapped the stack of file folders with his finger. "I guess we can take a look at these other items next time we get together. Unlike what we wasted our time talking about today, most of these cases are actually important."

"Until then," said Talbot. He walked rapidly away.

Morse turned in his chair and looked up into the eyes of the late J. Edgar Hoover. "Well, Jay," he said, "I'll bet my distinguished career against your well-deserved reputation for extreme paranoia that the Director of the CIA is already on his cell phone ordering his people to get somebody up to Belgrade, Montana. He'll easily succeed in putting an agent inside Kitty Carson's store hours before Jim Redline gets there. But that isn't going to help him at all, sir. Because I'm there *now!*"

Morse grabbed the phone on the conference table, punched three numbers and said, "Tell them to snatch the box immediately. I want it here tomorrow."

CHAPTER EIGHTEEN

Murray Klein was stark naked. Blushing furiously, he lurched across the room and toppled face first onto the bed.

"But why do I have to be nude just to get a massage, Helen?" he asked. "Why can't I at least wear my boxer shorts?"

"Relax, Murray," said Helen Rutz patiently. "I know what I'm doing." She was standing next to the bed reading the label on a bottle of edible massage oil. She noted that the main ingredient came from the petals of a rare Australian flower. "Don't worry about a thing. You're not allergic to flowers, are you?"

"No, but—"

The phone rang. Helen walked into the kitchen to take the call. It was Jim Redline.

"Well, I'll be damned," said Helen. "If it isn't Mr. Inconsiderate himself. I've chewed my fingernails to the quick back here waiting to hear from you."

"Sorry about that," said Redline.

"Are you on your way back to Florida?"

"Not yet. I'll be in Montana tomorrow collecting your jewelry box. This turned out to be easier than I expected, Helen. In fact, everything about this investigation has been a breeze so far. One of us must be living right."

Helen stamped her foot and whooped. "Hot damn! Tell me everything! How did the box wind up in Montana?"

"It's an interesting story and I promise to tell it to you one of these fine days," said Redline. "But not now. I called to ask you to do something for me. Move the General's notes out of your trailer. Stash them where no one would think to look for them. Do it today."

"Why?" asked Helen. She lit a cigarette and leaned against the kitchen counter. "Who'd be looking for the notes? How many people even know I have them?"

"This is just a precaution," said Redline. "Can you think of someone you trust who'd be willing to store the papers for you?"

"Sure," said Helen. "But this is weird, Jim. Am I in danger because the notes are in my trailer?"

"No," said Redline. "It's just how I do things."

"I'd appreciate having a more complete explanation than that someday," said Helen. She hung up, stubbed her cigarette out in an ashtray and returned to her bedroom.

Murray Klein was flat on his back, his erection pointing straight up.

"Now *there's* a muscle that's just begging for a massage," purred Helen. "What happened, Murray? Were you thinking naughty thoughts while I was gone?"

"I'm so embarrassed," lied Murray.

"You shouldn't be," said Helen. She sat down on the edge of the bed and sprinkled a few drops of massage oil on the palm of her hand. "Tell you what, Murray. I'll give you a special massage in exchange for a teeny-weeny favor. Would you let me store something in your trailer for a while? One little cardboard box? It would mean a lot to me."

"Hell yes!" gasped Murray. "Oh, Helen, you're so sure of yourself! Slower! No, faster! That's it! Perfect! Don't stop!"

Helen stroked Murray's penis while she stared into space and thought about all the things she was going to buy when she was filthy rich. A big house, of course, and an outrageously expensive automobile. Maybe two automobiles. Gobs of new clothes with matching jewelry. A country-club membership and a sea voyage to the tropics.

"Oh boy!" shrieked Murray. He pounded his fists on the mattress. "I love you, Helen! I love you!"

"Really?" asked Helen. She decided Murray deserved something special in return for his willingness to store her secret papers. She crawled up on the bed. "Well, yes, of course you love me, Murray," she whispered. "But let's see how much *more* you love me when I do *this*!"

*

It was midnight and Tom Sawyer was sitting on his toilet flipping through a well-thumbed copy of *Hustler Magazine*. When he heard his front door being ripped from its hinges, he sprang to his feet and pulled up his pants. "It's about time," he muttered.

Dude Daniels was sprawled on the ratty sofa in Sawyer's living room when the front door exploded into a thousand pieces and a huge man emerged from the rubble. Daniels was on his feet before the man had even wiped the sawdust out of his eyes.

"Tom!" bellowed Tiny. "Get your flabby ass out here!"

Sawyer peeked around the corner just as Tiny and Dude crashed into each other.

He tore his eyes away from the carnage, hurried into his bedroom and fumbled under the mattress for his bankroll. Pulling on his shoes, he glanced around to see what else he needed. Dude had disposed of his gun, of course, but he could get another one. While he scanned his meager possessions, a part of his mind was trying to calculate the odds that Tiny could subdue the powerful black man.

Too close to call, thought Sawyer. But not really my main problem at the moment.

Sawyer had to cut across the living room to make his way to the demolished front entrance and out into the safety of the night. He flattened himself against the wall and began to inch toward the jagged hole that was once a wooden door. Then he stopped and risked a glance at the snarling combatants.

Dude's nose was spread across his face like a red flower, blood pouring in two thick streams down his upper lip and into his gaping mouth. One of his ears had been ripped loose and dangled from a strand of gristle. A sliver of wood jutted from the corner of his left eye.

But the man was bouncing lightly on the balls of his feet, holding his fists in front of his chest like twin cannonballs, ready for more.

Sawyer couldn't tell if Tiny had been damaged yet. The big islander was in the act of swinging a metal lamp at Dude's head. Dude blocked it and simultaneously kicked Tiny in the crotch. Tiny gasped, bent forward and caught a fast-moving knee squarely under his chin. The force of the blow hurled him nearly all the way back to the front door. He skidded across the floor on his back, his round head bouncing on the carpet like a rubber pumpkin. He came to a stop within two feet of Sawyer and, upside down, made eye contact.

"Tom," said Tiny. He grinned and a tooth dropped out of the corner of his mouth. The flesh on his chin was shredded. Blood pooled on the floor beneath his head. "Give me a hand here, buddy."

Sawyer looked across the room at Dude. He had plucked the sliver of wood from the corner of his eye and was staring at it in amazement.

Tiny scrambled to his feet and ran at Dude. They collided in the middle of the room, fell to the floor and began punching, biting and gouging.

Sawyer hurried into the kitchen, stood on a wooden chair and pushed a greasy ceiling tile aside. He reached up and wrapped his fingers around a baseball bat duct-taped to a rafter. With the bat resting on his shoulder, he marched back into the living room and stood over the heaving mound of black and white muscle.

Tiny's hands were tightly wrapped around Dude's neck. Eyes bulging, Dude had Tiny by the balls. He was twisting them for all he was worth.

"Tiny," shouted Sawyer, "move back so I can clobber the big bastard!"

Tiny placed his hands in the center of Dude's chest and pushed himself as far away as possible. Just as Sawyer swung the bat, Dude grabbed Tiny by the front of his shirt and jerked him forward. The heavy bat caught Tiny squarely in the center of the top of his head. Blood burst from Tiny's ears and he went limp.

"Shit!" said Sawyer. Before he could swing the bat again, Daniels grabbed it, twisted it out of his hands and tossed it aside. Sawyer turned and tried to run but Daniels kicked his feet out from under him.

Sawyer's face slammed into the floor. He groaned, rolled over and tried to get to his knees. Daniels was on his feet now. He kicked Sawyer hard in the side of the head, knocking him out cold.

Daniels quickly checked both men for vital signs. Tiny still had a faint heartbeat. Daniels dragged the Samoan across the carpet and propped him against the sofa. Blood and brain matter oozed from a crack on the top of his skull. Tiny took one last ragged breath, let it out in a short liquid whoosh, and died.

Sawyer was barely alive, his neck bent at an impossible angle. He was gagging, his throat clogged with blood and bone splinters.

"Damn," muttered Daniels, "looks like I can't claim a paycheck for this fucked-up job. Well, it's like my momma told me long ago. Some days are better than others." He knelt on the carpet and smothered Sawyer with a sofa cushion. Then he noticed a bulge in Sawyer's pants pocket. He pried the roll of hundred dollar bills loose and counted them. "On the other hand," he said to himself, "the night isn't exactly a total loss, either." He clambered to his feet, stared at both dead men for a moment, and then eased through the shattered doorway and disappeared.

CHAPTER NINETEEN

Although eighty-two years old, Kitty Carson never slept past five o'clock in the morning. Even if she'd been taking inventory at her store until the wee hours or simply baking fruit pies until her fingers grew clumsy with fatigue, at five o'clock sharp her dark blue eyes snapped open and she was ready for a new day.

Kitty had not altered her morning routine in decades. Wearing a flannel nightgown and doeskin moccasins, she would shuffle out to the kitchen to get the coffee started. Then she'd open the back door, listen to the soothing rustle of the Gallatin River slipping along the edge of her property, sniff the crisp dry mountain air and let the cat out. A tall glass of orange juice, two pieces of sourdough toast and two mugs of strong black coffee constituted breakfast. Kitty ate while she listened to the news, weather and livestock report coming from the little red plastic radio above the stove.

By six o'clock, Kitty had let the cat back in, finished her bath, cleaned her teeth and brushed her hair. She usually dressed in a long-sleeved western shirt, jeans, cowboy boots and a colorful bandanna. Once in a blue moon, she'd substitute a denim skirt for the jeans and drape a heavy turquoise necklace around her neck in place of the bandanna. If it was snowing or raining, she'd rub mink oil on her boots and tug a wide-brimmed felt cowboy hat over her hair. When the temperature dipped below twenty degrees, she'd add a fringed deer-hide jacket and matching gloves to her ensemble.

Play the part, she often reminded herself as she checked herself out in the tall mirror in her bedroom. And the part I'm playing is the struggling Montana widow trying to make an honest buck selling Old

West antiques to bug-eyed tourists who couldn't tell an authentic pioneer wagon wheel from yesterday's cow pie.

Kitty drove a dark green Ford pickup truck. A loaded 30/30 Winchester carbine and a scoped varmint rifle stretched across a steel gun rack mounted in the back of the cab. Often in the pre-dawn hours on the long gravel road that meandered from her log house ten miles into the sleepy village of Belgrade, Kitty encountered mule deer or other edible wild critters. It was an odd month when she wasn't able to bag enough game to keep her freezer full of roasts, cutlets, drumsticks or ribs. The animals were usually taken lawfully, in season, and with appropriate licenses and tags.

Usually, but not always. Kitty Carson was a hard-nosed businesswoman with a clear sense of right and wrong. She never cheated on her taxes or lied to a customer. But she had lived in Montana long enough to fully accept the widely held belief that an occasional act of civil disobedience was not only permissible, but necessary. She and her friends were of the opinion that the law was a good thing and it mostly worked. But laws were written by ordinary people who could not be expected to anticipate every circumstance that might arise in the real world. Now and then, citizens had to exercise their own judgment, maybe even *improvise* a bit.

It was Tuesday and Kitty parked her truck behind her store on Belgrade's one block long Main Street. She unlocked the store's rear door and pushed it open just far enough so she could reach in and flip the light switch. Once inside, she quickly closed and locked the sturdy door. Although Belgrade had almost no crime at all, Kitty had a persistent fear that she would someday be mugged and robbed by a clever bandit who had studied her habits and figured out that she *always* came to the back door alone two hours before the store officially opened for business.

Kitty's Katchall started out as a gift shop specializing in Montana crafts and assorted "Rocky Mountain" candies, with a few antiques tossed in to give the place a bit of country charm. But over time, it had become apparent to Kitty and her late husband Steve that tourists were much more interested in Old West antiques than little chocolates shaped like trout or wall hangings made from dried tumbleweeds lashed together with a rawhide thong. They decided to double the antique merchandise in their inventory. Sure enough, within a year gifts had shrunk to less than twenty percent of the store's rapidly rising monthly sales.

The size of two single-story four-bedroom ranch houses, Kitty's store was the largest building in Belgrade. The exterior was paneled with weathered barn board to give it a rustic look. Rough-hewn wooden benches bracketed the front door. Under the front windows, large cedar flower boxes overflowed with bright mountain wildflowers in the spring and summer. When the flowers died in the fall, Kitty filled the boxes with fresh evergreen boughs, pine cones and multi-colored leaves.

Fastened to the wall next to the front door was a man-sized scarecrow stuffed with straw and draped in old cowboy duds. The six-foot straw man wore high-heeled boots, faded jeans, an old cowboy shirt, a fake snakeskin vest and a dusty ten-gallon hat with a bullet hole in the crown. Visitors loved to stand next to the big cowboy grinning like idiots while someone snapped their picture and said, "Honey, that old scarecrow looks more alive than you do! Now smile like you mean it!"

Kitty's Katchall had a cozy, warm ambience. People with no interest at all in buying antiques sometimes hung around for hours peering at the thousands of items on display in the twelve connected rooms that made up the retail area. Security was an issue that Kitty had never resolved to her complete satisfaction. There was no way she could keep an eye on everyone who came into the place. Mainly, she relied on the honesty of the average person to keep pilferage at an acceptable level. About once a month she caught someone stealing. When that happened, Kitty invariably went the last mile to see to it that the thief suffered as much as the law would allow.

The first thing Kitty did each morning when she was safely inside her store was to stroll through all the rooms checking on her goods. She walked slowly down the narrow aisles, her eyes flitting from object to object, her face beaming. It was the happiest time of her day. She loved to look at her possessions, to touch them, to revel in the sheer bounty that surrounded her. Keith, her only employee, was of the opinion that the store was embarrassingly overstocked, but Kitty did not agree. She loved the feeling she got from being surrounded by thousands of interesting objects and the certainty that no one could ever take from her every single thing on this earth that she valued. That feeling had become the controlling force in her life after her husband had been swept away from her forever by an avalanche so many years ago.

Kitty ambled slowly through her empire. The store smelled like linseed oil, old leather and wool. Her eyes caressed the wicker fishing creels, stone butter churns, Indian blankets and steel milk cans. She adored the dolls, stuffed fish, lamps, duck decoys, tea sets, flags, wreaths, birdhouses, chaps, clocks, spurs, hobby horses, baby buggies, sleds, saddles, lariats, books and tatty animal hides. She loved the faded sign tacked above a bleached buffalo skull that said, "Key Work Clothes," and the yellowed movie poster next to it advertising *Badmen of Arizona*, starring Buster Crabbe and Marsha Hunt.

Kitty completed her tour and headed for the front door. On the inside wall just above the door were two of her favorite tin signs. One said, "Enjoy Red Rock Cola," and the other said, "Cheese-Lard." She opened the front door and stepped outside to check out Belgrade's tiny business area. There were two pickups and one motorcycle parked in front of the café directly across the street.

First light, she thought, and per usual, Joe and I are the only ones in town at work. She tried to see through the front window of Joe's Bar and Café. Joe unlocked his door an hour before dawn or as soon as the coffee was ready, whichever came first. Kitty did not approve of the sign he kept in the window ("Likker In The Front, Poker In The Rear"), but she had to admit that more grinning tourists posed for pictures beside that sign than next to her handsome stuffed cowboy. For good luck, she ran her small hand behind the scarecrow's waist, as she did every morning, to feel the raised letters on the back of his wide leather belt, "S T E V E."

"You always wanted to be six feet tall, sweetie," she whispered to the stuffed cowboy. "And you finally made it."

Back inside, with the front door securely bolted, Kitty headed for her office. In the center of the main room, ten feet from the door and surrounded on four sides by a waist-high oak banker's wall, sat Kitty's scarred old desk. The big walnut desk was cluttered with invoices and correspondence and letter trays and candy dishes and calendars and pens and magazines and chewing gum and paper clips and hand lotion and lip balm and toothpicks and an Oxford English Dictionary and a stack of road maps. An antique executive chair leaned back from the desk toward two modern steel fire files crammed with business records. The file cabinets were separated by a large black floor safe. On a countertop that ran completely around the banker's wall were racks of candy bars, postcards, breath mints, designer soap, key chains, ashtrays, pocket mirrors and assorted odd gift items. Pushed up against the inside of the short wooden divider was a metal folding table that supported an electronic cash register and a merchant's credit card machine.

When Kitty was seated at her desk, she could easily look over the top of the banker's wall and observe the customers who came through the front door. If they looked decent, she greeted them with a cheery hello and then stayed at her desk and did paperwork while they moseyed around the store. She never tried to sell anyone anything because she believed that people shopping for antiques spent money when they were seized by irrational inspiration, not because a sharp-tongued sales clerk slicked them into it. If she saw someone step through the door looking a mite slinky-eyed, she got up and pretended to dust things as she followed them around. Nine times out of ten, they got the hint and left within a few minutes.

When there were so many customers in the place that Kitty could not keep track of all of them, she pushed a button under her desk and summoned Keith. He was usually working in his small shop in the back, repairing a damaged item or touching up old furniture, or he was in the basement where they kept duplicate inventory, business supplies, seasonal signage, shipping cartons, packing tape and rolls of bubble pack. Keith would lope through all the rooms, smiling and nodding, making his presence known. He was a tall, wide-shouldered, muscular young cowboy—an amateur bull rider—with large hands and a direct gaze. One glance at Keith and folks generally figured out that he was the bouncer at Kitty's Katchall.

Kitty sat at her desk sucking on a piece of peppermint candy left over from Christmas, rocking back and forth in her old chair, thinking about her troubled nephew, Gene Zane. She looked at her watch. Still an hour to go before she officially opened up for business. It was Tuesday and Gene had said he figured to show up Friday afternoon. She'd need a few extra pies around the house and maybe some store-bought chicken.

Although she hadn't seen him in forever, Kitty knew a lot about Gene and his present difficulties because Gene's mother filled her in each time they talked on the phone. Both sisters felt that family business was important to keep tabs on, even if family members lived hundreds of miles apart and hardly ever saw each other. When Gene's wife had died of cancer, his world turned to mud. Both women knew he was at a crossroads—he might get over Patti's death and get on with the rest of his life or he might just come apart at the seams. The jury was still out. Gene's mother was of the opinion that his strong sense of responsibility for Sissy and his grandson would eventually cause him to snap out of his deep blue funk. Kitty wasn't so sure. Two of Gene's cousins had reported to her that he had been drinking hard and had run up serious debts.

Stress, thought Kitty. No man can handle too much unrelenting stress or grief. Some of the strongest men who ever lived buckled at the knees when the yoke life forced them to carry was just too damned heavy. She thought it might be healing for Gene to go fishing with Keith, take his mind off his troubles for a few days, maybe get a sense of the value of kinfolk in hard times. Kitty was looking forward to talking with Gene and, if he really needed help, well, she had money. More than she would ever need at this stage of her life. Maybe they could work something out if he wasn't too proud or stubborn. He'd have to promise to lay off the booze first, of course. She wondered how Gene had come up with enough cash to take an unplanned vacation to Montana. He was driving up in his truck, probably charging his expenses on a credit card. I should offer to at least pay for his gas, she thought.

She looked at the jewelry box on her desk, the one Gene had sent to her from Germany shortly after she and Steve opened the store. He had asked her about it on the phone the other day and, though he had tried to sound casual, she had sensed that it was extremely important to him to discover that she still had it. He'd even said he wanted to buy it from her, for crying out loud. Fine by me, I'll take the box home tonight, she thought, and clean it up a little. Despite the fact that he wanted it back, it was important to her for Gene to understand how much the jewelry box had meant to her all this time. It had been within six inches of her hand for over thirty years and had become as reassuring as an old friend.

I'll need something else now, she thought sadly, to store my extra keys and loose change in. I could use an old candy jar or tobacco tin, I reckon. Then she caught her breath, her fingers twisting in the bandanna around her throat. Her eyes suddenly brimmed with tears and she thought, oh, I almost forgot! Steve, can you forgive me, sweetie?

Kitty jumped up and hustled toward the back of the store, pausing in front of the stairwell that led to the basement. She hit the light switch at the top of the worn wooden stairs and then cautiously made her way down into the huge musty old room, barely able to see through her tears.

It had been so very long ago. Shortly after Gene's gift arrived, customers began asking if the jewelry box on the desk, the one with the miniature painting of a castle on the lid, was for sale. Kitty had always said no, explaining that it was a personal possession, sent to her by a close relative. But Steve had remarked that if folks were *that* interested in European jewelry boxes, maybe it would be smart to have a few around. Hell, he had said to her, people are always trying to buy yours and it isn't even out on display. It's a hint, Kitty, he had said, charming her with his lopsided grin. Our customers are trying to tell us what they want to buy and we aren't listening to them.

But Steve, Kitty had protested, brand new European jewelry boxes? They don't fit with the theme of our store. There's nothing western about them and they're not antiques, either.

No, he had chuckled, wrapping his strong arm around her and nuzzling her cheek. But they're gifts, aren't they? And we sell a few gifts now and then, don't we?

A week after that brief conversation, Steve had stumbled across a line of European jewelry boxes while he was browsing through a gift mart in Denver, boxes that looked a lot like the one Gene had sent from Germany. Wooden jewelry boxes with fancy castles painted on their glossy tops. They weren't *identical* to Kitty's jewelry box, but close enough. Steve had returned from Denver with a cardboard carton that contained three of them.

If these three boxes sell, he had said to his doubtful wife, we'll buy more. He tossed the carton on the desk and reached for the ringing phone. Early the next morning, Steve and his skiing instructor were buried by an avalanche on Bridger Mountain. Weeks later, still dazed with grief and barely able to function, Kitty moved the unopened carton from her desk to the basement, dropped it on a cluttered shelf and promptly forgot it ever existed.

It took her fifteen minutes to find them. They were hidden behind a Pony Express pouch. Kitty slit the tape on the carton with her pocketknife, pulled out one of the small boxes and examined it. The box was in good condition—no rust on the hinges, no visible deterioration of the wood, the lacquer still smooth and shiny. She raised the lid and ran her fingertip over the soft cloth interior.

Then Kitty pressed the jewelry box to her chest and felt, for the first time in years, the deep sorrow that had been her constant companion after her sweet husband had been killed. She had finally learned to control it, of course, and had even found a way to be happy most of the time. But holding the little wooden box, hearing Steve's words, picturing his wonderful grin . . . it was just too much.

Dabbing at the corners of her eyes with her bandanna, Kitty took the carton upstairs and placed it in the middle of her desk. She removed several keys and a few coins from her old jewelry box. She dropped them into one of the new boxes and carefully set it on the exact spot previously occupied by the old one. Then she closed the flaps of the cardboard carton and set it on top of her safe. I'll hang price tags on the other two boxes later, she thought to herself, after I figure out which room they should be in.

She picked up her old jewelry box, walked it out to her truck and locked it in the cab. By the time she made it back to her desk, it was almost nine o'clock, time to open the store.

Kitty took a quick peek in a small mirror she kept handy to see if her makeup had been ruined by her tears. Then she unlocked the front door and stepped outside to make sure Belgrade was ready for business. Two tourists, a short bald man and a stout woman wearing new white tennis shoes, were standing on the sidewalk looking up and down the street, trying to decide where to start shopping. Behind her, Kitty heard the back door slam and knew that Keith had come to work.

As she turned to go back into the store, Kitty stopped and looked fondly at her favorite scarecrow.

"Steve, honey," she said seriously, "we're finally going to find out if those silly jewelry boxes you bought in Colorado will sell or not. Remember our deal? If they're still sitting on the shelf in two weeks, you're taking me out to dinner. A girl never forgets a promise like that, cowboy!"

*

As was her custom, Kitty walked across the street at noon to grab a bite to eat at Joe's. There were no customers in the store, but Keith moved up to her desk to keep an eye on the front door. He started another chapter in a paperback novel he'd been trying to finish for months. Kitty would be back in thirty minutes and then it would be his turn to amble over to the café. The doorbell at the rear of the store buzzed twice. Keith tossed his book on the desk and trotted back, expecting a freight shipment of some kind. He unlocked the back door, opened it and looked outside. There was no one in sight.

"Kids," he mumbled. "Got nothin' better to do on a summer day, I reckon." He hurried back to the desk, dropped into the chair and reached for his book. He didn't notice that the wooden jewelry box Kitty stored her extra keys in had vanished.

When Kitty returned from lunch, Keith reported that only one customer had been in, a young woman with a baby, and she had stayed no more than five minutes.

175

"She buy anything?" asked Kitty, sliding into her seat behind the desk.

Keith ran a comb through his hair, tucked in his shirt, checked the folding money in his wallet and headed toward the front door.

"Yeah," he said over his shoulder, "a candy bar."

Five minutes later Kitty noticed the small pile of keys and coins in the center of her desk where the new jewelry box should have been. Don't tell me, she thought. Today? A thief takes my jewelry box today?

Shaking her head, Kitty scraped the keys and coins into the center drawer of her desk. Then she removed one of the remaining two jewelry boxes from the carton resting on top of the safe and set it precisely where the missing box had been only moments before. She twirled the dials on the old safe, swung the heavy door open, removed the last jewelry box from its carton and placed it inside the safe. Then she closed the safe door and locked it. She wedged the empty carton into a large wastebasket in the corner of her office and walked outside to stand next to the tall scarecrow. Squinting in the bright afternoon sun, she looked up and down Main Street, hoping to spot the thief.

"Keep your eyes peeled, sweetie," she whispered, running her fingers along the back of Steve's wide leather belt. "Something's up in Belgrade, Montana and it sure as hell isn't jewelry box sales!"

CHAPTER TWENTY

Frank Tarelli leaned across the conference table and winked at Chief Dan Running Dog.

"I wouldn't worry about that if I were you, Danny," he said. "That's just *one* of the many things we're going to take care of for you people. Like I said earlier, we can deliver the whole casino package, soup to nuts."

"Yes, that's what you keep telling me," muttered the Chief. His deep brown eyes were looking at Tarelli but not seeing anything of interest. He twisted the heavy silver ring on his finger. "And what's your cut? How much are you going to take to do this so-called package deal, anyway?"

Tarelli waved his hand in a big looping circle over his head. "Hey, not to worry, Danny. We'll get into that later. Trust me, *whatever* small consulting fee we decide to charge for our expertise, the money will come back to you people many times. We can even put in your contract that, say, after a certain number of years, when you feel you truly understand how to make a profit at this casino game, you can boot us out and it'll all be yours. The whole shit-a-ree."

Chief Dan Running Dog looked at the stony-faced old men sitting around the table. All thirteen tribal leaders were there but, so far, they had remained silent. They weren't sure how this gambling business worked yet. Maybe it was a good idea for the tribe, maybe not. Indians liked to take plenty of time to make a decision like this one, the kind of time white people never seemed to have. White people were always in a hurry and, if money was at stake, always lying. The Chief could feel that the leaders wanted to slow this dialogue down, take a careful look at this casino proposition.

"Ah," said the Chief. He fanned the pages of a stack of computer printouts Frank Tarelli had handed him when the meeting started. Columns of numbers and a lot of technical mumbo-jumbo but no mention of prostitutes or drugs. Tarelli had casually remarked that he wanted to talk about those lucrative services, too, but he would not put anything about them down on paper.

Tarelli's cell phone vibrated. He smiled apologetically at the Chief, jerked the phone out of his coat pocket, flipped it open and turned his back on the Indians.

"I'm in a meeting. What the hell do you want?" he whispered, cupping the tiny instrument in his hand.

"Sammy just called," said Nick Genoa. "Said to tell you to come out of that meeting right now and call him back."

Tarelli blanched. "Gee, I hope no one was seriously hurt," he said slowly. He looked over his shoulder at Chief Dan Running Dog and made a sad face, shaking his head from side to side. "I'm on my way," he mumbled and snapped the phone shut.

Tarelli ran his fingers through his curly black hair and made a whooshing sound with his lips. He turned to face the table and ran his eyes over each bronze face.

"Gentlemen," he said solemnly, "I apologize for this unexpected interruption. There's been an accident and I have to leave right now. Danny, how about we take a break, you and your people look over those papers, talk to each other, and I'll come back later to answer your questions. Maybe next week. How does that sound?"

"Sorry to hear about the accident," said the Chief. He was tremendously relieved. He seemed to be looking at a spot behind Tarelli's head. "Be sure to call before you drive all the way back, Mr. Tarelli. In case we have gone to the mountains to cool off and can't be here to meet with you."

The Chief knew that no one from the tribal council would wait for Tarelli to return. They would all want to go someplace in the hills to discuss the casino project. There would be no whites there and the old men would talk for two or three weeks, maybe even two or three months. They would talk until they came to an understanding. Meantime, Frank Tarelli could twist in the wind for all they cared. Or go back to Las Vegas. No one on the council would give the aggressive Sicilian a second thought.

"Okay, uh, thanks Danny," said Tarelli. "Later, people." He hustled out to his big shiny car and roared away in a cloud of dust. Damn, he thought, these Indians are a tough sell. They never *say* anything. Can't read their eyes. Impossible to know if they understand what I'm telling them. What the hell are they waiting for, anyway? Crazy Horse to return from the dead and take back Montana?

Tarelli drove fifty miles along the northern edge of the sparkling Big Horn River to a cheap modular house near the eastern border of the Indian reservation. The house served as both a temporary office and a residence for Nick Genoa and himself. The flimsy building sat in dreary isolation in the center of a flat desolate prairie. The front yard was home to a small herd of antelope. There were no trees near the house to offer protection from the sun or the endless battering wind.

Tarelli jogged up the bare wooden steps. As he hurried through the front door, he saw Nick Genoa walking out of the kitchen, a meatball sandwich in his hand.

"What's up with Sammy?" asked Tarelli.

"I don't know. He didn't want you to call him on the cell phone. Said to be sure and use a landline so no one can listen in. I think he wants us to get in the car and go do something important. He said he'd give you the particulars. He's in a serious hurry, Frank."

Genoa took a bite of his sandwich and sat down on their cheap rented sofa. He used one hand to thumb through a fresh copy of the swimsuit edition of *Sports Illustrated*. He was a small man with tiny fingers, but when it came to dealing cards, he was a magician. He was paid a handsome salary to train the dealers in Sammy's casino and a hefty bonus to help the security people spot card sharks.

Nick Genoa was famous for two things in Las Vegas—his ability to manipulate cards and his insatiable lust for showgirls. His partner, Frank Tarelli, senior to Nick by a few months, was also famous for two things—his understanding of shady casino accounting practices and his hair-trigger temper. Tall and built like Rocky Marciano, Tarelli had the dark eyes, skin and hair of his Sicilian ancestors and a natural attraction to violence that, in his younger days, had earned him the moniker "Terrifying Tarelli." But lately, Tarelli had been working on modifying his tough-guy image so he could move up in the organization's management structure. He wanted desperately to be seen as a shrewd numbers guy with a good head for business, not as a goon.

Tarelli sat down at a cheap metal desk, grabbed the phone and punched in Sammy Manzitto's direct number.

"Yeah," said Sammy. Tarelli could tell Sammy had a cigar in his mouth. That meant no one else was in his office. Sammy, always a gentleman, never smoked cigars in his office unless he was alone. Or with a showgirl, which, he insisted, was exactly the same thing as being alone.

"Tarelli. What can we do for you, Sammy?"

"Whatever I want you to do, like always, Frank."

"Sure, Boss. What's up? I was in a meeting with the Chief and his deaf-and-dumb crew when you called. These natives aren't real quick at thinking things over. I get the feeling they're still celebrating their victory over Custer and haven't noticed the rest of the world has moved on."

Sammy grunted. "They can't make this deal work without us and they know it, Frank. Now, pay attention. I didn't call to discuss the problems you're having with the savages."

"I'm all ears, Sammy."

"A good friend of mine, very high up in the federal government, contacted me a few minutes ago. He wants to give us a break on the reservation casino thing, help us make the deal come together extra sweet. And this guy can do that, understand? We're talking expedited gambling licenses here, tax breaks, auditors who can't add and subtract and other good stuff."

"Holy shit. He sounds like a very good friend to have. What's he want us to do for him in return for all those goodies?" Tarelli tried to sound eager, but it wasn't easy. He could feel fat drops of sweat streaking down the back of his neck. Sammy was hot for this deal and that meant whatever he was going to ask Frank and Nick to do was major. Failure would not be an option. Failure could even be fatal.

"My friend needs something important done and he needs it done yesterday. I want you and Genoa to haul ass to a little burg called Belgrade. I mean the instant we get off this phone, you're gone, understand? Throw a toothbrush in the car and stand on the gas pedal with both feet. Belgrade is close to Bozeman, wherever the hell that is. Look it up on a map, Frank. How far is Bozeman from where you are now?"

"I don't know. Montana is a huge place, Sammy. Hey, Nick, how far is Bozeman from here? Ah, he can't answer me, his mouth is too full of meatballs. I'm thinking it might be two hundred miles, something like that. Less than three hours away."

"Genoa's eating?" asked Sammy.

"He's got so much food in his mouth right now his head looks like a bag of rocks," said Tarelli.

"Genoa don't look like he ever eats anything. Tell him I said that. Okay, Frank, here's what I want you to do when you get to Belgrade."

Frank listened carefully for several minutes, said goodbye to his boss and hung up. He turned to Nick Genoa. The smaller man was dabbing with a hanky at a blob of thick red marinara sauce that had fallen on his magazine.

"Sammy says you should eat more," said Tarelli.

Genoa took a moment to wedge an enormous chunk of food against the inside of his cheek with his tongue.

"I can do that," he said. "Hey, you seen this magazine, Frank? It's got them young swimsuit babes in it. Cover to cover. No sports stuff at all. Just great looking dames with little bits of see-through cloth pasted on 'em in strategic places."

"Sounds like a sport to me," said Tarelli as he stood up. "Go get your shaving kit, put on a clean shirt and meet me outside. We're outta here."

*

Tarelli and Genoa encountered a forlorn cluster of mobile homes, gas pumps and rundown bars ten miles east of Bozeman. It was two-thirty in the afternoon. Tarelli was driving his personal car, a white Lincoln Continental with Nevada plates. Genoa sat in the back seat, tapping a deck of playing cards on his knee, puffing on a stinky black cigarillo. He was blowing the bitter smoke through an open rear window. Tarelli could not abide tobacco smoke of any kind. Nick was sitting as far away from him as possible. Tarelli wasn't exactly his supervisor, but he was one mean son of a bitch.

"It's like a ghost town around here," complained Tarelli. "Where the hell is everybody?"

"This ain't a town," said Genoa. "It's just a watering hole. Speaking of which, let's stop. I need to take a leak."

"I got a brainwave happening here," said Tarelli. "Let's get some food and a six-pack. Take it down the road with us."

"You're a genius," said Genoa. He pointed up the road with his smoldering cigarillo. "How about that joint?"

"Get that stinking weed out of my face," snarled Tarelli.

A hundred feet ahead of them was a compact peeled-log building with a faded banner over the front door that read, "Grizzly Bar." There were neon beer signs in every window. A hand-lettered message tacked to a wooden pole by the entrance to the dirt parking lot read, "Buffalo Burgers. Onion Rings. Homemade Pie." Two pickup trucks were parked at odd angles in front of the bar, both plastered with dried mud, road bugs and prairie grass. One truck was loaded with straw bales. In the back of the other were two large ranch dogs.

"This'll work," said Tarelli. "Ever had a buffalo burger?"

"Buffalo are extinct," said Genoa.

"No, they're not. Buffalo meat is delicious. Sweet with very little fat in it," said Tarelli. He parked the Lincoln next to the truck carrying the two dogs. Both men got out and stretched. Genoa dropped his cigarillo on the ground. He hitched up his pants and looked around. The two dogs bounced up and down, whining, ears pricked forward. The biggest one bared his front teeth. Tarelli laughed and gave the dogs the finger.

"Probably smarter than their owner, but not by much," he said.

Frank Tarelli was wearing cream-colored golf slacks, a pale green polo shirt with a small alligator stitched over the pocket in dark green thread, and brown basket-weave loafers. He had a gold bracelet on his left wrist. Nick Genoa was wearing black slacks, a tan open-necked sport shirt and a light-weight black and tan checked sport jacket. He glanced at his platinum watch.

"Soon as we get inside," said Genoa, "I've got to make a beeline to the john. Just mustard on my burger, Frank, and an order of onion rings. No pie." He patted his sport coat to make sure the swimsuit magazine was still folded into the inside pocket.

"Take your time," said Tarelli. "I'll have a beer while they're cooking the food."

Tarelli and Genoa stepped through the front door of the Grizzly Bar and paused to let their eyes adjust to the dim light. The log walls were covered with elk, deer and antelope antlers. A half-dozen four-place tables bracketed a small parquet dance floor. A ceiling fan moved smoky air in a lazy circle over a stuffed black bear cub mounted on a wooden platform. Along the back wall stood a cigarette machine and an old jukebox. There were two customers in the bar, both cowboys.

One cowboy was seated on a stool at the bar, the other was standing in front of the jukebox, fishing in his jeans for change. The cowboy at the bar was thick and wide. He looked like he might weigh two hundred and fifty pounds or more. The other one was tall and wiry. Both men wore tattered straw cowboy hats stained black with sweat.

The female bartender looked to be about thirty years old. She was smoking a cigarette while she talked with the big cowboy. Her blond hair was cut short and she had circles of red rouge on her cheeks. She wore a plain white blouse and tight black jeans. She was leaning against a stainless steel beer cooler, nodding her head, smiling. Behind her, wedged between liquor bottles, a tiny television set flickered, the volume turned down low.

Genoa spotted a hand-lettered sign that read "Restrooms" tacked above a narrow hallway near the bar. Without a word, he hurried off in that direction, jerking his magazine from his coat pocket. Tarelli

183

walked to the end of the bar and rapped his keys several times on the scarred wooden surface. The woman gave him a quick disapproving glance, then turned her back and resumed her conversation with the cowboy.

Tarelli cleared his throat loudly and tapped his keys on the bar again. No one seemed to give a rat's ass that he was here and ready to place his order. Yokels! He felt the back of his neck begin to sizzle.

"Hey, lady," said Tarelli. He whistled and snapped his fingers. "C'mon down here and take my order. I haven't got all day."

The lean cowboy standing by the jukebox slowly turned around and gave Tarelli a long cold look. His unlit cigarette bobbed up and down in the corner of his mouth.

"John" he said softly, "why don't you see what that dude wants. He don't sound happy to me."

The big cowboy chugged his beer, slammed the empty bottle on the bar, slid off his stool and lumbered down to stand in front of Tarelli. The bartender sighed and lit a fresh smoke. She rolled her eyes at the ceiling.

"Here we go," she said under her breath.

Tarelli looked up at the cowboy and frowned. "John" looked like a young Brahma bull. He was in his late twenties, wind-whipped and covered top to bottom with pale range dust. His upper body was as wide as a barn door. He had piggy red-rimmed eyes, half hidden behind heavy pouches of wrinkled sunburned skin. His cowboy boots were smeared with moist animal dung. Even without his hat, he would have stood a good four inches above Tarelli. On his meaty right hand, he wore a ring shaped like a saddle, complete with pommel and stirrups.

"I'll take your order, Mister Dude," said John with exaggerated politeness. The pupils of his eyes had shrunk to tiny black specks, barely large enough to let the beer-fueled fury behind them funnel through. "But hurry the fuck up. You ain't the only customer needs service around here."

Tarelli leaned against the bar. It would be fun to whip this slow-witted saddle bum and he sure was asking for it. But Sammy Manzitto would be furious if he found out Frank had wasted valuable time thumping cowboys instead of staying focused on the job that needed to be done. On the other hand, this wouldn't take all that long . . .

Tarelli dropped his car keys on the bar, hooked his thumbs in his belt, locked eyes on John and said, "Two buffalo burgers. Two onion rings. One piece of apple pie. A six-pack of Bud. Bottles, not cans. That would be a take-out order, Hoss. If you didn't get all of that, I'll repeat it for you. Or, you could pull your finger out of your ass and print the order in that sheep shit drying on your boots. That way you could just read it to the cook."

John smiled and removed his filthy hat. He set it on the bar next to Tarelli's keys.

"Oh," said Tarelli, "and I'd like to drink a beer while I'm waiting." He snapped a fast look at the bartender. She was blowing a smoke ring at the ceiling. "In a clean glass," he said to her in a loud voice.

John puckered up and spit a thick stream of tobacco-rich saliva across the front of Tarelli's immaculate cream-colored slacks.

"Oops," said the cowboy. "Sorry about that, Mister Dude. Don't know how that happened. I was aiming for your eyes."

Tarelli caught John in the throat with a lightning quick right hand and then drove a pulverizing left into his rib cage. The big man sucked air and his head dipped slightly. Tarelli whipped an elbow across the bridge of his nose. John's hands flew up to his face and Tarelli stepped forward and drove a thunderous right into his gut. Then he hit him twice under the chin with short left and right hooks.

Tarelli danced back to admire his work and give John room to fall down. The cowboy had flopped against the bar, supporting himself with his elbows. His nose was broken and his upper lip was slimy with snot and blood.

"Must be expensive pants," John gasped. He wiped his mouth with the back of his sleeve and coughed.

The other cowboy had made it over to where John and Tarelli stood in three long strides.

"You got a nosebleed, John?" he asked. He was talking to the big cowboy but looking straight at Tarelli.

"I get the feeling this fella don't like me, Slim," wheezed John.

"Do tell," said Slim. He pushed his hat back with his thumb and dropped his unlit cigarette on the floor.

Tarelli couldn't tell if John was finished or not. He risked a glance at his skinned knuckles. They were beginning to swell. Genoa would come out of the can any minute now and even the odds. Tarelli tried to think of something clever to say to buy time. He opened his mouth to tell Slim he should go stand next to the lady bartender so he wouldn't get any blood on his pearl-buttoned shirt.

Tarelli's eyes shifted slightly toward Slim. That's when John hit him on the side of the head with a fist that felt like a hundred pounds of falling lead. Frank Tarelli had never been hit that hard in his life. His knees buckled and he stumbled forward. Slim snapped a vicious punch into Tarelli's face, then followed that with a bony knee to his crotch. Tarelli didn't feel any pain, but he heard someone moan and he knew it wasn't either of the cowboys. He saw John's huge fist rushing toward his head again, the one with the saddle ring on it, and he knew for sure he wasn't going to be able to finish the important job his boss had sent him to do. He felt the impact, heard skin rip, and went down hard, his head bouncing on the wooden floor. He rolled over on his back and hacked up a cup of blood.

"Cancel them buffalo burgers, Jenny," muttered John.

Through a veil of blood, Tarelli saw a dirty boot spiraling toward his face. He heard his cheekbone crack and seconds later he gagged on a stream of warm fluid gushing down his throat. Just before he passed out, Tarelli thought how ridiculous it would be if he drowned in his own blood on a barroom floor in Montana. His family and friends would never get over it . . .

Nick Genoa sauntered out of the men's room and heard something hit the floor with the sound of a car door slamming. He knew instantly what had happened. Frank Tarelli could not walk away from a fight, even when he was outnumbered or had far more important things to do. He was "Terrifying Tarelli" and that was all there was to it.

Genoa saw the two cowboys standing over Tarelli, totally absorbed in the task of kicking him to pieces. He slipped behind the bar, flattened the startled blond with a hard elbow to the jaw, spotted Frank's car keys next to a tattered cowboy hat, scooped them up and glided out the front door.

Genoa unlocked the Lincoln, got behind the wheel and cranked the ignition. He adjusted the air conditioning and rearview mirror. He lit a fresh cigarillo, opened the car's glove compartment, grabbed a compact automatic pistol and stepped outside, leaving the car door open. He laughed and blew smoke at the two dogs. The biggest one flashed long, curved fangs and snarled. The smaller one whined and wagged its tail. Nick shot both dogs in the head, eased back behind the wheel of the Lincoln and tossed the pistol on the passenger seat.

The front door of the bar burst open and the lean cowboy ran out into the parking lot. Genoa pulled the car door shut, jerked the gearshift lever, stomped on the gas pedal and made a fast illegal move across the median and out onto the interstate. He knew there wasn't a pickup truck made that could catch a powerful car like the Lincoln on the open highway.

Damn, thought Genoa, I'll have to come back and collect Tarelli after I'm done with this job. He'll be sitting in a wheelchair someplace, sucking tapioca pudding through a straw. When Sammy hears what he done, Frank Tarelli will be parking cars for the rest of his pathetic life. He might be better off if he just gave up the ghost right there on the dance floor.

Genoa took a deep drag on his cigarillo and checked his rearview mirror. Nothing behind him but empty highway. He grinned. It wasn't impossible to believe that two sweaty ranch hands full of beer could demolish a cocky has-been like Tarelli, he thought, but it would be just this side of a miracle if they could also figure a way to catch me out here in the wide open spaces.

Damn, he thought, I'm starving! I'd strangle my own sister to get my hands on just one deep-fried onion ring…

*

Nick Genoa drove down Main Street in Belgrade, scanned the shops and eateries, spotted Kitty's Katchall, saw a shady place to park

187

the big car, figured a way to get his hands on the jewelry box and did it all in the first two minutes he was in town.

The hard part was pulling off the necessary distraction without a partner along to help out. He looked at his watch. Four in the afternoon. Nice sleepy time of the day. Too early for happy hour, too late for lunch.

Genoa parked the Lincoln a hundred yards from Kitty's store under a cottonwood tree on a quiet residential side street. He tossed his sport coat over the pistol on the front passenger seat, locked the car, lit another cigarillo and walked casually down the sidewalk. He stopped and read the bawdy sign in the window at Joe's Bar and Café. Then he stepped across the wide street and walked up to the tall scarecrow next to Kitty's front door.

"Howdy, big fella," he whispered. "Care to join me in a smoke?"

Genoa leaned forward, placed the hot end of his cigarillo against the belly of the stuffed cowboy and puffed. The dry straw under the scarecrow's shirt caught fire immediately. Orange flames shot toward the sky.

Genoa jerked the front door open, poked his head in and looked around. There was an elderly woman sitting a few feet away behind a low wooden room divider.

"Hello," she chirped. "Step on in, stranger, I won't bite you." She grinned and rose to her feet. She wasn't much taller standing than she was sitting down.

"Afternoon," said Genoa. "Some kid put a match to that stuffed man you've got tacked to the wall out here. You got a fire extinguisher handy?"

Kitty Carson's face turned ashen white. She hit a button under her desk and yelled for someone named Keith. Then she grabbed a portable fire extinguisher from behind a file cabinet, slipped past Nick Genoa and darted outside. Seconds later a cowboy came on a dead run from the back of the store, shouldered Genoa out of the way with muttered apologies and barreled through the open doorway.

Genoa slipped into the store and walked rapidly toward what he assumed was the woman's office. He could hear her scream, "Steve!

Oh my God! How do you work this damn thing, Keith?" Smoke puffed through the doorway into the store.

The jewelry box was in plain sight in the center of the desk. Genoa looked at it just long enough to verify that it had a painting of a castle on its lacquered lid. He grabbed it, wheeled and trotted through the maze of cluttered rooms looking for the back way out. He unlocked the heavy door at the rear of the store and stepped outside into a small parking lot. There were two pickup trucks there but no people in sight. Genoa trotted along behind a row of retail shops in the general direction of his car. Ten minutes later he was heading east on the interstate, driving a prudent five miles an hour under the speed limit.

Genoa looked at his watch again and did some quick calculations. He could be enjoying a nice dinner at home in less than four hours. He'd come back and look for Tarelli next week. Give him time to heal up so he could handle the long drive back to the reservation.

But first things first, he thought. He had orders to destroy the jewelry box and call Sammy Manzitto to confirm that the job was done. He could just make out the sparkling blue waters of the Yellowstone River less than a quarter mile off the highway. Genoa took the first exit he came to and drove along a frontage road until he saw an official-looking wooden sign with the profile of a jumping trout carved on it. "Fishing Access," it said. He followed a bumpy dirt road several hundred yards through a grove of bright green aspens to a gravel parking area close to the river. A black Jeep Cherokee was just pulling out. The driver stopped, leaned out his window and waved a cheery hand. Genoa cursed, feathered the brake pedal, pushed a button to lower his window and faked a smile. His right hand drifted under the sport coat and rested lightly on the handle of his pistol.

"They're hittin' bait," said the driver of the Jeep. He was an older man with a snowy white beard and twinkling eyes. Santa Claus. "If you've got nightcrawlers or grubs, you're in business. Took my limit in less than an hour. Salmon eggs might work, too."

"Thanks," said Genoa. He decided not to ask the old man what a grub was. Santa Claus waved cheerily and drove slowly away. Genoa parked his car in front of an oily railroad tie. He returned the pistol to the glove compartment, tossed his coat in the back seat, and picked up the jewelry box. Then he took a small can of gasoline out of the trunk and walked toward a patch of scrub oak trees fifty feet away.

Genoa sat on a flat rock and watched the box burn while he dialed Sammy's number in Las Vegas.

"Yeah," said Manzitto.

"Nick Genoa. I'm sitting by the Yellowstone River warming myself in front of a little fire I got going here, Sammy. Made it out of a hunk of wood I found in Belgrade."

"They say Belgrade's a great place to get firewood this time of year," said Manzitto. "Don't forget to stomp on the ashes. Good work, Nick."

"Thanks," said Genoa. He looked at the fast-moving river and reached for a fresh cigarillo.

"Where's Tarelli?"

"Uh, I'll call you later and tell you what happened to him. You aren't going to like it," said Genoa.

"Terrifying Tarelli," snorted Manzitto. "I can't wait to hear what the dumb shit did this time. Okay, call me tonight." He slammed his phone down.

Genoa waited fifteen minutes to be sure the jewelry box had been completely consumed by the fire. Then he stuffed the empty gasoline can behind a bush, kicked dirt on the smoking ashes and began strolling back toward his car. He checked the time again and moaned. He was too hungry to drive all the way home without grabbing a snack someplace. Maybe Wong's in Billings. They had those juicy crab legs and those huge Idaho potatoes baked in aluminum foil.

Genoa slammed to a halt. There were two dogs draped across the wide front hood of the Lincoln and two cowboys resting against a mud-splattered pickup truck. A lean cowboy with an unlit cigarette in his mouth and another one who looked like a grain silo. The pickup truck was parked snug up against the Lincoln's back bumper.

Genoa felt a flutter in his gut. His first thought was that he might miss dinner at Wong's. His second thought was, don't panic, Nick, you can handle these two idiots. He rubbed his chin and tried to come up with a plan. The pistol was in the glove compartment. The trick was to

190

offer the two men money or something, anything that would let him get inside the car so he could get his hands on the weapon. Then, bam, bam, and he'd be back on the road. Crab legs and baked potatoes.

Genoa continued walking until he was standing beside the car door on the driver's side. He was less than ten feet from the cowboys. He could unlock the door and get inside the car very quickly. If he was good at anything, he was good at things that required speed and manual dexterity. He sized up the two men. They were watching him intently but didn't seem concerned about much. Saddle bums, thought Genoa. *Stupid* saddle bums, at that.

Genoa reached in his pants pocket and pressed the button on his key chain to unlock the car. Just as he heard the locks snap open, he saw that the window on the front passenger-side door had been smashed to bits. The glove compartment was open and Genoa didn't have to look to know that the pistol was gone.

Damn, he thought, maybe these particular saddle bums aren't as stupid as they look. I'll have to bluff 'em . . .

"Destruction of personal property," said Genoa sternly. He pointed a tiny finger at the two cowboys. "That's a felony where I come from."

As if on cue, both men began to saunter toward him. The big one reached inside his mouth with a curved finger and plucked out a wad of chewing tobacco as big as a bird's nest. He tossed it in the air. It landed on Genoa's shoe with a soft plop.

"You know," said the lean one, "I'd have to say the number one mistake dudes make when they come to Montana is they always think they're smarter than the locals. Would you agree with that, John?"

"Yup, I would, Slim," wheezed John. His nose was smashed flat and he had two black eyes. There was a piece of skin hanging from a big ring on his right hand. The front of his shirt was streaked with bloody slime.

"And," said Slim, "that pisses me off."

"Me, too," said John. "Then they shoot our dogs and drive off figurin' we can't find 'em."

"Exactly," said Slim. He dropped his unlit cigarette on the ground. "I reckon they don't realize we can track a ladybug fart across fifty miles of black ice. Blindfolded. In a blizzard."

"Done it a hundred times, Slim," agreed John. He grinned, showing crooked yellow teeth and bloody gums. "Come to think on it, just done it again."

"Back up a ways, mister," said Slim. Genoa took a half-dozen steps backwards. Using two hands, Slim grabbed the smaller of the dead dogs by the back legs and pulled it off the hood of the Lincoln. John put one huge hand around the back legs of the other dog and gave it a tug. It hung by his side like a forty-inch club, dripping dark fluid from a crusty round hole between its blank eyes.

"You boys are going to have to pay for a car wash," said Genoa, his voice shaking. "Look at the mess those dogs made on the hood of my car." He was trying hard not to throw up.

"We'll leave a couple bucks on the front seat," said Slim. "Now close your eyes real tight. You're fixin' to be the first visitor to Montana that ever got his ass beat to a pulp by two dead hounds. It's the least we can do for 'em."

Genoa shuddered, closed his eyes and jammed his hands into his pockets. No matter what happened, he wanted to be sure his fingers didn't get broken.

"Really loved this dog," said John. Genoa cracked one eyelid and saw John twirling the heavy dog over his head like a lariat. The dog's body hit Genoa in the throat, his knees gave out and he fell over hard on his back. He gasped and stared up at the spinning summer sky and thought about his mother.

Off to his left, Genoa could hear the river hurrying by on its long journey east to join the Missouri. He saw the smaller dog, bloody jaws hanging open, lips peeled back from its pink fangs, whistling toward his face. Genoa wanted desperately to put his hands up to protect himself, but they were wedged tightly in his pants pockets.

He had a split second to think about Sammy and how pleased he was that the jewelry box had been destroyed in spite of the complications created by the unreliable Frank Tarelli. By God, thought Genoa, that should count for something . . .

CHAPTER TWENTY-ONE

"Have another drink," said Lionel Cooper. "You look like you could use at least one more."

"The understatement of the year," muttered Dr. Irving Katz.

The two men sat across from each other in an elegantly furnished hotel suite in Manhattan. Dr. Katz stood, walked slowly to a small bar on the far side of the room and built himself another double bourbon on the rocks.

"I appreciate your coming here today," said Cooper. He was drinking decaffeinated coffee. "I know you're on medical leave from your important job with the CIA, but even so, I imagine you're a busy man."

"Please," said Dr. Katz, wandering back to his chair. "Don't patronize me. We both know I had no choice but to respond to your summons."

"That's true. The videotape is almost professional quality, don't you agree, Doctor? With very little editing, it could be ready for direct distribution to the porn trade."

Dr. Katz stared into his drink, his bearded face a map of despair. "If she ever finds out we were taped that night . . . for that matter, if anyone finds out . . . I'm . . . toast."

"My point exactly," Cooper purred. "She doesn't have to find out your illicit tryst was captured on tape. No one does. Not if you tell me what I want to know."

"How the hell did this happen?" whined Dr. Katz. "It was a long time ago. I wasn't the lead psychiatrist at the agency then. I wasn't important at all in those days. What possible reason did you have for spying on me?"

Cooper smiled. "I've made it my life's work to keep a close eye on key government officials in this country, Doctor. My readers expect me to tell them what's really going on behind all those velvet curtains in Washington. It's always easier to dig up dirt on the unwary subordinates than it is to catch the big guys. You'd be stunned if you saw the collection of filth I possess. By the way, so would my naïve staff. I pay them handsomely to conduct legitimate investigative research only. They have no idea that I maintain a secret stash of incriminating material that has only a slight chance of ever being useful. A, uh, friend purchases disgusting information for me—like your tape—from bottom feeders so unsavory I won't allow them to set foot on my property. Occasionally the stars line up in a certain way and a piece of information that's been gathering dust in my private archives suddenly becomes worth its weight in gold."

Dr. Katz took a deep breath and let it out through his nose. "I'd relish the opportunity to analyze you. If I could unravel your messiah complex, I'd achieve professional immortality. You're a self-appointed judge, jury and executioner when it comes to bringing down the rich and powerful. Totally ruthless in your zeal to crush public figures who don't meet your standards of behavior. How did you come to be the conscience of an entire country, Mr. Cooper?"

"Interesting question, Doctor. Perhaps at a more appropriate time we can discuss my personality at length. But right now we have other fish to fry. I'm going to ask you some questions and I suggest you answer them truthfully. Your ability to continue to trick your peers into believing you are an ethical psychiatrist depends entirely on what you say to me in this room today."

Dr. Katz, emboldened by alcohol, squared his small shoulders and thrust his chin in Cooper's direction. "If you think I'm going to compromise the security of the United States because you have illegally obtained a video of me having sex with a powerful statesman's daughter, you have grossly underestimated my patriotism, sir."

"We shall see. Brace yourself, Doctor. Has the president recently directed the CIA to do something for him personally? Something so risky he does not want anyone else to know about it? Let me be specific. Is the agency working on a special project connected to mind control and the JFK assassination?"

The air seemed to rush from Dr. Katz's tiny body. He stared at Cooper in horror. "You son of a bitch," he blurted.

"Here's an even more important question," said Cooper. "What is the goal of that project?"

"You're crazy," screeched Dr. Katz. "Only a madman—"

"Please control yourself and concentrate on answering my questions."

Dr. Katz hurled his drink to the floor and jumped to his feet. Even though he was standing, his frenzied eyes were barely even with those belonging to the seated Lionel Cooper.

"You cretin," shrieked the doctor. "There is absolutely no way . . . how you ever stumbled across . . . if you think for one moment that I would discuss with you . . ."

Cooper reached into the pocket of his silk blazer and withdrew a small packet of photographs. He held one up so Dr. Katz could see it. The doctor stopped in the middle of his tirade, his mouth hanging open.

"Surely you didn't come here thinking that video was all I had on you?" said Cooper. "Remember this particular evening, Dr. Katz? I don't pay much attention to popular culture, but even I know this man's name. What was going on here? Were you experiencing a little gender confusion that night? A regression to a time long ago when little Irving needed a big strong man to hold him close?"

Dr. Katz stared at the photograph until his eyes blurred with tears. Then he buried his face in his hands and fell back into his chair.

Cooper returned the photographs to his pocket. Using two fingers, he plucked the doctor's empty highball glass from the floor and sauntered toward the bar.

"I'll make this one a triple," he said.

*

Lionel Cooper, his head buzzing with ideas about how to use the astounding information he had extracted from a demoralized Dr. Katz earlier that day, loped past Tina Romero's open office door at four-thirty in the afternoon. Although the lights were on, she was not there. Probably in the john, thought Cooper. Snapping his fingers and mumbling to himself, he rode the mirrored elevator to the third floor. As he sat down behind his desk, his eyes were drawn immediately to the document Tina had placed next to the phone.

It was a faxed copy of a confidential report from an Arizona private investigator hired by Jim Redline. Cooper read it from top to bottom. Bonanza!

Jim will have the jewelry box soon, thought Cooper. His pulse quickened as he realized how close he was to knowing everything about what had to be the most absurd idea to come out of Washington D.C. in years.

Unable to sit still, Cooper jumped up and began to dance around his desk. He was still dancing when Tina Romero walked in with an ice bucket and a puzzled frown.

"You haven't had your first scotch yet and you're already partying?" she said.

"Sometimes a fellow just has to shake it," laughed Cooper. "And this is one of those times!"

CHAPTER TWENTY-TWO

Gene Zane sat down on a padded folding chair in the front row of the makeshift outdoor theater. The sighing wind blowing uphill from the tree-shrouded Little Bighorn River threatened to interfere with his ability to hear the lecture. Gene had a pad and pencil at the ready, binoculars dangling from a cord around his neck and a compact 35mm camera in his pants pocket. A noisy crowd of tourists began to file out of the visitor's center behind him and fill in the remaining chairs. They had all come to Montana's Little Bighorn Battlefield to listen to the "official" explanation of the most famous military massacre in the history of the Old West.

A woman sat down next to Gene, smiled and began to fiddle with her sunglasses. He glanced at her out of the corner of his eye. Mid-forties, pretty face, soft auburn hair, nicely dressed in tan slacks and a pink short-sleeved shirt.

A uniformed park ranger was standing patiently in front of the shuffling audience. He had given this speech many times and no longer required notes. He reached up with both hands and removed his wide-brimmed hat. The wind caught his hair, tossing it around in silky waves that matched perfectly the movements of the pale prairie grasses behind him. On a hilltop sixty yards beyond the ranger, just visible over his shoulder, was a cluster of closely grouped white crosses enclosed by a black wrought-iron fence. In the center of the short white crosses loomed a tall slab of black granite.

Gene shifted in his seat and peered at the dark monument through his binoculars. The name chiseled into the stone was General George Armstrong Custer.

197

"This place gives me the creeps," said the woman next to him. She had turned in her seat to look at Gene. "It feels weird. Is it the wind, the way it moans? Or is it just me?" She smiled and even though her eyes were almost completely hidden by her sunglasses, Gene felt a mild jolt. He didn't want the woman to smell beer on his breath, so he nodded without speaking.

"You know what I mean?" she continued. "Those young soldiers died here under such brutal circumstances. It feels almost like their ghosts are standing around watching us. Sad ghosts. And look at those white crosses. Not just the ones up there behind that iron fence but the ones scattered across the hills. So many boys died alone here, running for their lives, isolated from the others. They were probably hacked to pieces while they begged for mercy. It must have been dreadful."

"Must have been," said Gene. He pretended to be looking at an object of considerable interest through his binoculars. He was acutely aware of the presence of the woman. Something about her made the hair on the back of his arms prickle.

"Oh, excuse me. I didn't mean to jabber," said the woman apologetically. She turned and faced the ranger. Then she spun around to look at Gene again, as if she had already forgotten that she might be bothering him. "Are you a writer?" She pointed at the pad of paper on Gene's lap.

Gene blushed. "No. I'm a college professor. I teach Western American literature. Thought I'd take a few notes to use in class next semester." He had angled his face downward, hoping not to offend the woman with his breath. Maybe she couldn't tell he had downed three cans of beer for lunch less than an hour before.

"Oh," said the woman eagerly. "Do you—"

She didn't finish her question because the ranger began to speak in a loud voice. He introduced himself and took a moment to warn everyone that later, when they walked out to look at the crosses or to follow the narrow paths to various important battle sites, they should be on the alert for rattlesnakes. The audience tittered nervously.

"Many people think," said the ranger, "that General Custer and the men under his direct command died here because he was too arrogant to think that he could be defeated in battle by a ragtag bunch of half-naked savages armed with bows and arrows. Those people think that he rode into the valley of the Little Bighorn with a ridiculously small number of soldiers expecting the Indians to surrender immediately to the overwhelming authority of the United States government but discovered, to his eternal dismay, that his courageous adversaries had other ideas. Over the years, with the help of scholars and the descendants of both white and Indian combatants, we have been able to piece together most of what actually happened here on the afternoon of June 25, 1876. As you might imagine, the real story is quite different from the popular version. It will be my pleasure today to acquaint you with the sequence of events that resulted in what historians tell us was the most puzzling battle ever fought between the cavalry and the Indians."

Gene began rapidly scribbling notes. The hot summer wind blew harder and someone in the back of the crowd yelled, "Speak up! We can't hear you!" The ranger raised his voice several decibels and continued with his lecture.

"The reason the cavalry was out here scouring the hills for Indians," the ranger said, "was money. Gold had been discovered and settlers were swarming into Indian lands in search of wealth. The army was sent out to protect them."

The woman next to Gene leaned toward him and whispered, "So predictable! Money is always the reason men kill each other." She glanced at the pad of paper on his lap. "Can I look at your notes when this is over?" she asked, flashing a perfect smile. Gene caught a whiff of her scent. He nodded mutely and continued to take rapid notes in his abbreviated style.

Custer brings 7th Cav (600 men) to banks of Little Bighorn . . . scouts tell him "too many Indians" . . . massive Indian village nearby . . . maybe 8,000 women/children and 2,000 warriors . . . village completely obscured by dust . . . Custer doubts scouting report, splits Cav into three small groups . . . orders Reno to charge . . . Reno immediately encounters warriors led by Crazy Horse, is beaten back . . . Benteen and Reno are pinned down near each other for next two days . . . Custer and two companies of soldiers trapped, just north of

Reno/Benteen . . . huge force of Indian warriors, armed with forty different kinds of stolen firearms, surround Custer . . .

"Custer and his men," said the ranger, "retreated to that hill you see behind me. A few miles away, companies under Major Reno and Captain Benteen were dug in under heavy fire and did not know exactly where Custer was located or what his situation might be. This is where the General made a crucial mistake. He sent a messenger to tell Reno he was in serious trouble and needed immediate reinforcements. The messenger was an Italian soldier named Giovanni Martini. Giovanni had been in the United States about two months, spoke almost no English and, although he managed to find Captain Benteen, failed to make himself understood. Captain Benteen could detect no particular urgency in Giovanni's version of Custer's message and ultimately Reno made the decision that he and Benteen should stay put. That decision would haunt Reno for the rest of his life. While a relatively small group of warriors exchanged fire with the men under the command of Reno and Benteen, more than a thousand Cheyenne, Sioux and Blackfeet attacked Custer and, in less than two hours, killed the General and all the men fighting beside him."

Gene stared out across the hills at the white crosses poking up through the swaying prairie grasses and wrote: *Custer died because communications broke down . . . the wrong man carried the life-and-death message . . . this could never happen now . . . in the information age, everyone knows everything, sometimes more than everything . . . too bad George didn't have a laptop computer and a cell phone!*

"Did you know," whispered the woman next to him, "that after the battle the Indian women came up this hill from camp and jammed awls in Custer's ears to make sure he was dead before they mutilated him?"

"What?"

"It's a fact. My ex-husband wrote a book about it," said the woman. She took off her sunglasses. Gene looked into her sparkling gray eyes and swallowed hard. "My husband spent twenty years researching this stupid battle. If he had spent twenty years paying attention to me instead of trying to figure out what went wrong here, he might still be in my life. I read his book, of course, but until today I had never actually seen this place. My name is Terry Brooks. What's yours?"

"Gene Zane."

Terry Brooks smiled, touched the back of Gene's hand, slipped her sunglasses back on and turned her head to look out across the windy hills. The ranger had finished his talk and the crowd was breaking up. Most people were trudging toward the wrought-iron enclosure to take pictures of Custer's headstone. Others were walking up the trails that led to sites considered important enough to be marked with explanatory signage. Everyone was dutifully scanning the ground for rattlesnakes.

"It's too hot and windy to go out there right now," said Terry. "Besides, George isn't here anyway. Did you know the army took his remains back to West Point for burial in 1877? Let's go someplace and get a beer. I want to look at your notes. It'll be fun to see what a professor thinks is worth writing down. I can tell you what my ex-husband believed happened out here. His theory differs radically from the one the ranger just offered us. We can always come back later and you can take pictures of everything."

"How do you know I want to take pictures of everything?" asked Gene. He decided he liked Terry Brooks very much and that surprised him.

"Either that's a camera in your pocket," said Terry, grinning impishly, "or you're very pleased to meet me."

"Oh," said Gene, blushing. "Well, sure, I could use a beer." He stood up and looked down at Terry Brooks while she searched for something in her purse. She was beautiful. She drank beer. She was divorced. And he was on vacation. Gene felt his tired heart skip a beat.

*

Gene and Terry sat at a small table in a corner of the Bear Claw Bar two miles north of the Little Bighorn Battlefield. The Bear Claw was in a ramshackle plank building on a gravel frontage road close to the interstate highway. Ventilation in the bar was poor and the air was milky with stale tobacco smoke. There were a half-dozen people seated on stools at the bar playing a dice game that involved a leather cup, dollar bills and foul language. Two lean young cowboys were shooting pool and occasionally pumping quarters into the jukebox. A plump yellow cat slept on the end of the bar, oblivious to the thumping music and everything else going on around it.

"That cat has only one ear," said Gene. "Probably not a handicap in a place like this."

"I love Montana, don't you?" chirped Terry. She took a sip of her draft beer from a small frosty mug. "So authentic. Just look at that old bar. It could be a movie set. It's so rustic, so gritty. I wouldn't be surprised to see Lee Marvin having a drink in here."

Gene looked around. Maybe a really *bad* movie set, he thought. He drained his mug and waved at the waitress. "This is my first trip to Montana," he said. "And I'm barely over the border. I think I'll reserve judgment for now. By the way, Lee Marvin is dead. If you spot him drinking in here, be sure and let me know so I can take his picture."

"Your first trip to Montana? You teach the literature of the American West and you've never visited the Big Sky State before? Shame on you, Gene. What brought you up here this summer? And from where?"

"I'm on my way to visit an aunt I haven't seen in a long time. She lives in Belgrade, a little town near Bozeman. Thought I'd bunk in with her and do some trout fishing. I drove up from Arizona."

Terry smiled. "Belgrade. I know it well. They've got a snazzy little airport there."

"No kidding," said Gene innocently. "I'm looking forward to checking the entire area out from top to bottom. My aunt lives in a funky log ranch house out in the boonies someplace. The Gallatin River runs right through her property."

"Sounds like a good time," said Terry. She watched as Gene downed his second mug of beer in three quick swallows. "You're not married, Gene?"

"Widowed," said Gene, burping softly. He wiped his lips with the back of his hand. Then he flagged down the waitress, ordered another beer and a shot of bourbon.

Terry frowned. "Do I make you nervous? You're putting away a lot of alcohol in a big hurry. Not that it's any of my business."

Gene flushed and shook his head. "No, I just . . . um . . . I guess . . . well, I wasn't really counting . . ."

Terry looked at him intently. "Tell me about it, Gene," she said gently. "It's okay. I'm interested. What's it been like for you since your wife died?"

"Uh, well," said Gene, "Terry, I don't think I *can* tell you about that. I've never talked about that with anyone. But maybe . . ." He stared into Terry's calm eyes and felt a sudden, irrational urge to blurt out the whole story. For some stupid reason, he wanted to dump the crippling pain and endless confusion he felt all over this sweet, lovely woman. He looked at her moist red lips and soft throat. Deep inside his chest he felt something shift, then slide, then fall apart.

"Gene," said Terry, placing her hand over his. "I'm just guessing, but I have a feeling it would be a good idea for you to tell *somebody* how your wife's death has affected you. Maybe this isn't the right time or the right place, and I know I'm not the right person. But, trust me, you need to talk to somebody. You know that, don't you?"

Gene shrugged. "I know I can't talk about it cold sober." He chugged the bourbon and chased it with three long swallows of beer. His eyes darted around the room and found the waitress. She was leaning against the bar, watching him. He nodded at her and she turned and said something to the bartender.

Terry folded her arms across her chest. "Really? You'd have to get plastered in order to get it all out?"

Gene hung his head. "Maybe not plastered," he said. "But it seems like the only time I can think clearly anymore is when I've had a few pops. That's not good, is it?"

Terry Brooks examined her fingernails for a moment, a look of deep concern on her pretty face. She angled her wrist so she could glance at her watch. The waitress brought Gene a fresh mug of beer and another shot of bourbon. She smiled sympathetically at Terry before she wandered away.

"Here you are, sitting in this crappy old bar with me," mumbled Gene, "and just being here with you makes me want to talk about it for the first time ever. And that's amazing. There's something about you, Terry. I felt it the first time you spoke to me. You're like a dream person. Like the smell of smoke never sticks to your hair, like you're wrapped in an invisible force field that keeps all the terrible things in life away from you. You're fresh and pure, like a . . . like a . . . well, like a goddess. I do want to talk to you, Terry. I want to talk to you all night long. There's so much I need to say to you."

"All night long?"

"I *need* to talk to you, Terry," said Gene, clutching her wrist. "I'm so glad you came along today."

Terry gently removed her wrist from Gene's grasp. "Look, Gene, let me make myself clear. You need to talk to somebody who can really help you. But not me and certainly not tonight. You need professional help. That's what I'm trying to tell you."

Gene felt a bolt of panic streak across his chest.

"But I thought you said . . ." Gene fumbled for the exact right thing to say. What was it? How could he make her understand?

"Gene, I didn't know you were . . . I mean, I thought we'd get to know each other a bit this evening, maybe have dinner. But tonight is *not* a good night for you to talk about your problems. I see that now. Look at you. You're miserable and you're getting very drunk."

Gene gasped. "No! You're wrong! Tonight *is* the night, Terry. And you're the perfect person for me to talk to, I know you are. Can't you *feel* that we're supposed to be here right now and I'm supposed to talk to you until . . .until . . ." Gene grabbed the shot glass in front of him. "All I need is to relax a little more and then I'll be ready to talk. I can do it. Stay here with me, please. Honest to God, Terry, I'll mellow out in a few minutes, my head will clear up and we can just sit back like two old friends and talk this out. And then you'll know me. You'll *really* know me."

Terry Brooks pushed her chair back, stood up and stepped away from the table. Her eyes were clouded with disappointment and concern. She shook her head. "I'm sorry, but listening to you has changed my mind about tonight," she said. "I think I should be moving on. Talk to a doctor, Gene. I really don't think you know how much trouble you're in."

Gene looked up at Terry in shock and disbelief. "We're not going to talk tonight? You're leaving? Terry, are you leaving me?"

I'm coming apart, thought Gene. I'm falling to pieces in a shit-hole bar in Montana in front of the nicest woman alive and there's not a damn thing I can do to stop it. I can't even get up out of this chair . . . I can't think of a single sensible thing to say to her . . .

"Yes, I'm leaving," said Terry. "You seem like a very nice man, Gene. But you don't need just a friendly ear to pour your troubles into while you drink yourself to death. You need *real* help." She put her hand into her purse and came out with her car keys. "Goodbye, Gene. I hope things work out for you."

Terry turned and walked rapidly out of the noisy bar. The two young cowboys paused in the middle of their pool game to watch her go. The waitress waited until Terry was outside and then glided toward Gene's table. Gene felt tears running down his cheeks and dabbed at them with a cocktail napkin. He held the paper napkin against his nose and blew. The waitress floated up and placed her hand lightly on his shoulder.

"Well, there's good news and bad news, cowboy," she said brightly. "The bad news is your lady friend has gone home alone. The good news is you hung in there and made it to happy hour. Two for one! You ready, big fella?"

"Oh, yeah," said Gene, wagging his head enthusiastically. He peeled a wad of bills out of his wallet and tossed them on the table. "Bring 'em on!"

Through the cracked window next to his table he watched Terry Brooks get behind the wheel of her car. She really is a goddess, he thought. A painful lump formed in his throat as he watched her back away from the Bear Claw and bounce down the road toward the interstate.

And that goddess just drove away . . .

"Wanna talk about it?" asked a raspy male voice. A red-nosed, unshaven old man plopped down in the chair just vacated by Terry Brooks. He grinned through mossy teeth and pointed out the window with a nicotine-stained finger. "There she goes," he said, "like a bat outta Hell. Nice lookin' gal. Let's have a beer and you can tell me all about her, friend. I seen the whole thing from over there at the bar. Pitiful! She really worked you over."

The old man's watery eyes focused on the pile of cash Gene had tossed on the table. He lit a cigarette and signaled the waitress. She waved at him. The bartender looked over and then said something that made the waitress laugh.

"Finest lady I've ever met," muttered Gene. He was still staring out the window. "But I blew it big time. She was sitting right there where you're sitting now just a minute ago."

"Yup," said the old man. He peeled a ten dollar bill off the stack and gave it to the waitress in exchange for two full mugs of beer for himself and two more for Gene. "Keep 'em coming, Alice. Listen pal, you didn't do nothin' wrong. The woman ain't been born yet who could really understand a man, know what I'm sayin'? I've hooked up with a heap of 'em in my time and I know what I'm talkin' about. They just never seem to get it right. It's some kind of natural defect."

Gene took a long pull on his beer and squinted at the old man through a cloud of thick smoke. "I'm going to have a beer or two for the road, but then I have to get on up to Belgrade," he said cautiously.

"Belgrade!" boomed the old man, slapping Gene on the shoulder. "Hell, son, I was *born* in Belgrade! You got kinfolk up that way?"

Gene nodded. "Why, yes. My aunt lives there. Kitty Carson. You must know her. She's been in business there for a long time."

The old man swallowed a large mouthful of beer and rubbed his bristly chin on the back of his hand. "Kitty Carson," he said. "Let me think on it. Sounds mighty familiar. Tell me about her. I might recollect the lady. Been a while since I've been up in those parts."

Gene rambled on about his aunt, but his eyes kept drifting back to the window. The light outside was fading fast and he was hoping to see Terry Brooks coming in off the interstate, speeding down the frontage road, sliding to a dusty stop beside the Bear Claw. She'd come back because *this was the night.* He knew it and she had to know it, too. Something cosmic had happened between them and it had frightened her. She'd get a few miles down the road and then she'd realize that her fears were groundless. She'd hurry back and they would talk and Gene would tell her about his late wife and his brilliant grandson. He'd tell her how lonely he he'd been and how depressing it is to lose a mate to premature death. Terry would understand perfectly. She would lean over the table and kiss him full on the mouth. Her gray eyes would be clear as spring water . . . and filled with love.

The important thing was to stay here and wait for her. It would be terrible if she came back and he was gone. *This was the night . . . and this was definitely the place. Gene drained his beer and tried to make out the exit ramp coming off the interstate. I'm still here, Terry, he thought, right here at our table. I'm not going anywhere without you.*

"What say we have one more round," said the old man. He counted the money on the table, grunted, took a twenty off the stack and waved it at the waitress. "Your aunt sounds mighty interesting," he said. His bloodshot eyes narrowed into canny blue slits. "You say she's a widow? Hell, boy, I might just have to go with you to Belgrade! I ain't married myself and never figured to, but she sounds like she might cause an old fool like me to up and change his mind!"

Gene thought about calling Kitty, telling her he'd be in later tonight. No, better say early tomorrow morning. Or, hell, *sometime* soon. Exactly when would depend on what Terry Brooks wanted to do. She'd have ideas of her own. It might be good to let Kitty know he'd made it as far as the Montana border, though.

And then Gene remembered that Tom Sawyer would be waiting for him in a motel in Belgrade. It wouldn't be smart to let Terry meet Tom. He'd just have to think of a slick way to handle the situation if Terry came with him to Belgrade. And she probably would because once they talked everything through and she understood him and she had kissed him and he had said, wow, you taste like peppermint . . . she'd want to meet his family.

Gene tried to focus on the frazzled old man sitting beside him. Who the hell *was* this old fart, anyway? He looked like he'd been living in a boxcar.

"Do you know anything about the fishing up here?" Gene asked, hoping the bum would say no and go away.

"Fishing?" said the old man. He chuckled and tapped Gene on the back of the hand with a filthy fingernail. "Friend, we're in Montana! There's more fish up here than mosquitoes. More fish than elk, more fish than deer, more fish than ducks, more fish than women, praise the Lord. If you're born in these parts, like I was, you're half fish by the time you're five years old. You can think like a fish. I swear, us natives sometimes swim upstream in the spring and breed with the trout! Why, one time I . . ."

Gene drank another beer and listened with half an ear to the old man's garbled fishing tales while he waited for Terry Brooks. It was pitch black outside now. He looked at his watch. Maybe she was waiting for him up the road someplace. Maybe she wanted to see if he'd come after her. If he really cared enough to get up and walk out of this stinky bar like she had done. She could be sitting up ahead, eating dinner alone, waiting for him. Figuring that if this truly was a night set aside by Destiny just for them, well, he'd show up sooner or later. Damn! So hard to know what to do . . .

Gene suddenly felt lightheaded. A dull ache was spreading across his chest and his left arm throbbed. He put his head down on the table and closed his eyes. He needed to rest for a moment and think. It was hard to say what Terry Brooks expected him to do tonight. It was even harder to guess if she had driven north or south on the interstate. Why did things that mattered so much always seem to be impossible to figure out? Hell, Terry could drive for days before she realized she should have stayed here with him. And now it was so dark and there was so much pain . . . so much dark terrible pain . . .

The old man watched Gene for a while, then glanced around to see if anyone else had noticed that his drinking companion had passed out. It was late and the half-dozen people still in the bar were in the final stages of getting totally wasted. The waitress was shooting pool with a cowboy, her back turned, and the bartender was in the john. The old man quickly palmed the pile of cash in the center of the table, then reached over and tugged Gene's wallet out of the back of his pants. He glanced inside and smiled. Had to be five hundred dollars or more! The old man pressed his yellow fingertips against the side of Gene's neck. Shit, he thought, this bastard is so out of it, he'll be lucky if he ever wakes up! Quickly, he pawed through Gene's other pockets. He found a set of keys, a few wrinkled dollar bills and a small camera. Moving stealthily, he slipped out the front door and shuffled across the parking lot toward a dusty pickup truck with Arizona plates.

The keys fit the truck. The old man unlocked the front door and slid quickly behind the wheel. When the engine started on the first crank, he grinned and pounded his fist on the dashboard.

I told myself when I sat down at that bar, he said aloud, tonight was the night! Oh yeah! I knew it was tonight! He grinned, lit a cigarette, snapped on the radio, dropped the truck into gear and sped away.

CHAPTER TWENTY-THREE

Kitty Carson could not stop crying. As she drove into Belgrade early in the morning, tears streamed down her rouged cheeks and flooded her colorful bandanna. She gripped the steering wheel tightly and strained to see the road ahead.

This is ridiculous, she thought miserably. It was only a batch of straw and some ratty old cowboy clothes. But I loved that stupid thing!

She and Keith had prevented the burning scarecrow from catching the store on fire. But "Steve" had been a total loss. A half-dozen people from Joe's Bar had raced across the street to help. One of them had called her attention to a smoldering cigarillo on the sidewalk less than five feet from the scarecrow's burnt carcass.

After all the afternoon beer drinkers had wandered back to the bar, Kitty had carefully inspected each room in her store. But she knew that she would not find the peculiar little man who had told her that her best friend was on fire. For one thing, a quick glance had confirmed her suspicion that the jewelry box she had just placed on her desk had been stolen!

Kitty had promptly opened the safe, grabbed the remaining box and plunked it down in the same place the stolen one had occupied. Who knows, she told herself, maybe I'll get lucky this time and catch myself a jewelry-box thief red-handed! Keith can jump up and down on his gizzard until the mangy culprit tells me just what the hell is going on around here!

Getting old is a colossal pain in the butt, she admitted to herself. If I were young, I'd sit down with a pencil, a note pad and a cup of coffee and just logic this thing out. Multiple thefts of a worthless object that's been gathering dust on my desk for years can't be a chance happening. When Gene gets here, I'm going to make him tell me everything he knows about this fiasco, whether he wants to or not. That man has managed to get himself in a peck of trouble and now I'm in it with him!

Kitty parked her truck behind the store, dried her eyes, repaired her makeup and began her morning ritual. At precisely nine o'clock, she unlocked the front door and stepped outside. With the exception of the missing scarecrow, everything looked normal on Main Street. She sat down behind her desk and began comparing this year's sales figures to last year's results. Business was up. Enough to cover inflation and then some.

This is the year I buy one of those fancy electronic security systems that outfit in Bozeman is always trying to sell me, she thought. Because it damn sure looks like big-city crime has finally invaded my little town.

*

Jim Redline splashed cool water on his face in the pristine men's room at Gallatin Field, the picturesque airport on the outskirts of Belgrade. He noticed the man standing next to him was admiring himself in the mirror, adjusting his fancy suede bush hat, twisting this way and that to get a better look at his new outdoor threads. The man was wearing a sky-blue denim shirt with a bright yellow trout fly stitched over the pocket, a khaki fishing vest, twill cargo pants and lug-soled trail boots. A shiny metal rod case leaned against the wall. Although the man looked every inch a sportsman, he was clearly in no hurry to sally forth into the howling wilderness in search of something as slimy as a fish.

Redline stepped into the airport lobby. The interior of Gallatin Field had been designed by someone who knew exactly what people expect to see when they come to this part of America—a pleasing combination of rugged timbers and massive boulders. Just outside the restroom loomed a life-size bronze statue of a snarling grizzly bear with six-inch polished steel claws and menacing curved fangs.

Suspended above the bear on thin black wires was a flock of metal Canada geese winging their way majestically across The Big Sky.

A herd of energetic people in designer clothes galloped past Redline, some carrying fancy rod cases, others tooled leather golf bags or snazzy cameras. From somewhere nearby, he heard a woman speaking German. A tall man directly in front of him was conversing in Italian with a young boy. A cab driver strolled into the lobby holding aloft a hand-lettered cardboard sign that said, "Mr. Habib."

Redline spotted another bronze sculpture just outside the airport's main entrance. The larger-than-life work of art depicted a brawny man brandishing a fly rod, his floppy hat, bushy mustache, square jaw and toothy grin strongly reminiscent of Teddy Roosevelt. A metal dog lay at the feet of the immortalized fisherman, gazing up at him for eternity, eyes brimming with unconditional love.

Redline rented a compact sedan and headed west toward the tiny community of Belgrade, a scant three miles away. He drove slowly down Main Street and immediately spotted Kitty's Katchall. An ambitious enterprise, he thought, for such a one-horse burg. He noticed feathery black smudges on the silvered barn boards next to the front door. Smoke damage?

As Redline continued down Main Street, he quickly formed an opinion of the town. Belgrade is a rustic western village prospering from its fortuitous proximity to Gallatin Field, he thought. The stores are freshly painted. The wide streets are free of potholes and trash. Everything is bright and crisp and pleasing. Even the birds look alert and ready for business.

Redline parked under a beautiful shade tree in a residential area one block off Main Street and walked back to Kitty's Katchall. He opened the front door and stepped inside.

A few feet from the door, a small elderly woman dressed in fancy western garb sat at a desk just beyond a low banker's wall. She was on the telephone. And she was crying.

"Oh, I can't believe this," she said in a hoarse whisper. "In a bar? How can they be sure it's Gene if . . . oh, yes, I see. Well, at least they caught the thief."

212

That's Kitty Carson, thought Redline. And something's terribly wrong.

Kitty hadn't yet noticed him. From where he stood, Redline could see some of the antiques on display in an adjoining room. Scarred leather chaps, dented milk cans, weathered canvas mail pouches, coiled lariats. The store smelled of leather and dust. He scanned Kitty's cluttered desk. There was a shiny wooden jewelry box next to her telephone.

A tall, broad-shouldered young cowboy wearing a black western shirt and black boots came jogging from the back of the store. He glanced at Redline but then immediately turned his attention to Kitty. She muttered something into the phone and hung up.

"Keith, that was my sister," she said, dabbing at the tears in her eyes with a tissue. Her face was a study in grief. "Gene suffered a fatal heart attack last night in a bar near the Battlefield."

"Oh no," said Keith.

Kitty blew her nose. "I knew he wasn't in good shape but this is a shock. I'm going home to change into traveling clothes," she said. "Gene's remains are in the morgue at the hospital in Billings. They won't release his body until someone in his family identifies it. His parents are flying in later today. I want to meet them at the airport down there."

"Damn," said Keith. "Let's close the store so I can drive you to Billings."

"Yes," said Kitty.

Suddenly she looked up and saw Jim Redline standing just inside the front door. Without a moment's hesitation, she grabbed the jewelry box and held it out in front of her heaving chest. Then she screamed, "Who are you? Another goddamned jewelry box thief? Here, take it, you murdering bastard, take it!" She threw the box at Redline. It bounced on the worn plank floor and stopped inches from his feet.

Sobbing, Kitty Carson rushed out from behind her desk and disappeared into the back of the store. Keith turned around and looked at Redline. His hands balled into fists and his lean face darkened.

Redline bent down and picked up the jewelry box. He turned it over several times, then opened it. He held the box close to his face and sniffed. Finally, he inspected the shiny copper hinges.

Redline heard a door slam in the back of the store. "What did she mean?" he said to the young cowboy, trying to look offended. "Suggesting that I'm a thief? Who'd steal this thing? It isn't an antique."

Keith eyeballed Redline and opened his mouth several times to reply. Nothing came out. Finally, he sighed, rubbed his forehead, and shrugged. "Sorry about that, mister. Kitty just got some rough news. Mind handing that thing to me? It's not for sale."

Redline advanced and gave him the box.

Keith stared at it. "That's strange," he said.

"What?" asked Redline. "What's strange?"

Keith placed the jewelry box on Kitty's desk and plopped down in her chair. "Never mind," he said.

"I'm not much interested in antiques," Redline said. "Truth is, I didn't come in here to shop. Thought I'd inquire where a fellow could get a decent meal in this burg."

Keith propped his boots on the edge of Kitty's desk. "You can get a burger across the street at Joe's," he said. "But if you want a real meal, head west on Main Street. Place called Rusty's Roundup. Steaks as big as saddle blankets."

Redline thanked him. He tried to think of a plausible reason to hang around and talk to Keith about the jewelry box but couldn't come up with one. He walked slowly back to his car, thinking about what Kitty Carson had said—*What are you, another goddamned jewelry box thief?* And what about the weird smoke marks near the front door of her store? When Keith had looked at that brand new jewelry box and mumbled, "that's strange," he'd said plenty.

Someone stole the old jewelry box? That's more than strange. That's downright sinister. But who would steal it? Tom Sawyer, if he had a chance, but he's tucked away. Gene Zane dropped dead in a bar before he got as far as Belgrade. Keith obviously has no idea what's going on with the box. Kitty knows plenty but I can't question her today. She's too distraught over Gene's death.

Redline slid behind the wheel of his car and drove back down Main Street in the direction of Gallatin Field. He peered at Kitty's Katchall as he passed by. I figured this was going to be a piece of cake, he thought. Wrong as I've ever been. *I'll sure as hell come back someday and find out what happened. But I might as well go home now. Talk to Lionel. If someone else wants the box bad enough to steal it, that changes everything.*

CHAPTER TWENTY-FOUR

Charles Talbot stood outside the Oval Office waiting for the President to finish talking on the phone with the Secretary General of the United Nations. There were several important government officials conversing near where he stood, but he studiously ignored them. He was preoccupied with reviewing in his mind an important call he had received just moments before the President's secretary had summoned him for "a brief private visit." The call had come in from Las Vegas.

"May I assume," Talbot had said, "that you have good news for me?"

"Very good news," said Sammy Manzitto. "I thought you would want to know there was a small fire in Montana recently."

Talbot had swiveled in his chair so he could look through the bulletproof window behind his desk at the clear blue Virginia sky.

"How small?"

"About the size of a jewelry box."

"Any possibility the smoke from that fire was seen by unfriendly eyes?"

"No. The fire occurred in an isolated area several miles from the nearest town."

"What was the nearest town?"

"Belgrade."

Talbot had thanked Sammy and assured him that he could look forward to an appropriate gesture of appreciation for calling with such welcome information.

As Talbot waited, he considered whether to tell the President that, against all odds, something actually *had* surfaced that could have disrupted their sensitive plans. And then, when the Chief expressed alarm, reassure him that the threat had been neutralized immediately. After all, if Talbot didn't say anything about the jewelry box incident, he would never get credit for his quick thinking and decisive action. On the other hand, he knew better than to reveal the nature of the CIA's intricate relationship with organized crime. The last thing Talbot needed was for the President to start pondering all the ways the mob might be useful to *him*.

The door to the Oval Office opened and the President gestured for the CIA Director to join him. "The United Nations," snarled the President, "is a tar pit!"

"Has been since Day One," said Talbot. He walked past the President and sat down on a guest chair in front of the famous desk.

The President closed the door firmly and motioned to a group of upholstered sofas arranged around the oval rug in the center of the room. "Sit over here," he said. "I want to be as far away from that damn phone as I can get."

The President ran his fingers through his hair and groaned.

"How the hell can we be expected to successfully launch a sneak attack on our enemies if we have to call the UN first and ask a bunch of hostile foreigners for permission to do it?" he asked. "Do you realize we actually *pay* for membership in that organization?"

"We used to run things in this country our way," said Talbot. "No interference from the rest of the world."

"Globalization sucks," muttered the President. "Ah, the hell with it. Let's talk about something fun. What's the status of our, um, project?"

Talbot plucked an invisible piece of lint from the sleeve of his jacket.

"Sir, I must insist that from this day forward, you and I meet only in the presence of other top staff members and limit our talks to routine intelligence issues."

The President's eyes widened. "Really? You're saying it's a go? You want to avoid private contact with me so you can guarantee my total deniability on this thing?"

Talbot's nod was almost imperceptible.

217

"Hot damn!" exclaimed the President. "Your people have found a way to create—"

Talbot shook his head. "Trust me, sir, you don't want to know what my people have found. I will say this. We believe we now have the capability to solve your problem."

"Great! Let me ask you this, Charles. When will I know that a certain madman is finally on his bony knees in heaven begging Allah's forgiveness for not having me assassinated on national television? Are we talking days, weeks or months? I could use a good night's sleep. Tell me when you think the mission will be completed."

"I can't discuss our timetable, Mr. President," said Talbot patiently. "I want you to appear genuinely surprised—stunned, if you can manage it—when you hear the news that your most dreaded adversary has gone the way of all flesh." He pretended to consider his next remark carefully. "But it is important that you know this," he said, leaning forward slightly, a faint conspiratorial smile on his lips. "We're going to test our 'weapon' before we launch it at the priority target. That test will take place soon. After we're satisfied that the 'weapon' performed precisely as expected, we'll arrange for your enemy to come face to face with his creator at the earliest possible moment."

The President beamed and clapped Talbot on the shoulder. "Excellent! I couldn't be more pleased. Of course you should conduct a test before you launch your weapon at the real foe. You can't be too careful with something like this. May I ask if the test target is also someone I loathe?"

"Soon an individual you dislike intensely will meet his fate. Please consider his premature exit from the planet a token of my deep appreciation for your guarantee of future assistance with certain career plans I am formulating now."

The President jumped to his feet, cupped Talbot's elbow and guided him toward the door. "I wish I'd known about this a few minutes ago," he said. "If I'd been in a better mood, I probably wouldn't have told the Secretary General to bicycle over to the Rose Garden and kiss my sweaty white ass."

*

218

"The report states the chain of custody is not in question," said Conrad Morse. He waved a sheaf of papers over his head. "Unobserved, our agent stealthily extracted the jewelry box he found on Mrs. Carson's desk and had it in his possession from that moment until he arrived here. Never took his eyes off the thing. Am I correct?"

"Correct," mumbled a tall worried-looking man standing rigidly in front of the FBI Director's desk. He was the agency's senior scientist, responsible for authenticating obscure physical evidence. This was the first time in his twenty-five-year career that he had ever set foot in the Director's office. He was painfully aware that something about this particular case had caused an unexplained breach in the normal chain of command and placed him squarely in harm's way. He wiped his damp palms on his long white lab coat.

Morse cursed. "You found nothing at all in the box? No encrypted message? No safe deposit key? No photographs? And you're telling me the explanation for this failure is that the box our agent brought back is not the one we were after at all. Explain that."

The scientist cleared his throat. "Sir, the jewelry box I just examined was definitely manufactured during the same time period as the one we were hoping to retrieve and it fits the general description. But it has never been used. The information I have is that the box we are looking for has been sitting on Mrs. Carson's desk for over thirty years. The interior should show evidence of wear. The hinges should be coated with dust and grime. There should be scratches on the exterior and the lacquer should be faded because of long-term exposure to light. None of these conditions exist with the box the agent brought to me. And then there's the painting on the lid."

"What about it?"

"It is supposed to depict the famous castle that sits on a wooded mountainside directly above the city of Heidelberg. It doesn't. In fact, I have identified the structure as—"

"Well shit!" boomed Morse.

The scientist diplomatically waited a few moments and then said, "I believe the box our agent brought back has been in storage for years, sir. Probably sealed in a packing carton. That would explain—"

"Double shit!" yelled Morse. He waved the startled scientist out of his office and took two antacid tablets. Then he answered a priority call from the agent in charge of the New York City field office.

"Sir, you asked to be notified at once if Lionel Cooper was spotted doing anything out of the ordinary this week," said the agent. "This morning he met privately with Dr. Irving Katz at a swank hotel in Manhattan."

"And why do I care about that?"

"Until recently, Dr. Katz was the CIA's senior psychiatrist. He's now on indefinite medical leave. We don't know why Katz was suddenly relieved of his duties, but we do know he's not currently under a physician's care. He must have stepped on a very big toe and got himself benched. Our archivists tell me we have a file on this man that goes back many years. Katz is a sex addict. His hobby is philandering. If Cooper knows as much about Dr. Katz's dark side as we do, he's blackmailing him."

"Son of a bitch," said Morse. He hung up and immediately called the Assistant Director for Counterintelligence, Bill Williams.

"Bill, get up to my office as fast your stubby little legs will carry you," said Mr. FBI. "We need a new strategy."

CHAPTER TWENTY-FIVE

"Please tell me how this was accomplished," said Dr. Barbara Bowmaster. She removed her glasses and began polishing the thick lenses with a pink tissue. "How did you get Mustafa Rashid from his cell in a high-security federal prison to a safe house without some eagle-eyed reporter from CNN noticing that something was rotten in Denmark?"

Agent Orson Dean crossed his legs and rubbed the underside of his jaw with the back of his hand. He was an athletic-looking young man with hazel eyes and coarse black hair trimmed close to his square skull. "I'm not sure I'm authorized to tell you exactly how it was done," he said.

"Get serious," said Dr. Bowmaster. She replaced her glasses and stared at Agent Dean through grossly magnified eyes. "I've got the same security clearance you have and I'm part of this operation. Talk to me."

"If you insist. As you know, whenever Director Talbot invokes the phrase 'our national security is at stake,' everyone in the federal government conveniently looks the other way so he can do his black magic," said Agent Dean. "He ordered one of our 'doctors' to conduct a physical examination of Mustafa Rashid and find something seriously wrong. That resulted in Rashid being scheduled for a bogus operation to repair a bogus hernia. He was taken from his cell late at night and driven to the safe house in a prison ambulance. Simple as that."

Dr. Bowmaster chewed on a fingernail and tried to focus on what Orson Dean was saying, in spite of the fact that her conscience was busy shredding her already substantially depleted reservoir of self-confidence. This is a mistake, she thought. A *horrible* mistake.

"We've taken precautions to insure that the press doesn't know Rashid has been moved and that the inmates who saw him being taken away have only hazy information about his medical situation. Soon the inmates will be told he expired in the hospital following surgery. The press will find out about Rashid's 'death' only after he's been 'cremated,' of course, so they can't demand to see the body."

Dr. Bowmaster faked a smile. "Charles Talbot is a genius," she said softly. "We're all fortunate to be working under him."

Agent Dean returned her fake smile with one of his own. "Thanks to Director Talbot, Mustafa Rashid has now been spirited into the real world where we can use him for something besides a doorstop," he said. "You must be thrilled, Doctor."

Dr. Bowmaster shut her eyes. Talbot should have told me about this change, she thought. He had plenty of opportunities. Why am I the last person working on this project to find out the timetable has been advanced?

Agent Dean pretended to consult his watch. "We should head for the safe house now, so you can spend some quality time with Rashid. Director Talbot expects us to deliver him to the target's residence within forty-eight hours."

Dr. Bowmaster's eyes popped open. "What exactly have you been told Rashid is supposed to do when he accesses the target's house?"

"I don't understand your question, Doctor."

"How much do you know about Rashid's mission?"

"I know everything you know," said Agent Dean, "and more. After all, you won't be there during the covert action, Doctor, but I will."

"That's precisely what concerns me," said Dr. Bowmaster. As soon as those words left her mouth, she felt herself start to disintegrate. It was all she could do to keep from screaming at Agent Dean that they had to call the whole thing off. She had known for weeks that when the time for action finally arrived, she would have to confront her nagging doubts. There were certain things about this experiment that she had deliberately chosen not to discuss with Charles Talbot.

Foremost was her growing suspicion that, in spite of his frequent assertions to the contrary, Asad Rashid was lying to her. It was possible that he and Mustafa were silently collaborating, making plans to escape. She had kept her worries to herself in order to prolong the intensely pleasurable task of bringing Talbot the news he wanted to hear. But now her anxieties could no longer be repressed.

"How many agents will be available to prevent Rashid from slipping away if he decides to betray us?" Dr. Bowmaster wanted desperately to ask her question in a normal voice, but it came out in a pitiful squeak. "After all, he'll be alone for the first time in months. I can't predict with absolute certainty how he'll respond, consciously or unconsciously, when he grasps the fact that he's . . . free."

"I was told that's why we're calling this action a test," said Agent Dean. "And we all know that tests sometimes fail, Doctor. Surely, you're not concerned about this one? You're confident things will go smoothly, right? Isn't that what you told Director Talbot? That the outcome is virtually assured?"

"I know it's only a test. I didn't ask for a test, but Director Talbot insisted. And, as you say, everyone knows that tests sometimes fail." Dr. Bowmaster abruptly stopped talking aloud, but her lips continued to move.

Agent Dean got to his feet, pulled a set of keys from his pocket and jostled them in his open palm. "There will be armed agents controlling the site. Rashid will go in without weapons because we know he can dispatch this target with his bare hands. Hell, he could slap this old fart to death. If Rashid tries to escape instead of returning voluntarily to our custody, he'll discover that he's anything but free."

Dr. Bowmaster plucked a ballpoint pen from her desk and gripped it so tightly her fingers ached. "The Director mentioned to me recently that if . . . others . . . should happen to be in the residence when Rashid arrives, he must eliminate them, as well. No one who might be able to identify Rashid and compromise his critical future mission can be left alive. But if Rashid is sent in unarmed, won't he be vulnerable? He's not a large man. If he should encounter someone in that house he can't overpower without a weapon, what is he supposed to do? Call you and ask for assistance? Have you been ordered to handle that situation for him, Agent Dean? Is your team authorized to kill innocent American citizens in order to preserve the anonymity of this terrorist?"

Agent Dean was moving toward the office door. He turned and said stiffly, "I'm afraid that concludes the question and answer period for today, Doctor. Please allow me to offer you a bit of free advice. Never ask a field agent a question if you don't really want to know the answer. And never tell the Director of the CIA that you have a plan you are sure will succeed if you don't actually believe that yourself."

Dr. Bowmaster felt an infant migraine start to kick its tiny legs deep inside her brain. "Well, pardon me for being human," she said bitterly. "I'm just not thrilled with the idea that innocent American citizens may be sacrificed because they're in the wrong place at the wrong time. I'm a doctor, Agent Dean, not a . . . a . . . whatever the hell the rest of you are! I don't see why we have to treat a laboratory test like we're mounting an assault on Omaha Beach. Can't we disguise Rashid so no one can guess his identity? Can't we abort the mission if Rashid runs into unexpected problems? Why do we have to kill American citizens because an experiment fails?" With a groan, she hurled herself against the back of her chair and allowed her now fully mature migraine to run amok.

"If we leave without further delay," said Agent Dean, "we can get to the safe house in time for lunch. And this we want to see, Doctor. They're ordering in sausage pizza because nothing distresses Rashid more than the stink of cooked pig."

*

Lionel Cooper sat alone in his office reviewing, for the third time, the incredible CIA report Dr. Irving Katz had turned over to him. Unbelievable, he thought. Here we have an educated midget, a thumb-sized pervert, who had the audacity to make his own personal copy of a classified document. What the hell was Dr. Katz thinking? And the report really is dangerous, thought Cooper, but not because it's true. It's dangerous because it can never be proven untrue and, therefore, some people will insist on believing it no matter what. Like that imbecile sitting in the Oval Office picking lint out of his foreskin right now. When he read this report, he would instantly conclude that the outrageous assertions made by the KGB psychiatrist were not only factual but that it was his personal destiny to be the first President to employ that information in the defense of liberty.

Cooper had been constructing a theory about what might be going on in the White House. Dr. Katz had admitted that the President had ordered CIA Director Charles Talbot to try to create a robot assassin and then launch the hypnotized killer at a dangerous foreigner. The huge Mars Mission budget, strongly supported by the President, had provided Talbot with covert funding for his expensive research. Cooper believed he could guess the identity of the secret target. And if my hunch is correct, he thought, it means the President is willing to put the rest of us at risk in order to try to put down just one insignificant fanatic.

Of course, thought Cooper, the task confronting the CIA is impossible and Director Talbot surely knows that. Eventually, after he's milked the deal for everything he can, Talbot will tell the President that the concept of a programmable killer has no scientific validity whatsoever.

The important thing, Cooper thought, is that soon I will have under my roof not only this old intelligence report, but the jewelry box and General Rutz's notes, too. That evidence might enable me to force certain key individuals in Washington to validate all the dirty details of the President's mad scheme. And then, to the astonishment of my critics, I will prove that the coward leading this country is a demented narcissist willing to put all of us at risk just to save his own dimpled ass.

The intercom buzzed and Tina Romero said, "Jim is holding on line one."

Cooper grabbed the phone. "Jim, thanks for calling. Do you have the box?"

"Afraid not," said Redline. "I'm flying back to Cambridge from Belgrade momentarily. I want to talk to you as soon as possible. I'll be late. Wait up for me."

"I can't believe it," said Cooper. "This is terrible news. You were so sure you knew where it was. Do you think you can eventually find the box?"

"I honestly can't say," said Redline. "I believe the box has been stolen. Lionel, tell no one about this. Certainly not Tina or Lyman."

"Jim, you suspect someone on my staff is guilty of leaking information?"

"It's possible," said Redline. "If someone got up here before I did and took the jewelry box, then they had to be tipped off. Think about that. I'll talk to you tonight and we can decide what to do next. Sorry, my plane is boarding right now. Goodbye, Lionel."

Cooper hung up. Almost immediately, Tina strolled into his office. "Well, what did Jim have to say for himself? Was he successful?"

"Uh, he said the trout fishing is terrific in Montana," said Cooper. "I'm not sure when he'll be back."

CHAPTER TWENTY-SIX

Helen Rutz and Murray Klein stood toe to toe at the foot of her bed. They were arguing about West Nile virus while getting dressed.

"If even one infected mosquito pokes his beak into that bald head of yours," said Helen forcefully, "you'll be history within forty-eight hours, Murray."

"I will not," protested Murray. "Only elderly people with a weakened immune system succumb to West Nile. I'm younger than springtime and healthy as a horse." He pointed at the freshly rumpled bed and grinned. "As I've been vigorously demonstrating for almost an hour."

Helen blushed. "Murray, promise me you'll use mosquito spray before you play golf tomorrow. My doctor says there are more dangerous insects lurking around sand traps than breeding in the Everglades."

Murray grinned. "You're falling in love with me, Helen. Admit it."

"I admit nothing of the kind," said Helen. "For one thing, I'm sure as hell not going to fall in love with a man too dumb to take care of himself!" She tried to put a stern look on her face.

"What's going on, Helen?" asked Murray suspiciously. His eyes probed hers. "Why the sudden concern for my welfare? Are you in some kind of trouble?"

Helen dropped her eyes. "Maybe. I got a disturbing call just before you showed up to take me to dinner tonight. It was my business partner."

"Business partner?" said Murray. "I didn't know you even had a business partner."

Helen bit her lip and looked at the ceiling. Her eyes were damp. "Can you keep a secret?"

"Hell, yes," said Murray.

Helen took him by the hand and led him into the living room. She sat close to him on her old sofa, lit a cigarette and told him the whole story. The confidential notes written by Walter Rutz and sent to her by mistake. The old jewelry box and its possible connection to the JFK assassination. Lionel Cooper and his handsome young investigator, Jim Redline. Redline's promising interrogation of Tom Sawyer, the last man known to have the box in his possession.

At the top of his lungs, Murray expressed absolute amazement that all of this hush-hush stuff had been going on right under his nose! He rambled on and on about how incredulous he was at being kept in the dark. When Helen realized he was never going to stop complaining, she politely told him to shut up so she could finish her narrative.

"Jim called earlier today. You were here, remember, Murray? I took the call in the kitchen. He said he was closing in on the jewelry box," said Helen. "You can imagine my excitement. But then he called me again late this afternoon and said things had taken a mysterious turn. He refused to elaborate. Said it might be a false alarm or it might be extremely important. He advised me to get out of town for a while. Take a little vacation, he said. Just as a precaution."

"What do you think he was talking about?" asked Murray.

"I have no idea. But I know he failed to take possession of the box."

"The notes written by your late ex-husband about the contents of the jewelry box are in that cardboard carton I lugged out of here this morning, aren't they?" asked Murray. "The one you asked me to hide in my trailer?"

"Yes," said Helen. "That was another precautionary move Jim recommended."

"Wow," said Murray. "I'm neck deep in the JFK thing. Whether I want to be or not."

"Jim said he was flying back to Cambridge tonight to discuss the new development with Lionel Cooper," said Helen. "He said I should tell Rose Blanchard where I was staying and he would communicate with me through her. Said he'd contact me as soon as the coast was clear."

Murray put his hand on Helen's knee. "Sweetheart," he said softly, "We should do exactly what Jim said. Get the hell out of town immediately."

"What's this 'we' stuff, Murray? All I want you to do is keep that box hidden in your trailer for a while."

"No way," said Murray. "I can't bear to think of you hiding in some ramshackle motel while I cruise around Smithville alone and miserable. Let me take you someplace fun, Helen. Hey, how about Key West? I know it like the back of my hand. And it will be my treat."

Helen shook her head. "Thanks, Murray, but I'm not going anywhere. I've made up my mind. I don't care what Jim says. I refuse to run and hide. He might be a coward, but courage is my middle name. Besides, we aren't that far along in our relationship."

"Helen," said Murray, "do you know how many people connected to the JFK assassination have died under mysterious circumstances over the years? People who boasted they knew something no one else knew about that crime? People just like you? There have been a dozen books written about it. No way all those people died of natural causes. Statistically impossible! You're involved in something extremely dangerous, sweetheart. Jim Redline is trying to protect you until he can determine that it's safe for you to walk around in the open. He's just doing his job. And, I think our relationship was serious long before today. Am I right about that?"

"Statistically impossible?" asked Helen. Her hand fluttered across her throat. "People have died under mysterious circumstances?"

"Gobs of 'em," said Murray somberly. "All doing exactly what you're doing, honey. Threatening to reveal secrets the government and the underworld have sworn to protect. You think the West Nile virus is a mortal threat? Proving who killed JFK is probably the riskiest thing an ordinary person could do, Helen."

Helen stubbed out her cigarette and kissed Murray on the cheek. "You've convinced me, you silver-tongued devil. Let's drive to

Key West right now."

"Well, uh," said Murray, "hang on a minute. We have to pack first. I'll go home and throw a few things in a suitcase, cancel my golf match and come back for you, Helen. Shouldn't take more than a couple hours."

"Nonsense. I can go with you right now," said Helen, jumping to her feet. "I'm already packed."

Murray blinked. "What? How could you already be packed? Until I just talked you out of it, you were going to stay here and risk your life. I refuse to run and hide, you said. Courage is my middle name, you said. True or false, Helen?"

"True," said Helen, marching toward her bedroom. She looked over her shoulder and winked. "I said those things and I meant them. But somehow I knew you'd change my mind, Murray. You're the practical one in this family."

CHAPTER TWENTY-SEVEN

Asad Rashid stared at Dr. Barbara Bowmaster for a full minute before he answered her question.

"That is the first thing you have asked me since we met that I do not appreciate," he said finally. "What more can I say or do to convince you that I am totally at peace with your decision to test my loyalty in this way? Tell me and I will gladly say it or do it immediately."

Dr. Bowmaster shook her head. "I'm sorry, Asad. I know this is insulting to you. But it's nearly impossible for me to believe you're telling me the whole truth. If I were in your predicament, I'd say *anything* I thought would help me get free. If Mustafa has more influence over you than you're willing to admit, everything we're planning is doomed to failure."

"Please believe me," said Asad patiently. "When it comes to our plans, Mustafa is irrelevant. He no longer controls me, Doctor. I am too strong for him."

"See, that's what I mean, right there, what you just said," said Dr. Bowmaster sharply. "That is not possible. If you think you're too strong for Mustafa, then he's tricked you, Asad. I had hoped you might persuade him to allow you to function as the dominant personality for a short time, long enough to carry out one or two important missions for me. But I have always known you can never permanently overpower Mustafa. This is all very troubling."

Asad smiled. "Ah, now I see. You are a scientist. You must have absolute proof before you act. But we both know proof of the kind you require can be found only in deeds, Doctor. Therefore, you must allow

231

me to go forward with the test so I can demonstrate just how committed I am to you. There is no other way."

"I'm extremely uncomfortable with that proposition," said Dr. Bowmaster. "I have asked my superior for more time so I can determine precisely what your current relationship to Mustafa is, Asad. Failure at this juncture could have catastrophic consequences for all of us. I realize now that measuring your loyalty to me is not as important as I once believed. Not when I compare the temporary joy of believing that you are mine to do with as I see fit to the permanent horror of discovering later that I have been deceived."

Agent Orson Dean walked into the room. "I'm sorry to disturb you two," he said cordially. "But Director Talbot has asked me to inform you, Doctor, that your request for an indefinite delay is denied. I have been ordered to initiate the mission tonight."

*

Conrad Morse spun around in his chair and stared through the office window at the hazy late afternoon sun. His desire to find the original jewelry box had evolved rapidly into an obsession. He believed that once he possessed the elusive box, he could force Charles Talbot into revealing *what was really going on.* And knowing what was really going on was the only way to keep score in the intelligence game. Morse had decided to either win this shadowy contest or go down trying.

"Where is James T. Redline now?" he asked.

"Flying from Belgrade to Boston," said Assistant Director Bill Williams. He was seated in front of Morse's desk, flipping through a bundle of notes. "We can toss a net over him anytime you give the word."

"You're sure he has the original box?"

"No. And we cannot be sure until we talk to him. All we know is he went to Belgrade to get the box. We think Kitty Carson kept it in a safe place until he arrived. We assume he paid her a lot of money for it."

"There can be no witnesses to his arrest, Bill," said Morse. "It's important that the FBI's interest in this matter be kept secret. When Redline's plane lands at Logan International, track his every move. Make sure we have several people inside his home. And have a couple people keep an eye on the Cooper Building, too. He might go straight to his office. Contact Tina Romero and tell her to let us know at once if she hears anything at all from Redline."

"Right. Incidentally, Tina mentioned last night that she suspects Lionel Cooper is on the trail of a current government scandal with possible links to the old jewelry box," said Williams. "She has not yet been able to provide us with any useful details because Cooper has suddenly become extremely secretive. First time he has ever denied her access to his private activities."

It was all Morse could do to keep from screaming, "I knew it! I knew it!" He smoothed the hair on his temples with the palms of his sweaty hands and said calmly, "Tell Romero we must know the exact nature of the scandal as soon as possible. Authorize her to take extraordinary measures to find out what Cooper is up to, even if she has to risk losing her job to get the information. The FBI will reimburse her for any lost income."

"And the official reason we are detaining Redline, sir?" asked Williams.

Morse spun around and drummed his fingers on his desk. "We confiscate the notes and the box and tell Redline our actions are necessitated by a deep concern for national security. Then we hold him while our scientists inspect the stuff. If the box is empty, we return it and the notes to Redline, thank him for his patriotic cooperation and release him. But if the box contains even one of the conspiracy clues Helen Rutz claims it does, we go to Plan B."

"What exactly is Plan B, sir? To be honest, I don't understand why we're concerned about this flimsy conspiracy story in the first place. Is it because you know the box is tied to something even more intriguing than the JFK assassination? Is that why you've taken a personal interest in this matter? What's really going on here?"

In a frigid whisper, Morse replied, "Has it not occurred to you, Bill, that if it were important for you to know 'what's really going on here,' I would have filled you in a long time ago?"

A bubble of sour acid shot out of the Assistant Director's gut and slimed across the roof of his mouth. He knew he should back off immediately. But he also knew his boss had no respect for subordinates who lacked the onions to speak up in situations like this one. He flipped a virtual coin in his mind, lost, cleared his throat and blurted, "I believe I'm entitled to know more than I do about this operation, sir. Especially if national security is truly the issue."

Morse flashed Williams a look hot enough to melt his fillings.

"Is that so? Well, then, let's make a deal. In due time, if all goes well, and if, by some fucking miracle you're actually able to carry out the simple orders I just gave you, I might tell you what's going on. Or I might not. Is that clear?"

Bill Williams mumbled a few unintelligible words and duck-walked out of the office.

*

"You heard me right, sir," said Agent Mike Smiley quietly. He was murmuring into his cell phone. "There are four men watching Cooper's place like they were expecting the Messiah to walk out the front door any minute. Two of them are disguised as college students. Beards, funky clothes, knapsacks. Another guy is pretending he's changing a tire on a rusty old Volvo. He's changed it twice just since we got here. The fourth man is sitting on the ground, resting his back against the metal fence that surrounds Cooper's property. He's smoking and staring up at the night sky like he's getting paid to rename the constellations."

Agent Smiley was sitting in a black sedan with his partner, Agent Ralph Wilson, one block from Cooper's estate. Agent Wilson was peering at the scene through a pair of night-vision binoculars. He could see all four of the men clearly.

"These guys look like burglars to me," said Agent Wilson.

"Request permission to take the trespassers down," said Agent Smiley into the phone. "They may be burglars."

"You are on an important mission tonight, Agent Smiley, that does not include arresting burglars. How much help do you have available on-site?"

"Only Agent Wilson, sir. But he and I can easily handle these clowns. And I just heard from our people at the airport. Redline left Logan International a few minutes ago and is driving in the direction of his house. He's definitely not coming here, sir. In fact, the agents assigned to the airport watch are now taking an alternate route to his neighborhood so they can be in position there when he's arrested."

"Dare I ask how these four 'clowns' managed to get the Cooper Building staked out tonight before you savvy professionals were in position?"

"Uh, well, we were delayed by a snafu like you wouldn't believe, sir. See, what happened is, we were all ready to go when suddenly—"

"Spare me the details, Agent Smiley. Okay, based on the fact that Redline appears to be headed home rather than to his office, I'm authorizing you and Agent Wilson to vacate your post. Without alerting Cooper's slumbering neighbors that the FBI is on the scene, quietly take these four men into custody and drag them across the river for questioning. Let me know if you learn anything useful. It strikes me as peculiar that they would be there on this particular night."

"Very peculiar, sir. Thank you, sir."

As soon as Agent Smiley finished his call, Agent Wilson said, "Well, what did he say? Is he sending a helicopter over here to spray these assholes with Agent Orange or what?"

"He said, 'Smiley, I'm so glad you're in charge of this sensitive operation tonight and not that airhead Wilson.'"

"Yeah?" said Agent Wilson. "He actually mentioned me by name?"

*

Agent Orson Dean had slipped Asad Rashid inside the Cooper Building at precisely midnight. Agency technicians had provided

Agent Dean with the security codes that enabled him to open both the electronically locked front gate and the main door of the old building. The technicians told Agent Dean it was duck soup getting the codes from the private company that had installed the system. They simply informed the owner that national security was at stake and he instantly handed them Cooper's confidential file.

"This man was a genuine patriot," the technicians said. "As we were leaving his office, he bowed so low his sweaty forehead actually stained the carpet. He even gave us a copy of the special key to the elevator, so you guys won't have a problem getting to the target's pad on the fourth floor. The fire escape doors only open from the inside."

After disabling the security lights near the front gate, Agent Dean and Asad Rashid had shuffled across the darkened yard, then crouched next to the front door of the stone building.

"Listen to me, Asad," Agent Dean had whispered. "You get your oily butt in there, do the deed and come out through this door. I'll be waiting for you near the front gate. You're surrounded by armed CIA agents who have orders to shoot you dead if you try to escape. Do you understand?"

"It is not necessary to threaten me," Asad had responded quietly. "You will be very pleased at how efficient I am, Agent Dean."

"I'm already pleased," Agent Dean had responded, "just to have made the acquaintance of a high-caliber fanatic such as yourself, Asad. Remember, if you should encounter something or someone you can't handle, don't be a hero. Push the yellow button on the beeper in your pocket. We'll come in and take care of the situation for you."

"Maybe *something* unforeseen could temporarily stop me," Asad had whispered fiercely, "but never *someone!*"

"Oh, yeah, I forgot," Agent Dean had muttered. "You've never met an enemy you couldn't disembowel with just a flick of your dirty yellow toenail." He waited a full minute after the front door closed behind Asad, then scuttled back to his original position. Agent Dean sat down with his back against the iron fence, a few yards from the gate. He hadn't smoked in twenty years, but on this special night he lit a cigarette and blew tiny white rings at the moon.

*

Asad Rashid crouched in the dark just inside the Cooper Building. He could see a narrow band of light coming from a doorway a few yards down the hall.

"Mustafa! Come to me now. I must tell you I fear Agent Dean and his men have orders to kill us the moment we leave here. Dr. Bowmaster warned me about them. She said it was possible we would be executed, even if I complete the mission as instructed."

"Of course they're going to kill us," said Mustafa bluntly. "That has been their intention all along."

"I know nothing about violence, Mustafa. But you are a great warrior. Tell me what I must do to insure that we both survive?"

"We need weapons if we are to live through this night," said Mustafa. "As many as we can find. Normally, a hostage would also be useful. But hostages won't help us this time. Anyone unlucky enough to be in this building is without value to Agent Dean and his murderous crew."

"How do you propose I get my hands on weapons?"

"There will be weapons in this building, Asad. Americans fear the loss of their material possessions more than they fear the wrath of their merciless God. They are all armed to the teeth. However, this is not a task you can accomplish. It will be necessary for me to have total control now. I must ask you to retire so that I may operate without interference. Trust me, you do not want to be present while I am brutally sacrificing human lives in the name of Allah."

"May I remind you that Dr. Bowmaster said it is important that I complete this mission?"

"You will never see Dr. Bowmaster again," replied Mustafa. "Not on earth and certainly not in heaven. We are fighting for our lives and our eternal souls tonight, Asad. I do not have time to debate every ethical dilemma you perceive us to be facing. This is a holy war, my brother, and only I am trained to deal with it."

"I reluctantly agree, Mustafa. In my heart, I knew it would come to this. When you have successfully extricated us from this barbaric situation, what then?"

"As soon as it can be arranged by our sympathizers," said Mustafa, "we will return to our beloved homeland to live in peace and harmony for the rest of our natural lives. I will tell our leader that, because of your extreme heroism, we escaped the tyranny of the infidels. He will declare us to be martyrs so that we may spend eternity together in the lap of Allah."

"You swear it by all that is holy, Mustafa?"

"I swear it, Asad."

"I am confident you will prevail over the great evil that confronts us. I look forward to our next visit, Mustafa."

"As do I, Asad."

*

Tina Romero pressed her crotch against the back of the young man's neck and ran her fingers through his curly black hair. Then she stuck the tip of her tongue in his ear. He was seated in her office chair, fiddling with her computer. He reached around and slipped his hand under her skirt.

"You're sopping," he breathed. "We'd better get horizontal before that thing dehydrates you."

Tina giggled. "Control yourself, Greg! I don't want to do it here. Let's go to my apartment."

"Why?" said Greg. "Office sex is the best sex in the world." He stood up and dropped his pants. His erection jutted through the fly of his boxer shorts like a crimson cucumber.

"You beast," gasped Tina. "Okay, you talked me into it. But lock my door first. My boss is home tonight, remember?"

Tina peeled out of her clothes as fast as she could. Greg watched her until she was completely naked. Then he removed the rest of his garments and stepped toward the office door. He paused, looked over his shoulder at her and arched his bushy eyebrows. "Let's go up to Cooper's office and do it on his desk. Leave a couple sticky spots for him to puzzle over in the morning."

"Stop blabbing and haul that monster over here," said Tina. She braced herself against the wall, feet wide apart. "Let's see if you're strong enough to do it standing up."

"My dear lady," panted Greg. "I'm strong enough to do it in midair if it pleases you."

His hands slick with sweat, he fumbled with the door lock.

The door burst open and Mustafa Rashid raced into the room. He drove his elbow savagely into Greg's gut. Greg crashed to the floor, gasping and helpless. While Tina watched in horror, Mustafa took a pair of scissors from her desk and jammed the blades between Greg's heaving ribs.

It was over in seconds. Clutching the bloody scissors in his dark hand, Mustafa turned to face Tina.

Instinctively, she covered her breasts with one hand and her crotch with the other. She opened her mouth to scream for help, but she was too panicked to produce anything but a series of pitiful squeaks. Her knees gave way and she slid down the wall until she was flat on her back on the floor.

Mustafa stroked his beard with his left hand, the one that wasn't smeared with Greg's blood. He looked at the terrified young woman spread-eagled before him and smiled.

"My goodness," said Mustafa. "That really is tempting. You American females are so direct. Unfortunately, I must decline your proposition, my dear. You see, I am a happily married man."

CHAPTER TWENTY-EIGHT

Two blocks from his home, Redline abruptly pulled his car into a supermarket parking lot and came to a full stop. He glanced at the clock on the dashboard, then rested his forehead on the steering wheel and sighed. *I'm so exhausted, I completely forgot I asked Lionel to wait up for me. I'd better get over there or he'll be so pissed off he'll fire me before I get a chance to tell him I quit.*

Redline drove slowly through the quiet streets of residential Cambridge. One block from the Cooper Building, he pulled to the curb and stopped. Although he had been thinking about Kitty Carson and what she had said to him about the jewelry box, a part of his brain had automatically registered the fact that the security lights over the front gate were dark. As his eyes adjusted to the gloom, Redline made out several human shapes standing near the gate. He grabbed his cell phone and dialed Cooper's private number.

Cooper answered on the third ring. "Jim, are you finally here?"

"Arm yourself," said Redline. "Don't think, don't hesitate and don't ask questions. Stay alert until I get there."

"What?"

Redline tossed his phone aside, removed the fuse that operated his car's interior lights, quietly opened the passenger door and slipped outside. Moving quickly through the inky darkness, using the wealthy neighborhood's lushly landscaped front yards as cover, he was able to creep within a few feet of the people milling around near the gate. Kneeling behind a thick hedge, he watched and listened.

*

Agent Mike Smiley held his badge up a little higher so his prisoner could get a better look at it. The agent was standing a safe four feet from the seated man and had the drop on him.

"I don't think you heard me, sir," said Agent Smiley. "F, as in frog, B, as in bobcat, and I, as in disgusting insect. You're under arrest for trespassing. Now drop that cigarette, stand up and turn around."

"No, *you* did not hear *me*," snarled Agent Orson Dean. He tossed his cigarette aside and clambered to his feet. "You can't hold me at gunpoint, you idiot, because I'm one of the good guys. C, as in citizen, I, as in innocent, A as in damned annoyed. Now clear out of here before you screw up a Top Secret undercover operation! What the hell is the FBI doing here tonight, anyway?"

"Hey, hey, hey," said Agent Smiley. "Cut the amateur comedy act, pal. If you were CIA, the Bureau would know your agency was planning a dance here tonight. Remember the rules of coordination? The FBI competently handles domestic surveillance while the CIA routinely screws up the foreign stuff. Now turn around and show me your wrists."

Not far away, Agent Dean could see two of his people talking to a man in a dark suit. The man was brandishing a gun. As he watched, the man in the suit marched his compliant captives toward a large black sedan.

"That's right, we nailed your entire team," said Agent Dean. "The fourth burglar is resting comfortably in our vehicle right now, enthusiastically writing out his confession."

Agent Dean stifled a scream. "Listen to me! I'm Agent Orson Dean with the CIA. You're going to trash your career and mine unless you call this number immediately and verify what I'm telling you." He recited a phone number with a Virginia area code. He did it twice, slowly, like he was talking to someone suffering from a severe learning disability.

"Orson Bean? Wow! Weren't you one of the 'Hollywood Squares'?"

"Dean! Do I look like a burglar to you?"

241

"No, you look like a chain-smoking homicidal maniac to me," said Agent Smiley. "But I'm a reasonable man, Mr. Bean. I'll examine your identification. If it's legitimate, I might call that phone number. But if anything comes out of your pocket that isn't shaped like an authentic federal credential, I'm going to blow a hole in your chest the size of a manhole cover. Hell, I might shoot you anyway. I never liked Orson Bean."

Agent Dean groaned. "We're undercover. We don't carry identification when we're undercover and you know it. Okay, look, I'll let you cuff me if you'll swear on your mother's grave you'll call the number I just gave you. It's crucial that we be allowed to stay here and see this mission through. National security—"

"Is at stake," said Agent Smiley. "You desperately need some fresh material, Mr. Bean. However, you've persuaded me to dial that fictitious number. I'll do it as soon as you're no longer a threat to my physical person. By the way, my mother is still alive and kicking."

"You'll verify who I am if I let you put cuffs on me?"

"Cross my heart and hope to spy. Now turn around." Agent Smiley cuffed Agent Dean, frisked him, discovered a nine-millimeter pistol in an ankle holster, removed a thin wire and a tiny microphone from his shirtsleeve, spun him around and shoved him in the direction of the black sedan that had just come to a screeching halt nearby.

"You lied to me," hissed Agent Dean. "I can't believe this. You aren't going to call. You bastard. You can't deceive a federal agent. That's treason!" Agent Dean aimed a desperate backwards kick at Agent Smiley's shin. The FBI agent adroitly avoided the kick, grabbed the taller man by the neck and whacked him hard on the side of the head with the butt of his pistol. Orson Dean spiraled to the ground like a dying moth and lay still.

Agent Wilson jumped from the black sedan and trotted over to stand next to Agent Smiley. He looked down at the unconscious man sprawled in the grass.

"Big one," he said.

"Claims he's CIA," said Agent Smiley. "Know what, Ralph? I think he's telling the truth. But if this bum truly is a federal operative, his personnel file is already in the shredder."

"Which means he's having one of the more enjoyable moments of his entire future life right now," chuckled Agent Wilson. He jerked his thumb at the sedan. "The guys I nabbed didn't say squat. But they were impressively armed, Mike. They are definitely not burglars. They're either federal agents, mobsters, domestic terrorists or rap artists."

"Help me put this slob in the trunk," said Agent Smiley. He poked Agent Dean with the toe of his shoe. "Then let's drive this fascinating quartet across the river where we can question them in private. I sense something big is going on here, Ralph. Big, big, big."

Agent Wilson said, "I assume our people got Redline, too? At his house?"

"Who cares about him?" said Agent Smiley. "We made the top collar tonight, Ralph."

*

Mustafa Rashid stepped boldly from the elevator into an elegant apartment. Less than ten feet away, a lanky old man sat in a black leather chair. The man was wearing white terry cloth slippers and a white kimono decorated with red satin dragons. He held an iced drink in one hand and a pearl-handled pistol in the other. The pistol was pointed at Mustafa's chest.

"Stop right there or I'll shoot," said the man.

Mustafa froze. Agent Dean had assured Asad that the target was an elderly gentleman, frail and defenseless. But at this moment, this man looked anything but defenseless.

"Perhaps we can discuss this situation like two civilized men," said Mustafa calmly. He calculated the distance from where he stood to the black chair. *I can do this, he thought. If I can get three feet closer, he's mine. This old man is totally unprepared. Look at him! Actually holding the weapon right under my nose while he dulls his reflexes with alcohol! It's as if he has already conceded that I'm going to take the pistol from him!*

"Yes, let's do that," said the man. His shrewd eyes scurried across Mustafa's lean body. "Although I generally make it a rule not to converse at length with people if they're drenched in blood. I must say, you look damned familiar. Could you be . . . Rashid? Mustafa Rashid? I saw you on television so many times during your trial I almost feel as if I know you!"

Mustafa bowed. "Mustafa Rashid, at your service," he said. "And you are?"

"Lionel Cooper, internationally acclaimed author. Perhaps you're familiar with my work?"

Mustafa shook his head. "I am embarrassed to say I have not heard your name before tonight."

"Well," said Cooper, "perhaps I'm not as well known currently as I will be soon. May I ask what brings you to my home this evening, Mustafa? I don't recall inviting you."

"I bring greetings from the CIA," said Mustafa. "They delivered me to your door a few minutes ago and asked me to kill you."

Cooper did not respond immediately. His unblinking eyes never left Mustafa's face. A full two minutes elapsed. Cooper finished his drink. Still he did not speak. Mustafa used the time to examine the author's exquisite possessions, at least the ones he could see from where he was standing. *Look at all this wickedness, thought Mustafa. This infidel deserves to die!*

"That is a very troubling statement," said Cooper finally. "The CIA asked you to kill me tonight but they didn't even tell you who I am? Well, what can you expect from government drones, right, Mustafa? They're the same the world over."

"The drones in your government could be substituted for the drones in my government tonight and no one would notice," said Mustafa.

Cooper said, "The CIA doesn't care a whit about me. And they wouldn't smuggle you out of federal prison just to murder an old writer in the twilight of his career. So there must be something else going on here. Can you tell me what it is?"

With pleasure, thought Mustafa. Anything to keep you talking, old man. He spread his hands wide and took a small step forward. "I am part of a Top Secret experiment being conducted by your government. They wish to assassinate my leader. They plan to send a killer into the desert after him. Someone who cannot fail because he is in a trance."

Club Red is rising from the ashes once again, thought Cooper. *This is terrific.*

"A trance, Mustafa?"

"The CIA believes it has developed a sophisticated new way to manage human behavior through hypnosis. And they intend for some poor fool who is trusted by my leader to go forth and do the evil deed. They believe I am that fool."

"Oh my, what will these geniuses come up with next? A hypnotically controlled assassin? How original. I suppose I should ask you if they've succeeded? Are you in a trance tonight, Mustafa?"

Mustafa laughed harshly, waved his arms and slid his feet another few inches forward. "Certainly not! I am the master of my own fate! No man will ever control Mustafa Rashid!"

Cooper's expression turned serious as he formed his next question.

"Well, yes, but the CIA would not have delivered you here tonight with instructions to kill me unless they believed you would do it. They couldn't trust you with a potentially explosive mission like this if there were any possibility you had the will to resist them. How do you explain that, Mustafa?"

Mustafa rolled his eyes and moved ever so slightly forward. "That is difficult to explain, Mr. Cooper. The situation is complex. But perhaps this will help you to understand. They intend for both of us to die tonight."

"Oh, I see," said Cooper slowly. "CIA personnel are outside waiting for you to kill me? And then, when you return to their custody and report that the mission is completed, they will kill you, also? My goodness, Mustafa, you're in a bit of a pickle. Let me think about that for a moment. Hmmm. It is obvious you bargained your way out of prison with lies. You promised to kill me—to prove to them that you will do anything they suggest when you are under hypnosis—and you assured them you would happily go back to your homeland and assassinate your unsuspecting leader, too. But they don't believe you. They have failed and they know it. So they have no choice but to kill you tonight. I'm probably an afterthought. A target of opportunity."

Mustafa feigned extreme indignation and used it to mask another impulsive step forward. "Yes, I fooled my captors into releasing me. I would never harm my leader! But it would take hours for me to explain to you exactly how I tricked the CIA. Even then, you might not believe me."

"Trust me, I can spare the time to hear a fascinating story like that one, Mustafa."

"Unfortunately, you cannot," said Mustafa. "This mission is planned down to the last second. If I do not show up precisely when expected, the men waiting outside have orders to rush in here and kill us both."

"Of course they do," said Cooper. He scratched his chin with his pistol's shiny barrel. "I should have realized that. A bit more dangerous situation than I first imagined. While I'm considering our options, Mustafa, would you be so kind as to tell me why you're covered in blood? May I assume at least one of the CIA operatives who brought you here is dead on the floor downstairs with his throat ripped open? Perhaps more than one?"

Mustafa elevated his hands until they were directly in front of his eyes. He was painted in crimson from his fingertips to his elbows. He shrugged and took another tiny step forward. "What a vivid imagination you possess, Lionel Cooper," he said. "This tells me you are a brilliant writer of fiction."

Cooper leaned over to place his empty glass on the carpet beside the chair. He opened his mouth to deliver a witty response to Mustafa. But to his horror, he found he could not utter a sound because the savage terrorist, moving with incredible speed, was suddenly in the process of strangling him to death.

*

Charles Talbot sat in his study, pretending to read a book. Every few seconds his eyes strayed toward his telephone. *Soon they'll call and say it's all over. Mission accomplished! Mustafa Rashid, relentless enemy of freedom, dead as a mackerel. And Lionel Cooper, winging his way toward hell, too! When the President realizes that I have cleverly eliminated a citizen he believes is a serious threat to the security of the country he has sworn to protect, it will be easier for him to accept the sad news that my agency's best efforts have failed to produce a programmable assassin capable of attacking . . .*

The phone rang. With a cat-ate-the-canary smile on his handsome face, Talbot picked up the receiver and settled back to savor the news.

"Talk to me," he said.

"Good evening," boomed the familiar voice of Conrad Morse. "I knew you'd be up and about tonight. I also knew you'd want to hear this startling news only from me. We just nabbed four of your operatives conducting an illegal surveillance near Lionel Cooper's estate."

Talbot snapped upright in his chair with such force that the heavy book on his lap flipped end over end across the room and crushed one of his crystal golf trophies.

"What the hell are you talking about?" he hissed.

"Oh, come now, you know perfectly well what I'm talking about," said Morse. "What is your explanation for this outrageous covert action?"

"You can't seriously expect me to answer that question!"

"I realize it goes against all your instincts as a professional keeper of dirty national secrets, but this time you have no choice but to tell me the truth," said Morse.

Talbot cleared his throat. "Now see here, Conrad. I know this must look a bit peculiar but there *is* a rational explanation for it. As it turns out, the neighborhood near Lionel Cooper's residence is of paramount interest to us tonight. We have reason to believe a foreign terrorist is hiding there."

"A foreign terrorist is skulking about in Cambridge? Why wasn't I notified?"

Talbot's eyes were tightly closed. He was trying to invent a plausible story, one that would at least temporarily satisfy the suspicious FBI Director. "Because, against all odds and to my immense embarrassment, a terrorist in our custody escaped from a hospital in Washington. Following a tip that he might have fled to Cambridge, we set up a security net. By sheer coincidence, it happened to be close to Cooper's home. Naturally, we hoped to nab the man quickly and smuggle him back to his prison cell before anyone found out we had dropped the ball. You were the last person I wanted to know about this fiasco. Vanity, I suppose. Surely you can understand that?"

Morse chuckled. "A foreign terrorist slips out of your grasp and his first thought is, shit, I better get my ass to Cambridge? Why? Is he enrolled at Harvard?"

Talbot decided to try taking the offensive. "Wait just a damned minute," he said sternly. "What were *your* people doing hanging around Cooper's home tonight? I think it's *you* who owe *me* an explanation! Are you still investigating that ridiculous jewelry box story? Is that because you know something important about it that you conveniently neglected to tell me?"

Morse paused. "Don't play games with me! It's *you* who will tell *me* everything you know about Lionel Cooper and Helen Rutz and that jewelry box," he said. "And you will do it now!"

"Like hell I will!"

"You have no sensible option," continued Morse. "Tell me now or I'm going to alert the press that the CIA has misplaced a terrorist and is desperately trying to cover it up."

"I don't blame you for doubting me. But my foreign terrorist story is dreadfully close to the truth," said Talbot. "As close as I dare get. I must ask you to accept it as gospel for the moment. I am not at liberty to discuss any other details concerning this delicate matter. My lips have been sealed by the President himself."

"Damn you!" exploded Morse. "You and the President are working hand-in-glove, under the table, on something only the two of you know about? That kind of clandestine maneuver is frowned upon in a democracy, Charles."

"Of course it is," said Talbot. "But as you are well aware, it is occasionally necessary to improvise in order to preserve the security of this great nation. The President and I know exactly what we are doing. If you could talk to him about the situation we find ourselves in, I'm confident you would agree with our bold strategy. Incidentally, I recommend you do not contact him about this. Not if you value your job."

There was a long pause. "I'm, uh, extremely disappointed to hear you say that," said Morse. "But I'm also a realist. These things do happen. I've been involved in a couple of stealthy deals with the Big Enchilada myself."

"I know that. Please note that I didn't demand an explanation from you when I heard about those deals. Why? Because I knew you couldn't tell me what was really going on without incriminating the President."

Another long pause. "What can I do to help?" asked Morse.

Talbot felt the painful knots in his neck and shoulders relax. "Please release my operatives at once. There is a critical action in progress inside the Cooper Building. The slightest deviation in timing could prove fatal to the participants."

"Consider it done," said Morse. "You know, I was going to buy a pair of coconuts to dazzle you with when next we met in private. But now I'm convinced even coconuts would be too small to impress a man like you, Charles. I don't know what you and the President are involved in, but it surely requires nuts of a circumference I could never hope to match."

*

Conrad Morse hung up the phone and stared bleakly across his desk into the worried eyes of Assistant Director Bill Williams.

"Shit-oh-dear," said Morse. He slammed his fist down on his desk.

"Don't tell me we're going to let the prisoners go?" asked Williams. "If we keep the pressure on those men, they'll eventually crack and tell us everything we want to know!"

"Pipe down," said Morse. He put his feet up on his desk and closed his eyes. "Let me think."

Williams dropped his eyes and studiously examined the intricate pattern on his necktie.

Morse thought, *Charles Talbot said there was an action inside the Cooper Building tonight. Is he searching for the jewelry box? How could he know where the box is when I don't? Did Redline manage to slip past my agents? What's so interesting about that damned box, anyway? Why would both the President and the CIA Director risk their careers just to get a peek at it? For that matter, is it the jewelry box they're really after? Or is it something else entirely? Something they don't want me to know about?*

"Alright," said Morse. He opened his eyes and put his feet back on the floor. "Release the four men we arrested tonight."

Bill Williams made a face. "Damn it!"

"Don't ask me to explain," said Morse. "There's more going on here than I can tell you."

"I can see that. But you're okay with everything, sir? It all makes sense to you?"

"Of course," lied Morse. "I'm still in control of the elements that matter to the Bureau. How long will it take for you to process the prisoners and get them back on the street?"

"Not long. Why do you ask?"

"That might be a problem. If those men were still in our custody in, oh, I don't know, say another two hours or so. Get my drift, Mr. AD? Make sure the usual bureaucratic snarl is in full swing. Before you release those men, have Smiley and Wilson break into Lionel Cooper's residence and search it from top to bottom. Tell the famous man the FBI just got an anonymous tip that a terrorist is hiding under his bed."

"Wow," said Williams. He stood up and shook the wrinkles out of his slacks. "That's a good one. I know you can't tell me what's really going on, sir. But I'd give anything to know."

"I'll tell you this much, Bill," said Mr. FBI. He folded his hands behind his head and settled back in his chair. "An extremely arrogant man, who is currently so preoccupied with tuning his own fiddle that he hasn't noticed the world around him just burst into flames, has lied to me for the last fucking time."

CHAPTER TWENTY-NINE

Jim Redline barreled off the elevator into Lionel Cooper's apartment and beheld a macabre scene so unlike what he had expected that it took him a full two seconds to respond to it.

Sprawled awkwardly across a black leather chair, curiously dressed in a white silk kimono festooned with fire-breathing scarlet dragons, Lionel Cooper was being viciously assaulted by a small, olive-skinned, heavily bearded man.

In two strides, Redline erased the ten feet of space that separated him from the violence and grabbed the intruder by his shoulder and the seat of his pants. The man had a lethal grip on Cooper's slender neck. Redline caught a glimpse of Cooper's eyes—bulging blue marbles in a mottled face—enough to see that he was still alive and in a state of mortal terror. Redline jerked the attacker off his feet and hurled him through the air like a sack of garbage. The small man spun and landed lightly on the balls of his feet, ready for combat. He had Cooper's pearl-handled pistol in his hand.

"I didn't expect you so soon," said the intruder calmly.

Redline didn't answer because he was already flying through the air like a human torpedo, his powerful legs extended in front of his body like twin battering rams. The pistol cracked twice. The first slug zipped past Redline's ear. The second clipped the thick rubber heel on his left shoe and ricocheted away. Even as he fired the pistol, the bearded man was scrambling to avoid a collision. But Redline's left foot caught the man's shoulder squarely and the heavy impact jarred the pistol from his grip. The gun somersaulted across the room, bounced on the carpet and disappeared under a black sofa. Redline crashed to the floor, rolled, jumped up and prepared to charge again.

The intruder's expressionless eyes searched for his weapon, then swiveled and locked on Redline.

"Jim," wheezed Cooper, "don't underestimate that little shit! He's Mustafa Rashid!"

Cooper's chest was slick with vomit, his bottom lip split and swollen. Blood dripped from his nose into his open mouth. A stream of urine spiraled down his calf and into his white slipper. He was gulping air and coughing blood, trying desperately to hang on to consciousness.

"Fancy meeting you here, Mustafa," said Redline. "Out slumming tonight?"

Hands weaving a deadly design, fingers curved into talons, Mustafa Rashid crouched, waiting patiently for his opponent to make the first move.

"Jim?" said the terrorist, snapping a curious look at Cooper. "Jim *who?* You know this man, Mr. Cooper?"

Redline lunged at Mustafa, but the nerves in his left foot had been numbed by the force of the bullet hitting his heel. He momentarily lost his balance and sank to one knee.

In a flash, Mustafa vaulted over a glass coffee table and raced out of sight. Redline steadied himself, then quickly pursued the man down a short hallway. He could hear Mustafa slamming drawers in a room to his right. Redline eased around a corner into a brightly-lit kitchen. His back pressed against a stainless steel refrigerator, gripping a wicked-looking carving knife in his right hand, Mustafa smiled again. He tested the edge of the blade against his thumbnail and said, "Welcome to death, Jim Who."

Slashing the air in every direction, Mustafa crept forward. When he was close enough to kill, he executed an expert feint he had used successfully more times than he could count and drove his knife straight at Redline's pounding heart.

Redline twisted, jumped as high as he could and hacked at Mustafa's arm with the edge of his hand. The blow forced the tip of the knife down, but the blade sliced a long gash in Redline's thigh. Mustafa was too close to punch with his fist but Redline whipped his elbow around in a compact arc and connected with the side of the little man's neck. Mustafa staggered and nearly went down. Redline dropped his right shoulder and caught Mustafa under the chin with a crushing uppercut. Mustafa dropped the knife and fell to his knees. Redline wasted a precious moment pressing the palm of his hand against the stinging cut in his leg in a futile attempt to stop the bleeding. Barely conscious, Mustafa groped blindly for the knife, found it and made a desperate lunge at Redline's groin. Redline grabbed Mustafa's wrist, twisted the knife out of his hand, then kneed him hard in the face. Mustafa slammed over on his back and slid across the polished kitchen floor like a sack of grain. The top of his head collided with the narrow edge of the steel refrigerator door with a sound like a pumpkin falling off a two-story building.

Redline picked up the knife and limped over to where Mustafa lay in a heap. Clutching a handful of oily black hair, Redline jerked the terrorist upright. Mustafa opened his eyes and tried to spit in Redline's face but couldn't get the thick liquid beyond his own lips. Blood-streaked saliva dribbled through the coarse black hair of his beard in sticky threads.

"You may kill my earthly body, American," gargled Mustafa through a stew of clotted blood and phlegm. "But you can never destroy my immortal soul! I will enjoy eternity in a golden paradise a filthy infidel like you can never hope to see!"

"I'm happy for you, Mustafa," said Redline. He pressed the knife's razor edge against Mustafa's hairy throat.

"No, Jim, stop! I beg you!" Cooper staggered into the kitchen. He slumped against a marble countertop. "Mustafa is much more valuable alive than dead!"

Redline craned his neck so he could look over his shoulder at Cooper. "What the hell are you talking about? Everyone in the country wishes this psycho was dead!"

"Jim, there's so much you don't know." mumbled Cooper. "Give me a chance to explain. Please don't kill that man. I need him!"

Redline looked into Mustafa's flat black eyes.

"Jim, listen to me!" Cooper hung his head and coughed. Blood dribbled from his nose and splashed on the countertop. His knees gave way and he slid to the floor. "Don't kill him!"

"Sorry, Lionel," said Redline wearily. "You should have said something sooner. He's gone."

*

Redline gently scooped Cooper off the floor and carried him into the master suite. He laid him on the bed and then limped into the bathroom. He soaked a thick black bath towel in cold water, came back to the bedroom and cleaned the blood and vomit from Cooper's face, neck and hands. When he finished, Redline threw the towel on the floor, grabbed the phone next to the bed and punched in two numbers.

"Lyman," he said. "Wake up! It's Jim. I said, wake up, damn it! I'm in Lionel's apartment. He's injured. Bring the Land Rover to the front door and wait for us. Never mind! Just do it! We'll be down shortly."

"Can't go down there," mumbled Cooper. "We leave, we die. Mustafa told me there are CIA assassins waiting downstairs with orders to kill me if he doesn't do it first."

"If there are CIA assassins downstairs, how do you figure I got up here?" asked Redline. He returned to the bathroom, wet another towel and knotted it around the deep gash in his leg. Then he rummaged through the medicine cabinet and found a bottle of painkillers. He swallowed two pills, put the bottle in his pants pocket and came back to the bedroom.

Cooper had raised himself up on his elbows. "Right," he said, frowning. "The assassins are not downstairs or you wouldn't be up here. So where the hell are they? Did you kill them, Jim?"

"Try to stand up," said Redline. "We have to get out of here." He took Cooper by the arm and helped him off the bed. "Can you walk or should I carry you?"

"I can walk," said Cooper. "Actually, I feel much better now. But answer my question while I get some things from my safe."

"This is what I know. There were some strange men hanging around the front gate a few minutes ago," said Redline. He watched as Cooper twirled the dials on a wall safe that had been concealed behind a framed picture of Richard Nixon waving his famous two-fingered goodbye from the steps of Air Force One. "Two FBI agents collared them, stuffed them into a car and drove off. I heard one prisoner protesting vigorously that he was an undercover CIA operative. But the FBI either didn't believe him or didn't care. I caught most of what went down from behind some thick cover in Mrs. Randolph's front yard. Looked and sounded to me like a serious interagency squabble of some kind. If they get it straightened out before the sun comes up, they'll be back. The CIA can't leave Mustafa here. By the way, I heard my name mentioned. This isn't just about you, Lionel. What the hell is going on?"

"Yes, I imagine you're curious about why the CIA would send Mustafa Rashid after me," said Cooper. His distended lower lip wobbled painfully with every word he spoke. "Lionel Cooper, national treasure, revered by millions of loyal fans, right? Suddenly a target for CIA assassins? What crime against America has the great author committed?" He reached into his safe and extracted a thick bound document and several banded packets of currency. He held the document aloft and said, "Jim, this is a Top Secret CIA report created during the Cold War that, uh, conveniently fell into my hands shortly after you left to begin your search for Helen Rutz's jewelry box. Believe it or not, it's full of information about the KGB and mind control and Fidel Castro and, yes, Lee Harvey Oswald. This report—supported by the jewelry box and the general's notes—will enable me to pry the lid off a scandal in the White House so outrageous I think it will topple our reigning President and probably several of his allies. Biggest story of my life. And I have you to thank for it, Jim. If you hadn't taken an interest in the Helen Rutz inquiry, I would never have tumbled to this mad scheme."

Redline shook his head. "Are you serious? You want to take on the President of the United States because of an old jewelry box and a musty report? This is what almost got us both killed tonight? It's one thing to smear an occasional careless bureaucrat. Or even uncover a connection between the mob and our government. But confronting the top man in the entire civilized world? He'll kill you, Lionel. Or someone hired to protect him will kill you whether the President orders it done or not. And they'll probably take me out, too, just because I'm here."

"Could happen," said Cooper. His pale eyes were dancing. "Pretty damned exciting, isn't it, Jim? Oh, come on, admit it! You've been hoping something on this scale would come crawling out of the sewer one of these days. Are we big league now, or what? Hang on a moment while I get out of these disgusting rags. I can't think clearly when I'm filthy."

Cooper slipped out of his ruined garments, walked into a large closet and emerged dressed in a clean shirt, slacks and loafers. Despite his battered appearance, he seemed to be almost fully recovered from his ordeal. Even energized.

"Take this money, Jim." Cooper handed Redline two packets of cash. "We're going to have to go undercover to insure that one of us lives to tell this bizarre tale to the American public. In forty-eight hours or less we should be able to move around freely again. We can come right back here and put the finishing touches on the investigation. Believe it or not, in the last few minutes I've formulated a damned good plan for extricating both of us from this nightmare. I'll explain it to you as soon as we're safely away from the Cooper Building. Where's your car? Lyman and I can drop you there. We need to split up."

"And here I thought you and I would spend a quiet evening figuring out who stole the jewelry box," said Redline. "Or who told whoever stole it where the damned thing was. Silly me."

"We'll have that conversation soon, Jim," said Cooper. "Can you carry Rashid on that injured leg? He's proof that the CIA tried to kill me tonight. I'm going to hide the little bastard's body until I'm ready for him to make a prime-time appearance. Can you see it? National television? The notorious Mustafa Rashid, resting in a tub full of chipped ice, dead eyes staring straight into the camera? This incriminating CIA report perched on his chest? Dan Rather will crap a ring around the moon."

Redline sighed, closed his eyes and squeezed the bridge of his nose. "Yeah, I can see it. Tell me this. Where did you get that CIA report, anyway? Documents like that don't just fall out of the sky. Who gave it to you?"

"It's a fascinating story, Jim," said Cooper. "But too complicated to be told tonight."

"That's what I thought. Should we be worried about asking Lyman to help us out tonight? Remember, I think there's a good chance someone close to you has been leaking information to your enemies."

"Ha!" said Cooper. "Lyman? Tina Romero, maybe. No way it's Lyman."

Redline grunted and headed for the kitchen. "I can tell you're sure we're going to survive this thing," he said. "Know what I think? I think if we get past the front gate, it'll be a miracle."

Cooper tagged along and watched Redline drape Mustafa's body across his broad shoulder. "Oh, we're going to get through the front gate, Jim," said Cooper. "And then we're going to do a lot more than just *survive* this thing. A lot more! I feel it in my bones. Don't you?"

"I feel something in my bones alright," panted Redline as he limped toward the elevator. "Pretty sure it's panic."

CHAPTER THIRTY

Agent Smiley and Agent Wilson raced back to the Cooper Building. They found the front gate open, the front door unlocked They had been told that Agent Orson Dean and his team were, in fact, CIA operatives conducting an approved covert mission. Consequently, they would be released from custody and returned to the estate in approximately one hour. Agent Smiley and Agent Wilson quickly located two brutalized naked bodies in an office on the first floor. They jimmied the fire door, pounded up the stairs and, guns drawn, rushed into Lionel Cooper's apartment.

After a rapid room-by-room search, Agent Smiley and Agent Wilson thundered back down the stairs and raced down the long gravel driveway to the garage. Ten minutes later, a breathless Agent Smiley stood outside in the dark talking to Director Talbot on his cell phone.

"A young woman and a young man," he panted. "Dead in an office on the main floor. Naked as the day they were born and carved up like Christmas turkeys. No one in Cooper's apartment. Evidence of foul play in the living room, kitchen and bedroom. Bloody bath towels and a large kimono soaked in urine and vomit. Strong aroma of cordite in the living room. Someone recently fired a gun there."

"No sign of Cooper or the jewelry box?"

"No, sir. There is no one in the apartment over the garage, either. Agent Wilson and I surmise that Cooper somehow survived a murderous attack and fled the scene. We further surmise he may not be alone."

"I've just been told Redline never arrived at his house. He's probably with Cooper."

258

"Should we search the other rooms in the main building for the jewelry box, sir?"

"How long would that take?"

"Two days."

"Fuck."

"Yes, sir."

"This isn't going to work, is it?"

"No, sir."

"Alright, bail out. Leave everything just the way you found it. It was worth a shot."

Agent Smiley folded his cell phone, dropped it in his jacket pocket and looked up at the stars. "This is weird," he said.

"What now?" asked Agent Wilson. He turned his back and urinated on the gravel driveway.

"Pizza," said Agent Smiley. "On a night like this, you can't go back to the office without pizza."

*

A frustrated Agent Orson Dean pondered his new situation. In the middle of an intense grilling by a team of foul-tempered FBI agents, he and the three operatives under his command had suddenly been released from custody. No explanation for their change in status was given. A grim-faced uniformed FBI motor pool employee drove Agent Dean and his people back across the river in an unmarked van and dropped them in front of the Cooper Building.

As the van sped away, Agent Dean gave it the finger. Then he and his troops checked their weapons and jogged through the open gate and up to the front door. Agent Dean glanced at the glowing dial on his watch. Less than an hour before sunrise. The plush residential neighborhood that bordered Cooper's property would soon begin to stir. Agent Dean could think of no earthly reason Rashid would be loitering inside the building now. *That little sand rat, he thought. Thanks to the FBI, Rashid has probably snuffed a dozen innocent Americans by now and is halfway back to his desert hideaway. But it's worth a quick look. Besides, I have to be sure Rashid killed Cooper before he took off.*

"Okay, listen up," whispered Agent Dean. "We need to bring this mission to a close quickly. If, by some miracle, Rashid is still on the premises, I'll either shoot him or flush him out. If you see the little shit, kill him. No 'halt-who-goes-there' crap. We're here to make sure this madman doesn't leave the area alive. In fact, no one is to leave here alive tonight except the four of us. We're talking big-time national security, people. It would not be an exaggeration to say that the lives of countless innocent Americans may depend on the decisions we make here in the next fifteen minutes."

"Oh, great," mumbled one of Agent Dean's men. "No pressure there."

"Shut up, Douglas. Pressure is our friend. Keeps us sharp. We thrive on pressure."

"Yes, sir."

Agent Dean waited two minutes while the others dispersed. Then he glided into the dark building. He could not remember a time in his entire career when he had felt so jazzed. Weapon in hand, he quickly checked the office nearest the front door and then scurried down the carpeted hallway. He paused outside Tina Romero's office, listened for a moment, and cautiously opened the door. He used the barrel of his gun to snap on the overhead light.

"Holy crap," he whispered. He stared at the two naked bodies sprawled on the floor. *Rashid, you pervert,* thought Agent Dean, *you enjoyed this, didn't you?* He stepped back into the hallway, closed the office door and rapidly checked the remaining rooms on the first floor. He found nothing.

*

Fifteen minutes later, Agent Dean flopped down on a black suede sofa in Lionel Cooper's living room, put his feet up on a glass coffee table and punched a button on his cell phone to speed-dial Director Talbot.

"Report."

"I'm sorry for the delay, sir, but earlier tonight two idiots from the FBI—"

"Say no more about that. I'm the one who arranged for your release."

"Yes, sir. I'm calling from Cooper's apartment. Rashid is gone. And—"

"How did you get up there? I figured Rashid would disable the elevator when he left the building."

"Unfortunately, sir, I gave Rashid my only copy of the special key to the elevator earlier this evening. Luckily, the fire door on the main floor was open, so I took the stairs."

"That's strange."

"Yes, sir. No one up here, dead or alive. There are bloodstains in the kitchen, master bedroom and master bathroom. Plenty of evidence that at least one person suffered a devastating injury here tonight. I found a bloody knife on the kitchen floor. I smelled cordite but I didn't find a gun. Before I came upstairs, I discovered two naked corpses in a private office on the first floor. An adult male and an adult female. They were . . . well, sir, it was definitely Rashid's work."

Agent Dean could almost hear the gears grinding in Talbot's head.

"No sign of Lionel Cooper? That's bad."

"Even worse, it looks like whoever was still alive when the fighting was over just rode the elevator to the main floor and walked out the front door. Probably while my men and I were being roughed up by the FBI, sir. I asked one of my people to check the garage. He just called. No one out there, either."

"Damn," said Mr. CIA.

"Yes, sir. I just want to say, sir, if the FBI had not interfered tonight, I'm confident this mission would have gone off without a hitch. We had it planned so perfectly—"

"Can it," said Mr. CIA. "It's unprofessional to cry over spilt milk."

"Yes, sir. But at the risk of offending you further, may I remind you that my crew is on the grounds outside and dawn is only moments away. If someone in the neighborhood spots them and calls the local police, we're screwed. Unless you're prepared to go public with this action, I think we should depart immediately. It isn't necessary to sweep the second and third floors. There is no one in this building. No one still breathing, anyway."

"You sometimes state the obvious as if it were a divine revelation, Agent Dean," said Talbot.

"Yes, sir." Agent Dean tried to think of something brilliant to say that would salvage his rapidly vanishing career. Nothing occurred to him.

"You and your people get out of sight right now. As soon as you're a safe distance away, I want you to make an anonymous call to the Cambridge police and report suspicious activity at the Cooper Building."

"Could you repeat that instruction, sir?"

"Call the cops, Agent Dean. What we need now is help from local law enforcement. Unlike us, they can operate out in the open. Cooper is a national celebrity. When the Cambridge police find the two bodies on the main floor and realize that Cooper may have been kidnapped or killed, they'll call in the FBI. We have a friend in the FBI who is sympathetic to our needs. He'll make sure I'm kept informed about everything the FBI and the police are doing."

"We have a friend in the FBI, sir? How fortunate for us, sir."

"Cooper may have survived Rashid's attack. Or, Rashid might have killed him and hidden the body somewhere in the building or on the grounds before he ran off. It's also possible that Cooper is injured but still alive. When the police or the FBI find him, I'll know about it before anyone else does. If he's dead, the game is over and we win. But if Cooper is alive and conscious, he becomes a problem for us. Of course, he'll be traumatized. It should be easy to discredit any incoherent statements he makes during the first hour or so he is under the protection of law enforcement. Nevertheless, I want you to stand by, Agent Dean. Cooper cannot be allowed to live long enough to start making sense."

"Yes, sir! I would like nothing better than to be given a chance to complete this mission myself, sir. But what about Rashid?"

"Look for him in all the usual places," said Talbot, "and kill him if you find him. But if he vanishes into the woodwork, don't worry about it, Agent Dean. I can handle that.

CHAPTER THIRTY-ONE

Jim Redline drove his rental car around for almost an hour near Suffolk Downs in Boston looking for the perfect motel. Then he sat in his car outside the office of a particularly seedy place trying to decide if the joint was crummy enough that he could walk in looking like a serial killer and rent a room without being challenged. There were only three banged-up old cars in the gravel parking lot and not a single human being in sight. Good omen.

No guts, no glory, he told himself. He untied the towel from his gashed leg and briefly examined the wound. Finding that it had almost stopped bleeding, he tossed the towel on the backseat, got out of the car and limped into the office.

"Welcome to the Long Shot Motel," rasped a pale, emaciated young man. He had a navy blue five o'clock shadow, a lantern jaw and big ears shaped like conch shells. He lit an unfiltered cigarette, blew smoke through his red-veined nose, leaned across the battered wooden counter and gave Redline a thorough once-over. "Well, what I can do for you, Mr. Rockefeller," he said. "Want to buy a quart of plasma?"

"Looks worse than it is," muttered Redline. "I just need a room. Nothing fancy."

"You're telling me our bridal suite is beyond your budget. Got it. Twenty-four bucks if you plan to stay all night." The man grinned, exposing slimy gray teeth and puffy gums. "That would be cash, of course. We don't take credit cards, checks or beaver pelts. If you promise to bleed to death before morning, I can cut that price in half."

Redline handed the man a twenty and a ten. "Keep the change," he said.

"Thank you. Do you plan to fill out a registration card?" The man pointed his blue chin at Redline's ripped and bloody pants. "It's optional."

"I'd rather not," said Redline.

"If you're going to willfully circumvent the law by refusing to register, it will cost you another ten bucks," said the man cheerfully. He coughed hard against the back of his hand, pulled a plastic flask from under the counter and took a long pull. "Chronic allergies," he wheezed. "Booze is the only thing that seems to help. Hope it doesn't offend you that I drink on the job. My doctor ordered me to do it. He says I'm like those folks who are allowed to legally smoke marijuana to control their cancer pain."

"What's your name?" asked Redline.

"Wayne. What's yours?"

Redline produced another ten-dollar bill and Wayne pushed a flat metal key across the counter.

"Worked here long, Wayne?"

"Seems like forever sometimes. Room seventeen," said Wayne. "Straight across the parking lot. Television set's on the fritz but the shower works great."

"What time do you get off today, Wayne?" asked Redline. He pulled a fat roll of bills from his pocket and rolled it back and forth on the counter.

Wayne took a step backward. "Whoa, hold it right there, big fella! All my after-work companions have tits. So if you haven't got a nice set of jugs under that dirty shirt, we have nothing more to discuss about how I plan to spend my leisure time today."

Redline smiled. "I didn't mean that the way you took it, Wayne. I need someone to run a few errands for me. Pick up some personal items. I thought maybe you'd like to score a little extra money when you get off work today."

"Oh," said Wayne. A shrewd look flitted across his bloodshot eyes. He took a deep drag on his cigarette. "What kind of personal items? Never mind, I can guess. Cocaine? Meth? Hell, don't matter none to me, pal. Whatever your poison, I can damn sure get it for you."

"A six-pack of beer and a submarine sandwich. Some fresh clothes and a few toiletries." Redline put the roll of bills back in his pocket.

Wayne searched Redline's eyes. "No problem," he said. "But I don't work cheap, bubba. No minimum wage for ol' Wayne. Especially when I have no idea who the fuck you are. I might be taking a fatal risk here. You wanted by the law?"

"I'm wanted by an angry ex-wife," said Redline. "Step over to my room when you're finished here. We'll draw up the papers."

Wayne coughed. "Draw up the papers? Hey, that's pretty good! Like a couple lawyers, right? Yeah, good idea, write everything down for me, sizes and all that. My memory isn't worth a crap these days. They say severe allergies will do that to a man."

Redline tossed two twenty-dollar bills on the counter. "Maybe that will help you remember to stop by later, Wayne."

Wayne grabbed the bills and stuffed them into his shirt pocket. "How could I forget," he said.

Redline stepped outside, his face pointed toward the ground, hopped into his car, drove twenty feet and parked as close to the front door of Room Seventeen as possible. Still looking at the ground, he limped to the rickety plywood door, twisted the key in the lock and slipped inside.

*

Wayne lit a fresh smoke and propped his bony elbows on the counter, thinking about the big man and all his lovely money. Out of the corner of his eye, he caught movement in a dark hallway at the far end of the office.

"Did you get a good look at that guy, Selma? Big as a house and handsome, too. Reminded me of Matt Dillon. Remember him? Sheriff of Dodge City, Kansas? Tougher than baked shoe leather."

A short, heavy black woman eased out of the shadows. She put her hands on her ample hips and flared her nostrils. "I saw him," she said. "Matt Dillon was a character on a television show. That guy was the *real* law, Wayne. You in deep shit now."

"The law? No way! He's just a nice guy having a bad day. His ex-wife caught him with the maid and tried to cut his balls off. He's slumming until she cools down."

"Snap out of it, Wayne!" said Selma. "He mesmerized you with all that cash. I saw him waving it under your ugly nose. Your eyes bugged out like you was a starving rat and the money was a wedge of cheese. You an even bigger fool than I think you are if you go to that man's room tonight. Wayne, you *volunteered* to buy him hard drugs! He didn't have to use no fancy tricks, no entrapment, no nothin'! You already busted! You told that drug cop *exactly* how you really make money in this dump."

Wayne turned two shades paler. "What would a drug cop want with a little fish like me? I don't know jack! I just get useful stuff for people that need it."

Selma snorted. "You history, baby. Look like I'm finally going to get to work behind the counter."

"I better check this dude out," said Wayne. He coughed so hard he doubled over until his pimply forehead whacked the counter. "I'll get Manny to talk to him. He'll know right away if the guy's a cop or not."

"Manny? Manny a nut case! You put that fool in a room with a drug cop and the cop gonna leave feet first, Wayne. Manny gonna waste that sucker!"

Wayne took a pull on his flask, wiped his lips on his shirtsleeve and ground out his cigarette. He looked at Selma through half-lidded eyes. "So, what's your point, Selma?"

CHAPTER THIRTY-TWO

Stuart McManus and his buxom young wife Janice were eating an early breakfast on their deck. Just as Stuart was pouring himself a second cup of coffee, the maid appeared, apologized for interrupting them, and said, "Mr. Lionel Cooper has arrived and is asking to see you both. He looks . . . injured. I showed him into the den."

Stuart got quickly to his feet. "Lionel wouldn't come here at this time of day without calling first! What do you mean he looks injured, Daisy?"

"I think someone punched him in the face," said Daisy.

"Oh no," said Janice. "Shouldn't we call the police or an ambulance or something?"

"I don't think so," said Stuart. "If Lionel wanted help from the authorities, he would have taken care of that himself. Get our first aid kit and meet me in the den."

Muttering to herself, Janice raced off. Stuart gave his maid a stern look. She had wandered over to the deck's railing and was staring into space. "Pay attention, Daisy. Tell *no one* that Mr. Cooper is here until further notice. And allow no one to come into this house without my permission. Do you understand?"

"I understand," said Daisy. "Tell no one."

*

Lionel Cooper sprawled across a sofa, a thin gauze bandage fluttering from his lower lip. Janice McManus sat on the floor near him and gently stroked his hand. Stuart McManus stood at parade rest in front of a cold brick fireplace, listening intently while Cooper finished telling his startling tale.

"Until I inform the citizens of this country about the shockingly reckless activities of our President and his ass-kissing sidekick in Central Intelligence, I'll have a bull's eye painted on my forehead," said Cooper. "The national leaders want me dead and they came damned close to getting their way last night. If it hadn't been for the serendipitous intervention of Jim Redline, Mustafa Rashid would have strangled me in my own home and no one would ever have discovered what befell me."

"That's an incredible story," said Janice. "Even though I'm sure every word of it is true, Lionel, I'm having difficulty accepting it. Maybe because I don't want to live in a world that can be so treacherous."

"Stuart," said Cooper, "this all started when you told me about NASA's need to manage the moods of the astronauts training for the Mars expedition and the rumor about a connection between that need and information the government has been sitting on about Cold War mind-control experiments. I put your story together with something Jim and I are working on and it led to my startling discovery."

"It's a miracle that you escaped," said Stuart, "and found your way to our home this morning. I'm touched that you thought of Janice and me at a critical time like this, Lionel. We'll do everything we can to keep you safe."

"I know you will," said Cooper. "I can't imagine being anywhere else at this moment. When we left the Cooper Building, Lyman and I drove to, uh, a warehouse I own in Boston. We covered Rashid's body with dry ice and locked the CIA report in a safe. Then Lyman brought me here."

"Where's Jim Redline?" asked Janice. "Seems like he should be around to protect you."

"Undercover," said Cooper. "I told him to maintain a low silhouette until the coast is clear. One of us has to live through the next couple of days. If something happens to me, it will be up to Jim to get this story to the public. I told him where Lyman and I were going to put Rashid's body and the CIA report so he can retrieve them at the proper time if that becomes necessary."

"Wait a minute. You're expecting to be killed?" asked Stuart. "While you're a guest in our house?"

"Anything is possible," said Cooper. "I might be safe here. But the world's largest intelligence agency is looking for me, Stuart. And they're very good at finding people."

"Where's Lyman?" asked Janice. "He could have stayed here, too."

"At my insistence, he's on his way out of the country," said Cooper. "He'll live out his remaining years in comfort, thanks to the commissions I paid him over the years. He took many risks on my behalf."

"He wasn't just your gardener?" asked Stuart.

"No," said Cooper. "Lyman had invaluable connections to the underworld. He collected information for me about certain people in ways that I could not afford to have my enemies or public know about. The transactions were dangerous and expensive. Rarely could I use the information directly, but when I did, it was devastatingly effective. Jim Redline would not have done that kind of nasty work for me. I admire Jim but, like his late father, he operates under a set of rules that prevent him from doing anything that isn't above board. Lyman has a much more realistic view of the world. He and I understand each other perfectly."

"And the warehouse in Boston?" asked Janice. "That's where you keep this provocative information?"

"Yes, but the authorities will never link me to that warehouse," said Cooper. "In fact, I hadn't seen it before last night. Lyman has done a first-rate job of cataloguing the various tapes, films, photographs and confidential documents he obtained for me over many years. I'll decide later what to do with all that incendiary material, now that he is no longer here to watch over it."

"What did Jim say when you told him about the warehouse and your secret relationship with Lyman?" asked Stuart.

"Not one word," said Cooper. "I'm sure he was disappointed. But he said nothing."

"You trust Jim Redline?" asked Janice.

"Not really," said Cooper. "But I trust my ability to predict his behavior. If something happens to me, Jim will do everything he can to make sure the public finds out what I've discovered. He will simply consider it his duty."

"Tell us, if you can," said Stuart, "how a man as worldly as the President of the United States could fall prey to a myth as transparently false as 'total mind control.' If he thinks his enemies possess a hypnotic technique they can use against him, surely his advisors can persuade him of the scientific truth? That total mind control is impossible to achieve?"

"If only it were that simple," said Cooper. He debated the wisdom of telling Stuart and Janice about the tenacity of Club Red and decided against it. "The difference between *total* mind control and mind control that will permit a psychiatrist to influence a hypnotized subject in such a way that the subject feels compelled to carry out a deadly mission is just five letters. This whole thing boils down to a semantic riddle, Stuart, the solution to which even rational people can interpret differently. The President, a man who has often displayed an embarrassing lack of personal courage, looks out across the troubled planet from his rocking chair in the Oval Office and sees olive-skinned fanatics driving trucks loaded with explosives into our embassies and military barracks, blowing themselves to shreds and believing as they do so that their voluntary suicides will earn them eternal martyrdom and a seat in heaven next to Allah. Someone has persuaded them that dying in this particular way will be honored beyond anything they could hope to accomplish while alive here on Earth. The President— who would never volunteer to die for any cause, no matter how honorable—interprets that to mean that these killers, who were once normal people, have been transformed into unstoppable weapons by an evil alchemist who uses black magic to take over their minds. The Chief trembles at the thought that the devil orchestrating these insane suicides is now whispering into the ear of the same wealthy foreign terrorist who has publicly vowed to assassinate him. He'll get me for sure, thinks the President, unless I get him first."

"That's nuts," said Stuart.

"I agree," said Cooper. "The President is so consumed with irrational dread that he has begun to make decisions that imperil every American citizen. He lacks the courage to lead us through these uncertain times."

"I suppose this is a stupid question," said Janice, "but could the President be right? Wouldn't any reasonable person conclude that suicidal killers are not exercising their own free will? That they are doing someone else's bidding because their ability to choose has been taken from them by force or deception?"

Cooper smiled, winced, touched his mangled lip and made a mental note not to smile again. He took a moment to appreciate Janice's familiar cleavage. "There is nothing stupid about that question, Janice," he said. "It's true that some observers will conclude the crazed killers being hurled at western civilization like cannon shells these days are being manufactured en masse and against their will by a purposeful, intelligent and diabolical process of some kind. But since most people are taught that free will is the one gift all human beings are guaranteed by an otherwise detached and silent universe, the majority of us categorize suicide killers as deadly, but statistically insignificant, psychological anomalies. We all know that human beings can choose good over evil. Sometimes we forget that history teaches us people are also free to choose evil over good, and often do so. Convinced that he will soon be swept away by forces beyond his control, the President has interpreted extreme human behavior as a sign that his enemies have found a way to permanently put an end to choice. In effect, he has been psychologically dismantled, not by truth, but by nightmares of his own design."

"I hope you're right," said Stuart. "If I thought there was any chance that my mind could be hijacked by an enemy of the United States and then turned into a weapon, I'd . . . I'd . . . jump off a tall building!"

"Me too," said Janice. "That's the scariest thing I've ever heard."

"Stuart, I need to ask you now for a huge favor," said Cooper.

"Anything, my friend," said Stuart. "Anything at all."

"I want you to organize a press conference to be held on your front lawn tomorrow morning," said Cooper. "Instruct your press agent to tell his media contacts that you are about to be named the new chairman of the Federal Reserve System."

Stuart gasped and said, "But . . . but, Lionel, that position isn't vacant. And I don't want it anyway. I told Congress—"

"I know that," interrupted Cooper. "The point is to get the press curious so they'll come here tomorrow morning to record whatever you're going to say, no matter how preposterous the idea sounds to them. We need national coverage, all of it centered on you. But when the big moment comes for your speech, it will be Lionel Cooper who steps to the microphone. I can talk to the entire country, Stuart, tell them what has happened. As soon as I've finished, I'll be a free man again. No one will dare harm me once the truth is told. Certainly not the CIA."

"Wow," said Janice. "What a great idea!"

"Are you sure?" asked Stuart. "The press will demand proof of your accusations against the President. Can you meet that demand by tomorrow morning?"

Cooper shook his head. "No. I have the proof, but tomorrow is not the time to drag it out before the viewing public. The purpose of tomorrow's press conference is simply to insure that I'll live long enough to do what needs doing."

Stuart stared at Cooper for a long time. Then he gripped the mantel of the fireplace and opened his mouth. Nothing came out.

Janice squeezed Cooper's hand. "You're brilliant, Lionel. Brilliant! There is no one else in the world who could do this."

Stuart McManus turned and walked out of the room. No sooner had he left than Daisy entered the den and said, "You might want to turn on the television, Mrs. McManus. The Cambridge police and the FBI are talking to reporters about some dead people they found in Mr. Cooper's building this morning."

*

"Peterson Detective Agency. How may I help you?"

"This is Daisy Williams. I need to talk to Pamela Peterson immediately. Tell her it's an emergency."

There was a clattering sound and Pamela Peterson's voice said, "Daisy? What's up?"

"I know where he is right this minute," said Daisy. "That has to be worth a lot more than you were going to pay me just to dish a little dirt on the poor guy. I mean we're talking dead people and the FBI and the whole nine yards now. Not just kinky sex with his best friend's wife."

"How the hell can you know where he is right this minute?" asked Pamela. "Haven't you been watching the news? The man is missing and presumed dead. Not even the FBI can find him."

"He's as alive as you are," said Daisy, snapping her gum. "But I want money first. Twice the amount we discussed. Then I'll tell you what I know."

"This is nuts," complained Pamela. "Okay, Daisy, I'll take a chance that you're telling me the truth. The money will be in your account in the next thirty minutes. Get in touch with your bank and confirm that. Then call back and tell me what you know. If you're lying, Daisy, I'll tear your tits off with my bare hands. I swear I will. I don't care if you are my cousin."

Pamela broke the connection and immediately dialed her client.

"Yes," said a soft voice.

"Pamela Peterson, at your service. Hang on to your ass because you're not going to believe this. You hired me because you want to write an unauthorized biography based on confidential interviews with Lionel Cooper's secret enemies, right? But as everyone on the planet knows, things changed dramatically yesterday. The man is all over the national news now. Even the FBI's involved. That means everyone who can spell his name is going to write a book about him. You need an edge, something really special, if you want your book at the top of the list. And what could be better than this—exclusive access to the man himself before anyone else even knows he's still alive?"

"What . . . you're . . . saying . . . can't . . . be . . . true! I'm watching CNN right now, Pamela, along with half the civilized world. The police say they're sure Cooper was murdered in his apartment last night. They expect to locate his body soon. Why would you torture me with false information at a time like this? Are you trying to extort more money from me because you think I'm going to tell you to drop the investigation now that the man is dead? Well, let me explain to you what happens to unethical private detectives who screw around with people like me, young lady . . . "

"Listen to me, you little shit," hissed Pamela. "I'm the professional this time, not you, and I know exactly what I'm doing. If the individual who called me says Cooper is alive and she knows where he is right now, then the son of a bitch is alive and she knows where he is right now! End of story! I'm going to pay her a big chunk of your money so she'll fork over the details. Stay by the phone. You're going to spend the rest of your life thanking me for this or my name isn't Pamela Peterson!"

"If you're lying, Pamela, you'll spend the rest of your life regretting it!"

"Just stay sober and wait for my call, asshole." Pamela hung up and gave the phone the finger. Then she grabbed her purse and ran out of her office like the building was on fire.

CHAPTER THIRTY-THREE

Locked inside his grimy motel room, Jim Redline collapsed on the creaky narrow bed and promptly fell asleep. A pounding headache woke him two hours later. He limped into the bathroom, removed his pants and examined the deep gash in his leg. It was crusted with blood and pus. He wrapped a thin washcloth around a sliver of soap and scrubbed the cut clean.

Then he crawled back into his stiff, blood-soaked pants and sat on the edge of the bed, holding his throbbing head in both hands, thinking about Lionel Cooper, Lyman Wolfe, Mustafa Rashid and everything he had learned in the past few hours. It didn't take long to work it out. This can't fly, he thought. Lionel has finally taken his self-appointed role as national judge and jury too far. The CIA is going to try to kill him. And if they succeed, I'll have to decide whether to finish what he started or walk away. Only a suicidal idiot would . . .

Someone rapped lightly on his door.

"It's me, Wayne," said a muffled voice.

Redline opened the door a crack. Wayne was standing there, his cadaverous blue jaw split by a self-conscious grin.

"Ready to draw up the papers, big guy?" chuckled Wayne. He coughed against the back of his hand and spit a gob of phlegm at the ground.

"Get in here, Wayne," growled Redline. He unhooked the security chain and stepped back.

Two burly police officers shouldered past Wayne and stormed through the doorway. One cop had his revolver drawn, the barrel pointed at the floor. The other one gave Redline a steely look and said,

"I'm Officer O'Neill. This is Officer O'Toole. Put your hands in the air where we can see them."

Officer O'Neill quickly determined there was no one else in the motel room. He nodded at Officer O'Toole. "Clear."

"Have I broken a law, officers?" asked Redline.

"Hell yes, you've broken a law!" yelled Wayne. He stood in the doorway. "This is about you soliciting illegal drugs from me, you stupid shit! I could lose my job!"

Officer O'Neill said, "Could I see some identification, sir?"

Redline fumbled for his wallet and produced his driver's license."You're James T. Redline?" Officer O'Neill flashed the driver's license at Officer O'Toole.

Officer O'Toole raised the barrel of his weapon until it was pointed at the center of Redline's chest. "Well, I'll be damned," he said. "I think this just went from a possible drug bust to World War Three."

"What happened to your leg, Mr. Redline?" asked Officer O'Neill. He removed a pair of steel handcuffs from his belt. "Cut yourself shaving?"

"Listen, officers, Wayne misunderstood me. I did not solicit drugs from him."

"He's lying," shrieked Wayne. "Guy's loaded with cash! Check it out!"

Redline studied Officer O'Toole. *I'm one hiccup away from getting drilled. This rookie is about to shit in his pants . . .*

"There are some very important people downtown who want to talk with you, Mr. Redline," said Officer O'Neill. "But I think you know that. Now face the wall and put your hands behind your back."

Officer O'Neill cuffed Redline and all three men walked out of the room. Wayne lit a cigarette as he watched Officer O'Neill put his hand on Redline's head and guide him into the back seat of a police cruiser. Officer O'Toole radioed the station to say they were bringing in a man identifying himself as James T. Redline.

"Mr. Redline is injured and may require medical attention," said Officer O'Toole. "And we need a tow truck over here." He gave the dispatcher the address of the motel and the license plate number on Redline's rented car.

Light bar flashing, the cruiser sprayed gravel across Wayne's feet as it sped out of the Long Shot Motel's parking lot.

Wayne stood around for a few minutes, smoking and coughing, hoping someone would come out of one of the rooms and ask him what had just happened. No one did. He took his time strolling back to the office. Selma was leaning on the counter.

"You a natural born idiot, Wayne," she said. "Only an idiot would have called the cops. They'll be back, asking questions about this place. Then what you going to do?"

"What in the world is a 'natural born idiot,' Selma?" asked Wayne. He checked his pockets to make sure he had his car keys and the folding cash Redline had given him earlier. Selma had laid this line on him many times. Wayne enjoyed the familiar ritual because he figured it meant that Selma was secretly hot for him, even though she vigorously denied it whenever he got drunk and tried to put the moves on her.

"Mean no one had to show you how to be stupid," said Selma angrily. "You was born already knowin' how to do the dumbest possible thing every chance you get."

Wayne lit a fresh cigarette, blew Selma a kiss and sauntered out the door.

*

Two hours after he was booked, Redline was taken from his cell. Wrists and ankles securely manacled, he was driven in a police ambulance to an unoccupied clinic in a rough part of Boston. Three husky cops walked him into the building through an unlocked back door. The cops pushed him down a dimly lit hallway and into a small room. They forced him to recline on a padded examining table, then secured his arms and legs with heavy elastic straps. Only then did they remove his wrist and ankle restraints.

One of the cops said, "Relax, Mr. Redline. The doctor will be with you shortly."

The three cops walked out of the room laughing.

Twisting his neck, Redline inventoried everything he could see from his position on the table. There were two wheeled carts littered with bedpans, syringes and shiny metal instruments. Colorful charts on the wall displaying human anatomy. Shelves with rows of big glass jars containing pale organs suspended in clear fluid. The stale air reeked of formaldehyde.

The door opened and a man stepped into the room. He closed the door, then walked briskly to the examining table and peered down at Redline. He was wearing a charcoal gray suit and a red tie. The man had wavy silver hair, prominent cheekbones, thin liver-colored lips and electric blue eyes.

"Hello," he said. "How are you feeling?"

"Terrific, thank you. Mind if I use the phone? I'd like to call my attorney."

"You require the services of a doctor," said the man. "Not an attorney."

"You're not a doctor," said Redline.

"Are you feeling any pain?" asked the man. "Dizzy from loss of blood?"

"You're not a doctor," repeated Redline. "I insist that I be allowed to call my attorney."

"You're sure I'm not a doctor? Well then, what am I?" The man strolled around the small room. He stopped next to one of the wheeled carts and picked up a syringe.

"Probably CIA," said Redline. "Maybe FBI."

The man gently put the syringe back on the table. Then he dragged a straight-backed chair next to Redline and sat down. "It's truly a pleasure to meet you, Mr. Redline," he said. "In spite of the fact that you're employed by Lionel Cooper, my sources tell me that you're a pretty decent young man. That makes me confident you and I can settle this mess right now, before the big boys from Washington get here tomorrow morning."

"You're not a big boy from Washington?"

"Actually, I *am* from Washington," said the man. "I'm temporarily in Boston supervising the investigation into the unexplained disappearance of Mr. Lionel Cooper. The other Washington people

278

plan to be here bright and early tomorrow morning. They are quite . . . agitated about all this. You'd be smart to talk to me tonight, Mr. Redline, clear all this up now. Before they get here."

"What's your name?"

"You can call me Dan."

Redline stared at the perforated ceiling tiles above his head. "Well, Dan," he said, "why don't you begin this illegal interrogation by telling me everything I want to know."

Dan laughed out loud. Then he stood up so Redline could see his face. His neon blue eyes were totally mirthless.

"That was damn funny, Jim. May I call you Jim? Tell *you* everything you want to know? One of the best lines I've heard in a long time." Then Dan paused, rubbed his chin. "Well, why not? We're all alone here. What is it you want to know, Jim?"

"You're FBI?"

"Of course. Haven't you been watching the news?"

"No. I've been, uh, a little preoccupied lately."

Dan frowned and crossed his arms over his chest. "So, you're saying you don't know what's been going on? Don't know about the two young people who were slaughtered in the Cooper Building yesterday? Tina Romero and her friend Greg Young?"

Redline blinked and tried to stay focused on an ugly water stain on one of the ceiling tiles. Apparently, the blood on Mustafa Rashid's hands had not come just from Cooper's nose, he thought. Did he kill Tina before he attacked Lionel? Or did the CIA shooters do that?

"And you're going to tell me that you don't know what happened to Cooper, right? Where he is now? Or whether he's dead or alive? Because you weren't there?"

"Right," mumbled Redline.

Dan began to stroll around the room again. "Well, then, I don't like this little game anymore," he said. "New rules, Jim. It's time for you to tell *me* everything I want to know. So, please start talking now."

Redline had absolutely no idea what he should say or do next. "I have the right to consult with an attorney, Dan. And this would be a good time for you to show me some identification. I'm a United States citizen. My civil rights are guaranteed under the Constitution. Or had you forgotten that annoying little detail?"

Dan returned to his chair, plopped down and folded his arms across his chest. "I have some bad news for you, Jim. The rules that protect an ordinary citizen in situations like this have been waived in your case. You have the honor of being classified by the highest possible authority as a potentially serious threat to national security. That means we can take from you the information we need without your permission and without regard for the effect our methods might have on your health. In other words, sooner or later, you're going to tell us everything we want to know."

"You're bluffing," said Redline. He tested the elastic bands that held his arms down. They didn't budge. "Don't try to intimidate me. Threatening an American citizen with physical torture is against the law in this country. Period, end of story."

Dan chuckled. "Sure, but you're not in this country right now. You're in a place most people don't even know exists. It's a special place we designed where dedicated guys like me are free to pry the truth out of stubborn assholes like you. And look how easy you've made this! You voluntarily slipped below the radar. You did such a good job of making yourself invisible that, for all practical purposes, you might as well be dead, Jim. Now is that convenient or what? If we announce to the world tomorrow that Jim Redline died while trying to escape from the law, the world will believe us. So where does that put you? Let me spell it out. It puts you flat on your back under the federal microscope, buck naked and spread-eagled. I can take you apart one cell at a time until you tell me what I want to know, Jim, and no one can stop me."

Redline felt no fear. Only rage. Limitless, searing rage. It felt good. He flexed his powerful muscles against his bonds again, realized that was not the way out, and forced himself to try to buy time. "And what exactly do you want to know, Dan?"

Dan leaned over the examining table and whispered, "There's an old wooden jewelry box, Jim. You know where it is. If you take me to it right now, good things will happen. You won't die fleeing from the law after all. Instead, you'll go home, keep your big fat mouth shut and live a long, happy and prosperous life."

It took Redline several seconds to process what Dan had just told him. *This is about the box? I'm going to die in the back room of a run-down clinic in Boston because I went looking for that stupid jewelry box? The government is willing to kill Tina Romero and Lionel Cooper and me just because of what might be inside that box?*

Redline lowered his voice to a near-whisper. "Is that all, Dan? Well, why didn't you just say so before?"

Dan put both his hands on the examining table and positioned his face directly above Redline's. His breath reeked of stale coffee and fried food. "Very good, Jim," he said. "You've decided to cooperate with me. Not because you're a decent, law-abiding citizen. Uh-uh. Nope. Because you don't want to get your eyelids ripped off. So, talk to me, tough guy. Tell me exactly where that fucking jewelry box is. Right now, before old Dan loses his temper and does something rash with that big needle over there."

"Sure thing," said Redline. He raised his head and spat straight into Dan's sparkling blue eyes.

CHAPTER THIRTY-FOUR

The President was alone in an elegant Victorian suite on the top floor of the Brown Palace Hotel in downtown Denver. He was sitting in a wing chair, watching CNN and nibbling his fingernails to the quick.

An aide glided into the room. "Sir, the governor has arrived and is waiting downstairs with members of his staff and the national press. He asked me to inquire—"

"I need to speak to Director Talbot," said the President sharply. "Tell the governor I'll join him shortly."

The aide vanished for a moment, then returned and pointed to the red telephone next to the President's hand.

"Director Talbot is on your secure line, sir."

"See to it that I'm not disturbed until I complete this call," said the President. He grabbed the phone and barked, "What the hell have you done now, Charles?"

"I beg your pardon, sir?"

"The Cambridge police and agents from the FBI are crawling all over Lionel Cooper's mansion this morning. CNN says two people were found dead in there and Cooper is missing. Tell me this disaster is not connected in any way to our little experiment."

"Relax, Mr. President," said Talbot. "There's no way the events in Cambridge can be connected to either of us."

The President spit on the Persian rug beneath his feet. "I knew it. The other day when you said a 'test case' was necessary, I thought of Lionel Cooper immediately. But I never dreamed you would actually select him. What the hell were you thinking? I detest the man but most

Americans believe he's a national hero! Are you trying to get me assassinated by my own constituency? That is not the path you want to take to the White House, Charles."

"Sir, there is nothing to worry about. I have the situation under control. When Cooper's fate is revealed to his anxious public, the furor will quickly die down."

"And just when can we expect that to happen?" The President jumped to his feet and inspected himself in a large antique wall mirror. He adjusted his Jerry Garcia necktie, smoothed his hair with the palm of his hand and polished his front teeth with the tip of his finger.

"As soon as they locate Cooper's body," responded Talbot. "Apparently he crawled off, like the rat that he is, and croaked behind a garbage can someplace."

"And when they find him dead," whispered the President, "will that be the final proof that your 'test' was an unqualified success? We can proceed immediately with the primary mission?"

"Well," said Talbot, "I must reserve judgment about that until my people have had a chance to analyze the performance of the . . . weapon, sir. I'm afraid considerable patience will be required of you."

"Patience my ass," growled the President. "I get gas when people tell me to be patient."

"It might be wise if you stayed out of Washington for a few days," said Talbot.

"Why?"

"It's important that you distance yourself from the media frenzy that's about to erupt, Mr. President. Some difficult questions will surface in the next few days. People are going to imagine all kinds of unsavory scenarios. They'll make totally unfounded accusations, point fingers in all the wrong directions and look for a scapegoat."

"You think they'll point fingers at me?"

"You know how it goes when a front-page murder isn't solved quickly, sir. Conspiracy theories spread like wildfire. And you can believe me when I tell you this particular murder mystery will never be solved. Some nut case is sure to declare that the government arranged Cooper's death because he had become a big thorn in our collective paw. You are the government, Mr. President. Your enemies in the media are going to ask you some very rude questions. You shouldn't submit to that kind of inquisition before you've had adequate time to fashion an airtight response. After Cooper is found, you and I must review this matter in private before you say one word about it publicly."

Phone in hand, the President strolled over to a large picture window and peered through a layer of yellow smog drifting across the inner city. In the distance, he could just make out a majestic mountain peak.

"Let's cut to the chase, Charles. You're scared shitless. I can hear it in your voice. Something's gone horribly wrong, hasn't it? We're in trouble."

"I just need a little time, sir, to see if . . . I mean, uh, well, to fix anything that might need fixing. It would be a great help to me if you could stay out of town for a few days."

"I've been thinking of going up to Alaska," said the President. "Tag a salmon or two. Bless the oil fields. Make sure the grizzly bears are being protected from tourists."

"They say it's gorgeous up there this time of year."

"I don't like the situation you've put me in," said the President. His voice had turned frigid. "If you trip over your own dick and go down because of this fiasco, Charles, I'm not going down with you. Do you understand that? When I get back to Washington, this problem had better be resolved or you're going to discover that my phone number is suddenly unlisted."

"Trust me, sir, I will protect you no matter what."

"I know you will, Charles." The President's voice mellowed. "I'm about to do high tea in the lobby of this magnificent old hotel with the governor of Colorado. We're having those little tea sandwiches. They slice the crust off the bread, cut the sandwiches into triangles and stack them on top of each other like cocktail napkins."

"I love tea sandwiches," said Talbot. "Enjoy your morning, sir. We'll have a pleasant and productive talk when you return from Alaska."

The President hung up, then called his aide and told him to make arrangements for an unscheduled flight to Alaska.

*

Dr. Barbara Bowmaster stumbled around her apartment in her fuzzy pink bunny slippers, mumbling to herself. She had dutifully dressed for work but changed her mind when she turned on the news and saw what was happening in Cambridge. She called her office to say that she was ill and would be out for the rest of the week. Then she promptly opened a fresh bottle of vodka and made herself a Bloody Mary.

"Early reports indicate that popular author Lionel Cooper is missing from his residence and could be injured or even dead," the blond CNN anchor was saying. "Police have found two badly mutilated bodies in the building but say they have not been able to locate Mr. Cooper. The FBI has been called in because evidence found at the scene suggests the wealthy writer may have been kidnapped. A police spokesman said authorities fear the worst and are asking the public to help them track down the perpetrator—or perpetrators—responsible for this heinous crime."

Dr. Bowmaster dabbed at her eyes with the sleeve of her blouse. "You idiots," she moaned and began to weep. For ten minutes, she cried as hard as she had ever cried in her life. Then she abruptly stopped, blew her nose and built herself a second Bloody Mary.

Oh, the hell with it, she thought, taking a sloppy gulp of her drink. So Orson Dean and his team of bloodthirsty commandos are going to get away with murder. I did my best to stop them. The instant Cooper was dead, they probably terminated Asad, too. Charles Talbot will call me one of these afternoons, tell me the grand experiment in mind control has ended rather awkwardly and thank me for my hard work. After that, I'll never hear from him again.

Barbara stared into her glass. Two fat tears rolled down her cheeks, squeezed beneath the frames of her thick glasses and plopped into the tomato juice. Whatever made me think I could run with the big dogs, she thought. Everyone knows the way those dogs got so big in the first place was by gobbling up all the little pups like me.

*

Murray Klein and Helen Rutz sat in patio chairs on the deck of their motel room in Key West drinking coffee and eating fresh donuts. The sun had just peeked over the far horizon.

"I wonder why old people get up so early," said Murray.

"Because they have to pee," said Helen. She licked chocolate frosting from her fingertips and then lit a cigarette. "Go see what the Weather Channel says it's going to do here today, Murray. Maybe we should rent a sailboat."

Murray wandered away. He was back in less than a minute. "Helen! Get in here! You've got to see this! It's unbelievable!"

Helen scrambled to her feet and looked around in wild-eyed panic. "What? I don't see anybody."

"Not out here. On the television. They're saying that writer might be dead. Lionel Cooper. And two other people. Murdered!"

Helen followed Murray inside. Waves of anguish washed over her as she stared at the dramatic images flickering across the television screen. Helicopter shots of Cooper's beautiful estate, crawling with police. Two bodies being wheeled out of the Cooper Building. An old video of Lionel Cooper accepting an award from Harvard University, followed by some footage of him traveling in the Orient. A file photo of Cooper exiting a famous Cambridge restaurant with Jim Redline. Then someone began a live interview with a twitchy police detective about the search for Cooper.

"All I can say at this point is that he's not in the pond," said the detective. "But he could be under the flowers that border the iron fence that surrounds this property. The dogs are starting to work that area now."

"Under the flowers?" said Helen. "Murray, they think Lionel Cooper is buried under his own flowers! And they're not saying anything about where Jim is!"

Murray sighed. "What the hell have we gotten ourselves into, Helen?"

CHAPTER THIRTY-FIVE

CIA Director Charles Talbot started his work day on his knees in the master bathroom in his home, holding his necktie aside with one hand, clutching the toilet bowl with the other, energetically regurgitating the previous evening's supper—beef stroganoff, spinach salad and Dutch chocolate cake. Even as he emptied his nervous stomach, he was calculating the odds that he would survive as head of the world's largest intelligence agency once the President fully understood the significance of the events that had taken place at the Cooper Building.

Talbot brushed his teeth and gargled with an antiseptic mouthwash. He stared balefully at his reflection in the mirror above the sink. *Cooper is out there someplace getting ready to tell the world that he was criminally assaulted in his own home by a man who looked just like the most famous foreign terrorist ever captured in the United States,* he thought. *Of course, I'll nullify the credibility of that future claim when I issue a press release later today stating that Mustafa Rashid died seventy-two hours ago, the unfortunate victim of an errant blood clot following routine surgery to correct a strangulated hernia.*

There was a light tap on the bathroom door. His wife said, "Are you okay in there, dear? Sounds like you're sick to your stomach."

Talbot jerked the door open and glared at her. "Damn right I'm sick to my stomach," he snarled. "I told you last night that stroganoff tasted funny."

"I ate the stroganoff, too," said his wife defensively, "and I feel fine. But the cake was very rich and you ate two pieces of it even though I reminded you that chocolate plays havoc with your digestive system. Do you want some dry toast and a cup of mint tea before you go?"

"What do you think?" said Talbot. He stormed out of the bathroom, grabbed his briefcase and stomped outside to his waiting limousine.

As his driver maneuvered the sleek black car through heavy traffic, the Director sucked on a breath mint and peered through the tinted bulletproof windows. I can't let this catastrophe affect my behavior, he told himself. I have to pretend that everything is just fine. I can't do anything about Cooper now, anyway. What I *can* do is competently handle the things I still have control over. Like the press release about Mustafa's death. And the invention of a credible explanation for the President about how the comprehensive experiment to build a controllable assassin has come to its disappointing end.

As a result of our painstaking research, Mr. President, I can say with confidence that you have nothing to fear from those working near you. We have established beyond any doubt that the core elements of the human mind are permanently protected, sealed away for eternity by the hand of God. They can never be more than marginally influenced by mere mortals. The man has not been born who can totally control the mind of another. Certainly not that camel-kissing zealot whose own thought processes are so warped by his rigid belief in a set of primitive superstitions that he can't appreciate the glory of the modern world. Unfortunately, our research also confirms that we cannot launch a hypnotized assassin at your priority target with any reasonable expectation of success.

Damn, thought Talbot, not bad for a first draft!

*

FBI Director Conrad Morse was in his office in the Hoover Building talking on the phone to the Assistant Director for Counterintelligence, Bill Williams. Williams had been in Boston less than an hour.

"Old Blue Eyes got his hooks into our prime suspect last night?" asked Morse. "How the hell did that happen? The plan was to let Redline marinate in his own anxiety in the slammer all night so he'd be easy meat for your interrogation this morning."

"That was the plan," confirmed Willliams. "But Old Blue Eyes was here supervising the investigation into Cooper's disappearance. As soon as the police realized they had the same Jim Redline we were after, they reported his arrest to our Boston field office. Old Blue Eyes was there reading the sports page and he pulled rank. Demanded immediate access to the prisoner. Convinced the Boston SAIC that if Redline could be persuaded to reveal Cooper's location, we might be able to take credit for a life-saving rescue. Old Blue Eyes was alone with Redline for several hours."

"Damn it."

"I got a peek at Redline through a one-way mirror at the police station just a few minutes ago," said Williams. "I've seen Holocaust survivors who looked better, sir. But whatever Old Blue Eyes did to him last night, it didn't work. Redline has revealed exactly nothing so far except an ability to hurl saliva with uncanny accuracy."

"I've been studying his file," said Morse. "Redline is tough as nails. We could stab him in the heart, bring him back to life and he probably still wouldn't tell us what we want to know."

"That might be a little extreme," said Willams nervously. "Even for us."

"I'm just trying to make a point here. Slapping a man like Redline around will only irritate him. What did Old Blue Eyes think he was doing, anyway? He knows better than to try something like that without clearing it with me."

"He was sure Redline would crack like a rotten egg," said Williams, "and reveal the location of the jewelry box. Old Blue Eyes is bucking for a promotion, sir. He figured if he walked into your office this morning and handed you the box before you'd poured your first cup of coffee, you'd be grateful as hell."

"How far away can I send that sadistic son of a bitch? Have we perfected interstellar travel yet?"

"The word around the water cooler is he's morbidly afraid of being assigned to Africa," said Williams. "He thinks all the insects there have AIDS."

"Perfect," said Morse. "Old Blue Eyes will be in the Congo by this time tomorrow. I'll put him in charge of the mosquito census."

"Not to change the subject," said Williams, "but I've come up with a much better way to get Jim Redline to tell us what we want to know than slapping him around."

"Spit it out."

"I have a copy of his file, too, and you're right, he's as rugged as they come, especially if he's angry. It could take weeks to pound anything useful out of the guy. But, although he may have absorbed some of Lionel Cooper's radical ideas about corruption in the federal government, I'm thinking Redline is not even close to being an enemy of the state. His father was a Marine and so were two of his uncles. Redline was a star football player for an ivy-league college. He votes in every election and he's proud of the fact that he can trace his family's roots back to the American Revolution. That tells me how he wants to be treated by his government. I suggest we wrap this whole thing in the American flag and play taps over it. Tell him we have had no choice but to take extreme measures to secure the jewelry box because it may contain information that threatens our national security in ways he is just not privileged to know."

Morse quickly analyzed what the Assistant Director had recommended and was surprised at how well it stood up. "That could work. Okay, Bill, go for it. Clean Redline up, have one of our doctors fix anything that Old Blue Eyes broke, get a hot breakfast in the poor bastard and start treating him like the honest American taxpayer he is. Within reasonable limits, of course. Answer some of his questions, but don't reveal everything. Make him see that the smartest thing he can do now is give up the location of the jewelry box, even if he's already sold it to someone for a fortune. I believe he'll feel a tremendous sense of relief if we offer him a dignified way out of the mess he's created. Oh, and don't forget to have him sign a secrecy pledge."

"This should work, sir, but what if he refuses to cooperate with me no matter what I say?" asked Williams. "Redline has to be furious by now. He just went through three hours of pure hell at the hands of Old Blue Eyes. What if he just gives me the finger?"

"Never happen. He'll fold like a wet newspaper," said Morse. "But if he's too stubborn to take the bait quickly, explain that what Old Blue Eyes did to him last night is only a tiny sample of the kind of misery that can befall a citizen who doesn't listen closely when his government tells him it desperately needs his help."

"You're serious?"

"Yes. If Jim Redline balks after we offer him a perfectly sane reason to help us, then he will be subjected to our most extreme methods of information extraction. Make sure he understands that."

"Yes, sir, will do."

"Have a great day, Bill. And congratulations on designing an excellent strategy for bringing James T. Redline to his senses and Helen Rutz's jewelry box into my office."

*

For the twentieth time since he had first jotted them down, Lionel Cooper reviewed his notes. Each word had to be perfect. Cooper wanted every single person who heard his speech to clearly understand two things: *what* the President was trying to do and *why* he had to be stopped before it was too late.

Gently massaging his tender black-and-blue lip, Cooper peeked through a crack in the curtains of his room on the second floor of Stuart McManus's elegant Boston home. The crowd of television and newspaper reporters on the huge front lawn below had doubled in size since he had last checked. Stuart was scheduled to come out at ten a.m. to clarify his dramatic statement, made late yesterday in a cryptic press release, that he was about to take over as chairman of the Federal Reserve System . . . despite the fact that the presiding chairman appeared to have no knowledge of any official change in his status and had expressed outrage that the famous economist would attempt to oust him with a populist coup!

"Well, Lionel, it worked exactly as you said it would," said Stuart McManus. "Everyone showed up." He had quietly slipped into

Cooper's room. He moved to the window, pulled the curtain aside and peered down at the excited throng trampling his lawn. Daisy was gliding through the crowd, serving coffee and tea. Stuart knew that Janice was watching through the peephole in the front door.

"Of course," said Cooper. "Incidentally, the intense reaction of the media to your bogus announcement should give you some idea of how easy it would be for you to actually become the chairman if you ever decide to do so, my friend."

Stuart looked at his watch. "I suppose. But it's your show today, Lionel, not mine. In ten minutes I'll go down and let them in on the big secret. Are you ready?"

Cooper endured sharp pain in his split lip so he could smile. "Yes, but I doubt anyone else is ready for what I'm going to say. Certainly not that coward sitting on his powdered ass in the Oval Office. What I wouldn't give to be able to see his face when he finds out I'm on to him."

Stuart sighed. "I wish you had taken seriously my idea about hiring private security guards for your protection. The CIA could have a sniper hiding on a roof across the street."

Cooper shook his head. "If the CIA knew I was hiding in your house, they would have crept into my room last night and cut my throat with a dull shoehorn."

Stuart McManus shuddered from head to toe. "I've finally lived long enough to witness the impossible. Even you, one of the most creative thinkers in the world, could not have conjured up a plot to rival this one, Lionel. A terrified President twisting in the grip of the enemy's evil psychological campaign to turn him into a machine, using nothing more sophisticated than the *rumor* that they can assassinate him whenever they wish because they know how to control the human brain. A CIA Director slavishly bowing to the President's insane instructions, even though his actions clearly put at risk the lives of countless innocent Americans. Surely this is the darkest hour in our country's political history."

Cooper nodded somberly. "But perspective is everything when it comes to dramatic moments like this one. We must never give in to despair, no matter how hopeless the immediate situation appears to be.

Courage is mankind's best protection from a world filled with uncertainty and danger. I have made an excellent living spying on the ambitious people who inhabit the corridors of power in Washington and I often feared my unwholesome occupation would eventually plunge me into such deep cynicism I might never recover. But, happily, it did not. I have never told anyone this before, old friend, because I thought it might be interpreted as a sign that I was weakening. But I must say it now. If I have learned one important thing from my work, it is this—the vast majority of our leaders are excellent people. They truly are the best and the brightest. But, alas, leaders are only human and occasionally arrogance or greed, or, as in this particular case, fear, sneaks through the defenses of one of them and runs amok. And when that happens, *someone* must do something about it before that individual does irreparable damage to the country."

Stuart smiled. "Thank goodness we have you, Lionel, to do this difficult work for us."

Cooper parted the curtains again and said, "I'm ready to do it now, Stuart."

*

Bill Williams made arrangements for Jim Redline to be hastily examined by a doctor, then smuggled into a deluxe suite on the top floor of the Hilton Hotel near Logan International Airport. Flanked by two husky FBI agents, a male nurse pushed Redline into the suite in a wheelchair and placed him at a round oak dining table. On the table were serving dishes overflowing with hot food. Dressed in white hospital pajamas, his hands and feet securely manacled, Redline stared dully at the steaming dishes—scrambled eggs, bacon, fried potatoes, pancakes and toast.

The nurse left and Williams entered the room moments later. He sat down at the table directly across from Redline. The two dark-suited agents stood at attention in the hallway just outside the door.

"Good morning, Jim," said Williams. "I'm here representing the FBI. You may call me Bill."

Redline blinked groggily but said nothing. Blood was beginning to seep from some of the small punctures in his body, staining the fabric of his pajamas.

Williams tugged a sheet of paper from his coat pocket and squinted at it.

"Jim, I am aware that one of our senior agents, acting on his own authority, attempted to coerce information from you last night. That was a regrettable misunderstanding caused by an unavoidable breakdown in communications. Please accept my apology. Now then, our physician's report states that you have no broken bones or seriously damaged major organs. But you are suffering from painful needle punctures in and around the main nerve centers in your torso. You have some muscle bruises caused by blows from a fist or blunt instrument. You also have a nasty cut in your thigh that is no less than thirty hours old and could not have been inflicted by our agent. You have been given a massive dose of penicillin to prevent infection in your leg. The cut has been cleaned and sutured by the examining physician. Hmmm, what else does he say? Oh yes, you are dehydrated and have not eaten solid food in more than twenty-four hours. And you're suffering from exhaustion due to stress and sleep deprivation. Does that about cover it, Jim?"

Redline slowly raised his manacled wrists and pointed a thumb at the food on the table. "If you intend for me to eat some of this," he said in a creaky voice, "you'll have to feed me."

"That would be awkward," said Williams. "Even though you are obviously a powerful man when you're feeling well, Jim, you don't look like you could crawl out of here on your hands and knees today, let alone mount a serious escape attempt. Do I have your word you won't try to smother me with one of these pancakes if I allow you to feed yourself? I'll take your silence as a yes."

Williams mumbled something into a mike hidden in the sleeve of his coat and the two agents guarding the door burst into the room, guns trained on Redline's broad back.

"Remove the cuffs from this man's wrists. Jim, allow me to introduce Agent Smiley and Agent Wilson. They have orders to shoot you dead if you try to escape. Gentlemen, please resume your stations in the hallway."

Moving his hands with great deliberation, Redline put eggs and potatoes on his plate and poured water into a tumbler. Although the food tasted like paste, he forced himself to eat.

"Jim, the government's definition of terrorism has evolved dramatically from what it was just a decade ago. That's why we've found it necessary to keep a close eye on Lionel Cooper for quite some time now. Cooper is considered to be a genuine threat to national security because of his inflammatory and irresponsible criticism of important elected officials. His personal assistant, Tina Romero, kept us advised of his every move. As you know, she was tragically murdered by an unknown assailant on the same night that Cooper disappeared."

Redline pushed a mouthful of food into his cheek. "Tina was on your payroll?"

"Yes. That's how we found out about your recent discussions with Helen Rutz and her claim that an old jewelry box she once encountered in Germany might put the JFK assassination in a whole new light. And, of course, Cooper's intense interest in locating it."

Redline picked up a piece of toast. He wanted to spread butter on it, but there was no knife on the table. Just one fork and one spoon.

"Thanks to your experience of last evening, you know that the FBI is extremely interested in obtaining that jewelry box, as well," said Williams. "I can't tell you why we want it, Jim, but believe me when I say that only a concern for the security of our nation would cause us to intervene in the affairs of private citizens."

Redline chewed his food and looked into Bill's foxy bureaucratic eyes. He was thinking it would be fun to throw Bill out the nearest window. Redline began to inventory all the objects in the suite, looking for something that might serve as a weapon.

Williams produced a pocketknife and used its longest blade to butter a slice of toast. He cleaned the blade on a cloth napkin and then bit the toast in half. With his mouth crammed with bread, he mumbled, "So, where is the jewelry box now, Jim?"

Redline took a sip of water. "Don't you want me to tell you what happened to Lionel Cooper the other night? I was there, you know. I saw everything."

Williams finished the toast and reached for a piece of bacon. "Eventually. But first I want you to tell me where the jewelry box is. When you answer that question—and we actually retrieve the box— then I'll listen to the rest of your story. It's a credibility thing, Jim. If you tell us the truth about the box, then we might believe what you tell us about Cooper's abduction."

Williams buttered another slice of toast and slathered it with orange marmalade.

"I'm puzzled," said Redline. "You say the FBI wants the box, but you can't tell me why. And, notwithstanding your humble apology about the inexcusable abuse I suffered last night, I'm still being treated as if I have no legal rights at all. Seems to me I should be talking with my attorney this morning, not volunteering information."

Williams swallowed, poured himself a glass of water and prepared to deliver what he believed would be the most important words he would ever say in his official capacity as Assistant Director of Counterintelligence. Words that might someday put him in the Director's chair.

"I understand your frustration, Jim. But here's the bottom line. I need to take possession of that jewelry box *today*. It's a matter of tremendous importance to your government. I urge you to reveal the location of the box immediately. If you will do that one thing for me, I promise you will walk out of this hotel a free man." Williams leaned forward and gave Redline the most solemn look he was capable of faking. "After you sign a secrecy pledge, of course. Jim, if you love your country the way I think you do, you will cooperate. Your late father was a Marine. I'm sure he would have wanted you to do whatever was best for America. Am I right, son? Semper fi?"

Redline smothered the urge to scream. I have to get away from this crazy asshole, he thought, or I'm going to kill him. "Let me finish my breakfast," he said in a strangled whisper. "I'm still too weak to think clearly. Would you butter some pancakes for me?"

Williams frowned. He had expected Redline to capitulate instantly. He reached for the butter dish. "Take a little time to think, Jim, but consider this while you're pondering your options. *I must have the box.* In plain English, that means you will either do what's right voluntarily or people much less civilized than me will make your ordeal last night seem like child's play."

With a shaking hand, Redline poured syrup on the buttered pancakes. And on the tablecloth. And on the floor.

"Reluctantly, of course," continued Williams. He reached for another slice of bacon. "Only as a last resort."

"Thanks for sharing that with me, Bill," said Redline. "It certainly makes my decision a lot easier." He surveyed the suite again. There was a pewter vase filled with fresh flowers on a lamp table less than ten feet from his wheelchair. Maybe he could knock Bill unconscious. But then what?

Williams looked at his watch. "Ten minutes, Jim. Take ten more minutes to eat your fill and then tell me where the jewelry box is or . . . well, I've already explained what will happen next. By the way, the reason I chose this particular hotel for our meeting is that I have a helicopter and a jet plane warming up right across the street. If the box is not in Boston or Cambridge, we can fly to wherever it is."

"Terrific," said Redline.

William's cell phone chirped. He pulled it from his coat pocket, snapped it open and hissed, "Don't you people know I'm busy? What the hell is it now?"

"Are you watching television?" asked Conrad Morse.

"Uh, no, sir. I'm having breakfast with James T. Redline. He's still considering our offer."

"Listen carefully. We just got a call from a Boston television station. Lionel Cooper is alive and getting ready to screw the government again. He's about to make a televised speech from the front lawn of no less a personage than Stuart McManus! You're five minutes away by chopper from where Cooper is standing right now. Get your ass to the McManus residence and make sure we have

Cooper under our control before he disappears again. Keep Redline in the hotel suite until Cooper is no longer a threat. I guarantee you, Redline will talk like a magpie when he finds out his boss is in our custody."

"Yes, sir," said Williams. He closed his cell phone and muttered into his sleeve. Agent Smiley and Agent Wilson crashed through the door again, guns drawn.

"I have to leave for a while," said Williams. "Keep a sharp eye on the prisoner until I return, but do not speak to him." He stood up and hurried toward the open door. Then he spun on his heel and glared at Redline.

"You knew Cooper was alive, didn't you? You knew he was going to hold a press conference this morning. You sat there playing with your food like a naughty kid, knowing exactly what was about to happen."

Redline pointed at the dishes on the table with his fork. "Should we save any of this for you, Bill? You haven't tried the eggs yet."

"Fuck you," growled Williams. He raced off, slamming the door behind him.

Agents Smiley and Wilson holstered their guns. They gave Redline the evil eye for a moment, then ogled the food. Redline was staring at his fork. It was of exceptional quality. Nothing but the best at the Hilton, he thought. You could pitch hay with this damn thing.

"I just realized I'm famished," said Agent Smiley.

"Is this a lucky break or what," said Agent Wilson. "I was about to soil myself out there. Keep an eye on this desperado, Mike. I have to take the mother of all dumps." He hustled down a short hallway. Seconds later, there was the sound of a door being closed and locked. An exhaust fan whirred.

"No problem," said Agent Smiley. He slapped Redline on the back. "You don't look so good, pal. It's amazing to me you can even chew that soggy flapjack after what you've just been through. Oh, and look at that. Tsk tsk. Your jammies are all speckled with fresh blood. Well, what can I say? Life is brutal for the unwary. You aren't going to eat all this grub yourself, are you? That would be downright selfish, especially since the government is paying for it. Here, let me give you a hand."

Agent Smiley rested his left hand on the table and leaned over to reach for a slice of bacon. Redline slammed his large fork through the back of Agent Smiley's hand with such force that the sturdy tines were driven halfway through the surface of the table. Agent Smiley opened his mouth to scream but Redline had already cleared the wheelchair and had him by the necktie, twisting violently, shutting off his air. With his left hand pinned to the table, Agent Smiley tried to hit Redline in the face with his right fist. Redline slipped the punch, jerked Agent Smiley's gun from its holster and clubbed him on the ear with it. Agent Smiley's eyes fluttered and he dropped facedown into a plate of fried potatoes. Redline whacked him on the back of the head with the gun to make sure he was out. Nauseous from the sudden exertion, he tugged a set of keys from Agent Smiley's coat pocket and unlocked his ankle cuffs. Then he lurched down the hallway and flattened himself against the wall next to the bathroom door. He heard the toilet flush.

Whistling softly, Agent Wilson stepped into the hallway, drying his hands on a small towel. "Oh, shit," he said, just before Redline smashed Agent Smiley's heavy gun against his jaw. Agent Wilson crumpled to the floor.

A few minutes later, wearing Agent Smiley's snug-fitting dark suit, scuffed wingtips and mirrored sunglasses, Redline limped down the fire stairs to the main floor and then strolled casually through the kitchen of the Hilton Hotel, waving a gold badge at the curious employees. He exited through a back door and walked in the direction of a parking lot on the airport side of the building. He spotted an elderly man standing next to a new midnight blue Cadillac. The old man punched a button on his key chain and the car's trunk sprang open.

Holding Agent Smiley's badge case over his head, Redline walked straight at the man and yelled, "FBI! I need your vehicle, sir!" When he reached the car, Redline closed the trunk and swung around to face the old man, making sure the big gun in his shoulder holster was plainly visible.

The man staggered and nearly lost his balance. "FBI? You're confiscating my car?"

Redline grabbed the key chain dangling from the man's hand and nodded. "Yes, sir. Sorry, but we're about to have a national emergency."

"Damn!" wheezed the man. He stared at Redline in amazement. "There's blood all over your shoes! What's happening? Is the country under attack?"

"Not yet," said Redline, sliding behind the wheel. He cranked the powerful engine. Then he pulled two twenty-dollar bills from Agent Smiley's wallet and lowered the window. "Take this and use it to pay for a taxi. Go home and wait for someone from the government to contact you. You'll be compensated for your inconvenience. Please tell no one what happened here today."

The old man attempted a wobbly military salute. "Yes, sir! Oh my God! This is frightening! Tell no one! Uh, not even my wife?"

"No one." Redline dropped the car into gear and drove rapidly away.

The old man watched his Cadillac blend into the morning traffic and disappear from view. He took a handkerchief from his back pocket and mopped his perspiring face.

"Gee, I think it would be okay if I told my wife," he muttered. "What harm could that do? She died two years ago."

CHAPTER THIRTY-SIX

Stuart McManus scanned the expectant faces of the newspaper journalists, television reporters, camera operators and technicians who had gathered on his front lawn to record his remarks. The television crew had set up a podium and attached a bank of microphones to it. A fleet of satellite trucks was parked bumper to bumper on the curved driveway in front of his stately house. As he stepped to the podium, Stuart saw Janice guarding the front door. When he gave her the signal, she would open the door, reach inside for Lionel Cooper's hand and solemnly escort the distinguished author through the amazed crowd.

The murmuring gradually settled down, until finally the only sound was the aggressive mating call of a robin perched in a nearby tree.

"Good morning," said Stuart. "Thank you all for coming here today. I have something to say of such staggering importance to the citizens of this country that it's difficult to find appropriate words with which to begin. No, I am not referring to my audacious statement of yesterday in which I announced I was about to assume control of the Federal Reserve System. Please forgive me. I said that because I needed to get you here this morning."

Several reporters grabbed their cell phones and began madly punching numbers. The camera operators edged in closer. One woman near the back of the crowd tried to rush forward, snagged her heel in the grass and lost her balance. She splashed boiling hot coffee on a small bearded man standing next to her. The man was staring intently at Stuart McManus and did not appear to notice that he had just been scalded.

Stuart paused to sip cool water from a paper cup Daisy had thoughtfully placed on a shelf beneath the podium's slanted top.

"Yesterday the Cambridge police and the FBI jointly announced that my good friend, esteemed author Lionel Cooper, had disappeared from his estate under suspicious circumstances. They asked everyone in the country to assist in their search for him. I have wonderful news for America. Lionel Cooper is alive and well. He is here, in my home, and in just a few moments, he is going to speak to you."

Silence. No one seemed able to fathom what McManus had just said.

"Lionel Cooper believes he's a marked man. He has told me he will be fortunate just to live through this day. I have provided him with a safe harbor so that he can tell his riveting tale to the people of America and the world. I believe we must rally around this wonderful man and protect him until the full truth can be revealed. When you learn *who* his enemies are, *who* is trying to silence him and *why,* you will understand that it will take all of us to save him."

A dozen hands were in the air. "I will take no questions at this time," said Stuart firmly. "After Lionel has delivered his remarks, we will both be available to make sure you do not leave here until all your questions are answered." He locked eyes with Janice and inclined his head. With a dramatic flourish, she opened the front door.

"Ladies and gentlemen," said Stuart, his voice breaking, "may I present a national treasure, the most honorable man to live in America since Abraham Lincoln, Mr. Lionel Cooper."

Side by side, Janice McManus and Lionel Cooper posed while television cameras transmitted their images to every network in the country. Then Janice looped her arm through Cooper's and they began to walk slowly toward the podium.

Someone in the crowd clapped. Then several people stood up and began to applaud energetically. There were whoops and whistles and cheers as the reporters came to the full realization that the white-haired patriarch passing by them truly was Lionel Cooper.

When they reached the podium, Janice kissed Cooper lightly on the cheek and, dabbing at her eyes with a tissue, turned and walked away. Lionel shook hands with Stuart and muttered something in his ear. Stuart retreated to a position behind and to the left of the podium. Cooper faced the cameras and the astounded representatives of the media. He tried to smile, winced, touched his badly swollen lip with the tip of his finger, pulled his notes from his pocket and spread them out on the podium.

"My God, he's been assaulted!" cried a front-row reporter. The cameras zoomed in on Cooper's pendulous purple wound. He nodded at someone he knew. Then he tapped one of the microphones sharply with his fingernail. All random conversation ceased.

"There is much to say," said Cooper. "I must deliver my message quickly and trust that I will survive long enough to validate my shocking statements later with the kind of irrefutable supporting detail that you are accustomed to getting from me."

Cooper raised his voice a notch. "As you know, I abhor melodrama. So, please believe me when I say that I truly have no idea how long I will be able to stay on the air before someone breaks in here to take me into custody or kill me on the spot. Listen and learn what the enemies of freedom and truth have always understood—the most potent weapon in the world is *fear*. Only the most courageous among us is immune to its toxic power. Unfortunately, the current President of the United States is so lacking in grit that he has become an unwitting tool of our enemies. Literally terrified out of his mind and acting impetuously through his willing agent—the nakedly ambitious CIA Director, Charles Talbot—the President has recently authorized an attempt on my life. I was assaulted in my own home by an internationally renowned killer brought there in the dead of night by CIA assassins. Only the intervention of my bodyguard allowed me to escape with my life. As we now all know, two other innocent persons who happened to be in the Cooper Building that evening were not so lucky."

What Cooper had just said was so unexpected that the people standing on the lawn could not process it. They stood like marble statues, paralyzed, barely breathing, intent on absorbing every single word of a speech they now understood might change the world forever.

"Why did this happen? It happened because our spineless President, convinced he has been targeted for assassination by a fanatical foreign terrorist, is collaborating with the CIA Director in a scheme involving mind-control experiments, an absurd attempt to create a 'programmable' assassin capable of removing this alleged threat to his life. Needless to say, this idea is preposterous. It is nothing more than the diseased spawn of sheer desperation, a last-ditch strategy only a man who has completely relinquished control of his faculties could believe in. Worst of all, if the President's sick plan were actually put into play, it could eventually place all of us at mortal risk. I have acquired abundant and incontrovertible physical proof that what I am saying to you is true. The CIA tried to kill me in order to keep me from presenting the damning evidence I have in my possession to a court of law, or even to the court of public opinion. What I need from each of you this morning, and from all freedom-loving citizens everywhere, is protection from the powerful forces that seek my death. It is vital that my story be heard so that, collectively, you can create a human barrier, an impenetrable shield between me and the imperious men who—"

Cooper abruptly stopped speaking. The small bearded man had worked his way from the back of the crowd to a position directly in front of the podium. At first, Cooper could not believe what he was seeing. Then he stepped back from the microphones and pointed at the grim-faced man.

"What the hell are you doing here, you pervert?" asked Cooper menacingly. "Stuart, please escort this man to—"

With a shriek, the man jerked a pistol from under his shirt, pointed it at Cooper and fired.

A dozen people screamed as Cooper, a look of astonishment on his face, raked his fingernails across a ragged patch of blood forming in the center of his chest. Then he took two faltering steps in the direction of a horrified Stuart McManus and fell on his face in the grass.

Panicked people hurled whatever they were holding in their hands to the ground and dove for cover. Suddenly, a helicopter thundered into view and began to descend toward the yard. Dr. Irving Katz turned and looked up at the hovering chopper. The letters "FBI" were stenciled in yellow on its gleaming black body. Dr. Katz jammed the barrel of his gun between his smiling lips and pulled the trigger.

*

It was nearly midnight when the Assistant Director Bill Williams met with Conrad Morse in the Director's hushed office on the seventh floor of the Hoover Building.

"Tell me everything you know," said Morse. His face looked like an ice sculpture.

"We flew straight to the McManus residence," said Williams in a soft voice. "But we were too late. You've seen the tapes. The killer shot Cooper through the heart with a .38 caliber pistol at point-blank range. Cooper was dead before he hit the ground. And then there was the suicide."

"The killer was a CIA employee?"

"The shooter has been identified as Dr. Irving Katz, a CIA psychiatrist."

"I know that name," said Morse. "Katz had several private meetings with Cooper not long ago in New York."

"The CIA admitted Katz had been suffering from severe depression. He was on extended medical leave. They surmise he stopped taking his medicine and flipped out. And they now claim he is responsible for the earlier botched attempt to kill the author in his own home. When that effort failed, Katz somehow tracked Cooper to the McManus residence and finished the job."

"Clever," said Mr. FBI. "In other words, they want the public to believe that Cooper drew outrageously false conclusions from his near-fatal encounter with the disturbed Dr. Katz the other evening, including all that balderdash about mind-control experiments and foreign terrorists and a cowardly President and so on. Okay, enough about Katz and the CIA's public smoke screen. Tell me why James T.

Redline is not here with us this evening, Bill, wrapped in an American flag, whistling taps. Tell me why the jewelry box is not sitting on my desk tonight along with his signed secrecy pledge. Tell me why we aren't recording his voluntary statement about what this clusterfuck is *really* all about!"

Williams had difficulty meeting the Director's death-ray glare. "As you know, sir, Redline escaped from the Hilton Hotel while I was en route to the McManus residence. I swear he appeared to be too weak to raise a water glass to his lips, let alone try anything heroic, thanks to the painful torture he had undergone at the hands of Old Blue Eyes just a few hours before I met with him. Nevertheless, he somehow managed to overpower the two experienced agents who were guarding him and vanish."

Morse took a moment to check the condition of his fingernails. "And I'm told he did it with surprising ease. I'm further told the reason Redline had any opportunity to escape at all is because *you* instructed Agents Smiley and Wilson to remove his wrist restraints. You did that so he could feed himself?"

"I cannot deny that, sir. The fact that Redline is not here with us right now is entirely my fault. We'll find him. I have every law enforcement officer in the United States looking for him."

Morse snorted. "Good luck. How are the injured agents doing?"

"Agent Wilson has a broken jaw and a concussion, but he's alert and taking nourishment. Agent Smiley also has a concussion and is scheduled to have surgery in a few hours. The fork did some nasty nerve damage to his hand, but the doctors believe they can repair it. Frankly, sir, the humiliation factor is worse than their physical injuries. I'm not sure they can continue to function for the Bureau. Or pee standing up, for that matter."

Morse sighed. "It was reported to me our people had to pull the fork out of the table with pliers. They said it looked like the damned thing had been forced into the wood by a machine. How strong does a man have to be to do something like that?"

"Redline mustered unbelievable strength," admitted Williams. "At least for a few seconds. Scary to think what he's capable of doing when he's in shape."

"Or when he's *really* pissed off," muttered Morse.

Williams cleared his throat. "Has the President called you, sir? Demanded an explanation?"

Morse laughed bitterly. "The President will not call me and he will not call Charles Talbot, either. He doesn't have to call us. He can sit in his office polishing his halo, waiting for us to present him with a brilliant solution to this entire fiasco. And if we can't come up with one, he'll simply demand our resignations."

"I'm sorry, sir. I am responsible for this entire debacle."

Morse stood up, stretched, turned, folded his hands behind his back and looked out his window into the darkness. "You certainly are responsible for this entire debacle. So let's jump to the obvious question, Bill. Did you do *anything* today that would argue against me firing you on the spot?"

"Perhaps," said Williams meekly. He opened his briefcase and removed some papers. "By the time my chopper was on the ground at the McManus residence, most of the reporters were preoccupied with checking Cooper and Katz for vital signs. Mrs. McManus had fainted and some people were attending to her. A few of the cooler heads were on their phones telling their station chiefs what had just taken place. No one paid any attention to me. I ran straight to the podium and secured Cooper's notes."

Morse spun around. "I assumed someone from the media had confiscated them."

"No, sir."

"Well, I'll be damned," said Morse. He was genuinely awed. His shrewd eyes narrowed. "You didn't read the speech, did you?"

"Of course not. I knew you would want to be the first person to do that," said Williams. What the hell, he thought, I'm history anyway. What's one more lie?

Morse reached eagerly for the papers. "And thus," he said, "the wily Assistant Director for Counterintelligence pulls his fat ass out of the fire one more time."

"I certainly hope so, sir."

"I confess I'm quite impressed with your clear thinking and quick action in circumstances that would have befuddled a less experienced man. You may have saved your job. Depends on what I find when I read this. I order you to go home and get drunk while I digest what the late, great Lionel Cooper had planned to say to his many fans about the 'cowardly' President and the 'nakedly ambitious' Director of the CIA."

CHAPTER THIRTY-SEVEN

It was a long, dreary flight back from Ethiopia. By the time the wheels of the Boeing 747 touched down at Reagan International Airport, Bret Barringer was thoroughly drained. During the drive to his secluded residence on the outskirts of Falls Church, Virginia, Barringer asked himself for the thousandth time—why do I continue to do this crappy work? I'm getting too damned old to fly around the world and deal with crummy food, lumpy mattresses, primitive plumbing and *uncivilized* people. And lately, it seems the "big" stories CNN asks me to investigate are just boring replays of "big" stories I've done hundreds of times before. If I have to look at one more starving African child or interview one more corrupt Third World despot, I swear I'm going to lose my mind!

Barringer continued his depressing interior monologue as he rolled his luggage up the wide flagstone sidewalk leading to the front door of his country home. I know why I persist, of course. It's because I don't know what else to do with myself. How would I spend my time if I quit this horrible job? Hit the talk show circuit? Write a tell-all book? Run for public office? No way! *Run for public office?* Ha! I'd rather lose my mind!

He unlocked the front door, tossed his bags in the corner, snapped on the overhead light and immediately spotted the note on the console table in the foyer. It was under Lillian's favorite glass paperweight on a sheet of her special stationery. Even from five feet away, Barringer recognized her loopy script. It appeared to be a long message. Suddenly anxious, he grabbed the note and tugged his reading glasses from his coat pocket.

309

"Welcome home, darling. Sorry I'm not there to give you a hug. Confession time. I've been corresponding with a doctor in Atlanta about Norma's condition. I know you think she'll always be slow. Norma and I do not accept that. We've decided to take a trip to visit Doctor Braun. He says he can help Norma using new drugs and a technique he is pioneering called precision testing. His peers tell me he is cutting edge, a true genius. I have a good feeling about this, Bret. I'm doing this for Norma. And for us, too, dear. Please don't hate me. We'll return soon. We both love you. Lillian."

At the bottom of the message, Lillian had jotted down some information about the Atlanta hotel where she and Norma had reservations. Next to that she had drawn two smiley faces and put big X's and O's under them.

Barringer groaned and did what he always did when something disturbing like this happened. He hurried into the kitchen, dipped his hand into an enormous ceramic jar and grabbed six gourmet chocolate chip cookies. Another wild goose chase, he thought, chewing furiously. One more outrageous medical bill to pay. Norma was born retarded and she'll always be retarded! Why can't Lillian accept that? Why does she feel compelled to run all over the country looking for . .

A large man walked into the kitchen. He was wearing a navy blue suit that was one size too small for his wide frame. "Good evening, Mr. Barringer," he said. "Do you recognize me? I am—I mean, I was—Lionel Cooper's chief of security, Jim Redline."

Barringer's mouth was so full of cookies he was unable to speak for a moment. Which was fortunate because it gave him time to recover from his heart-thumping shock at seeing the intruder. And time to think. When he had finished chewing and swallowing the cookies, he said, "Yes, I do remember you, Mr. Redline. I've seen you several times before tonight. You have my deepest sympathy, sir. I've been out of the country, but my office contacted me on the plane by satellite phone just a few hours ago to brief me about Lionel's death. Brought tears to my eyes. A tragedy for the whole country. I respected that man and his work."

"Thank you," said Redline. "I didn't know Lionel was dead until a few hours ago myself. I drove straight here from Boston, never got out of the car except to fill it with gas. Heard the news on the car radio."

"Mind if I ask how you got inside my residence, Mr. Redline? I recently purchased a new security system. State of the art, the salesman told me. There should be a dozen armed guards jumping all over you right now."

"Um, I'm quite familiar with how 'state-of-the-art' security systems work," said Redline. "But I do apologize for the unauthorized intrusion. I rang the doorbell. No one responded. Seemed like the thing to do was let myself in and wait for you."

"I see. Is that blood on your shoes or did you drop a bag of tomatoes?"

"Let's talk about that later," said Redline.

"I take it the authorities are looking for you?"

Redline nodded but did not offer to explain.

Barringer studied Redline. His face was a bit drawn, like he hadn't slept in a while, but even stuffed into the ill-fitting suit, he still looked like he could throw a car over the house with one hand. A rugged, physically intimidating man. But he also looked honest. The kind of man you could trust. His gaze was intelligent and reassuring. And he was unusually handsome. Of course, thought Barringer glumly, I've just described Ted Bundy, too.

"May I ask why you came here?" asked Barringer. "Is it because you have an especially good story to tell me? One that couldn't wait until tomorrow?"

"I'm afraid I have an especially *bad* story to tell you," said Redline. "Maybe the worst story you've ever heard. Also, I need your help tonight. Tomorrow may be too late."

Barringer pointed at his cookie jar. "Then I suggest you fortify yourself with a cookie or two before we talk, Mr. Redline. I made these myself. They're delicious."

*

FBI Director Conrad Morse waited impatiently in his limousine in the parking garage next to the Army and Navy Club on 17th Street in Washington, DC. His driver and two of his personal bodyguards stood at parade rest near the vehicle. It was one o'clock in the morning.

He knows I'm out here cooling my heels, thought Morse, but he's taking his sweet time anyway. He probably bought everyone in the Eagle Grill a round of drinks after he finished his speech. I'd do the same thing, of course. Can't rush off after these grizzled old warriors give you a standing ovation. Have to show appropriate gratitude to our supporters now and then.

CIA Director Charles Talbot walked into the garage, flanked by two bodyguards, and slipped into the back seat of Morse's limousine. The two men shook hands. The four bodyguards arrayed themselves near the vehicle, trying to keep at least one eye on every dark corner. Morse's driver lit a cigarette and moved discreetly away.

Talbot's clothes reeked of cigar smoke. He said, "What, no cashews? No cold drinks? You've lost your respect for ritual, Conrad. I'm disappointed."

"Good evening," said Morse. "Sorry for the late hour, Charles, but I wanted to personally thank you for eliminating Lionel Cooper. And my budget director thanks you, too. Now we don't have to spend a fortune every year keeping an eye on the demented old fart."

"Think nothing of it," said Talbot. "I do an occasional favor for people I like. Actually, to be serious about it, I had nothing to do with Cooper's unfortunate death. It was just an odd twist of fate that his killer was employed by my agency."

"So you say. Could be true, I suppose. Tell me if you agree that the following things also could be true. In order to stay away from the media until you get things tidied up around Washington, the President has extended his Alaskan trip. Meantime, both of our agencies have presented carefully coordinated and manicured stories about the Cooper disaster to the media. Your agency reported that Dr. Katz was suffering from extreme depression brought on when his lifelong addiction to sex came to the attention of his superiors. He was put on indefinite medical leave. Apparently, he suffered a psychotic break and went on a rampage that resulted in the deaths of Tina Romero, her lover and, eventually, Lionel Cooper. Your experts further stated that Dr. Katz and Mr. Cooper—who were recently seen together in a New York City hotel—were probably having a kinky sexual tryst when something went dreadfully awry. Your experts went on to say that Cooper's bizarre declarations about the President and secret mind-control experiments and foreign terrorists are impossible to decipher now that he is dead but were most likely just the panicked excuses of an embarrassed and frightened old man. His last desperate attempt to conceal his scandalous personal life from his adoring public and offer them a plausible explanation for why he'd been brutally assaulted in his own home. In a separate press release, seemingly unrelated to the Cooper incident, your agency quietly announced that the international terrorist Mustafa Rashid—also a small, bearded man—had tragically died from a surgical accident several days *before* Cooper was assaulted. Without actually saying so, the CIA thus adroitly protected itself in advance from any possible rumor that Rashid might have been the one to assault Cooper in his home, rather than Dr. Katz. How am I doing so far?"

"Couldn't have said it better myself," said Talbot. "Every time I hear those beautifully crafted stories I find myself wanting to believe them all over again."

Morse handed Talbot a long envelope. "It appears you will never stop lying to me, Charles. Here is a copy of the handwritten speech Lionel Cooper had with him when he was gunned down. One of my top people confiscated it at the scene."

Talbot frowned. "Why should I care about Cooper's speech now? Words never said can't hurt any of us. Not even the few idiotic things Cooper did manage to blurt out are being taken seriously at this point. He was obviously raving. McManus and his wife now admit the old man seemed confused and irrational when he showed up at their door."

"Aha," said Morse. "Good point. But you haven't yet read his amazing speech, Charles, and I have. Before you read it, answer just one question for me. You lied when you told me your agency had no interest in Helen Rutz's old jewelry box, right? You were stunned when I told you about it."

Talbot, genuinely surprised at the question, silently debated whether he should tell Morse that he had ordered the box destroyed. *What the hell, he thought. Let the little shit suffer a bit longer. I'll tell him. But not now. Not while he's digging at me like a rabid badger!*

"What the hell are you talking about?" said Talbot. "The jewelry box is of no importance to me or anyone else in my agency. I told you that."

Morse raised his eyebrows. "You are lying, sir. I know for a fact that the box is central to everything we're discussing. Furthermore, thinking that Jim Redline, Cooper's security chief, had found the box and was bringing it back to Cambridge, I ordered my people to intercept him when he arrived at the Cooper Building. Cooper's undelivered speech reveals that Redline was lurking in the shadows at the very moment my agents surprised your undercover operatives. Redline saw and heard enough to realize that the FBI and the CIA were *both* spying on Cooper's estate. While my people were interrogating your people in Boston, Redline rushed into Cooper's apartment where he encountered Mustafa Rashid in the very act of strangling the old man. Not Dr. Katz, but Mustafa Rashid! Redline killed Rashid and, with the aid of the gardener, Lyman Wolfe, helped Cooper escape. So that he could produce them later as evidence of your agency's complicity in the attempt on his life, Cooper hid Rashid's body and an old CIA report somewhere in Boston. The mysterious report contains a line-by-line record of a long-ago interrogation of a certain KGB psychiatrist—I think we both know who that was, thanks to Helen Rutz—and strong evidence that mind control played a role in the JFK assassination."

"Cooper could not have that report in his possession," barked Talbot. "I shredded the damn thing myself! You're making this up!"

"No, I am not making this up. It appears Dr. Katz made his own copy of the report. I believe Cooper blackmailed the doctor into handing it over," said Morse. "There are many other amazing statements in the undelivered speech. Surprising revelations about your mind-control project and the President's role in it."

"That demented little shit!" shrieked Talbot.

Morse watched Talbot twist in the wind for a while. Then he said quietly, "That isn't your worst problem now. Not by a long shot. There's a very dangerous man running around loose who wants to tell the world all about your scheme. That man is Jim Redline. He not only saw your operatives being taken into custody by my people, he then killed Rashid with his bare hands. And Cooper showed him the incriminating CIA report provided by Dr. Katz. I think we can also safely assume Redline knows where the CIA report and the terrorist's body are hidden. It's just a matter of time before he surfaces and blabs everything he knows to the press."

Talbot frantically searched Morse's steady eyes. He found nothing helpful there. "Why are you telling me this? To torture me? Where is Redline now? Do you know?"

"No idea," said Morse. *I had him and I lost him, you arrogant prick, but I'll be damned if I'm going to tell you that! Not when you continue to lie to me!*

Talbot pointed a trembling finger at Morse. "You're enjoying this, aren't you? You don't give a damn about national security or our careers or anything else tonight. You just want to watch my face as you tell me this shit."

"Normally," said Morse, "I would relish watching you suffer. But, we're *both* in trouble this time. I made some mistakes, too. Trust me when I say that I need to find and stop Redline just as badly as you do. It won't be fun, Charles, but we have to help each other if we're going to survive."

Talbot turned his head and stared through the tinted window of the limousine for a long time. "We're not going to survive. We're fucked. And so is the President."

"Not yet," said Morse. "It comes down to this. If we can stop Redline before he talks, we skate away clean."

"What are the odds we can find him?"

"Pitiful. But we can't let that stop us from trying. Agreed?"

"Agreed. What do you need from me? Manpower?"

"Obviously."

Talbot turned and searched Conrad Morse's eyes again. "Do you have any clue where Redline might be hiding? What he's wearing, how he's getting around, anything useful at all?"

"I do know some things about Redline." Morse folded his arms across his chest.

Talbot waited. When Morse said nothing more, he asked, "But before you share those things with me, you want something, don't you?"

"You are most perceptive when you're cornered, Charles."

Talbot rubbed his face with both hands. "You want to know what's really going on. Not just what Cooper wrote down in his speech. He couldn't know everything. He had to be guessing about a lot of it. Only I know everything. And you want to know everything I know."

"Exactly."

Talbot shrugged. "Okay. You win. What's your first question?"

Morse was so excited, he could barely speak. "What is it about that damned jewelry box that's so important to you and the President? Why did you risk everything to try and find it?"

Talbot slapped his knee and laughed until tears actually rolled down his cheeks. "Oh, my God! I can't believe this! You really think the jewelry box is the key to understanding what's going on? I had that box destroyed just hours after you first told me it existed. My people burned it to a crisp on the banks of the Yellowstone River in Montana! I didn't believe the box contained any important or new information about the JFK assassination, of course. But I was concerned that you had decided to let Lionel Cooper find it and write about it. Remember what you said? In your opinion, unless the box was important to my agency, then Cooper was free to write about it if he wanted. Well, I couldn't let that happen. I knew it would be extremely *inconvenient* for Lionel Cooper to speculate in print about JFK and mind control and all of that old conspiracy crap—even if it was bullshit—at the same time the President and I were covertly working on a way to manipulate the human mind. You see that, don't you, Conrad?"

Morse suddenly felt sick to his stomach. He whispered, "Your people burned the box?"

"Yes, we burned the fucking thing! It's a fact!"

Pale and shaking, Morse nodded. "Yes, of course you did. I see it now, Charles. It makes perfect sense because . . . you couldn't let anything interfere with your experiment. If only I had known, I could have moved faster than I did . . .or, better yet, just stopped worrying about . . . "

Morse's voice trailed off and he slumped in his seat. After a few minutes, he whispered, "Forget what I said earlier. I don't need to know any more about what's really going on than I already do. Let's concentrate on how we can keep Jim Redline from ruining us both."

"Excellent idea," said Talbot. "Let's start by reviewing everything you know about the man and go from there."

CHAPTER THIRTY-EIGHT

Bret Barringer and Jim Redline sat across from each other at a long gleaming table in Barringer's formal dining room. Redline had just bolted down two peanut butter and banana sandwiches, a bag of potato chips, four chocolate chip cookies and a quart of milk. He wet the tip of his finger and used it to snare a few rogue breadcrumbs. Barringer fiddled with a legal pad, two ballpoint pens, a glass of milk and a dinner plate heaped with cookies. After he had everything in its proper place, Barringer slumped back in his chair, folded his hands over his ample paunch and said, "Okay, Jim, let's hear it."

"Hang on a minute. Is that your family?" asked Redline. He pointed to a framed photograph of two females on a nearby étagère.

"Wife and daughter," said Barringer. "They're out of town. Incidentally, I have the next four days off. I've been slogging around in Ethiopia chronicling the AIDS epidemic. Have to take a break when I get back from a brutal trip like that to recharge my batteries. In the old days, I'd be in the office already, filing my report, screaming for extra airtime."

"Do you own a video camera?"

"Everybody owns a video camera."

"Good," said Redline. "I want to get some things on tape tonight. Could you bring the camera in here now, please?"

Barringer exited the dining room and returned a few minutes later with a compact video camera. Redline was standing beside the dining room table clad only in his jockey shorts. His impressively muscled body was peppered with raw bloody dots. There were enormous black bruises on his arms, legs and chest. The long sutured gash on his thigh was smeared with yellow antiseptic.

"Jim," gasped Barringer, "let me call a doctor! You should have told me you'd been in an accident!"

"Don't call anyone," said Redline. "A government doctor examined me this morning, pumped me full of antibiotics and assured me the puncture wounds and bruises will heal quickly. I'm fine, Bret. Well, 'fine' may not be the best word to describe how I am, but I'm not in serious trouble. Believe it or not, the pain is bearable. But please don't say anything hilarious tonight. It stings when I laugh. By the way, these injuries are not the result of an accident. A man did this."

"A man did that?"

"An FBI agent," said Redline. "He used a needle and a rubber hammer. He desperately wanted some information I was reluctant to share with him. When he threatened me with torture, I spit in his eye. Guy went ballistic. Knew exactly where to put the needle to cause pain without actually injuring me. And he resisted the temptation to damage my face. But he was out of shape and not able to beat me for long. Later, I encountered a couple of his associates. I was a little irritated myself by then. I put them both down. Commandeered a citizen's vehicle and drove here."

"You killed two FBI agents?"

"No. I've killed only one man in my life, Bret, and that was not intentional. Just a little over twenty-four hours ago, in fact. His name was Mustafa Rashid. The FBI agents are damaged but they'll live."

Barringer looked sick. "Slow down, Jim. I can't process information as quickly as I used to. You say the FBI tortured you? That's hard to believe. And Mustafa Rashid? You must be mistaken. He's in prison. I interviewed him in his cell less than a year ago."

Redline pointed at the camera. "Turn that thing on. I'm only going to say this once."

*

An hour later Barringer placed the camera on the dining table and sat down. "That's actually not the worst story I've ever heard, but it's probably in the top five. And it's quite creative. I'm sorry to say this, Jim, but I don't believe a word you said."

"You've heard worse stories than that one?"

"Sure. Remember Watergate?"

"Not really," said Redline. "A little before my time." As he talked, he dressed himself, then resumed his seat at the table.

"Watergate happened because Richard Nixon was paranoid," said Barringer. "His gang of merry pranksters were breaking into private offices all over Washington trying to dig up dirt on the Democrats. The President not only condoned their behavior, he encouraged it. I earned my spurs covering that story. When Nixon was forced to resign, tears of joy literally streamed down my cheeks. I was there when he handed Jerry Ford the keys to the Oval Office, strutted to his plane, gave America his famous two-fingered salute and roared off into permanent notoriety. One of the happiest days of my young life."

"You'll top even that day if you help me with this mess," said Redline. "If the current President and his pals have committed serious crimes—and it certainly appears to me they have—we should go after them," said Redline. "It's the right thing to do. We owe it to the country."

"It's the right thing to do? We owe it to the country? Are you crazy? Mind control? The JFK conspiracy thing *again*? Stealth and deception in the White House? I'm not sure the country wants to know that kind of stuff, Jim. Besides, you're talking about trying to take down some extremely powerful people. Dangerous people."

"But in the eyes of the law, those people are just men, right?"

"No. One of them is as close to being as immune from prosecution as you can get," said Barringer. "It's infinitely harder to convict the President of the United States than anyone else in the world. The President has a virtually impenetrable shield to hide behind. He has dozens of minions who do nothing all day but manufacture ways to provide him with plausible deniability in case he commits a felony. Consider that Nixon was the first President to face impeachment in one hundred years, Jim. If he hadn't recorded himself authorizing the Watergate cover-up, his enemies never would have succeeded in driving him out of office. Even though they knew for sure he was guilty as sin."

"But we have what Lionel used to call 'incontrovertible physical proof,'" said Redline. "We've got Mustafa Rashid's corpse and a copy of the Cold War CIA report. To say nothing of my eyewitness testimony concerning Rashid's assault on Lionel Cooper *and* the FBI's illegal inquisition against me. If we can get just that much of the story out there, the judicial system will probably take care of the rest. It isn't up to us to decide who's guilty here and who isn't. We just need to do our part. And maybe you'll get another Pulitzer to put in your trophy case, Bret, instead of diabetes from sitting around on your butt eating cookies all day."

"That's a terrible thing to say to a fat old man," said Barringer. He stuffed two cookies into his mouth at once. "I'm not going to do it, Jim. We try to move this story and you and I will be dead meat. That's a promise not a prediction."

"Why do you say that?"

"Because the President and his men will kill us," said Barringer. "I guarantee you the government has dropped a security net over the entire world by now that the Invisible Man couldn't slip through. If I call my boss right now and try to tell him what you just told me, the government will know about it within ten seconds. CNN has an obligation to cooperate with the government if national security is at stake. A military satellite will launch a rocket at my house and you and I will vanish in a cloud of pink vapor before I get halfway through the conversation."

"I know a way to get this message safely delivered to the world no matter how tight the government's net is," said Redline. "I figured it out on the drive down here."

Barringer guffawed. "You're wrong, Jim. We're like two flies trapped in a spider web. If we so much as scratch our nuts, the spider will instantly know where we are."

"Then we don't scratch our nuts," said Redline. "Come on, Bret. Trust me. We can do this."

"Jim, I'm not going to help you and that's final. First of all, in spite of your honest face, I don't believe you. Even if I thought some of what you said tonight was true, I still wouldn't risk everything I've worked for all my life to help you. I'm constitutionally unable to act when all I have to go on is the word of one irritated, injured and confused young man. I'm trained to observe the events taking place in the world and report only on what I personally see and believe. Now, please leave at once before I come to my senses and remember that I'm supposed to call the cops when a fugitive from justice breaks into my home."

"You refuse to help me?"

Barringer threw his hands in the air and bellowed, "That's right! Listen to me, Jim! I'm not going to help you! How many times do I have to say it?"

Redline's eyes chilled and darkened, as if black snow had drifted in behind them. He reached under his coat and removed Agent Smiley's pistol from its holster. Carefully, so as not to scratch the wood, he placed the gun on the dining room table. "I'm sorry, but you are going to help me, Bret," he said. "You're going to see and you're going to believe. And then you're going to help me."

"See and believe what?" asked Barringer, his eyes glued to the gun.

"You're going to see Mustafa Rashid's body," said Redline. "You're going to read the CIA report. Then I'm going to ask you one more time to help me."

"And if I say no?"

"You're not going to say no," said Redline.

Barringer sighed. "You said on the tape that Rashid's body and the CIA report are hidden in a warehouse somewhere in Boston. And you think we can get to that warehouse without being captured?"

"Yes," said Redline. "Even if we are picked up, it's me they want. I'll tell them I took you hostage at gunpoint. You'll walk away."

"I strongly disagree with your logic," said Barringer. "But let's assume we make it to the warehouse and I see the body and I read the report. What do you expect me to do then?"

"Then you deliver the tape we made tonight to a particular individual," said Redline. "Conveniently, he lives in Boston."

"And after I deliver the tape? You let me go so I can make an appointment with my psychiatrist and then start writing my memoirs?"

"After you deliver the tape, you'll arrange for me to meet an important politician in Washington, DC," said Redline. "That could be tricky, but it has to be done."

Barringer shuddered. "FBI headquarters is in Washington. You're walking us right into the lion's den. Furthermore, you're absolutely wrong, this does *not* have to be done. At least, not because 'it's the right thing to do,' as you claimed earlier. Cooper told me about you, Jim. He said you are an extremely angry young man. And he told me why. He said you don't realize how angry you really are down deep. This 'has to be done' because Lionel Cooper has been killed and you've been tortured and now you're way past being just another angry young man. You're furious. You want personal revenge. Am I right?"

Redline looked at Barringer for a long time. "Don't you ever get angry, Bret?"

"Not really. I used to get angry every day. I'd come home and stomp around the house and yell and scream and hate the world and everyone in it. But then, happily, I discovered the joy of cookies. Nothing like a fresh warm cookie to take the edge off my day. I literally chew my anger up and swallow it, Jim. Works great. You should try it."

"Thanks for sharing that with me," said Redline, grinning. He slipped Agent Smiley's gun back in its holster. "You just told me how to control you without resorting to violence. No more cookies. Not so much as jam on your toast in the morning. Not until we're finished in Boston. By the time we get to Washington, Bret, I want you so angry you can't see straight."

*

At her posh Boston health club, Janice McManus spent fifteen minutes bouncing around in a jazzercise class and half an hour gabbing in a sauna with three acquaintances. Then she squandered twenty minutes with a massage therapist, who not only poked and patted her pampered muscles until they were completely tension free, but also worked two pints of an exotic lotion into her golden skin. After some time in the hair salon and a quick trip to the juice bar for a papaya smoothie, Janice felt ready to face what was left of her morning.

She strolled across the parking lot behind the club toward her new Lexus sedan. A plump little man wearing a floppy-brimmed fishing hat, sunglasses and a wrinkled trench coat stood beside her car.

Damn it, thought Janice, not again! *Another sleazy reporter trying to get an exclusive interview with me about Lionel Cooper's death?* Don't these creeps ever give up? This guy has to be from one of the cheaper tabloids. That's the worst impression of Columbo I've ever seen!

"Hello, Janice," said the man. He touched two fingers to the brim of his hat.

"Look," said Janice, "I don't give interviews in parking lots. Certainly not to strangers dressed like *that*! I'm sorry, but if you're not Peter Falk, this conversation is already over."

The man pulled a wrapped package from inside his trench coat.

"This is for Stuart," he said. "It's a videotape. Jim Redline asked me to bring it to you. You remember who Jim Redline is, don't you, Janice? Lionel Cooper's bodyguard?"

Janice took a step backwards. "I, uh, I've never actually met Mr. Redline. I mean, yes, I know who he is. How did . . . what does he want from me?"

"Courier service," said the man. "Please take this package to Stuart and ask him to read the note inside and then watch the tape. It's very important that he do it today."

"Why should Mr. Redline . . . um, never mind. I understand. I'll see to it that my husband, that is, Stuart, uh, yeah, okay, I'll take it to him right now."

The man pointed a stubby finger at Janice. "Tell no one about this, my dear. We can't guarantee your safety if you do."

"I recognize that voice. Are you—"

"Good-bye, Janice," said the man. He turned and walked rapidly away.

324

That was Morley, thought Janice. No, wait. Morley is a lot taller than this fellow. And Morley wouldn't be caught dead in a wrinkled trench coat . . .

CHAPTER THIRTY-NINE

Stuart and Janice McManus sat side by side on the sofa in their den. He was holding the wrapped package in his hands, staring at it like it was a bomb.

"If I had a brain in my head," he said, "I'd call the FBI right now. Tell them Jim Redline just delivered this to me. Back away before I make a fatal mistake."

"Is that what you're going to do?" asked Janice.

"I don't know, but that's what a smart man would do."

Janice patted her husband's hand. "Honey, one of our best friends was murdered on national television in our front yard. Gunned down by the CIA! And then those grumpy FBI people questioned us for hours, trying to trick us into telling them what secrets Lionel had revealed when he showed up here. Lionel wouldn't lie to us. The President is up to something illegal and dangerous. Turning this package over to the FBI would be like, oh, I don't know, like aiding and abetting a criminal or something."

"Maybe," said Stuart. He opened the package. "I'll read this note while you get the VCR ready."

The cassette was wrapped in a sheet of lined paper. Stuart unfolded the paper and began to read the note neatly printed on it in blue ink. Janice slipped the videotape into the VCR and then wandered into the kitchen. In a few minutes, she returned to the den and put a carafe of coffee and two china cups on a low glass table in front of the sofa.

"I miss Daisy," she said. "Her coffee tasted a lot better than mine."

Without looking up, Stuart muttered, "I had to fire Daisy. She betrayed our trust. She somehow contributed to Lionel's death and she damn well knows it."

"Well, *you* don't know it," said Janice. She filled both cups. "Not for sure."

"I don't know anything for sure," said Stuart, "but I do what I think is right anyway."

Stuart finished reading the message. He sighed, put the sheet of paper down and picked up his coffee cup. "Well," he said, "here we go again."

"What did the note say?" asked Janice. She handed Stuart the remote control unit. "Am I allowed to know or is it a secret message intended just for you?"

Stuart looked at the shiny blank television screen and saw the fuzzy reflection of his own serious face staring back. It's like seeing myself as a ghost, he thought. Dead and dark and wispy. "Jim wants me to make five hundred and forty-five copies of this tape. And have the copies promptly delivered to five hundred and forty-five separate locations."

"How in the world did he come up with that precise number?" asked Janice.

"One copy for each senator and for each representative. That's five hundred and thirty-five tapes right there. The remaining copies go to radical Internet sites in the U.S. and Canada that are equipped with something called 'streaming video' technology. He says they'll distribute the contents worldwide. The idea is for me to get all of these tapes to these locations on the same day, at nearly the same time."

"Damn," said Janice.

"It's a planet-wide information blitzkrieg," said Stuart. "Jim is after the same thing Lionel was seeking when he came here—protection from certain people inside the FBI and the CIA. He says when nearly every ordinary human being on Earth has seen this tape, it's unlikely the federal agencies will use deadly force to keep him from testifying before a grand jury."

"Is he right about that?"

"I don't know."

"Why did he send the tape to *you*? Do you know each other that well?"

"He doesn't know me very well," said Stuart. "We shake hands once in a while and talk about the Red Sox. But he believes I'll do what he's asking me to do once I've seen this tape."

Janice stirred cream into her coffee. "How can you get hundreds of copies of that tape made and delivered? You can't even program the VCR."

"I most certainly can program the VCR," said Stuart. "I mastered that dumb machine a long time ago."

"I missed my soap opera this week because you mistakenly taped a tennis match."

"Sorry, dear, but that was no mistake," said Stuart. "In any case, Jim explains in the note exactly how I can get the tape copied and delivered. This is going to cost big bucks, Janice. Not copying the tape. That's a pittance compared to the money I'll be forking over to pay a fleet of greedy lawyers to defend me when the government finds out I'm the one who performed this act of treason or civil disobedience or whatever the hell it is."

Janice kissed her husband on the ear. "What good is money, anyway, if not for keeping lawyers clothed and fed and off our streets?"

"Easy for you to say. You'll be at your health club drinking yogurt smoothies while I'm making pea gravel out of granite boulders in a gay penitentiary someplace."

"Is that truly a worry?" asked Janice. "Or are you just saying that to scare me?"

Stuart pointed the remote control unit at the VCR and pushed the power button. "Let's look at this thing before I answer that question."

*

The President sat behind his desk in the Oval Office peering at Charles Talbot over the top of his half-moon reading glasses.

"You look like a man in the last stages of a horrible illness, Charles. Am I in trouble again because you've pulled another brainless

328

stunt? What the hell have you been up to while I've been tagging moose in the Klondike? Speak up, man!"

Avoiding the President's probing gaze, Talbot tapped the crystal on his watch. "I didn't sleep well last night, Mr. President. I'm expecting a critical phone call any second now. It should put me in a position to give you an up-to-the-minute briefing before you attend your press conference later this afternoon. It's vital that you respond confidently to every question reporters throw at you about the late Lionel Cooper's outrageously inaccurate accusations."

Talbot dropped his eyes and shuddered. He and Conrad Morse had one last chance to avoid catastrophe. The previous evening, operating on a strong tip, they had dispatched people from both agencies to a remote farm in Illinois. A county sheriff had spotted a man who looked a lot like James T. Redline hiding in a barn.

"I thought that was over and done with," said the President.

"Up to now, the press has quietly accepted the explanations we've given them. But they haven't had a chance to talk directly to you since Cooper died. I don't trust them, sir. They're vultures. They've probably saved their meanest questions for this afternoon."

"Don't bullshit me," said the President. "You're expecting bad news. It's written all over your face. Either that or you need to fart something awful."

"I'm not expecting bad news."

The President rubbed his eyes and yawned. "Well, then, fart, for Christ's sake. I can stand it. Tell me something, Charles. Why is it that these 'critical' phone calls always seem to come in at the last possible moment?"

"One of the great mysteries of all time, Mr. President."

The President stood, pushed his hands against the small of his back and walked to the tall glass doors at the rear of the Oval Office. "It's going to be a gorgeous day. Don't ruin it with bad news."

Talbot's cell phone chirped. He flicked it open, turned his back and took several quick strides away from the Chief's desk.

"Yes," he said quietly.

"Get your parachute out of the closet," said Conrad Morse. "Illinois was a dead end. The guy at the farm did, indeed, look like

329

James T. Redline, but he was just an escaped convict. Redline slipped through our net and put out a videotaped statement early this morning that nails all three of us to the cross. The chief of staff will be in the Oval Office in ten minutes to inform the President."

"How the hell could Redline do something like that? We told every media outlet in the world that any suspicious information was to be turned over to us for screening before it was made public!"

"He didn't bother with conventional media," said Morse. "He put it out on the Internet. Not only that, every member of Congress got a personal copy of the tape first thing this morning. My teenage son, whom I suspect is an amateur hacker, showed the tape to me before breakfast this morning. Headhunters in Borneo are probably watching it even as we speak. Hey, why don't you already know about this, Charles? Are your people asleep at the switch again?"

"I instructed my staff that I was not to be interrupted this morning."

"Well, then, you heard it here first. You are officially fucked."

"And I heard it from a world-class idiot. You're responsible for this disaster, Conrad!"

"Me? I'm responsible? At the risk of bruising your delicate ego, let me point out that if you had trusted me enough to be candid about your plans to destroy Helen Rutz's old jewelry box, none of this would have happened! It was your compulsive need to keep every single secret you know to yourself that has brought us to the gallows. Why you would lie to me when we're supposed to be a team is something I will never understand."

Talbot's cheeks prickled with rage and humiliation. "Damn it, you know I was under orders from the President to tell no one what he and I were working on. That included you! I trusted you to keep your big fat nose out of what was clearly not FBI business. That was my fatal mistake. In fact, it was my only mistake! Your perpetually suspicious mind coupled with your unbelievable incompetence as an intelligence officer are what delivered us to this point!"

"The only mistake you made was trusting me? Are you nuts? Your ludicrous decision to smuggle Mustafa Rashid into Lionel Cooper's home is the clearest example of reckless incompetence I have seen in all my years in this wretched business! Denial can't shield you from your own colossal blunders any longer, Charles. The truth will out! Furthermore . . . oh hell, what difference does any of this make now? We're both history."

"Any suggestions about what I should tell the President? I'm with him in the Oval Office right now."

"You're asking me? How the hell would I know what to tell the President? I'm unbelievably incompetent, remember?"

"Actually, I'm not asking you. I accidentally said aloud what I'm asking myself."

"Well, for what it's worth, all three of us are going to need the best lawyers money can buy. You could start by telling him that, I suppose. I called my lawyer before I left home this morning and invited him to lunch."

"You called your lawyer before you called me?"

"He can help me. You can't. So long, Charles. Barring a miracle, I'll see you in court. I promise not to tell the judge I think you're a gold-plated lunatic unless my lawyer advises me that by doing so I might avoid a double hanging."

Talbot dropped the phone into the inside pocket of his expensively tailored suit coat. The cords in his jaw had drawn painfully taut and his brooding dark eyes were fastened on something far away. Something ghastly . . .

"Well, I see you got your call," said the President. He had returned to his chair behind the big desk. He clasped his hands behind his head and smiled. "I'm ready to be briefed. What do you recommend I say to that flaming asshole from CNN when he asks me how much I know about your agency's off-the-books effort to develop psychological weapons of mass destruction? Or some obnoxious variation of that question?"

Stone-faced, Charles Talbot retrieved his briefcase, squared his shoulders and began walking resolutely toward the exit.

"Where the hell do you think you're going?" yelled the President. He jumped to his feet. "You don't leave this office until I say you can, mister! We're not finished talking!"

"Oh, we're finished talking, Mr. President," said Talbot under his breath. "We are definitely finished talking."

CHAPTER FORTY

Senator Quentin Baldwin from Nebraska, Senator Patty Jacobs from Vermont and Senator Dennis Wirtz from Idaho were seated around a conference table on the fourth floor of the Hart Senate Office Building in the nation's Capitol. The senior senator from the Cornhusker State was the ranking member of the minority party and one of the President's most intrepid foes. In the outer office, just beyond the locked conference room door, a dozen members of Baldwin's staff were working feverishly. Phones were ringing, fax machines were chattering and important people were lined up hoping for a chance to spend a few minutes with the influential politician.

"We've got that arrogant son of a bitch this time," crowed Baldwin. "It makes my mouth water when I contemplate all the horrible things that are about to happen to that insolent prick."

"How can you be so sure?" asked Jacobs. She sipped from a bottle of spring water. "He's the President. He can survive anything but a nuclear attack. You know something we don't?"

"You saw the tape," said Baldwin. "You saw and heard what Redline said, yet you aren't convinced we've got the President by the short hairs? Watch it again, Patty. And tune in to what the political sharpshooters have been discussing on the talk shows for the last two days. The President is in stinky poop up to his armpits. It'll be over his eyebrows by the time I get done with him. I can guarantee you that!"

"I wish I could agree," said Wirtz. "The tape raises some interesting questions about the President's recent behavior, but it's just one baby step in a complicated process that could take months to resolve, Quentin. And he'll be a wily foe. You don't drag the chief executive of the United States out of the White House for a public flogging just because one outraged citizen alleges the man has been up to no good. We'll have to mount a full-scale investigation. Special prosecutor, grand jury, the whole nine yards."

"Hell, I know *that*, Dennis," said Baldwin impatiently. "The tape hit town just forty-eight hours ago and the committee to manage the investigation has already formed. In fact, I'm the chairman of that committee. Mark my words, when this investigation is over, the President will walk the plank. Silver-tongued devil that he is, he can't talk his way out of this quagmire."

"Be serious, Quentin," said Jacobs. "Do you believe the President would give a moment's thought to an old superstition like *mind control*? Everybody knows the man's a coward, but he's not stupid. I think this is a trap. Somebody on his staff dreamed this whole thing up to make fools out of us. We'll look ridiculous if we say we believe the bizarre allegations on the tape before we have proof that they're true. And we'll certainly risk the goodwill of the President and our colleagues in his party if we appear too eager to believe that he's guilty as charged only to discover later that it's just an elaborate fraud. Who the hell is this Jim Redline character, anyway? Let me answer my own question. He's a handsome and muscular fugitive from justice and he worked for that scalawag Lionel Cooper! What does that tell you?"

"Tells me he was in the thick of this," said Baldwin. "Tells me he saw and heard everything."

"Well, what it tells me is that Redline is probably a conspiracy freak," said Wirtz. "Just like his late boss. Cooper never heard a rumor about a sitting President, no matter how outlandish, that he didn't believe. I heard Redline was Cooper's bodyguard. Plenty of muscle but short on brains. And no one has actually talked to him yet. Or cross-examined him. Or checked his urine for drugs."

"I agree with Dennis," said Jacobs. "Redline is undoubtedly an extremist. By the way, if he is forced to pee in a bottle to have his urine checked for drugs, I want to be there. The man is gorgeous."

"Before you come to any negative conclusions, consider these well-established facts," said Baldwin patiently. "The President is not only frightened of his own shadow, he's famously gullible, too.

Especially when it comes to things that involve his worst nightmare—assassination. The man would take seriously even a semi-credible rumor that a psychological weapon based on some form of mind control is available to his enemies. I'm right and you both know it."

"I'll agree that the President lacks personal courage and everything *could* have happened exactly as Redline said it did," said Jacobs. "But even if these stupid things did occur, will we ever be able to prove it? Absolutely not."

"That's right," said Wirtz. "There's the truth about life that we all come to understand as mature adults. Then there's the truth about life as defined by our legal system. Those two truths rarely match up. Never, in cases involving powerful people."

Baldwin waved his hand through the air like he was scattering pesky insects. "We don't have to be concerned about philosophical distinctions like that in this particular case," he said, "because somebody is going to crack like a piece of defective pottery and confess. That's all it will take to guarantee a legal victory for our side. One weak subordinate who can't stand the moral pressure that comes from knowing the scandalous facts. Or, better yet, a crafty survivor who gets good legal advice and agrees to trade incriminating information for immunity from prosecution before it's too damned late." He glanced at his watch. "In fact, I'll bet you two millionaires the most expensive lunch in Washington that the Attorney General has already been contacted by a couple of whistleblowers who match those descriptions to a fare-thee-well."

"Wait a cotton-picking minute," said Jacobs. "You're too cheap to make a bet like that unless you know you can't lose. Come on, Quentin. What's up?"

Baldwin produced a fat cigar and wiggled it like W. C. Fields. "Okay, you've forced my hand. I got a call from a confidential source in the Attorney General's office shortly before you distinguished lawmakers walked in here. Two people have already notified the AG that they are willing to fall on their swords in order to see justice done in America. Not one, mind you, but *two*! More are sure to follow. Remember Watergate? As soon as the pressure reached the boiling

335

point, the whistleblowers started coming out of the woodwork like cockroaches."

"That is a good sign," said Jacobs. "And everyone knows the AG hates the President. She has been quite clear about that."

"Your words, not mine," said Baldwin smoothly.

"Wow," said Wirtz. "Whistleblowers already? That must be a record for the fastest capitulation this town has ever seen! Did your confidential source identify the squealers?"

Baldwin plucked a piece of paper from his shirt pocket. "Yes, and I wrote it down. One is a female psychiatrist who works for the CIA. She claims that, at the urging of the Director himself, she put Mustafa Rashid in a deep hypnotic trance in an effort to influence him to become an assassin for our side. She says she will testify that Rashid was taken to Cooper's apartment by CIA operatives. He had orders to kill anyone he encountered there. It was a test to see if the mind-control experiment was working. By the way, she also remarked that, in her professional opinion, the concept of total mind control is patently ridiculous."

"Holy cow," said Jacobs. "The CIA arranging for the assassination of an American civilian? Isn't that against the Geneva Convention or something?"

"Who's the other sniveling coward?" asked Wirtz. "Excuse me. I meant to say, who's the other national hero?"

"Although his name was never uttered, my source managed to convey that it's the FBI's Assistant Director for Counterintelligence, Bill Williams. Williams says his boss became so obsessed with locating a strange antique jewelry box that he violated every law known to man. The box allegedly contains proof that mind control played a part in the JFK assassination. Cooper and Redline were also chasing that box. Conrad Morse believed Charles Talbot was desperate to get his hands on it, too. Williams says Morse ordered him to ignore the Constitution and basic human decency and take whatever risks were necessary to find the box. Apparently one of the things Director Morse tacitly approved was the brutal torture of Jim Redline during a botched attempt to get him to reveal the location of the damned thing."

"Heads will roll if we can prove the FBI tortured a civilian," said Jacobs. "Big, fat, stupid heads. That said, I remain skeptical about all of this. By the way, I collect antique jewelry boxes. If that one shows up, I'd like to have it."

"I'm way beyond skeptical now," said Wirtz. "No way any of this happened. It's science fiction. I mean it, Quentin. The more you talk, the more sure I am that we're being set up by someone in the other party. If we fall for transparently bogus crap like this, we deserve to forfeit our seats in the Senate come election time."

"You're right, Dennis," said Jacobs. "Something strange is going on here, but it isn't what we think it is. Can't be. Too weird, even for Washington."

"You are both dead wrong," said Baldwin. He watched them through half-lidded eyes, like a lizard.

Wirtz scrambled to his feet. "It wouldn't be the first time I was wrong. I hate to run off, but I'm chairing a meeting that started without me ten minutes ago. In parting, let me say this. It's possible that the FBI and the CIA, while performing their normal duties, screwed up a sensitive operation in some way and Redline is massively pissed off about it. But that doesn't mean the President will go down the drain if an investigation reveals his intelligence agencies dropped the ball. If he authorized both Directors to proceed with whatever it was they foolishly agreed to do for him, then you can bet the farm he arranged for full deniability first. Whatever it was he wanted them to do—mind-control experiments or neutralizing Lionel Cooper or whatever—you'll never prove in court that the President had advance knowledge about any illegal methods they were forced to use."

"Correct," said Jacobs. She got up, too, and began to move toward the door. "If I were President—and I will be someday—and I wanted something illegal or immoral done, I'd make damn sure there were no footprints leading back to me before I gave the project the green light. I have to go now, Quentin. Important people are waiting for me across town."

Senator Baldwin rolled his unlit cigar under his nose and sniffed loudly. "Enjoy your meetings today, Senators. Go make useless new laws or waste a few more bales of taxpayers' money on pork projects for your home states. The business of running the country into the ground won't wait while us canny old-timers arrange for a trivial matter like the impeachment of the other party's top man."

Jacobs took a baby step back toward the conference table and pointed her water bottle at Baldwin like it was a deadly ray gun.

"I recognize that sniff," she said. "Out with it, Quentin."

Wirtz said, "Are you still trying to get us to buy your lunch, or do you really know something juicy?"

Baldwin propped his double chin on his blubbery chest and folded his hands across his belly. "Well, there *was* one other minor thing. On a hunch, I called the man who is responsible for keeping the 'black books' in which the CIA hides a significant portion of their operating budget. I refer, of course, to funds they secretly cobble together each year from anonymous sources inside the federal bureaucracy. Unreported, cleverly disguised funds that make it possible for the agency to finance their most delicate operations without having to tell anyone in Congress a damn thing about what they're up to or what it's costing the taxpayers. I've known this particular source for many years. As soon as I heard his voice on the phone, I could tell he was wallowing in disgust."

"We know all about the secret intelligence money, Quentin," said Jacobs. "What did your disgusted friend tell you?"

Baldwin closed his eyes and let a full twenty seconds elapse before he spoke again. "He said if Congress were to take a peek at the CIA's black books right this minute, we'd have a new Chief in the Oval Office before you could say 'mind control' three times."

Jacobs and Wirtz trotted back to their seats.

"What are you planning to do with *that* information?" asked Wirtz.

"Now that you know the President is *at least* guilty of financing the mind-control experiments?" asked Jacobs.

"First things first," said Baldwin. He leaned forward so he could talk softly and still be heard. "Ask yourselves this question. Should we be sitting idly by while the FBI and the CIA try to find and arrest and perhaps kill Jim Redline, or should we be offering this brave young man sanctuary so he will live to tell a grand jury what he knows about this fiasco?"

"Oh, I get it," said Jacobs, nodding her head. "Until you talked to your friend about the black books, you didn't consider sanctuary for Redline because, like both of us, you feared he might be part of a politically motivated hoax."

"A hoax that would only become visible after a protracted and massively expensive government investigation," said Wirtz.

"When it comes to accusing a sitting President of a felony, any prudent person would hesitate until he was sure," said Baldwin. "And I'm nothing if not prudent. However, now that I've satisfied myself that Redline is the real deal, I'm ready to act decisively. Even risk my career. I believe Jim Redline can help us put together an investigation that will result in the speedy removal of Conrad Morse and Charles Talbot, as well as the eventual impeachment of an unfit president. And, incidentally, put *our* glorious party back in power."

"You're going to offer Redline sanctuary immediately?" asked Jacobs. "Without collecting any additional evidence to bolster your theory?"

"Are you *that* sure, Quentin?" asked Wirtz.

"No, I'm not that sure," confessed Baldwin. "I'd prefer to make a hundred more phone calls, triangulate a bunch of facts and lock down my proof tighter than a tick on a hog's ass. Unfortunately, I don't have the luxury of time. To quote a great Cornhusker football coach, 'It's late in the game. Three yards and a cloud of dust just won't get us where we need to go. We have no choice but to throw a Hail Mary!' In other words, something has to be done *today*, Senators, because the man we're depending on to change the course of political history could be in a sniper's crosshairs even as we speak."

"But, to do *anything*, you'd have to find Redline first," said Wirtz. "If the FBI and the CIA can't locate this guy, what makes you think you can?"

"You believe I can't find him, Dennis, because you're a coward. If you were Jim Redline, you'd be in Aruba today, pickling your liver with rum punch, hoping to kill yourself with booze before a government assassin cut your throat," said Baldwin. "But if you could think like a brave man, just for a moment, you'd know that I don't have to find Jim Redline."

"What the hell are you talking about?" asked Jacobs.

Baldwin finally lit his cigar. Then he looked at his watch again. "Think about it. In spite of the incredible risks, Jim Redline is determined to stand and fight. He's living proof that good things happen when ordinary individuals find the courage to do the right thing. We need more citizens like him. In fact, we need a president like him."

Someone rapped hard on the office door.

"Excuse me," said Baldwin. He walked to the door, unlocked it, opened it and stood aside as two men stepped into the room. One was short and plump. He was dressed in wrinkled slacks, a pink polo shirt and a faded blue blazer. His press credentials were pinned crookedly to his jacket pocket. The younger man was tall, broad-shouldered and good-looking. He wore dark glasses, black jeans, dirty sneakers and a sweat-stained baseball cap with the CNN logo stenciled on it. He held a professional-grade video camera in his hand.

"Senator Jacobs, Senator Wirtz, I'm sure you both know Bret Barringer."

Barringer muttered an unintelligible greeting.

"And this young gentleman with Bret," said Baldwin, "cleverly disguised as his cameraman, is the fellow we've been talking about all morning."

Neither senator spoke or moved for a moment. Then Senator Jacobs dropped her water bottle on Senator Wirtz's foot as she rushed to embrace Jim Redline.

CHAPTER FORTY-ONE

The President traveled by limousine to his personal attorney's sprawling Maryland home at three o'clock one moonless Saturday morning. He knew it would be politically damaging to meet openly with his attorney in the Oval Office or the residence or Air Force One. In fact, anyplace where curious staffers or members of the press might see them together and speculate about what was up.

Preston Howard was waiting just inside the open front door. He wore a dark blue suit, white shirt and red tie. The President was dressed casually in a bright orange satin jogging ensemble, a gift from the board of directors of the Special Olympics. Howard solemnly shook hands with his famous client and walked him into a comfortable book-lined study.

Outside, two Secret Service men bracketed the front door. Two other heavily armed agents guarded the President's vehicle and tried to sort through all manner of peculiar night sounds.

The President and his attorney sat across from each other in big leather chairs. After a few moments of awkward silence, the President cleared his throat and began.

"Sorry to bother you at this ungodly hour, Preston," he said. "Frankly, I didn't think this annoying problem would ever reach my level. Now I wish I had consulted with you months ago. Where should I start?"

"Mr. President, I must know the truth," said Howard gravely. "The raw, unvarnished, perhaps even embarrassing truth. For purposes of this first discussion, talk to me as if I am the most trusted friend you have in the entire world. When you're finished, I'll leave to brew a pot of coffee. When I walk back into this room, I'll no longer be your friend. I'll be your attorney. It will be as if we had never discussed this matter before. The truth, as you understand it, will be irrelevant. As your attorney, my focus will be restricted to how I can mount a winning defense if formal charges are brought against you. In other words, during our second discussion, I'll determine what is true and what is not."

"Agreed," said the President.

"Naturally," Howard continued, "I have been tracking the cases pending against FBI Director Conrad Morse and CIA Director Charles Talbot. Neither man has said anything yet that is fatally damaging to you. I say yet, because rumor has it that Talbot is contemplating a deal offered to him yesterday by the special prosecutor. If he agrees to testify about what you knew and when you knew it, and confesses to several lesser crimes, the prosecution is prepared to drop Talbot's worst nightmare, the attempted murder charge."

The President nodded.

"It appears Talbot has little choice in the matter. If he does not cooperate with the prosecution and is eventually convicted of sanctioning the attempted murder of Lionel Cooper, he could be looking at life in prison," said Howard.

"Charles will take that deal in a heartbeat," said the President. "And he'll lie in order to satisfy the special prosecutor's sinister expectations concerning my culpability. Charles Talbot is a spineless worm."

"Yes, but he's a crafty spineless worm with only one goal—to survive this train wreck no matter who he has to sacrifice," said Howard. "Fortunately, Conrad Morse has no damning first-hand information about you that he can trade for favors. Thanks to the testimony of James T. Redline and numerous disenchanted subordinates inside the Bureau, Morse will be writing his memoirs in prison."

"How much damage can this Redline fellow do to me? He said things in his tape that, although false, may sound convincing to the special prosecutor. I find it amazing that an ordinary citizen, one I've never met and for whom I bear no animosity, would willingly tell such outrageous lies about me."

"James T. Redline is not a direct threat to you," said Howard. "Although, if he were not in the equation, none of this would be happening. He set the stage for the destruction of Morse with his grand jury testimony. And he badly wounded Talbot when, to the amazement of everyone, he actually produced what he said he would—a copy of the Cold War CIA report and Mustafa Rashid's corpse. But everything he has said about you he got secondhand from the late Lionel Cooper. In other words, in a court of law, his accusations will be dismissed as hearsay. His statements are dangerous to you only in that they will tend to nudge the special prosecutor in a particular direction when he begins his investigation into your possible role in all of this."

"Redline is merely a catalyst?" asked the President. "His personal experiences and controversial allegations have created a potentially harmful curiosity among my enemies about my part in this farce, but he's not in a position to testify against me?"

"Correct. Incidentally, Redline is an accidental catalyst," said Howard. "It's clear to me he's a player in this case only because he was in a certain place at a particular time. In fact, this entire brouhaha is a classic example of what can transpire when random events come together in an unpleasant way, Mr. President. You're here this morning because you've had a run of exceptionally bad luck, sir."

"I guess there's a first time for everything. I've never experienced bad luck before, Preston. I don't like it."

"I hear you," said Howard. "Now then, please tell me how this all got started, Mr. President."

The President took a deep breath and tried to relax. He knew that Preston Howard was a lawyer who would do absolutely anything to win a case. He was physically impressive, brilliant, experienced and ruthless. Howard had the look and bearing of a highly successful man who could prevail over any real-world problem that came his way. Assuming his client could afford his astronomical fees, of course.

The President folded his arms across his orange chest and sighed theatrically.

"It began quite innocently, Preston. The head of NASA told me that he had inside information that there was a CIA report hidden away someplace that contained credible evidence that absolute control over at least one human mind had long ago been achieved and documented. Of course, his interest in the report had to do only with his desire to find the best way to manage the behavior of bored astronauts on future space voyages to Mars. But I immediately saw other possibilities. I decided to find out, once and for all, if mind control was fantasy or fact. That might sound absurd to you. Most people assume mind control is pure science fiction. But I felt it was my duty as Commander in Chief to know if a dangerous weapon like that existed anywhere in the world. I asked Charles Talbot for help. He quickly located the last copy of the old report."

"I see," said Howard. "The last copy."

"The report is controversial, to put it mildly."

"Quite," said Howard. "As I understand it, not everyone present for the KGB psychiatrist's interrogation agreed with his allegations concerning his success in programming Oswald. In fact, more than half of the medical people there said it was balderdash. Right?"

"Yes, but real leadership requires unbounded imagination, Preston, not blind allegiance to the opinions of people who will never experience the global perspective a man in my position enjoys. I read the report carefully and interpreted it as, well, promising. I asked Charles to run some experiments using modern drugs and new hypnotic techniques in combination with the detailed clinical information provided by the KGB doctor."

"Sounds logical to me," said Howard. "You had a responsibility to ignore conventional wisdom and determine if your adversaries might possess psychological weapons that would be impossible to detect until it was too late. The recent rash of foreign 'suicide bombers' certainly supports the notion that some form of mind control is in play overseas. You wanted Talbot to find out what the art of brainwashing looks like when it's taken to its absolute limits. Tell me exactly what you were thinking when you asked him to try to build a 'controllable human assassin.' What did you expect him to produce?"

344

"I did not think I would see a man in a trance, someone completely at the mercy of a human master, come stumbling out of a CIA laboratory. Nothing like the robotic monsters you see in the movies."

"Of course you didn't, Mr. President. You're far too sophisticated for that. Unfortunately, the lab results could not be satisfactorily evaluated after Mr. Redline killed the experimental assassin in self-defense. What did you intend to do with a totally programmable assassin, Mr. President, if one were made available to you?"

The President smiled. "I know that Redline said on his tape that Lionel Cooper believed I intended to direct the new human weapon at a terrorist leader hiding in the Middle East. A madman who has told the whole world that he will see me dead if it's the last thing he ever does. I admit the thought of using the assassin against that individual was my original incentive for investigating mind control. Staying alive so I can continue to lead the Free World in my own unique way is a responsibility I take seriously. Charles Talbot will testify that even though he was locked away in a federal prison, Mustafa Rashid was selected for the experiment because he had an intimate relationship with the terrorist lunatic. He was the only person under our direct control who could get close enough to do the deed. And Charles would be telling the truth because, as far as he knew, that was still my plan."

"But something changed? Something you didn't share with Talbot?"

"Yes. By the time the experiment had reached the point where the only thing left to do was test it, my thinking had evolved. I realized that using the new weapon to kill that particular enemy was not an option. For reasons I will never understand, that villain is a hero to over a billion people in his part of the world. If even one tiny mistake compromised our clandestine effort to take him out, the result could be retribution against the entire United States. I could not risk that just to protect myself. Had Charles come to me with the news that his people had perfected mind control, I had decided to tell him to abort the original mission. He would have been disappointed, of course, and would have begged for permission to proceed. But, even at the risk of sacrificing my own life, I would have said 'no.'"

"You're saying Talbot was eager to run the mind-control experiments when you asked him to do so? You didn't have to offer him any kind of personal incentive, Mr. President?"

The President adroitly covered his distress at this perceptive question by laughing out loud and slapping his knee. "Absolutely not. Charles could hardly wait to get started. And he was quite confident that he would succeed."

"Congratulations, Mr. President. Like all great leaders, you eventually came to the correct decision. The courageous decision. It's a shame you never had the opportunity to discuss that decision with Director Talbot. On the record, so to speak."

"Yes," said the President, frowning. "A real pity."

Howard was silent for a moment. Then he said, "How did you fund this project?"

"I pressured Congress to approve NASA's proposed Mars expedition. Then I authorized Charles to siphon a portion of that money into his black books."

Preston Howard pursed his lips. "Bad idea, Mr. President. Your enemies can track that money. They'll know you made those resources available to fund the experiment."

"Yeah," said the President. "Is there anything you can do about that?"

"Maybe," said Howard. "As long as everything else you did was legal and above board, I might be able to sweep that under the rug."

"We'll be fine, then," said the President.

"Sir, you are obligated to discuss a project of this magnitude with your National Security Advisor, the Vice President, the Chief of Staff, the Attorney General and key members of Congress. Yet you chose to go it alone. Tell me why you made that decision."

"I had no choice but to exercise personal authority in this case," said the President. "The information in the CIA file strongly suggests that both the Russians and the Cubans were directly involved in the assassination of President Kennedy. If that information had leaked during the Cold War, it could have provoked a nuclear showdown. President Johnson feared that possibility so much he ordered the report and all related documents destroyed. When I learned that one copy had miraculously survived, I made the decision to conceal the new mind-control experiments from everyone on my staff in order to minimize the possibility of a security leak that might have dire political consequences. Even now, when Communism no longer poses a serious threat to America, there are those in my administration who would insist on an invasion of Cuba if they thought Castro was responsible for Kennedy's death."

"I don't understand," said Howard. "You chose to keep secret an unconfirmed rumor about a foreign conspiracy to murder JFK? Mr. President, rumors like that are legion. And no sensible person would have taken this particular version seriously. It's too far-fetched."

The President bristled. "It's not what really happened in Dallas that we have to fear, Preston, it's what people are willing to believe really happened. It's clear we must continue to use the shield of 'national security concerns' to keep unreliable people with loose lips from finding out about the contents of that report."

"We can try," said Howard. "Now I must ask you the most difficult question of all. When did you know that Charles Talbot planned to test the results of his experiment by ordering his assassin to kill Lionel Cooper?"

"Not until it was too late to prevent it. During a private conversation, Charles told me he had to test the weapon before he could be sure that it was foolproof. He didn't reveal the identity of the individual the assassin was going after. I had demanded full deniability from the beginning of this sensitive project, of course. Charles knew better than to say anything I shouldn't hear. I just assumed the weapon would be dispatched to destroy someone on our approved target list. A minor foreign dictator or a troublesome spy or even another assassin. Someone I wanted dead."

"You did not want Lionel Cooper dead?" Howard's eyes narrowed as he studied the President's reaction to his question.

The President shifted his gaze to a magnificent painting on the paneled wall directly behind Preston Howard's head. "Lionel Cooper is not on any approved government hit list. Therefore, it did not occur to me that Charles would select him. I was horrified when I learned that a distinguished American citizen had been chosen as the target.

Speaking of distinguished American citizens, is that an original Andrew Wyeth painting, Preston?"

Preston Howard stared at his client for an uncomfortably long time.

He's trying to read my mind, thought the President. He's looking for the fatal mistake, the lie he can't cover up. He won't find it . . .

"Yes, it's an original Wyeth," said Howard. "A present from my wife."

"Must have cost a fortune," said the President.

"Why would Director Talbot order Mustafa Rashid to murder Lionel Cooper if he had even a tiny suspicion that you would disapprove? Was he under the impression that you would be pleased to discover that this man, considered by many Americans to be a relentless foe of political corruption, was dead? If so, how did he arrive at that conclusion? As you have pointed out, Talbot had any number of politically acceptable targets available. How could a man of his experience make a terrible error in judgment like that? I ask the question, Mr. President, because I believe the most formidable challenge for the defense will be convincing a jury that the decision to kill Lionel Cooper was made by the Director of the CIA alone, without your blessing."

"Give me a moment to think," said the President. "Let me try to recall exactly what I said to Charles and what he said to me."

Preston Howard watched as the President silently composed his response.

"As I said earlier, although I knew in advance that Charles intended to test his new weapon against a real target, I assumed he would try to take out a foreign threat to the security of the United States. Someone whose death would be welcomed by the intelligence community but go unnoticed by the average citizen. I was in Denver when I heard that Lionel Cooper had disappeared under mysterious circumstances. I phoned Charles immediately—"

"Why?" interrupted Howard sharply. "Why would you think there might be a link between the disappearance of Cooper and the mind-control experiments?"

The President was surprised by the question. "It just seemed too coincidental. I think anyone walking around with the kind of information I had in my head would have suspected a connection. I called Charles and demanded to know what was going on. I don't remember exactly what he said, but he let me know that Cooper's fate was tied to the mind-control experiments. I expressed outrage. Charles seemed surprised that I was upset but told me not to worry. He said he would take care of everything. Then he suggested I fly to Alaska for a few days and avoid answering direct questions from the press about the matter."

Preston Howard removed a handkerchief from his pocket and swiped at some invisible dust on the toe of his shoe. Then he stood and extended his hand. "Mr. President, that concludes the first part of our discussion. Please relax while I fetch some coffee. Oh, I almost forgot to ask. How are you and the First Lady getting along these days?"

The President smiled as he shook Howard's hand. "We're getting along great, thank you. In fact, I'd say the glory that quite naturally comes with my office has had a positive effect on my wife's libido. You know what they say, Preston. The best aphrodisiac known to man is power."

*

Preston Howard stepped into his kitchen. The coffee was already percolating. He opened a door leading into a small soundproof room adjacent to the kitchen. Two young people were seated at computer stations. The man looked up and smiled. The woman continued to stare intently at her computer monitor.

"Who do I thank for starting the coffee right on time?" asked Howard.

"You can thank me," said the young man. "I lost the coin toss. The computer has just finished compiling the information the voice analyzer recorded as you and the President were talking."

"I'm printing it for you now," said the woman. "When the President tells the truth, the analyzer prints his words in blue. When he lies, the words are in red."

"And the words in yellow?" asked Howard, peering at the pages rolling from the printer.

"Yellow means the President didn't know the truth but felt the need to say something anyway," said the man.

Howard quickly scanned the six-page printout. "No surprises here," he said. "Well, maybe the part about his relationship with his wife. Everything else matches my sense of his performance. But it's reassuring to have confirmation from a machine that has no party affiliation. My next discussion with the President should conclude rapidly. As soon as he leaves the house, I'll join you two in the kitchen."

*

Preston Howard returned to the study and resumed his seat. He was conspicuously empty-handed. He smoothed his tie across his belly.

"Where's the coffee?" asked the President. "Been so long since you made it yourself you forgot how to do it, Preston?"

"Mr. President," said Howard, "I am speaking to you now as your attorney, not as your friend. In my professional opinion, if we're forced into court, we'll lose. I see only one reasonable option, one opportunity for you to avoid impeachment or even imprisonment. I must call the special prosecutor this morning and tell him you have agreed to resign your office within the week. I'll tell him you are resigning not because you're afraid to face your accusers and certainly not because you're guilty of a crime, but in order to save the nation from the emotional stress and economic turmoil that would accompany a long and bitter trial. I'll say that your selfless act is also motivated by your responsibility as Chief Executive to protect the nation's security by seeing to it that certain potentially volatile state secrets are never discussed in open court."

The President gasped and jumped to his feet. He began walking awkwardly around the study. "Holy shit," he said. "This is not my fault, Preston. I didn't do anything wrong. Surely you see that?"

Howard stood up, too. "Yes, Mr. President. This is incredibly unfair. You are in an impossible situation. Naturally, I will help you make the same arrangements with your vice president that Richard Nixon did with Gerald Ford. That is, I will encourage her to pardon you shortly after she is sworn in. Mr. President, I urge you to go home and build a museum to house your important papers and awards. When this unsavory chapter in your long and honorable political career has been reduced by time to an obscure footnote, you will be welcomed back to Washington as a respected member of the most elite club in the world. And you will be remembered almost exclusively for the countless good things you did for this country. In fact, sir, you will not only survive this moment of undeserved suspicion, you will be regarded by generations to come as one of the most effective presidents in American history."

The President shuffled around aimlessly and then stopped in front of the Andrew Wyeth painting. As he studied it, he clasped his hands behind his back. "I don't know if I believe everything you just told me, Preston, but one thing is clear. History will remember me as the man who finally did what everyone feared might never happen in this country. I will put a woman in the White House. That's a pretty decent legacy, is it not?"

"It's a wonderful legacy, Mr. President."

The President leaned forward and carefully removed the large painting from the wall. He admired it for a moment and then smashed it repeatedly against his raised knee. The gilded oak frame snapped and the protective glass exploded into tiny fragments. With great deliberation, the President tore the delicate canvas to shreds. Then he dropped the tattered remnants of the priceless American masterpiece on the floor at Preston Howard's feet.

"You can bill the Vice President for your loss, Preston," said the President as he walked away. "You're about to become her new best friend."

EPILOGUE

Jim Redline and Senator Quentin Baldwin sat enjoying a private lunch in the politician's cramped office in downtown Omaha, Nebraska. It had been raining hard for hours. A fierce wind rattled the windows. There was a tornado watch in effect across the entire county.

"I can't do it, Jim," said Baldwin. He dabbed at the corners of his mouth with a paper napkin. "It's against the law for me to disclose privileged information to a citizen who does not have a clear need to know."

"This is privileged information, too," said Redline. He held up a manila envelope. "And I'm offering it to you in exchange for what you know about the jewelry box and the CIA report. Seems like a fair deal to me."

Baldwin tugged a plastic toothpick from his shirt pocket and began to explore the spaces between his teeth. "You want me to tell you everything I learned about the fate of the CIA report and the jewelry box during the closed-door testimony given by Conrad Morse and Charles Talbot? You expect me to risk my exemplary political career in exchange for that silly envelope, which you claim is full of potentially incriminating information about me? Horrible stuff you say Cooper and his slimy gardener collected over the years? That's blackmail, Jim. You should be ashamed of yourself."

"It isn't blackmail," said Redline. "It's a quid pro quo, a game you told me you invented years ago."

Baldwin snorted. "I was pulling your leg, Jim. Quid pro quo was invented by Julius Caesar's great grandfather, Moses."

"Look at it this way," said Redline. "I risked death when I crept back to Boston and smuggled this information out of Cooper's warehouse. I did that *before* Bret Barringer contacted you seeking protection for me. I was thinking of your welfare, Senator, even when I wasn't sure I'd live another twenty-four hours. Thinking of you and realizing I had to purge the files in that warehouse in case Lionel had information about you that could be harmful."

"And he did," said Baldwin uneasily. "Or so you say, Jim."

"I wouldn't lie to you."

"No? Listen, you went back to Boston to pack Rashid's decomposing body in fresh ice," said Baldwin, "and that's all you intended to do. And then you couldn't resist taking a peek at Cooper's secret files. Miracle of miracles, you found one with my name on it and had a brainwave."

"I had three things on my mind before I walked into that warehouse," said Redline. "First, I wanted to make sure Rashid's body was adequately cooled. Second, I wanted Bret Barringer to read the CIA report, cover to cover. But my third reason was to find and remove any incriminating information about you that might be stored there. Seemed like the right thing to do. Of course, if you had refused to provide me with sanctuary, I might have been forced to drop the quid pro quo card on you right then."

"You ever play chess, Jim?" asked Baldwin. "No? Too bad, you'd be a natural at it. You're six moves ahead of everyone else all the time. And you're stubborn as hell, too. Don't you ever take 'no' for an answer? I told you an hour ago I wouldn't do this. And I meant it."

"I wasn't ahead of everyone in this game," said Redline. "Someone got out in front of me and derailed my search for the jewelry box."

"Wait a minute," said Baldwin, pointing his toothpick at Redline. "Didn't I hear that you and Barringer are co-authoring a book? What did my assistant tell me about that? Barringer's agent was quoted in *Publisher's Weekly* as saying the title will be 'Club Red.' Did I get that right, Jim? What the hell does that mean, anyway?"

"It's a book Lionel intended to write a long time ago," said Redline. "I discussed the concept with Bret and he agreed to help me.

You'll have to read 'Club Red' to find out what the title means, Senator."

"Oh, I'll read it, Jim. But I better not see anything in there that sounds like what I'm going to tell you today. This is strictly confidential. Just between us boys. You tell anyone about this and I'll live out my few remaining years snacking on bugs in the rain forests of Borneo."

"I'm here only to satisfy my curiosity, Senator, not to gather material for 'Club Red.' You have my word."

Baldwin sighed. "Okay, here goes. Under oath, Conrad Morse stated that at the request of the President he had been secretly keeping tabs on Lionel Cooper for years. He said his mole, the late Tina Romero, alerted the FBI about the jewelry box caper. Following an intense conversation with Charles Talbot, Morse ordered his people to pursue the box with a vengeance. He believed if he could get his hands on it, Talbot would have no choice but to tell him the truth about 'certain things.' When he was asked *what* 'certain things,' Morse played dumb. Finally, he said 'the truth about what was really going on. Talbot was lying to me about something and I couldn't abide that.' But guess what, Jim?"

"What?"

"Director Morse failed. Charles Talbot testified that he sent people after the jewelry box within minutes of first hearing about it. Claimed the box was a pile of ashes just hours later. Said he did that because he believed Morse intended to let Cooper bring the stupid thing to the attention of the public. Talbot thought that could negatively affect the secret mind-control project he was working on for the President. He didn't tell Morse what he had done. So Morse spent a ton of money and broke a lot of rules in a futile effort to acquire the box. Morse's people *did* come back from Montana with a jewelry box, but the Bureau's scientists quickly determined it wasn't the right one. That's when Morse decided to focus on you, Jim. He believed you either had the real box or knew where it was."

"Charles Talbot said his people stole the original box and destroyed it? And then an FBI agent brought a bogus box back to Washington?"

"Yes," said Baldwin. "Furthermore, as soon as the judge realized that the alleged contents of the jewelry box had no specific relevance to the crimes committed by Morse or Talbot, he instructed everyone in the courtroom to forget they had ever heard about it. Same thing with the CIA document. The judge said the report was classified government property. He said President Johnson had ordered it destroyed for a damned good reason and the court would honor that order. Then the judge instructed the bailiff to remove the document from the evidence table and have it shredded at once. He also remarked that Director Talbot had done the government a big favor by burning the jewelry box."

"Very interesting," said Redline. "Exactly when did Talbot's people grab the original jewelry box? Date and time, if you have it." He had his pencil poised over his spiral notebook.

"You're addicted to meaningless details, Jim." Baldwin jerked open a drawer in his desk and removed a file. He opened it and impatiently flipped through some papers. "Believe it or not, I took notes that day. Never had to do that before because I always had my secretary at my side. But this time they wouldn't let anyone in the courtroom except me and one other member of my investigating committee because . . . okay . . . here it is. I jotted down the date and the approximate time." He recited the details of when the original box was destroyed, according to Talbot's best recollection. "And here's when Conrad Morse said his agent grabbed a jewelry box he *thought* was the correct one."

Redline scribbled in his notebook. Then he compared Baldwin's information to what he had recorded a year earlier when Dan Maples of Javelina Investigations had provided him with the exact date and time Gene Zane had phoned Kitty Carson to tell her he wanted to buy the old jewelry box back. He put his notebook in his pocket, stood up, handed the manila envelope to Baldwin and said, "Burn this before you look at it."

Baldwin scowled, grabbed the envelope and tossed it on his desk. "Very funny, Jim. Anything else I can do for you today? How about a pound of flesh?"

"No thanks, I've got a plane to catch. Think the airlines will fly in this weather?"

Baldwin pretended to be shocked by the question. "Weather? What weather? This is Nebraska, Jim. We breed thunderstorms and tornadoes like cattle here. Perpetually depressing atmospheric conditions keep our lovely state from becoming overpopulated with criminals looking for a safe place to sell drugs. The governor permits the sun to shine in Nebraska only when the Cornhuskers are playing in Memorial Stadium. And it always shines into the eyes of the opposing quarterback. I thought everyone knew that."

*

It was three o'clock in the afternoon. The Oldies But Goodies Café was empty. Rose Blanchard sat at her favorite table near a corner window. When Jim Redline, Helen Rutz and Murray Klein walked into the café, Rose jumped up so fast she knocked her chair over.

"Holy cow!" she yelled. "A genuine celebrity! Right here in my little café!"

She tore across the room and gave Redline a crushing hug. "You know what, Jim? You look even better on television than you do in real life!"

"I assume that's a compliment," said Redline. "Nice to see you, Rose. Coffee and a slice of key lime pie, please."

"Me, too," said Murray. "Whipped cream on mine, Rose."

"I'll pass on dessert," said Helen. She lit a cigarette and waggled her new engagement ring under Rose's nose as she did so. "Trying to stay trim until the wedding."

Rose gave Helen a nasty look, then lumbered off toward the kitchen.

When everyone was seated, Helen said, "So, you say Tom Sawyer is dead, Jim. You're sure about that?"

"Yes," said Redline. "I've recently been in touch with a man in San Diego who, uh, was with Tom at the end. Tom has gone on to his reward, Helen."

"And what are you going to do now, Jim?" asked Murray. "Now that all the fuss up in Washington is over."

"Write a book," said Redline. "That should take a year or so. And then I'm going to travel. Lionel Cooper was a generous man. He left me a substantial amount of money. Enough that I can take a couple years off to ponder my career options."

"Be sure and visit Key West," said Helen. "Murray and I are going to move there right after we're married." She kissed Murray on the cheek. "We might buy a big boat and sail around the world."

"But we don't know that for sure," said Murray. "That's under discussion."

"I'll certainly visit Key West," said Redline. "Helen, I have a confession to make. This is not strictly a social visit. I came here to ask you a serious question. You had a contract with Lionel Cooper. I feel an obligation to honor the terms of that deal. The first time we met, you told me this was about getting your hands on some big money. That hasn't happened."

"So what's your question?"

"Do you want me to continue to search for the jewelry box?"

"What?" asked Murray. "I thought . . . well, I don't know what I thought."

"There's a chance the box is still out there," said Redline.

"Who gives a damn," said Helen bitterly. "I'm done with this thing. It went in directions I never imagined. People died just because I wanted some money. I sent Walter's papers back to his attorney two months ago, Jim. Told him they meant nothing to me and should be included with his other memorabilia. But before I did that, I destroyed the parts that mentioned the jewelry box. I did that to keep peace in the world." She kissed Murray on the cheek again. "Besides, I don't need money anymore. I have love in my life now. Turns out it's even more valuable than money."

Murray dropped his eyes and fiddled with his napkin.

Rose Blanchard charged up to the table, looking like a summer storm cloud in a white tent dress, white seashell earrings and grubby white sandals. Her toenails were enameled bright green. "Coffee's percolating," she said. "But I'm plumb out of key lime pie, boys. I do have fresh carrot cake."

"Fine by me," said Murray. "Put whipped cream on mine."

"Jim?"

"I'll try the carrot cake. Hold the whipped cream."

"Will you autograph this for me?" asked Rose. She handed Redline a stained dinner menu. Then, blushing furiously, she stampeded back to the kitchen.

"Okay," said Redline, as he scrawled his name on the menu. "I just wanted to make sure I knew how you felt about the jewelry box, Helen. I'd resume the search if you asked me to."

Helen energetically stubbed out her cigarette. "Let's talk about something else," she said. "Something interesting."

"Jim, Helen's trying to tell you she's done forever with the JFK thing," said Murray. "Too damned dangerous."

Redline reached in his pocket, retrieved a long white envelope and handed it to Helen. "Maybe you'll find this interesting."

"What is it?"

"A wedding present," said Redline. "Two round-trip tickets to paradise."

*

Later, while Murray was in the men's room and Rose was phoning her friends to tell them that a genuine celebrity was eating carrot cake in her café, Helen squinted at Redline and whispered, "Jim, please tell me you're not going to look for that damned box."

"Loose ends keep me awake at night," said Redline. "It's a family curse."

"But why do you care about that box now? Is it because you want to pry it open and see what's inside?"

"No," said Redline. "I don't care about that."

"Then what?"

Redline shrugged. "I can't explain it. Let's talk about something else, Helen. Are you and Murray planning to have children?"

*

Kitty Carson smiled at the young man standing in front of her desk. "If I've seen you before," she lied, "I can't remember where or when."

"It was about a year ago," said Redline. "I walked in here just after you got a call from someone who told you that Gene Zane had died of a heart attack on his way to Belgrade. A young man named Keith was here, too. You yelled at me. Implied I might be a jewelry-box thief. And then you jumped up and ran away, crying your eyes out."

"Well, I don't remember exactly what I said to you that day. I apologize if I was rude. But if you know my nephew's name was Gene Zane, then I can guess why you're here. You want to talk to me about the jewelry box. And now I recognize you, Mr. Redline. I've seen you on television several times in recent months."

Redline pointed at the shiny jewelry box sitting in the center of Kitty's desk. "Where is the original box, Mrs. Carson? The one Gene Zane sent to you from Germany?"

"Poor Gene," said Kitty. She blinked back a tear. "Too young to die, that boy. At least his daughter and grandson are secure for the moment. He had life insurance, you know. And a house worth quite a bit."

"That's good to hear," said Redline. "Mrs. Carson, I know someone stole a jewelry box from your store last year. In fact, two jewelry boxes disappeared in a short period of time. But I'm not sure the thieves got the one that sat on your desk for three decades."

"Is the jewelry box part of that mess back in Washington, Mr. Redline?"

"Everyone in Washington believes the original jewelry box was destroyed by the CIA," said Redline. "Case closed. No one from the federal government is going to show up in Belgrade and cause you trouble."

"That's good to know. But you're here," said Kitty. "Are you going to cause me trouble, Mr. Redline?"

"I'm here because I want to know if you still have the original box," said Redline. "That's all. You have nothing to fear from me, Mrs. Carson."

Kitty's heart was beating a mile a minute. She sighed and said, "Do you want the box?"

"I don't want it," said Redline quickly. "I just want to know if you still have it. And, if you do, where it is now."

Kitty studied Redline for a long time. "If I show you where it is, you'll go away?"

"Yes," said Redline. "And never come back. That's a promise."

Kitty looked at her watch. "It's time to close up shop. Come with me."

Kitty and Redline stepped outside and stood in front of the new mannequin she and Keith had attached to the barn-board exterior wall of her store. The straw-stuffed cowboy wore a black Stetson hat, a red bandanna, a leather vest, a white shirt and blue jeans. His black high-heeled boots matched his wide black belt.

"Just before he went off to college in Colorado, Keith soaked the straw inside this old wrangler with a chemical that resists fire," said Kitty. "I asked him to do that because the last cowboy I put out here was torched by a vandal."

"He's very authentic looking," said Redline.

"He sure is," said Kitty. "I even gave him a heart of gold." Kitty took Jim's hand and placed it in the center of the mannequin's straw chest. "Can you feel his heart in there, Mr. Redline?"

Redline pressed down and felt something firm embedded in the straw. He traced its familiar rectangular shape with his fingertips. Then he smiled, put his arm around Kitty Carson and kissed her cheek.

Kitty watched Redline walk away. She watched him until he disappeared around the corner. Then she slipped her hand behind the dusty cowboy's back and traced the name stenciled on his belt.

"Steve," she said, "I'm going to hold you to our deal. You owe me a night on the town, honey. I never sold a single one of those jewelry boxes."